Praise for Freya North's *Little Wing*

'A terrific family drama of secrets . . . and so cleverly plotted'
Graham Norton

'A completely compelling story of family secrets, courage and resilience – the sense of place is just so powerful'
Fearne Cotton

'Moving, intriguing, and beautifully written, this is a story about coming home'
Katie Fforde

'A beautifully written and poignant exploration of family secrets spilling through the generations. Immersive and compelling'
Elizabeth Buchan

'A tender exploration of family secrets and healing, it is the perfect read for our troubled times'
Lucy Atkins

'Immensely enjoyable and absorbing . . . infused with empathy and a great sense of place'
Erica James

'A delicate, tender novel about love, about the paths that lead us to those we love, and how we cross the missing steps to reach home'
Carol Drinkwater

'Tender and touching. Keep the tissues close
for this poignant story'
Good Housekeeping

'I can't remember the last time I read a book
in one sitting or sobbed so hard at the end
but *Little Wing* is a really special novel'
RED

'What a treat: moving, emotional and tender.
This filled my heart with joy and occasionally
my eyes with tears; it is beautiful'
Prima

'Absolutely exquisite and the story is stunning'
@shortbookandscribes

'No review could do it justice . . . I devoured this book'
@zoebeesbooks

'Emotive, heart-warming, bittersweet, beautifully
written and pretty much perfect'
@whatchrissiereadnext

'What a blindsider of a read! Emotional, poignant, tender'
@hook.me.a.book

'This story was an absolute beaut . . . Freya will definitely
be an auto-buy author for me from now on!'
@tillylovesbooks

'If you love multigenerational stories then this one is for
you . . . I'll definitely remember the characters and their
stories for a long time'
@livreads_

The Unfinished Business of Eadie Browne

Also by Freya North

Sally
Chloë
Polly
Cat
Fen
Pip
Love Rules
Home Truths
Pillow Talk
Secrets
Chances
Rumours
The Way Back Home
The Turning Point
Little Wing

Freya North

The Unfinished Business of Eadie Browne

MLP

Copyright © Freya North, 2024

The right of Freya North to be identified as the
Author of the Work has been asserted by them in accordance with the
Copyright, Designs and Patents Act 1988.

First published in 2024 by
Mountain Leopard Press
An imprint of HEADLINE PUBLISHING GROUP

2

Apart from any use permitted under UK copyright law, this publication may
only be reproduced, stored, or transmitted, in any form, or by any means,
with prior permission in writing of the publishers or, in the case of reprographic
production, in accordance with the terms of licences issued by the Copyright
Licensing Agency.

*All characters in this publication are fictitious and any resemblance
to real persons, living or dead, is purely coincidental.*

Lyrics from *Just Like Heaven* by The Cure © Robert Smith, Simon Gallup, Boris
Williams, Laurence Tolhurst, Porl Thompson. Reprinted with kind permission from
Universal Music Publishing Group.

Cataloguing in Publication Data is available from the British Library

Hardback ISBN: 978-1-80279-300-0
Trade Paperback ISBN: 978-1-80279-301-7
Ebook ISBN: 978-1-80279-302-4

Jacket design by Alexandra Allden
Jacket images © Shutterstock.com

Printed and bound in Great Britain by Clays Ltd, Elcograf S.p.A.

Headline's policy is to use papers that are natural, renewable and recyclable products
and made from wood grown in well-managed forests and other controlled sources. The
logging and manufacturing processes are expected to conform to the environmental
regulations of the country of origin.

HEADLINE PUBLISHING GROUP
An Hachette UK Company
Carmelite House
50 Victoria Embankment
London EC4Y 0DZ

www.headline.co.uk
www.hachette.co.uk

*For Emma O'Reilly
with my love and gratitude for decades of
memories and true friendship*

Part I

Prologue

1976

'Eadie Browne has a hole in her cheek.'
I was not yet seven years old when I experienced love and hate for the first time, and both in a single day. There would be two occasions in my life when Patrick Semple would touch my face, uninvited. This was the first time and I was six. I was fairly sure I did not have a hole in my face, but Patrick sought to prove otherwise. Into my cheek, midway from my mouth to my ear, between the upper and lower rows of my teeth, he shoved his grubby, nail-bitten finger. We were in the school playground and Patrick, still poking at my face, regarded our circling classmates, triumphant. Everyone was crowding around and looking at me as they might a reptile in the zoo. Though I wanted to glower at him, instead I found I could only smile blithely at the lot of them.

'It's not a hole,' said Josh and he pulled Patrick's hand off my face and pushed him away from me.

There would be many times in my life when Josh Albert would come to my side. This was the first.

'It only happens when she smiles,' Josh told everyone. 'Look.' He gave my shoulder a small shake and spoke to me, earnest and softly. 'Stop smiling, Eadie,' he said.

Josh was a quiet boy and kind. He was reasonably good at everything and he performed all these everythings in a mild and unassuming way, which was why he had no enemies. So when he told me to stop smiling, it felt safe to do so.

Everyone gathered even closer.

'See,' said Josh. 'No hole.'

No one was looking at Patrick any more. Everyone seemed entranced by the magic powers of my face.

'Anyway, it's stupid to have a hole when you smile,' said Patrick, now on the edge of the throng and veering off the radar of my classmates. 'It's disgusting.'

'No it isn't,' I said. 'It's a dimple.'

'A *dimple*.' Josh verified the word which was then passed around my classmates in an appreciative murmur.

'Anyway,' said Patrick, now smarting, 'your parents are *dead*.'

They hadn't been when I'd left them at home for the short walk to school that morning. Suddenly, a terrible scorch of panic wiped the smile off my world and I started to cry. I scoured the playground, terrified that our headmaster Mr Swift would come for me like he had for Emma when her mum was rushed to hospital to have her baby brother. But that was different. That was about life. This was about death.

'No they're *not*,' I choked through tears, 'my mum and dad aren't dead at all.'

'Well, they are either dead or they are *Draculas*,' Patrick said, revelling in the swivel of attention back to him. He sighed, as if he was finding everything to do with me very tedious.

'Eadie Browne lives by the graveyard,' he told everyone, rolling his eyes as if I really wasn't worth talking about. 'And her parents only come out at night.'

This was one hundred per cent true.

And I really loathed that boy just then.

Eadie, 7 a.m. 15th June 1999, home

We're not going in to work today. We have a day off. Not the regular type of day off when you don't set an alarm – I had to set ours for half an hour earlier than usual and it's just sounded. One snooze cycle allowed. I'm trying to shut my eyes against the day but I'm wide awake. My husband sleeps on and I nudge him, huff at him, tug the corner of his pillow to disrupt his snoring. He can sleep through anything – including, it seems, our marriage.

We went to sleep cross with each other last night but just now I can't remember why and I can't remember who started it. It's hard to pinpoint, these days. I'm thinking I'm thinking but I can't recall. Recently there've been many nights when we've broken the rule of not going to sleep on an argument. To be pedantic, actually we've only bent the rule because it's never really an argument. Arguments, by definition, are about something; they have opposing sides and the potential for resolution. We just snipe and niggle over a whole lot of nothings and it's not nice yet we can't seem to stop. Ours is not so much a vicious circle but more of a grating cycle. What *was* it that set us off yesterday, which made us take to the opposite outer edges of our bed without so much as a sombre '*night*' being said?

A tear inches a lonely path down the side of my face and I don't know who it's for. Let him snore, Eadie. Give him a break. The alarm will go a second time in a minute. I envy him the absolute peace and respite and ignorance that sleep provides, as well as those blissful moments of reverie that are next for him when all is calm and soft and forgotten. I had that five minutes ago. Then I woke up and now I can taste the discord I went to sleep with.

But – such a long day ahead. A lot of driving which he's going to do. The weirdest of days, really. I switch off the alarm before it sounds and quietly face my husband. He is asleep, still defiantly turned away from me. God, he can snore. Much as I want to give him a shove, I place my hand gently between his shoulder blades and give a little push instead. I move to his arm and give a little pull.

'Hey,' I say. 'Time to wake up.'

We're going to bury the dead today. It's been a long time coming and we have one heck of a journey stretching before us.

Eadie

1976

It wasn't quite right to call it a graveyard, it was Parkwin Garden City's multi-faith cemetery. But kids always called it the graveyard because the word itself, as much as the drum-roll of tombstones, promised far more drama and darkness and menace than 'cemetery'. I lived right next door and it didn't bother me at all, in fact I liked my quiet neighbours, many of whom I considered friends.

Nor was it quite right to call Parkwin Garden City a *city*. Parkwin was a small town planted onto the Hertfordshire–Bedfordshire border in 1929 by Edweard Fairbetter who we were always learning about in school. He was a protégé of Ebenezer Howard, the gentleman with visionary ideas about town planning who founded the proper Garden Cities like Welwyn and Letchworth where the merits of city life and industry were wed with the virtues of the countryside. Over and above their historical significance, Welwyn and Letchworth also had theatres and lidos, restaurants and big shops and fast trains into decent hubs, and Parkwin residents were always grumbling about that. But when I was young, I thought I was growing up in the most perfect world. There was order and calm in the anodyne crescents and avenues, and an ice-cream van which trundled along them daily from May until September, that's all I needed to know.

But the factory had recently closed and there was loitering by those who'd lost their jobs. There was unrest in the sprawl of 1960s hasty housing which slunk like oil spillage over the intended town boundary into ugly brownfield. Divisiveness was developing between the original residents and newcomers, the young and the old, the employed and the jobless. But none of that registered when I was little. When I was little, Parkwin seemed a perfect and benevolent world to me. Which made Patrick's hostility all the more shocking.

We lived in the very last house on Yew Lane, between the cemetery gates and the small fenced-off scrap of land commandeered by the squat and windowless Electricity Building which, to me, was far more sinister than anything in the cemetery. The barbed wire and the warning signs. Risk of Death. A skull and crossbones. A stick figure being struck by what I thought was a thunderbolt from a furious God.

Our house was unique because it was the only bungalow on our street. It was the only bungalow in Parkwin. Along Yew Lane, the even numbers were on one side, odd numbers on the other until the pavement petered out to hedgerow on the left and the Electricity Building on the right. We should have been number 38 but, oddly, we were number 41. My father was always honing witticisms about this – about us being from The Other Side, about there being something Slightly Odd About The Brownes. But my father could take an idea and run with it for a long, long time; it was one of the many things he did which he wasn't paid to do. My mother said he was like a terrier when it came to ideas and I always thought how fitting it was that his name actually was Terry. Which is what everyone called him, including me.

Terry was taller than he seemed on account of him always tilting his head when he spoke. His hair, black-brown and with grey streaking through it like midwinter rain, was wild and occasionally long enough to be worn in a poor excuse for a ponytail which my mother regularly chopped off. My father wore ancient slippers with soles that had come right away from the toe so that they opened and closed like a mouth; when I was very young and very short, sometimes I thought it was them talking to me, not Terry. His words, which rattled out at an exhausting pace, were always fascinating and always made sense until later, when everything remembered was incomprehensible. I can write as fast as I think, he'd proudly declare but I'd sneak a look at his files and papers and I'd worry that the spiked and juddered scrawl choking every page expressed relative chaos in his mind.

Terry didn't like going out. He just didn't. He liked staying in, at 41 Yew Lane. He liked being at his desk in the corner of the sitting room, reading and writing during every moment of daylight.

My mother was round and shiny and pink and smiley. Give her a pair of ears and a fluffy tail and dress her in a frock and an apron and Beatrix Potter might have featured her as a mummy mouse. Her hair was a mass of small, neatly curled bubbles which hugged her head so efficiently she had no need for a hat in winter. She had a desk in the sitting room too; an ancient school desk with a lift-up lid and a surface that sloped towards her and there she sat, all day long, conjuring words that one day might, or might not, make it all the way into a completed poem.

My mother didn't like going out either. She liked staying in, at 41 Yew Lane. She just did. She needed it to be day outside to throw light on the blank pages of her book so that she could commit the words as methodically and thoughtfully as if she was building a bridge by hand.

And me. Me with my one dimple, hair as unruly as Terry's handwriting which not even my mother's gentle brushing could tame or soften. There wasn't a name for its colour, it was just nothingy. I once heard my parents refer to it as Unfortunate Hair. Well, I knew the story of Dick Whittington and how fortunes could change so I took to wearing the widest of Alice bands while I awaited such a time. It looked as though the front and back of my head were held in place by a bandage.

I didn't have a desk in the sitting room, there wasn't the space, but I had my favourite spot on our sofa between its arm and the heaps of mail and washing and the inevitable overflow from Terry's desk and all the newspapers and magazines with articles he had yet to clip out and stick elsewhere. From this vantage point I could look at my books and keep an eye on my parents and make sure we were all fed at a reasonable hour.

Like Terry and my mum, I also loved 41 Yew Lane. I loved the constant warm smell of toast which permeated and I loved my spic-and-span bedroom looking out to the garden, but I liked being outside more. I just did.

I'd always been happy with my silent neighbours in the cemetery. As soon as I was considered old enough, when I could walk and talk independently, I was allowed to go through the gate in our garden wall which led into the grounds. Until I went to school, my friends in the cemetery were the only friends I had. Sometimes, my mother would say, Eadie Browne – will you not give those poor souls a moment's peace? And Terry, looking up from his books and his files and his papers and notepads, would call over to her, they're dead, dear – as if my mother hadn't noticed. It struck me that at 41 Yew Lane we called our living room the Sitting Room and, for me, the cemetery had always seemed like an extra room in my home. However ironic, I thought of it as the Living Room.

My parents believed that our particular world of 41 Yew Lane and Parkwin Garden City Cemetery was a safe and bountiful place for me to roam and scamper and speak to strangers all by myself and, by the age of five, I was doing precisely that. I had no brother or sister so I was to make friends where I could find them and the cemetery was an excellent location for this, whether they were walking and talking – or dead and buried. I'd practise my songs between the furthest avenue of graves and the fence to the arable fields which stretched benignly towards the horizon; I'd try out cartwheels on the rolling green yet to be dug down, or I'd just sit awhile by the older pitted headstones lulled into daydreams. There were dozens of graves known personally to me and I'd spend time at each, having lengthy chats with the residents. I also had a favourite bench on which I'd lay out my colouring book and crayons and another on which to climb. But if I saw people visiting a grave near to where I was I'd stop playing and smile kindly – which along with *don't touch the flowers* and *don't go in the chapel* were pretty much the only rules my parents had set. Just smile kindly. Let them have quiet.

My very earliest memories are of standing on a chair by the window in our sitting room quietly watching the funeral cortèges as they passed by 41 Yew Lane. While my mum provided anecdotes and random facts about the dead person's life, Terry would stand beside me like a Master of Ceremonies.

'Mr Andrew Smythson. Eighty-four. Family flowers only.'

'A good age,' I'd proclaim, having been taught how to respond to the brute facts of death. Other reactions Terry had impressed upon me included *too soon* and *terrible, really* and *a merciful release* and *how desperately sad* and, on the rarest occasions, *good riddance*. Terry and I would count the cars in the procession and pass judgement accordingly on whether the turnout was good, disappointing or downright pitiful. I learned to read, to count, to tell the time because of the comings and goings at Parkwin Garden City Cemetery. Most of my lessons in humanity started there.

Once the mourners had left to eat curled sandwiches and drink warm wine and weak tea in a church hall or community centre, then we would walk through the gate in our garden wall. Solemn and quiet, we would stand at the new grave and contemplate the flowers; a coverlet of colour with heartfelt words crying out from the little cards. Draped over the dug ground, they formed a patchwork of emotion threaded through with fragrance that the recipient would never smell.

'See *here*, Eadie,' Terry would say. 'Here lies the meaning of *life*. This is what it's all about.'

So I grew up amongst the living and the dead and there was companionship to be found with both. My silent conversations at gravesides were just as fulfilling as those with my other friends there. George the caretaker and his wife

Mrs George. Michael the gardener. Barry, Joe and Abdul the gravediggers. And, when the occasion warranted it, Ross McIver the bagpiper.

But Michael was my best friend. I estimated that Michael was one hundred and fifty years old and the notion was comforting. He was so ancient, he might even have risen from a grave. His cloth cap, which he wore all year round, appeared to have grown out of his head like a puckered mushroom while his pipe, always crooked into the corner of his lips, had pulled one side of his mouth permanently downwards though I always knew when he was smiling. Every now and then he let me have a puff too; sometimes the pipe was lit, sometimes not. Pipe-smoking, I deduced, was good for the thoughts. It appeared to help people breathe in and breathe out.

I liked to accompany Michael Pipe as he went about his work. Up and down the rows we'd go, stooping for stray ribbon, righting lopsided flowers, raking leaves, collecting snags of cellophane and twigs. We kept busy with secateurs and shears which I handled expertly from a young age, tending to what Michael called the Shrubberies of Sympathy which were planted at regular intervals to soften the march of all those graves. Keeping the place tidy, keeping the place nice – both of us believing this was to be done mainly for the benefit of the dead.

'What ho, Eadie,' Michael would murmur every few minutes though mostly we worked wordlessly.

On the day when Patrick poked my face and told the class my parents were dead, I ran home from school and hurried into the house. And there they were, my parents, completely alive and just as I had left them eight hours earlier. Terry was still at his desk navigating his way between one pile of papers and another, as if umpiring a battle of wits between whichever writers he was analysing. And there was my mother, pen poised for her poetry – hoping, always hoping, that today would be the day when words might flow like ink from her nib. They only briefly noticed that I was home so I ran out to our garden and through our gate and into the cemetery, to pour my heart out at the graves of my various friends. And that's where Michael came across me.

What ho, Eadie. What ho.

Sometimes Michael gave me a trowel, at other times a rake, garden ties, or a black bin bag, perhaps the wheelbarrow, the secateurs.

That day, he fetched me the broom with the handle cut down to my size. Furiously, I brushed and swept my day away.

'And how did you hurt that knee of yours?'

I didn't want to talk about it and just then I didn't want to do gardening either. I didn't want to brush leaves or pick up pieces of plastic or gather twigs. I wanted to think about it and not think about it. I wanted my very own pipe to suck on and puff until the answers came.

'I fell over.'

But the truth was that Patrick had tripped me up as the bell sounded for the end of break. And he hissed at me I hate you Eadie Browne, I *hate* you. And now I hated him too.

To Michael Pipe I just said I fell when I was playing chase.

'You'll live,' he said. And then he said school days! He gave a long, thoughtful sigh and he said school days are the best days of your life.

'No they're not,' I said. 'They're the *worst*. I hate school,' I said. 'I hate it hate it hate it.'

'Now now, Eadie Browne,' Michael said.

And I said to him, I said now now *nothing*, Michael Pipe.

Just like that he had become another grown-up. I threw down my broom and turned away from him and the futility of tending the grass of people too dead to care.

Michael's hand on my shoulder, a little squeeze. But my eyes were hot with tears I didn't want to fall. My voice was knotted around my neck.

'What's all this, Eadie, what's all this?' he said while he ruffled my hair which was the kindest thing anyone could do on account of me having the Unfortunate Hair which grew like it was arguing with itself and was the colour of parched ground and about as dry.

'I *hate* Patrick Semple!'

And Michael hummed and puffed at his pipe and he handed it to me to do likewise. 'Is this what's – who's – making you hate school? This Patrick?'

I had a smoke and, placated by the sweet tobacco, its tickle and warmth, I nodded.

'Semple Semple,' he muttered. 'There's Semples over there – Row F. No one visits. Nettles and weeds drive me mad.'

'Well, I hope Patrick dies!' I said.

And Michael said now now, Eadie Browne.

And I cried out now now *nothing*.

Off I stomped, ignoring the graves of all my friends whom I'd promised to visit. I went to the part of the cemetery where the sunshine never reached, not even in high summer. An area pocked with bare earth, where thistles prospered and the air chilled a dullness to the grass. Right here, I earmarked a grave for Patrick Semple.

Back in my house, I went to my bedroom without either parent looking up. I sat on the edge of my bed and shone my torch into the wound on my throbbing knee. There, in the graze, tiny insidious shards of playground dirt were specked. I thought about calling for my mum but I could hear her getting ready, now, to go out to work. And if I asked Terry he would want to know how I'd done it and I'd have to tell him about dimples, death and Dracula and he'd veer off so steeply on tangents that he'd miss the point entirely. So I took my teddy's paw and dipped it into my glass of water from last night and then I stroked it over the graze on my knee again and again. And as I did so I thought to myself, if Patrick Semple is telling people that my mum and dad are dead, or something even worse, then I'm going to have to think of other things that my parents can be from now on.

And that's how it all began.

Mum and Terry worked nights, that's all it was. They worked nights because it enabled them to answer their true callings from their worlds in our sitting room during daylight hours. Terry the philosopher; a miner of concepts, an excavator of notions, an archaeologist of thought. While he chased that elusive publishing deal, he proofread other people's books along the way and cross-checked the appendixes of massive tomes. I'm an ideas man, he liked to say. These ideas, on reams of paper and the backs of envelopes and old Christmas cards and till receipts, were stuck all around his corner of the room like a clamouring audience. However, when he wasn't working with words by day, he was packing and unpacking and doing as he was told and often told off at the new supermarket on the edge of town by night. He'd been happy enough with his shift at the factory but the factory had closed and he had to remember he was one of the fortunate ones with a job to go to. But how he hated that new place. Terry said the supermarket would be The Death of The Independents and I'd lie awake worrying about where we'd put them all in the cemetery.

My mother cleaned offices, out of hours. If you asked her what she did, that's what she'd tell you. She never once described herself as a poet. She was resigned when she left for work and deflated when she arrived home but, once back at her desk in the sitting room, she perked up like daybreak. While my father was waiting for his talent to be recognized, my mother undersold hers. So my parents did these things at home during the day because they needed the light – for my mother to write, for my father to think. And they did these things elsewhere at night because they needed the money. But, at school, I now made sure they did other things entirely. I didn't do it to gain friends – I had enough of those in the cemetery – I did it to win a reprieve from being the weird kid with the single dimple who lived next door to the graveyard. I did it to keep Patrick at bay.

Our school was called the Three Magnets Primary School. An odd name unless, like us from the age of dot, you knew all about Edweard Fairbetter who founded our school and named it after Ebenezer Howard's diagram which laid out the Garden City principle as three magnets: *Town, Country, Town-Country* – and, at the centre, with the will to choose, *The People*. The school emblem, with those three magnets embroidered in yellow on our brown blazers, looked a bit like a mouse's face. School was at the end of a leafy road; lots of children walked themselves there and back and I was one of them.

Mr Swift was our headmaster and we all loved him. He ended every assembly – and wrote on every end-of-year report – *Read And So You Shall Fly* and he himself looked like a bird, a fantastical and majestic one like a carving on a totem pole. He was a solid block of a man with large hands and wide-open eyes whose all-seeing alertness was exaggerated by perfectly round spectacles which straddled his nose and clung to his ears, indenting his cheeks on the way. But those eyes of his never seemed to be looking in my direction when Patrick Semple was about, and the rest of the staff appeared blind to it too.

In assembly, before the Read And So You Shall Fly bit, Mr Swift spoke of Imagination and Endeavour and told us that these were the Unsinkable Ships of Purpose and I think I understood what he was talking about. I think he was telling us that it was OK to make stuff up if it was put to good use. So, in breaktime, when Patrick approached me with a leer and a snarl and something clenched in his fist, I turned away from him, sailed into my imagination and endeavoured to make everything sound plausible.

I called out that my father had been a Russian spy. I said that he could speak twelve languages. My father, I said, had invented a famous, unbreakable code. And suddenly I had my audience in a ring around me, wanting more and keeping me safe for as long as my imagination lasted.

And so it was that I placed Terry in the Secret Service. Sometimes the Navy. Often he was in Buckingham Palace, by order of the Queen, overseeing her forthcoming Jubilee and all her other things made of silver. Once or twice I forgot about all of that and put him in charge of a network of secret tunnels stretching from the Irish Sea to Welwyn Garden City.

My mother I crafted into an attractive hybrid of Florence Nightingale, Julie Andrews in *The Sound of Music* and a *Blue Peter* presenter. I packed her off to a Dickensian London where, each night, she gathered up street urchins, fed them kippers and bran mash, taught them to read and stitched their clothes for them by morning.

The Brownes are not dead, I said. The Brownes are not Draculish. The Brownes just happen to live by the cemetery because it's close to the Electricity Building which isn't even for electricity. I told the kids in my class how my great-great-great-grandfather had built it by order of the King. We are the only people who have the keys, I told them. And that's the real reason why I have just the one dimple – because it's a sign that I'm one of *them*, one of the few who can enter the Building. And not just the one next to our house – also the other twenty-nine that are dotted from here to Liverpool.

Before long, when my teachers called out Eadie Browne! stop daydreaming! stop gazing out of the window and *concentrate* – as they frequently did – many of my classmates would sneak a look too, believing there to be secret codes I was reading in the clouds or covert messages in the branches which I was surreptitiously deciphering.

When you are nearly seven years old and you live in Parkwin Garden City, it is with the belief that life is thankfully unspectacular. Therefore, my classmates gladly flocked to my fabricated world which, in turn, kept Patrick Semple beyond arm's length. If I had people around me listening to me, then he couldn't shove me quite so often, he couldn't hit my lunch to the ground, or grab my apple and whack it against my head, he couldn't snatch my biscuit or knock against me when I drank at the water fountain, he couldn't trip me up or hold on to my satchel until the strap bit into my neck. He could still hiss at me when I least expected, or pinch the back of my arm, twisting at my skin like a jammed key, but I learned to keep my cries silent and my smarting eyes hidden. I convinced myself they belonged to Eadie Browne, not E. D. Pistachionovsky – my alter ego which the class now believed was my secret but actual name.

However, all of this was akin to running down that steep hill by the ponds – when my legs would suddenly gain a momentum beyond my control, an independence from my torso, a life and a will of their own. Sometimes they carried me fast but sometimes they ran away from me and I'd fall and I could never tell which it was to be. So too I feared my stories intertwining like the gloves on elastic in the snaking coat sleeves which entangled us at home-time. I didn't want to come undone but I knew I was only an errant detail away from it. And Patrick, always Patrick, calling me a liar and telling me he hated me and me believing him because I knew both to be true.

'I'll keep your secrets for you, Eadie,' Josh whispered one day, positioning himself between me and Patrick as we readied ourselves for home-time. And I realized in that moment that the secrets he said he'd keep weren't about the tunnels and the unpronounceable surname and the street urchins and the espionage. Rather it was the fact that all my stories were made up. Josh and Patrick, my chum and my nemesis, the two people who knew the real me.

7.55 a.m. 15th June 1999

Ten minutes behind schedule and already we're blaming each other which is stupid, we know, but predictable. There's tutting and huffing when really, we're not even late. The van hire place doesn't even open until 8.00 and it's only a short walk away.

We'll be gone just for the day and yet we're looking around our flat and double-checking the smallest of things as if we're off for a month. We've both fed the cat. I've closed the sitting-room curtains, my husband has opened them but I close them again. It's a beautiful day, he remonstrates. It'll be dark when we're home, I say. And he's patting himself up and down checking for keys while I roll my eyes and point because the keys are where they always are, in the dish on the kitchen table. And I say, I need the loo. And he says, Jesus, you've been about ten times already. And I say, who are you, the Bladder Police? and actually that's quite funny and we laugh which stills us and lets us take a quick shy look into each other.

'Have you checked—?'

'Yes.'

'Hang on two ticks—'

'—Eadie, will you stop faffing and come *on*.'

'I'm not faffing.'

But actually I am.

I go to the loo, again.

'God's *sake*, Georgia Gee – let's *go*.'

Huh? Who?

He's holding my jacket. The label, designed to look just like an old-fashioned school uniform name tag, reads *Georgia Gee*.

'Is this new?' he asks and there's just a touch of accusation in his tone because we're meant to be saving, not spending.

'No, it's not new.'

Well, it is new – but it's second-hand-new and I bought it last week just for today. I mean to parry back and tell him all of this but suddenly I'm lost in thought, catapulted back through the years to the playground of Three Magnets Primary School. How, once a term, a teacher took me and Emma Rogers – how did I even remember her name – to The Hut.

'Eadie.'

'*Eadie.*'

And I'm slipping on the Georgia Gee jacket that I bought especially for today, for the funeral. My husband is ushering me out, locking the door, unlocking it to rush back in and fetch his glasses and, as we walk away into the day, I gladly veer away from thinking about funerals, remembering instead The Hut and all those years ago and the time when I first met Celeste.

The day the new girl arrived in our class was to become one of the worst days of my life. It was the day we were given our first exercise books. The covers were a dull, gritty orange and there was a grid on the front in which we were to write our names. Inside, the paper was lined, nice and wide, with a faint red margin to the left. The new girl was told to sit by me and over she glided, all tall and flinchingly pretty and her neat, glossy ponytail made my thatchy hair itch. Her shoes hadn't a single scuff and her socks were pristine white and stayed in place just under her knees; mine were an odd pair and one had gone pink in the wash. She had a pencil case overstocked with every colour imaginable and, from the zip on its own little fancy rope, a tiny koala swung. I watched from the corner of my eye as her fingers riffled through all her pencils and she wrote her name neatly in rainbow colours. I'd had to take my pencils from the chewed-down surplus in the mug on Terry's desk and I kept them in an old cigar-box.

Celeste Evangeline Walker. In perfect joined-up handwriting. I hated her. I loved her.

Eaddiee Racheline Pistachionovsky.

Browne.

I had to spill over onto the second line. I knew Celeste was reading my every word. I had no idea how to pronounce Evangeline. And whether or not she knew how to pronounce Pistachionovsky was swiftly irrelevant because our teacher swooped on my book and told me off, plonked two white stickers over my name and hovered while I wrote it again.

Eadie Browne.

The stickers were lopsided. My letters were on a slant. It was a mess.

Celeste was immediately popular, partly because she was beautiful and partly because she gave her stuff away: crisps, scented erasers and sheets of glittery stickers. When she ran out of these, she took orders from the class for what they wanted her to bring them the next day.

'I like your real name,' Celeste said to me. I didn't know which one she meant.

For so long, the universe had simply been my house, 41 Yew Lane. With school, my world expanded further because not only were there roads to be crossed but I had to navigate around people who weren't like me at all. 41 Yew Lane, though, remained at the epicentre for me, and I liked to envisage the world at large radiating out in ever-increasing circles. That was back when I believed that proper countries had to have 'land' in their name. After all, Yew Lane was in England. The rest of the world was therefore Scotland, Ireland, Iceland and its opposite Greenland, Swaziland and its cousin Switzerland, New and Old Zealands, Legoland and Heligoland and also Holland which belonged to the many Neverlands. But in class that day Patrick Semple called me stupid when I said America wasn't a country.

The teacher, however, told him I was quite right – America was a continent. Patrick hated me all the more for it.

'Have you heard of Finland?' Celeste asked me at the end of the lesson. 'How about Poland?'

'Of course I have,' I said. It was lunchtime. I grabbed my blazer but it fell to the floor and Celeste picked it up.

'Maureen McCann?' She read the name tag out loud. 'I thought you were Eadie Browne or Eadie the Other Name.' She started laughing. 'Who *are* you?' she said.

Patrick had the answer to that one.

'She's poor and she stinks,' he said. 'She has to have second-hand clothes because her parents don't love her,' he said. And he pointed to The Hut in the playground. 'They take her in there,' he said, wrinkling his nose.

The Hut was just a wooden shed, a depository for donated school uniform sold on to raise money for the school or given away to families who couldn't afford new. I would go in wearing one set of clothes and come out in another, kitted out top to toe, as if I was in an episode of *Mr Benn*. My entire uniform came from The Hut. Skirts with mountain ranges where the hems had been taken up and let down multiple times, sweaters with cuffs that had probably doubled as nose-wipes, sports kits stained grassily with triumph or defeat. Blazers with pencil sharpenings in the pockets – and everything with someone else's name sewn in. It made it more interesting, I didn't mind it at all. Until that day, until Patrick spelled it out, I had never felt anything other than perfectly content that my uniform came from there.

'Eadie wears old clothes and someone else's dirty pants,' he told Celeste while everyone else gathered around. 'That's why she smells. She smells of second-hand poo and wee.' Then he said, 'She smells poor.' And then he said, 'She smells of dead babies.'

I knew very well the quiet area of the cemetery where the little ones were buried in a peaceful nursery of their own. Under the trees and with the best view, they were cosy together, all of them, sharing their invisible play and soundless chatter for ever more. I had often seen the parents stand and stare in disbelief at the ground, at the solid earth that kept their silent children from them. And so it was in their memory that I flew at Patrick that day, with my nails and my teeth and a sound in my voice that squeezed up from my stomach where my insides felt like they were on the outside; a sound I didn't know I could make.

I was taken to Mr Swift's office and he said really, Eadie Browne, I expect so much more of you, as he handed me a letter to give to my parents. I had to apologize to Patrick in front of everyone and his eyes glistened darkly with pleasure and untold revenge. For the rest of the day I sat under the teacher's nose while everyone stared at my back but no one wanted to catch my eye. Only Josh.

'I'd've done the same thing, Eadie,' he said at home-time. I didn't believe him. His uniform came from a special shop in Hitchin.

Josh and I watched Celeste cross to the other side of the playground where the parents with cars were waiting. We saw her go up to a willowy woman wearing very high heels and a dress that clung to her for dear life, enormous sunglasses, a cigarette, hair piled high like golden candyfloss. And away they went, gliding along the road in a car the size and shine of which we'd never seen. I didn't have a car to take me to and from school, I had my legs. Josh whistled long and low and we walked away together before going our separate ways at the end of School Lane.

I walked back feeling ashamed. Just then, I hated my mum for forgetting to remove Maureen McCann's label and sew in one that said me. It had been such an odd day, the day I'd been told off for fighting Patrick Semple, the day I'd met Celeste Evangeline Walker. I arrived home to 41 Yew Lane, to my indoor parents with the bowed heads and the piles of papers and the untold tales and the mute poetry. I held Mr Swift's letter and wondered which parent to give it to but neither looked up from their work. I stayed where I was, praying for the X-ray vision I'd told all those kids at school I possessed as I tried to see through the envelope to the words inside. Without Terry or my mum appearing to notice my entrance or exit, I went to my bedroom taking the letter with me, but I could no more bring myself to open it than to throw it away.

But then came music to my ears. Bagpipes bellying their way from a graveside through my window, played by Ross McIver who always called me Wee Eadie Browne, rolling the 'r' as if tumbling it down some distant glen of his memory. As soon as the pipes stopped, I rushed through my garden, through the gate in the wall, into the cemetery grounds and over to the caretaker's office where I knew Ross would be waiting, all sporran and kilt, the socks and the skean-dhu, silver embossed buttons, a black Glengarry cap with the toorie on top. I gazed all the way up his six-foot-four-inch frame to his moustache, which crested like a wave almost down to his chin. Ross, to me, was King of Scotland and just to stand by him was to believe that all would be well in the world. He could easily pick up Patrick in one hand

and toss him like a caber. Ross looked down at me and I looked up at him while wondering what words of wisdom might filter their way through those great stacking whiskers of his.

'Will I walk you home, Eadie?'

Ross said it as if my house was miles away, as if I needed escorting and, as always, I took him the most circuitous route I could devise to delay our parting. Up and down the rows of graves we went and I ensured we double-backed frequently, down one path and up another, circumnavigating a Shrubbery of Sympathy unnecessarily, strolling right over to my garden fence before making a brisk about-turn away from it.

'Did someone Scottish die?' I asked.

'Aye. Donald Mackenzie.'

Eighty-five. A good innings. A fine turnout too.

'And how is life with Miss Eadie?'

'Very very good, thank you.'

'How are your ma and pa?'

'Very very good. They're inside.'

'And school?'

'Very very good.'

'Oh aye,' Ross said. 'Eadie Browne's world is very very good.'

I took Ross's aye for an eye and sensed that he was staring straight at the heart of the matter.

'Actually, I only sort of quite like school,' I mumbled.

'*Sort of,*' Ross said thoughtfully and he stopped awhile. '*Quite like.*'

'Sort of – quite like,' I repeated.

He started walking again. 'And your friends?'

I searched around for an answer and a friend.

'Well, here's one right here!'

We were at the grave of Alfred Pennyfeather 1880–1951 of whom I was particularly fond on account of him having Fourteen Great-Grandchildren and being The Inventor of the Appellex Modern Tynogrille, according to his gravestone. And nearby lay my friend Mildred Robinson who devoted her life to teaching. Loved by all. Next to her, Joy Trimble who always made me feel happy. And look – Michael, just over there, raking.

I don't know why Ross seemed so perplexed. I thought Michael was a friend of his as well.

'No, Eadie, I mean your wee pals – at school.'

But I didn't want to think about school. I wanted to escape with Ross to his world of Highland flings and golden eagles, whisky smuggling and the terrifying vaults under the streets of Edinburgh, the capital of Scotland. In return, I could update him on all the stories I told at school. All the pretend stuff which always made him laugh his deep, melodic, swelling laugh. That's what we were about, Ross and I, equals in storytelling.

'Are you OK, Eadie Browne? Is everything OK – at school?'

I caught Michael's eye but he didn't return my wave. Instead, he pulled his cap down even lower, turned his back and mooched off. He's told Ross, I thought, he's told Ross my secrets. Ross was looking at me in that way grown-ups can; pulling words out of me like a snake charmer.

'Is this about Patrick pinching me? Because like I told Michael it doesn't even hurt.'

He took some time to think about it. 'Have you told your ma and pa?'

'About the secret codes and the whisky stills?'

'The what? No, Eadie – about this Patrick.'

I hadn't said a word to my parents about anything, but back at home there was a letter from my headmaster that would tell them the lot.

'I hate school,' I said. 'I hate it I hate it I hate it. And I hate Patrick Semple most of all.'

I don't know why Ross took so much time to think about all of this.

'Will you do something for me, Eadie Browne?' he said and I watched his moustache move with his thoughts. 'Will you tell your ma and pa about this wee boy? Will you just try to be the real Eadie Browne at school and not the made-up one?' He brushed the shoulders of my Maureen McCann blazer like he was sending me off into the world. 'Stories are stories but.' It wasn't even a sentence.

At my gate, he paused. 'You know, Eadie, people often aren't who they seem. This laddie – maybe you don't know his real story. People often aren't who they seem – never forget that, aye?'

As I went through the garden and into the house, I thought to myself aren't grown-ups a crashing disappointment. I didn't much like Ross or Michael just then. And, with the song of the bagpipes in my soul, I took Ross's words one by one and removed them from my mind.

But what was I going to do about Mr Swift's letter? And what was I going to do instead of going to school the next day? I thought about that as I laid the table for dinner, opening a can of tuna and one of sweetcorn and standing on the stool so I could reach the butter and the cheese in the fridge. There were tomatoes and a cucumber too, I took those out and scrambled up onto the kitchen counter for one of the knives which were kept on a shelf out of harm's way.

'Supper's ready,' I called to my parents, though I had little appetite because I was full to bursting with all these horrid-tasting feelings which I wanted to spit out.

After we'd finished our main course, I went to the freezer and brought out the Viennetta. There was still some left from Mum's birthday and it was being saved for the next significant event.

My parents laughed and clapped and asked what the occasion was.

'I have a letter from Mr Swift, the headmaster,' I told them darkly, serving them each a slice.

'That's fantastic!' said Terry.

'Oh, Eadie!' said Mum, delighted.

But if they read it, all this joy would be crushed. After all, it was Terry's night to go to work and in his supermarket uniform, he always appeared to shrink a little. I didn't want to make things worse. I didn't want them to read it.

'I hate school,' I mumbled instead, knowing that they'd have something to say about that. 'I don't want to go any more.'

And they both said but school days are the best days of your life and after that I just stopped listening.

Mr Swift said good morning to me the next day so cheerily it was as if the letter and the reason for it had been forgotten. But Patrick drove a pencil into my thigh as we all trooped into our classroom.

'I'll get you,' he said. 'I'll get you.'

'Get her what? A bunch of flowers? A box of chocolates?'

I turned and there stood Celeste with her hands on her hips until Patrick skulked away.

'Ignore him,' Celeste said. 'I.G.N.O.R.E.' I could spell that too. 'By the way, is Pistachionovsky a Russian surname?'

She pronounced it so fluently that it sounded real and not made up.

'No,' I mumbled at her shoes. 'It's from *next door* to Russia.'

Celeste scrunched her eyes half shut as if flipping through an atlas in her mind's eye. 'Ah!' she said and she gave me the most lovely smile. 'That makes sense. Also, will you come to my house, Eadie? Like after school one day? Maybe? If you're not busy, that is?' It appeared she thought it impossible that I'd be free.

I spent the rest of the day avoiding her and instead I followed in Josh's shadow wherever he went. Celeste was too beautiful, too popular, too friendly towards me; I didn't trust her. At home-time, I waited for her to take her opposite route across the playground. However, at the far gate she turned, scanned the playground and located me.

'Eadie!' she called at the top of her voice, waving.

Her mother peered over her sunglasses in my direction but I don't think she knew who she was meant to be looking at.

'Eadie!' Celeste waved again.

I could sense other kids staring at me so I cupped my hand over my ear and bowed my head as if intercepting secret conversations on my imaginary spyware, and I walked away like that until my neck ached.

The first I knew of the invitation was a few days later, when Terry and Mum actually stood up from their desks and beamed at me just as soon as I was home from school and I thought for a moment they were going to burst into applause.

'Mrs Walker phoned!'

'You're going to Celeste Walker's after school tomorrow. Staying for supper!'

'How about that?'

'How *about* that!'

'Loveliest accent, hasn't she, Terry?'

'*Très chic.*'

I didn't know my father spoke French and I really didn't want to go to Celeste Walker's house on the other side of town, a world away. I didn't know what my parents would do without me and it was unfathomable that they'd agreed to send me away. I hadn't been in many other houses than 41 Yew Lane, and certainly not to eat.

My classmates found out, of course they did. Suddenly, my stories were irrelevant – now my fame and future fortune revolved around being the chosen one, the one who was going home with Celeste, to her mansion of the many swimming pools. Make sure you look at all her stuff! See if you can count how many toys she has! Remember everything you eat and if the plates are gold or silver! Bet she gives you things! Patrick though, Patrick gave me a Chinese burn and told me I was a lezzo though I had no idea what that meant.

Josh found me at the outer reaches of the playground at breaktime and we sat beside each other in our companionable way, doing those little dances with our shoes. If my feet stopped, his would nudge them back into action. He had lace-ups. He'd been tying them expertly by himself for as long as I'd known him.

'Josh – I still haven't given Mr Swift's letter to Terry and Mum.'

'Eadie Browne,' he sighed with a shake of his head. He sounded about thirty years old.

'And also I don't want to go to Celeste's after school.'

'Why not?'

'I don't even know,' I said. 'What's a lezzo?'

Josh frowned and shrugged. 'French, I think. Maybe Celeste's mum will know.'

'Wish you were coming with,' I said and I could see in his face that he wished so too.

'Maybe one day you can come over to my house.' He paused. 'Though I don't have any swimming pools.'

Mrs Walker dipped her sunglasses down her nose to take a good look at me and she cooed stuff mostly in French. Her English sounded beautiful too, and I decided that from then on I'd carry my satchel just like she carried her handbag, slung with nonchalance over my crooked arm. Celeste noticed and then she did it too and we copied her mother's slinky walk to the car where there were biscuits waiting on the back seats and I thought maybe it wasn't so bad to go to their house. Maybe it would do Michael good to have a day without me, he could pick up twigs and old bleached ribbons himself and see how boring that was. And perhaps it would make my parents miss me all the more, now that they had no one to say when it was time to eat, to lay the table and make the meal.

I'd grown up a walking distance from most things but from Celeste's car I watched the film of our town play out as we drove through areas I'd never known about and along streets where there was so much more space between the houses. And all the while Mrs Walker sang from the driver's seat or cursed at other motorists and to my ears everything sounded so much better in French.

A tour of 41 Yew Lane would have lasted one minute. It seemed to me we were walking for miles through Celeste's house. Everything was supersized, there was no clutter and a silky calm infused the rooms like fragrance.

'What is a *family room*?' I asked, because Celeste, like me, was an only child and this room was an immense lonely space with just a giant TV in its own grand wardrobe and a sofa the length of my street.

'Oh – I suppose it's the opposite of the drawing room,' said Celeste, ushering me into a vast room where empty armchairs appeared to be in pointless conversation and the sofas were even longer and everything was so spotless it was obvious no painting or drawing had ever taken place in there.

'Are we even allowed in here?' I asked.

Celeste laughed. 'I like the family room better because the settee is more squashy.'

I'd never heard of a settee.

'Ta-da – my bedroom.'

She kicked off her shoes and rubbed her feet like I'd seen women do in films so I copied her and we laughed about that as we fell backwards onto her bed. From a nest of cushions, we gazed up at clouds that someone had actually hand-painted on her ceiling.

'I don't have clouds on mine,' I said. 'I have cracks.'

Mrs Walker, who told me to call her Sandrine, was in the kitchen with her sunglasses now propped up on her head as she prepared a vast array of food on a queue of chopping boards. There were vegetables I'd never seen in colours I'd never imagined possible, named after people I'd never heard of like Oboe Jean. And I said to myself I could be very happy here, with these people and their interesting food and never-ending rooms and oversized furniture and a staircase that swept around the entrance hall like a huge comma.

'*Où est Papa?*' Celeste asked.

Sandrine lit a cigarette and sucked at it. It smelled so different from Michael's pipe and I held out my fingers to try it, surprised that she roared with laughter. I was given a slice of melon and a kiss on the cheek instead.

'I don't know,' Sandrine said. 'Working late – you know your father.'

I glanced at Celeste and from her expression it appeared that perhaps she didn't.

'What do your parents do?' Sandrine asked me and I loved the way the 'r' vibrated at the back of her throat, it sounded even better than Ross's rolling of his tongue around it.

'I told you!' Celeste jumped in. 'They are in the super-secret Secret Service. Tunnels! Russia! Orphans and waifs! You wouldn't believe what they have to do!'

'*Waouh!*' Sandrine clapped. 'I must watch what I say, no?'

And just like that, despite all that was on offer, my appetite went. I looked at Celeste and I looked at Sandrine and then I stared down at my plate. It struck me that they liked the fabricated Eadie and my deception suddenly mortified me. They didn't even know there was a real me. I wanted to go home just then but my house felt to be a planet away. I thought to myself if only Patrick was here. If only he was here to pinch me because when Patrick pinched me, I managed to fight tears. So I tried to pinch myself under the table, but that didn't work and I watched a tear plop onto Oboe Jean. Then another onto Harry Covair. And another. And another.

'Oh no!' Sandrine said. 'No, no no – my dear!'

'But Eadie,' Celeste wailed.

'It is my cooking?'

'Do you want crisps?' Celeste asked. 'We have them all. Every single flavour.' She paused and continued quietly to herself, 'Because I never know which flavour the kids at school might want.'

I didn't dare look up, I could only watch my tears adding too much salt to Sandrine's divine cuisine. I felt very, very far away from home. From my real home with not many rooms and with my actual parents and all the piles of paper and towers of books and other stuff of great importance which had priority over our furniture. I didn't want to be here and yet I never wanted to leave and how could I make sense of that, much less explain it? I wanted to be in two places at once yet I longed for there to be just one of me. I wanted the Eadie of 41 Yew Lane to be here. Not the spy with the lies.

Sandrine came and sat beside me. She tucked my hair behind my ear in that motherly way and gently put her arm around my shoulders. Under her touch, my Unfortunate Hair might well have been spun silk.

'Do you want me to telephone your parents?'

I shook my head.

'Do you just want to go home?'

I nodded.

We all sat there for a moment, flinching as tears caught in my breath.

Sandrine gave me a kiss. 'But perhaps first a little chocolate mousse?'

I didn't know how to move my head in response to that.

Probably at any age, chocolate in most forms makes things better, but that evening a rich, home-made mousse had truly healing properties. Just then Sandrine, she of the slinky walk and the high heels, the elegant accent and the sunglasses, the posh car and cigarettes, the glossy house and multicoloured banquet – she grinned at Celeste and me through a mouthful of mousse.

Terry never knew when he had food stuck to his teeth. Sandrine did, and she was disgusting and wondrous with it. Celeste went one step further and squeezed the mousse through the gaps in her teeth. And the Walkers looked at me with their matching mother-daughter eyes, imploring me to let go, let go of the tears and the worry and whatever else it was. Let go,

Eadie, open up and grin your mousse. Stay a while. Stay with us in this huge perfect lonely place.

And when I opened my mouth into a toothsome smile oozing with chocolate, they applauded.

And so I stayed.

'I don't really have friends, Eadie. Just a load of kids pretending to be so that I'll give them stuff.'

Celeste and I were sitting cross-legged on her bed, digesting this fact along with the mousse. I wasn't really bothered by all her toys and trinkets and neither, it seemed, was she.

I thought about Josh. I thought about what Celeste had just said.

'I get my friends through pretending,' I said and my face started to burn as my words rang loud even though I was whispering. 'I mainly invent stories to stop Patrick,' I told her. 'The others come to listen and they are like a fence – with him on the outside.' I could sense Celeste go very still. 'So I don't have proper friends either,' I said. 'Apart from Josh.'

'And now – me,' Celeste said.

'Are you going to tell your mum about my lies?'

Celeste thought about it. 'But they're not lies, Eadie. They haven't hurt anyone. They've looked after you.'

I looked at her. 'It's still a load of rubbish.'

It felt like I'd been in a foreign country and away for a year and a day when I climbed back into their car for the journey home. We listened to Sandrine sing and swear in French as she drove.

'How is the little sheet?' she asked. *'Comment s'appelle t'il?'*

'Patrick,' Celeste said, glancing at me guiltily. 'I told my mum about him last week – when you fought him. Sorry.'

There was still an unopened letter all about that hidden in my bedroom.

'He is just a little sheet,' Sandrine said again and still I was none the wiser. 'And you are a brave young woman.'

'*Maman!*' Celeste said, pointing out of the window. '*Regarde ça!*'

The Electricity Building had come into view.

'Secret HQ?' Sandrine gasped, rolling down the window for a better look. She turned to me and pulled an imaginary zip across her lips and Celeste kissed my cheek and I knew then that they didn't believe me. I could tell that none of that mattered to them and, as I watched them stare and marvel at the building, I realized that they very much liked what they knew not to be true.

At 41 Yew Lane, the sitting-room light was on. I could see the silhouette of Terry watching at the window, waiting for me to come in. He'd have been on his own for the first time in forever, his wife gone to work, his daughter out at her other best friend's.

So Josh and Celeste and I became inseparable. The three of us would sit in the playground in a circle with our legs wide and our feet touching, creating a force field to repel Patrick Semple. And though he stood a little way off, all on his own, no audience, we knew he was like a hyena just waiting to separate one of us away.

He knew he'd pick us off, one by one, eventually.

So too did we.

Firemen, accountants, solicitors, bankers, farmers, garage attendants, delivery men, builders, plumbers and a cook. These were the trades of our fathers.

'My dad is ...' I looked around at my classmates, nausea welling that the plain truth would destroy my fantastic stories and I'd be back to being Patrick's target with no one interested in protecting me.

'Eadie?' my teacher prompted. 'Stop daydreaming.'

'My dad ...' My head fuzzed and my face felt too hot. The teacher came in and out of focus and the sounds of the classroom were distorted. 'My dad,' I said. 'My dad ...'

'Works in the Secret Service!' Liz called out.

'He goes on missions to Russia!' Gary called out.

'He designs tunnels – from here to Liverpool!'

'He speaks several languages!'

'Master and Commander!'

'Code breaker!'

'Code maker!'

'And you haven't even asked about Eadie's *mum*!'

But we weren't being asked about our mums. Only our dads. Which seemed unfair on Tabby because she didn't have one.

And we were being asked about our dads because next week we had to bring them in; a sort of living show-and-tell hell.

'My dad's a boring accountant,' Josh said at lunchtime while the three of us tried to suck down warm yoghurt and slithery tinned peaches off the slightly roughened school spoons without gagging.

Celeste was very quiet. I don't think at that stage she even knew when her father would next be home, let alone what he did for a living.

'My dad doesn't really exist,' I said darkly.

In they came, the dads, in groups of four, every day for a week. Each man seemed to fill the classroom, bringing with him the scents and sounds of a wider world we hadn't had cause to imagine. Some looked identical to their kids, just a lot bigger. Others were a total surprise. Jenny's dad was white while she was black. Oliver's father was fat but Oliver was stick scrawny. Richard's dad was also called Richard and he was quiet and pale and neat in his suit whereas his son was the noisiest, muckiest boy in class. Josh's dad really was quite boring and I felt for Josh because the stifling of yawns was as audible as yawning itself. Some of the fathers came in uniforms, some brought in the tools of their trade, some gave out free pens or pads with their workplace logos. Saffron's dad called us 'guys' and played his guitar. None of us had heard of his band but we were all fans by the end. He kissed the teacher on his way out and she wasn't quite right for the rest of the day. However, there wasn't a single spy amongst them and none worked nights in a supermarket.

* * *

I had been watching Terry like a hawk for days and I sat at Alfred Pennyfeather's grave confiding that I'd been praying for a mystery bug to have Terry bedridden. I envied Mr Pennyfeather's daughters having a father who'd invented the Appellex Modern Tynogrille – while I'd invented a man who wasn't my father. I thought how I'd much prefer to take Ross in instead. He could play his bagpipes and blow Patrick's eardrums when he teased Ross for wearing a skirt. On my way home through the graves to our gate in the wall, I spent some time with Noel Ellington 1903–1969, Philosopher. I told him my dilemma and tried to tune in to his concepts on the matter. He was particularly quiet that afternoon, but I read and reread the inscription on his grave.

It is not because things are difficult that we dare not venture.
It is because we dare not venture that they are difficult.

I already knew it off by heart but whether I said it out loud or quietly to myself, still it made no sense to me. My other friends in the cemetery weren't forthcoming either and I left without a single new idea how to prevent Terry from visiting school.

At home I prepared supper, lighting the stove, setting three eggs to boil in one pan and some potatoes in another. I washed lettuce and took a packet of ham from the fridge and made tubes from each slice. Three for Terry, two for Mum and one for me. I laid the table and plumed kitchen roll into the water glasses. When I announced grandly that dinner was served, my parents looked up from their work astonished, delighted, as if seeing me for the first time in years.

Terry sliced into the ham and pushed it against his fork with some potato and a mound of salad.

'Blimey, Eadie,' he said. 'How much salt did you use? Are you trying to kill me?'

I couldn't remember the last time Terry had walked me to school and I refused to take his hand. My mind whirred with hasty ideas, the best of which was to somehow inform everyone before he uttered a word that this man wasn't really my father, but a stand-in on account of my father's identity being a matter of national security. Mr Swift was in the playground and with a lurch I remembered the letter he had sent home, for the attention of my parents, which still remained unopened and was currently tucked away on my bookshelf between *James and the Giant Peach* and *Fantastic Mr Fox*, as if the envelope contained an entire and terrifying tale of its own.

It was Friday and though there'd be chips at lunchtime that was hours and hours away. I stared at the clock willing the hands to move as Jenny's dad was introduced to the class. He was wearing a white coat and goggles because he was a scientist but I thought he looked like he was dressing up. Ian's dad was like a perfectly scaled-up version of Ian. He said he had two degrees in the arts but currently he was a househusband which was a very taxing, very tiring and underrated career, and the other dads looked at him with a mix of horror and sympathy.

'Patrick,' said the teacher. 'Would you like to introduce your father?'

Patrick went to the front of the classroom. He seemed half the size he was usually.

'This is my father Mr Barry Semple,' he mumbled and his dad told him to speak up while he rolled his eyes at the other fathers as if to say, kids – eh? the buggers.

'I'm Barry Semple – dad to two squirts, Patrick being squirt number one.' We all laughed at that. 'I'm an inspector. Not a police inspector. Not a bus inspector. I inspect places – offices, restaurants. I check up on the people who work there. I make sure all the rules are obeyed. Nothing gives me more pleasure than giving people what-for if they've messed up, done a bad job, broken the rules.'

He went on to list all the punishments and fines he dished out to rule breakers. It seemed preposterous to me that Mr Semple should have a son like Patrick and Patrick a dad like Mr Semple.

'Put it this way,' he said, quite forgetting he was talking to kids. 'It's a bit like me giving Patrick a hiding when he's out of line – it works. Right?' He looked at the other dads, at the teacher, then he looked at us. 'You do something wrong – you pay the price.' He shrugged, like it was the simplest concept. I don't think anyone in the class wanted Mr Barry Semple's job. I don't think any of us wanted to swap our dads for him. I glanced at Patrick, he was staring at the floor and there was a grubby track down his reddened cheek from a hastily brushed-away tear. For a moment, I felt for him but it was a strange feeling to have so I turned away from it quickly.

Terry was the last dad of the day, the final dad of the week. I glanced at the clock which was ticking far slower than usual.

'This is my father,' I said, not looking at him because I was staring at the floor willing a gap to open up and suck me down.

'Terry Browne,' he said and he bowed, he actually bowed. 'Father to Eadie. Husband to Jill.' I'd almost forgotten Mum had a name. He always called her *dear*. 'What. I. Do. For. A. Living,' he said and then he fell absolutely silent. Still the clock's hands hadn't moved.

I felt my father looking at me and I refused to return his gaze. I wanted to put my forehead down on the table. I wanted to curl up on the beanbag at the back of the room which smelled comfortingly of biscuits and warm bananas.

'I'm not an inspector,' he said. 'Nor am I a scientist. I'm not a house-husband like Ian's dad here, I'm not nearly skilled enough to be one of those. Hats off to you, sir, hats off to you.' And then Terry simply stopped while my heartbeat stormed ahead. 'I do *not* work in a supermarket,' he said eventually.

The air in the classroom was thick with expectation. I wanted desperately to go home.

'I do *not* work there.' Terry's voice wasn't working properly. 'I mean,' he said, 'I do go there to work – but it isn't *work* work.' His shoulders sighed and his backbone appeared to crumble. He was glancing to and away from all of us, from our teacher, like a dog about to be beaten. His head drooped and everyone could see how my dad needed a haircut. His arms were lifeless by his side while the hands on the clock hadn't budged. Nothing was happening. Nothing. People started to fidget. The other dads looked embarrassed.

'It's a cunning disguise, isn't it! So that no one will know!' I spun round to see Josh calling out.

And then Celeste leapt up. 'Tell us, Mr Browne!' she cried. 'About being a top-secret agent!'

And Terry looked at Celeste. And then he looked at Josh. Then he looked at all the expectant faces willing him to divulge. Finally, he looked at me. And the strange thing was, when he looked at me it was with a smear of guilt, a plea for apology. As if I was to excuse him for what he was about to say.

No one moved an inch when the bell sounded for break. Terry was still in full flow about his career as an international spy; about being an expert in deciphering the moral code, how a double agent had taught him Double Dutch, about his Great Escape from Alcatraz, about the Bridge over the River Wye, and about all those damn Busters he'd had to train for Operation Mince Pie.

Questions were fired at Terry as if from a Gatling gun and, though she smiled, the teacher looked at me every so often with an expression of intrigue and despair, as if she now knew why I was the way that I was and that she'd be helpless to do anything about it.

Josh's question was the best. Was it true, Josh asked, that Terry was a Dracula who lived in a graveyard and only came out at night?

Terry laughed so much that everyone joined in.

And that, at long last, was that.

The day that the stake was driven through the heart of my own personal Dracula was also the day when I was trusted to take a detour after school with three pound notes to collect our order from the Shop. Luckily, Josh lived that way so we ambled off together.

'Your dad was amazing,' he said.

'Thanks to you,' I said. 'And Celeste.'

'Race you to the corner.'

Josh won.

'Wish I could've taken my grandpa in instead,' he said.

'I wish I *had* a grandpa,' I said. 'Anyway – why?'

Josh nodded towards the end of the street. 'Because he owns the Shop.'

I paused only a split-second. 'Liar!' I laughed.

'It *is* called *Albert's*, Eadie.'

I'd forgotten that bit. Everyone only ever called it *the Shop* and I'd never seen Josh in it. I hadn't been there in ages.

'Is your grandpa called Albert Alberts?'

'No, his name is Reuben. Or Grandpa Ruby to me.'

'When you grow up – will you work there?'

'Well, I'd like to,' Josh said. 'But I have to be a doctor. According to my grandpa, owning a shop is good for grey hair just not so good for grey matter.'

'What's that?'

'Brainpower,' Josh explained.

I thought about that. 'Well, perhaps you can find a cure for grey matter and *then* own the Shop.'

We discussed this for a while as we zigzagged and kicked a pebble between us.

'Race you to your grandpa's shop!' I said.

He let me win.

Reuben looked like he'd stepped from the pages of a fairy tale; the kindest face with the right amount of wrinkles in the best places and glinty eyes like a slightly sad dog. His hair leapt from the side of his head in silver puffs and he wore a small velvet cap in rich bright blue decorated with silver thread. On his feet were corduroy slippers, it was as if readying himself to tell the best of bedtime stories even though it was only teatime. Reuben took my hand like a courtier might a queen's and he bowed. His accent, melodious and expressive, foreign and exotic, became my third favourite after Ross's and Sandrine's.

'Eadie's come to collect the order for the Brownes,' said Josh and he sounded so grown-up and professional to me.

'*This* is the Browne girl? Of 41 Yew Lane?' Reuben seemed amazed. 'Rachel! Come! This is Miss Browne. Of 41 Yew Lane,' he announced, as if I was a dignitary.

A lady breezed through the candy-coloured strips of plastic that demarcated the Shop from some secret world beyond. She wore an apron around her waist that matched the stripy screen. It had a big pocket, like a kangaroo's pouch, and there was something spiky in it.

'No!' she exclaimed. 'Really?'

I wondered why everyone was having such a hard time believing it was me. I'd been to the Shop before though usually I'd loitered outside.

'This is my mum,' Josh said. 'Mum – this is my friend Eadie.' He turned to me. 'My best friend.'

'I've come for the shopping,' I said, hoping to sound experienced at this. 'Browne. 41 Yew Lane.'

Reuben nodded and saluted and walked through the screen of plastic strips to return with our order in a bag emblazoned with the face of Donny Osmond. I recalled Sandrine saying she loved Donny more than life itself and I looked forward to giving her the bag. Mrs Albert seemed to give me a lot of change from our pound notes, which I put in my cigar-box pencil case.

'You must be starving,' Reuben said to us. 'A week of studying. Eat! Take!' He said it as if our grey matter depended on it.

Josh nudged me and nodded as he chose a Texan bar. 'Choose whatever you like, Eadie,' he said while his jaw worked this way and that.

Set in a U-shape with the till on the counter at the centre, the Shop was shelved wall to wall, ceiling to floor and crammed with goods, while the fridge unit, every inch filled, groaned intermittently. Eventually, I chose one of the knotted bread rolls speckled with poppy seeds which huddled like pups against the large plaited loaf on the counter. I sifted through my cigar-box where the coins were now covered with shards of pencil lead and flits of eraser rubbings.

'Put your money away, Eadie-leh.' Reuben tapped my hand and I noticed a line of numbers written on his arm. He must be as bad at maths as I am, I thought, and I liked him all the more. 'This is the girl?' he whispered to Josh only it wasn't a whisper at all. 'This is the Eadie that the schmuck messes with?'

I watched Josh nod. He turned to me and mouthed *Patrick*. I thought of Sandrine referring to Patrick as a little sheet. Now Reuben Albert was calling him a schmuck and I didn't know what that meant either but the bread roll tasted all the sweeter for it.

'I like your grandpa's little hat,' I said as Josh walked me to the end of Link Avenue.

'Jews often wear them.'

'Oh, is he Jewsy?'

'Jew*ish* – yes.'

'Is your mum too?'

'Yep.'
'So why doesn't she wear one?'
'Women don't wear them,' Josh said. 'Only the men.'
I thought about this. 'For their bald heads?'
Josh thought about that. 'Well, my dad doesn't wear one and he's bald.'
'But is he Jewish too?'
'Yep.'
'Do you think you'll also want to be Jewish some day, Josh?'
'I *am* Jewish, Eadie.'
My very best friend and I did not know that.
'That is absolutely amazing,' I said. 'My parents and I are Centrists – that's what they tell me.'
'*Centrists*,' said Josh.
'Yes,' I said.
'I don't know what those are,' Josh said.
'Neither do I really,' I said and we thought about that. 'Do you have a little hat too?' I asked.
'Yep.'
'But doesn't it bounce off all your curls?'
'I fix it in place with a hair clip.'
'A special Jewish one?'
'Actually, just a girl's one.'
I said I didn't believe him.
He said it was true.
We laughed about it a lot before I stopped in my tracks.
'Don't let Patrick ever know about that,' I said.

So after the best day at school ever, I'd completed my first solo mission to the Shop, accruing gifts along the way. I was entrusted to walk home from there; from the end of Link Avenue, left along Woodland Rise to cut across the park to the E-shaped streets that met Yew Lane. Donny Osmond wasn't all that heavy despite being filled with all that goodwill and generosity that no supermarket could ever stock. I smiled all the way home. It was perhaps the first day that there was no need for the goings-on at the cemetery to even cross my mind.

Our cemetery was multi-faith and I grew up unwilling to differentiate between religions because I had seen at firsthand how death was wholly unifying. I saw Christians sent on their way in polished wood coffins with gleaming brass fittings, Jews buried in plain pine boxes with rope handles, artists and agnostics in wicker caskets, and sometimes Muslims went into the ground in only a shroud. Whoever you'd been when alive, however much money you'd had, wherever you'd lived, whoever you'd worshipped – none of it really mattered when you were dead because you shared your subterranean world alongside the broadest spectrum of our town's population. Neither the degree of orthodoxy, nor the merits of one faith against another, guaranteed better soil. There wasn't a sliding scale of quality according to piety, it was all exactly the same. Earth was earth and deep down in it the dead were laid to rest.

I learned that one religion did not elicit deeper mourning than another and that atheists were grieved for just as much as the devout. Grief, it seemed to me, united people – it was indistinguishable between one set of mourners and another. Traditions differed; some came to lay flowers on a grave, some placed just a humble pebble, some brought food, toys, letters, even alcohol, but what was identical was the pull to remember, to honour, to mark with love.

Hate was something not visited upon the cemetery. Nobody brought hatred to the graves they'd come to visit. There were graves that were neglected, that were no longer visited, but Michael and I made sure these were kept neat regardless and I'd often call by just to check in with whoever lay there. I felt a responsibility towards Ruth Birch who had died in 1965 at the age of seventy-three. Her headstone carried only her name and her dates, no mention of family who'd gone before or those she'd left behind. I often made a detour to her plot, to regale her with the goings-on at school because I felt that someone with so few details could do with lots of them. Sometimes I'd put a pebble on top of Thomas Jefferey's headstone; it was engraved that he was a much-loved father and grandfather but perhaps his progeny had all moved far away because there was no sign that anyone visited. There were other graves which appeared to be forsaken and lonely but never, it seemed, from wilful neglect. Hatred was an emotion absent from the grounds.

But not from school. It thrived at school for the rest of that year; secretly snaking its way in through the gates, tripping up children as they played, winding through the corridors and coursing into the classrooms, hissing its presence through the scrape of a chair, the slap of a ruler, the slam of a desk lid, the slice of an insult, the scorch of a sudden pinch, a shoe stamping down on a biscuit, on an entire sandwich, kicking hard against a shin – always beyond the teachers' radar, operating on a frequency grown-ups couldn't hear, utilizing signs they couldn't read.

I knew Patrick hated me because he meted it out almost every day. He also wrote *Rich Bich* on the front of Celeste's exercise book but Josh pointed out to her that it was spelled wrong and therefore didn't count. Anyway, Patrick had used pencil so Celeste just rubbed it out with one of her strawberry-scented erasers as if it was little more than an accidental scribble. But he attacked Josh with a force that was harder to repel.

'You're brave – why not just tell him to shut up?' Celeste asked as the three of us walked to the Shop one day after school.

Josh took some time to think about it. 'It stops him picking on other people.'

And I knew he meant me.

'Maybe tell your parents,' I said.

'Do you tell yours about all the stuff he's said and done to you?'

The three of us pondered over this. The thought of any of it reaching any of our parents was almost worse. I'd sworn everyone to secrecy, even Michael and Ross.

Much as Josh and I lapped up the Frenchness at Celeste's, so Celeste and I drank in the Alberts' expressions. Chutzpah and schlep and meshugas and tuchus were naturally added to our lexicons. Mazel tov I said to Terry when an agent expressed interest in his work. Soon enough Josh proclaimed Celeste and I to be Jew-ish. I'm afraid you can't be Jewish, he told us, you have to be born so. But you two can be Jew-*ish*, he said and we were delighted. So perhaps that's why Celeste and I felt it so acutely, a few weeks later, when Patrick did what he did to Josh. Maybe that's why we broke the code and, behind Josh's back, we went to see Mr Swift.

The headmaster's office was all the browns; wood and leather and old books and it was fragranced by all three. There was a clock that tocked slowly with a slight echo that made time seem on our side and two tub chairs conversed with the headmaster's desk.

'Please, ladies – take a seat.'

Though our legs did not touch the floor, Celeste and I sat tall. Our teachers had taught us to add up and take away, to read and write and spell some quite difficult words – but our friendship had taught us right from wrong.

'Patrick Semple has written the word *Yid* on Josh Albert's arm,' Celeste said and we watched a grey pain instantly traverse Mr Swift's face. We told him how Patrick had pinned Josh down and dug the biro in hard as he also drew a spiky star which was nothing like a Star of David.

'And the thing is,' I said, 'it's not so much the word, Mr Swift. It's the fact that Patrick has written it on Josh's *arm*.' I showed him where on my own skin, tracing the word with my fingertip.

'It's just that we know Josh's grandpa,' Celeste said. 'His name is Reuben Albert.'

'Josh's grandpa Reuben Albert has writing on *his* arm,' I said – and with my finger I again traced an approximation over mine. 'He has a number,' I said.

'A tattoo,' Celeste said, 'from the camp.'

'The concentration camp,' I said. 'Where he wasn't a person – he was a number.'

We watched the muscles flex and twang in Mr Swift's cheeks. Celeste and I knew that no matter how mad Josh might be if he ever found out about this, we would never regret our visit to the headmaster. Three musketeers. Three sides of a triangle. Three magnets. One for all, all for one. Josh Albert. Celeste Walker. And Eadie Browne.

* * *

So Mr Reuben Albert came in to school the following week for a special assembly. He told us about his country before the Second World War. About his house and his family and his dog called Dudel. His big sister Leah and little brother Jonas. His parents and grandparents and his great-grandmother. The house where he was born, with the bedroom window which looked out over rooftops and trees to distant hills. He told us, softly, of his sweetheart Ester.

And then he told us about the ghetto, about people being so hungry that they sucked the leather of their shoes and belts for the tiniest amount of nourishment. He spoke of the night of shattering glass and the banging on the front door and having no time to do anything. He told us of being marched through snow, about being herded and jammed into trains. *Like cattle, children, like cattle* he said and it sounded like kettle but none of us giggled. None of us moved, none of us made a sound. We learned the word Auschwitz. We heard the words Six Million, but in numbers of people it was impossible to compute. We learned that he was the only member of his family to survive, that he never saw Ester again. We learned a lot that day. Lice. Starvation. Hatred. Gas. Death. Courage. Faith. Survival. *Arbeit macht frei*. But that we are never free of memories and nor should we be.

'As a Jew you learn to forgive – but it is important never to forget,' Reuben Albert told the school. 'How can I forget?' he said and it was then that he rolled up his sleeve to reveal the numbers tattooed on his arm.

I looked around for Patrick Semple. I saw him. He was sitting there and it looked like he was closing in on himself, as if some invisible vacuum was sucking the life right out of him. We locked eyes, I refused to let his go.

'Forgiveness,' said Reuben and I don't know if he was talking to us or himself. He was looking out of the window, over our playground to the park and woodland beyond. When I gazed out of windows it was because I was lost in thought. Reuben, it seemed, was staring straight at the truth.

'Forgiveness is what makes us human. It is our greatest gift. To others. To ourselves.'

Patrick didn't return to school in Junior 3, but it had nothing to do with him pinching me or tripping me up. It wasn't because he sent my lunch flying or called me all sorts of names – usually to do with how I looked. It wasn't because he said I hate you I hate you and made personal remarks about my dimple, my hair or my legs which mottled in the winter and became dirt brown in the summer. It didn't have anything to do with him slandering my parents for where they lived or what they did or vilifying them for being unable to afford brand new uniform. It wasn't because I was naturally much more able in the classroom than he. It wasn't because he talked about tits and boobs all the time – but accused me of having neither as if it was a repellent disability and not because I was simply eight years old. Most of the girls in our class were his target for their lack of tits and boobs. Patrick didn't leave school because he called Celeste and me lezzo, lesbo, lezzer, lezbicans, lesbeens. And it had nothing to do with Josh, because if Patrick had been thrown out of school then surely it must have been for that.

But Patrick wasn't expelled. He simply left. He left and he never came back.

At the start of Junior 3, Patrick Semple just didn't show up. There was a new kid in our class making up our numbers, Jonny McMahon who had a permanently runny nose. Patrick Semple had left Parkwin for good. His family had gone and they'd taken him with them; Alice in our class lived on the same street and she'd seen boxes and crates being loaded into a lorry from the Semples' house. She saw the family leave, she watched Patrick try to go back to the house, as if he had forgotten something special, but his dad yanked him away. Alice watched a new family move in the very same day.

It didn't take long for us not to think of Patrick and though we probably weren't ready to forgive him, soon enough we forgot about him altogether. And, for the two years we had left at Three Magnets Primary School, there was no mention of ugly poor Eadie Browne, or of Yids or lezbicans. Instead, those were halcyon times of snow days and proper summers, prize-givings and day trips on coaches, school plays and sports days and being allowed to give up playing the recorder. We grew bigger and the younger years grew smaller. It was exactly how school should have been.

Another year on and autumn whispered in once again and our shoes were too tight because we'd been barefoot for six weeks. My mother unpicked the hems of my uniform and the ensuing ridges on the fabric documented my growth spurts as the rings of a trunk age a tree. It was now our final year at Three Magnets and the concept of The Next Step became a looming shadow over everything we did. Mr Swift taught us in Junior 4 and made it his mission to educate us beyond the constriction of the local education authority. Deftly he wove together all the colourful strands that made up the wider populace of the school. His own father came in to meet us all, in his wheelchair with his wavery voice and his shaking body, and we patiently pieced together his stories about being a pilot. I hated that Mr Parkinson for giving Mr Swift's dad his disease. Reuben Albert made his annual visit to the school now, to talk to the upper years about what had happened to his family during the Holocaust. Primrose, everyone's favourite dinner lady, took to the stage sharing her experience of emigrating from Jamaica and sailing to England in a huge boat, telling us how hard it had been for her parents, how to this day people were still unkind because of the colour of her skin.

None of this was on any syllabus, it wasn't part of the curriculum, but these sessions were what made us feel too old for primary school. We came to see how different we were but how unique that made us and how our community was the richer for it. We didn't know that there were Quakers amongst us, that there were so many different types of Christian. We learned the word Zoroastrian and that Anahita was one of those. There was another Jewish family at the school whose grandparents were expelled from Egypt, given just a day to leave. We discovered that Cassie, in Junior 2, had two dads and I know that Celeste envied her because she felt she didn't even have the one. Rachel in the year below us brought in her older brother who was deaf and they showed us how easily they could chat and laugh using their hands. They could speak so much faster than any of us. Mr Swift said if there was enough interest, he'd set up a sign-language course. There was and he did. He also organized for a lady he knew to visit each classroom with her guide dog Ella. Ella was probably our favourite guest. Her owner passed around

Charlie and the Chocolate Factory in Braille and we all marvelled at the feel of it. That's what we did at our school. At Three Magnets Primary School we learned to feel.

And to think how I had once resented Michael for saying school days were the best days of my life. You were right, I told him. You were right and I was wrong. I love school, I told him. And he straightened the brim of his cap, smiled and pointed me in the direction of Ernest 'Ern' Daylesford's grave who'd been a teacher of science for fifty-five years. Not many people came to visit him now. There was usually a scraggle of weeds meandering around his grave as if half listening to him. These I dug up with the trowel Michael had given me for my tenth birthday.

And to Ross I started to say that it was OK, he didn't need to walk me all the way to my gate, but if he insisted then I tended to take him a fairly direct route. I didn't want to hurt his feelings but invariably there was homework to be done. And as soon as it was done I could head for the Shop with Celeste, step through the portal of candy-coloured strips to join Josh and Reuben in the back to Sort Stuff Out. Sometimes, Josh and I would go to Celeste's for a swim and these days the pair of them were often at 41 Yew Lane where we'd sit in the garden and chat about all-important nothings while we plucked at the grass and sensed Terry and my mum behind the net curtain, marvelling at the sight of us.

But I never once took Josh or Celeste into the cemetery. It wasn't a place for children, that much I knew.

If Mr Swift brushed his magic over all of us, it was certainly dipped in gold when it came to Josh who won a scholarship to a boys' school a long bus-ride away. It was the first time I truly experienced what Reuben called *nachas* – the utter joy one can feel for another's good fortune. He hugged all of us equally, as if Josh's success would not have been possible without his two best friends.

'But what will happen to the Shop?' I asked.

'The Shop?'

'Our jobs – as Employees?' I said. 'What happens to that when we go to secondary school?'

While everyone laughed tenderly at me, I wanted to cry and shout can't you see! Can't you see it's all unravelling? I feared that the next time we went through those candy-coloured plastic strips everything would be different. Things would look the same on the surface but the packets and boxes and jars and Donny Osmond bags would be empty. The contents would be gone.

'We'll always be best friends,' Josh said.

'That goes without saying,' Celeste said.

But it must be said, I thought, it must, or it will go.

We linked our little fingers and closed our eyes and took a long, deep breath and promised and prayed.

And we did believe it. We didn't doubt it. We weren't remotely interested in a world without each other. Our friendship had been the colour to our days and the glue for everything. We didn't doubt that it could withstand distance and newness and time. We were brother and sisters in all but blood. Our friendship was gravity.

In our last weeks at school, we became acutely aware of a huge world lying in wait outside Three Magnets, stretching far beyond the limits of our comprehension. At breaktime, we sat quietly with our backs to the fence that separated the school grounds from the woodland where we'd gone hunting for bugs in Infant 3, where our Junior 2 teacher had let off rockets to teach us about trajectories and angles, where the whole school went in the autumn to scavenge for leaves and twigs to make our collages for Harvest Festival. And I wondered how I'd ever find my way beyond this leafy, sing-song enclave, outside the safety and familiarity of being little and knowing everyone and everything I thought I needed to know.

8.10 a.m. 15th June 1999

I think to myself, I could do with a smoke. Then I laugh out loud. I don't smoke. I tell people I kicked the habit by the time I was in double figures. And, standing alone in the van rental car park, I suddenly think about Michael. Dear Michael with your stoop and your barrow and your sweet-smelling bacco and your what ho, Eadie, what ho.

What was the brand he packed into his pipe? I can see it – a nest of golden shreds in a dark round tin, edged in orange. A coin-twist lid which required levering off. Three Nuns! That was it. *Three Nuns – None Nicer.* Michael and I would often cogitate and discuss whether there was none nicer than those three nuns – or if it was just the tobacco which was nicest of all and the nuns themselves were horrid. And I remember Ross one time buying Michael a Dunhill's blend called Baby's Bottom. I was so horrified and disgusted I didn't dare try that one, though its fragrance was richly sweet and spicy and tempting.

'I can't believe I smoked a pipe,' I chuckle to myself.

'You talking to yourself again?' My husband's suddenly next to me. He waggles the keys to the hire van and Michael and Ross disappear in a puff of smoke.

'Pretty much,' I say and as we walk across the parking lot, I tell him about being a child pipe-smoker. He knows the story well but still he laughs at it. Quite often, recently, we've tended to over-laugh on occasion, as if it might make up for the disconnect and curtness which discolours so much.

I'm quietly wondering whether the rental office has a loo; I don't think I need it but what if I do? Oh, but we'll stop en route – it's a four-hour journey. Of course we'll stop.

Four hours in a van together and such a big day ahead; there's so much we should talk about and yet we'll probably say little. He puts his hand lightly against my back for a moment as we walk. I move in to him, just a little. He says come on, Eadie, we need to be on the road.

'We need a map, we need a compass,' Celeste said on our first day at secondary school.

'We need more than that,' I said. 'We need to stop right now.' And I said, we need to go back in time.

Classes twice the size of those at Three Magnets and three forms for each year group. Swarms of people, hundreds of them, and the noise, so much noise. I found the din deafening. The grating of chairs and the screech of shoes, doors banging, lockers slamming, and the shouting and the chanting and the chattering and the clattering and the droning whine of students remonstrating against the thunderous admonishments boomed out by the staff. Even in lessons the cacophony elsewhere could be heard.

The pace of it all.

The chaos in the cafeteria at lunchtime.

The footballs flying at my head in the playground at break.

The barracking and the jeering and sometimes the fighting.

More shouting.

The sinister looks from the third years loitering under the horse chestnuts.

Swearing. So much swearing.
    Fucksake get out of my way.
        Fuck this fuck that fuck you what the fuck.
        You're shitting me.
            Shit head.
                Knobhead.
                    Dickhead.
                        Cock.

Teachers turning a blind eye, a deaf ear. Teachers too jaded and inured to it all. Teachers losing the plot. Teachers who were beyond caring what my name was.

Celeste and I were in the same form only for registration and English lessons. Sometimes we'd pass by each other as we legged it from one building to another and our faces wore the mirror image of pure shock. We'd find each other at break, at lunch, at home-time and say to each other we should never have left Three Magnets. We should *never* have left! And we knew it was ridiculous but that was how we felt. Once I had felt tall, now I was tiny and school was huge and hostile with sharp edges and concrete stairs and labyrinthine routes and not enough time to make it from one lesson to another.

I changed my mind about growing up. If I could have frozen myself, Celeste and Josh at Three Magnets eternally turning ten years old I would gladly have relinquished my future life.

'You think *your* school's bad,' said Josh. 'You want to spend a day – even an hour – at *mine*.'

It was finally half-term and we were lolling in Celeste's bedroom, cross-legged in a circle, our knees sometimes touching, running our hands absent-mindedly over the luxuriant carpet.

'At my school they're all obsessed with balls,' Josh told us. His hair had just been cut and it served to accentuate the hollows around his eyes. 'And I don't mean rugby, football, and some weird game called Fives where you wear a manky glove and whack a ball around a strange room. What I mean is they just don't shut up about the *other* balls too – nads, bollocks, goolies.' He merrily quoted the language of idiots. 'Sweasticles, pesticles, ballsacks, scroggs.'

Celeste and I giggled.

'They're always calling each other tits and twats, like their actual gender hasn't occurred to them.'

We'd been having an ongoing *my-school's-worse-than-your-school* contest with Josh for weeks. Over the phone. By letters written on the bus, written in break, written surreptitiously in RE or double maths. And now finally, gloriously, in person.

'Boys!' I sighed, exasperated.

'Boys!' Celeste said, rolling her eyes. We often overlooked that Josh was a boy but he never seemed to mind.

'*And* they all give each other girls' nicknames,' he said. 'Betty. Nora. Fanny – predictably.'

'What's yours?'

'Juliet.'

'Romeo!' I cried, leaping up with one hand to my heart and the other to heaven. 'Wherefore art thou!'

'*Jew*-liet,' Josh said. 'JewJew, obviously, for short. Or, just Jew.'

Laughter shut down suddenly and the ensuing silence was sharp.

'It's fine,' Josh said. 'They're just— And anyway, there are a few of us Juliets there.'

The three of us sat and thought about it.

'Maybe Reuben could go in,' I said, 'and give his talk?'

But Josh's look said not likely, not at this school. 'And don't say a word to my family, OK? Promise? Say you promise.'

We promised.

'Well, what a bunch of imbeciles,' Celeste said, sounding at least thirty years old.

'Tossers,' I said.

'Dicks.'

'Wankers.'

'Bastards.'

'Knobheads.'

'Cunts,' Josh suddenly said and it sounded so wrong coming out of his mouth.

But Sandrine came in balancing a tray laden with chocolate and crisps and lemonade in champagne flutes with glacé cherries speared by cocktail umbrellas which made everything better. She looked so thin and chic and tired and beautiful and I could sense Josh gazing at her too. She looked nothing like any other mother we knew. She settled herself right down next to us.

'I was thinking, tomorrow I can take you to Welwyn. And maybe Wednesday I will take you to London,' she said. 'And you can stay for a sleepover. Pizza. Video.' She took a long sip from her glass. I didn't think it was lemonade in there.

'Actually,' Celeste said, 'Reuben has given us our old jobs back at the Shop. So we'll be busy.'

And we were so thrilled about tomorrow that none of us noticed the sadness wash over Sandrine as if she was a colour photo fading to black-and-white.

So we worked at the Shop each morning and Reuben paid us in kind with snacks which we took to one house or other.

A bottle of Tizer, Primula squeezy cheese in a tube, Matzo crackers and Nutella and, on our last day, a large jar of pickled herring rollmops for me. At 41 Yew Lane my parents were, of course, always home. But Celeste and Josh were used to popping their heads around the sitting-room door to be stared at like they were the most beautiful aliens on earth, as if their very existence was a stunning surprise to those two people stationed at their desks who lived a life thinking they were the only souls in the world.

I had come to understand that some people have outdoor parents and some have indoor parents and that was just a fact of my life. When Celeste and Josh came over, my mum never wafted into my bedroom like Sandrine. Terry never interrupted us to do chores like Reuben did. No one disturbed us. Time was ours to while away as we pleased. That week, in my bedroom, Josh spent an entire afternoon making a ball out of elastic bands and a long chain out of paper clips while Celeste sucked her hair and dotted the freckles on her arms with Tipp-Ex and I just sat between them feeling that everything was complete.

We felt older than we did when we were at school.

We felt happier than we had for weeks.

We felt our grey matter resting and recharging.

We tried not to think of next Monday.

The day before we went back to school, finally I found time to do my rounds at the cemetery. Michael waved to me from a little way off, standing beside an impressive pile of leaves he'd raked up; all the colours of beautiful autumn. It was a never-ending task, this time of year, that I knew. I should have helped him, he probably needed it more than Reuben needed help with unpacking boxes. Michael held his pipe aloft, gesturing for me to join him. But just then I shuddered at the thought of sharing that stem, of sucking through that same hole. I shook my head and tapped my fingers against an imaginary watch on my wrist and headed home. I hadn't visited half the graves I'd intended.

It wasn't about the smoking or lung cancer and emphysema and horrible black tar and all the other shocking things we'd learned about at school. It was that I no longer wanted to put my mouth where Michael's grizzled old one had been. And, as I went through our garden gate and into my bedroom where all the last-minute homework awaited, I thought how sometimes I felt young, sometimes I felt old, but at the moment neither felt particularly like the real me.

As school hauled us along, Josh's strategy was not to take things personally, Celeste's was to be brilliant at sport, while mine was to blend into the background. I'd done a collage in art where I'd stuck different pieces of wallpaper on a sheet of card over which I'd drawn an outline of a girl, an outline of me. That's the way I'd like to be, I thought: here – but not seen. So I taught myself to laugh alongside my classmates just loud enough not to be listened to. I refined my schoolwork so that it was unspectacular but warranted little attention from my teachers. I said forgettable things in class when I was asked. I kept everything to myself and to everyone at school I was neither hip nor square, I was neither here nor there. I don't think any of them knew I was Eadie-with-an-'a' and no one passed comment on my dimple or my hair and none of them cared where I lived.

My sole purpose was to go unnoticed and this I perfected. While Celeste leapt through the ranks of the netball teams, I discovered a place which suited me perfectly and that was backstage where I became crew for the school play. Neither of us was aware of the actual day, the first time, that we didn't sit together at lunch but it happened. It was the start of something different. Occasionally, we'd catch each other's gaze in the dining hall and, for a held moment, we'd send over a smile that could work its way above all the heads and hairstyles, through the noise and beyond the smell of undercooked chips and cheap bolognese, all the way back through the years.

With Josh, the three of us continued to find our nourishment in our friendship as well as at each other's tables. Friday Night Dinner at Josh's, with the two tall candles and the pair of plaited cakey challah loaves and clear chicken soup that Reuben called *Jewish penicillin*, remained our favourite. There, Celeste and I could indulge in a complete family who chatted and argued and teased and listened; a family messy with love.

At Celeste's we didn't see much of Mr Walker, he wasn't home that often but there was a cold chill throughout their house when he was. I didn't like their house with him in it; he made it seem emptier, colder, hollow. When he was there, even though Sandrine had another grown-up for company, she spent more time talking to herself, and angrily at that. I didn't like the effect Mr Walker had on his very own daughter, how Celeste's eyes were always darting about as if keeping watch in case he disappeared without saying goodbye again. We could always depend on Sandrine to make the most visually beautiful platters of miniature food that she never touched which left all the more for us. Mr Walker never ate with us anyway. That's not food, he said, that's a fucking joke.

It was in the kitchen at 41 Yew Lane, however, that the three of us held court, perfecting the division of labour as we cooked supper together. Fish fingers and peas. Frozen pizza and peas. Crispy pancakes. And peas. Sliced cucumber, quartered tomatoes, salad cream and always a tower of Mother's Pride slathered with marg. Celeste laying our table, me dishing up, Josh calling through to my parents *dinner is served!* We added salt and ketchup to everything, tucking in with appreciative hums while Terry and Mum regarded us in awe as if we'd been through culinary school; always applauding our dessert whether it was bananas with squeezy chocolate sauce, Birds Eye Supermousse or just tinned peaches. My parents were a pleasure to cook for, really.

By the second year, although it added almost two miles to my walk home and meant I had to forfeit my weekday visits to the cemetery, I'd taken to doing my homework at the café because at least I got a table to myself which I never had at 41 Yew Lane. I found the bland background noise of the café preferable to hearing Terry huff and exasperate his way through his writing while my mother cleared her throat every few minutes and muttered. Also, it meant on these evenings that one of my parents had to be in charge of supper, not me. At the café, I could crack on with my studies whilst learning to drink coffee which I knew to be necessary for adulthood though I found the taste gruesome. And so it was, that on the day that I'd managed to reduce to just three sugars, Sandrine walked in.

For a long while, she didn't appear to see me, fixated instead by the middle distance, a slice of cake uneaten right in front of her, a cup of black coffee untouched.

'Sandrine?' I brought her back to the present with a mighty jolt and she hugged me like she hadn't seen me for ages, though I'd been there for a sleepover the previous weekend.

We left the café and walked to her great glide of a car which had a parking ticket that she scrunched up and dropped in the gutter. I was looking forward to her impassioned Franglish road rage, *merde*-this, fucker-that, but it never came. She didn't even honk once, nor did she play any of her Johnny Hallyday tapes for us to sing along to. Through town we drove in steady silence, alongside the shops, the fountain, the park and the streets and on to Yew Lane. We passed the mirror-matching houses at the start of my road and then the ugly Electricity Building which, legend had it, had been the HQ of a top-secret covert tunnelling society such a long time ago. Sandrine pulled up outside number 41 and I said *merci beaucoup* and leant in for a double kiss but she took my hand in hers instead and held it to her cheek, the flesh of which appeared to have been scooped out with a spoon. There were tears caught in her lashes like silver shoals of fish slipping through a net. Her head dropped and her shoulders shook and she wept quietly into her hands leaving me no clue what to do. For a few moments I just sat there pretending it wasn't happening.

'Are you OK?' I asked eventually, even though clearly I could see she was anything but.

She chastised herself in French while she rummaged for a tissue. She continued to sob softly, hiding her face from me while I sat there, appalled. I'd seen grown-ups cry, of course I had – my next-door neighbour was a cemetery. But I knew the purpose of those tears, tears that were shed out there in the open, next to a grave where the loved lay dead.

'Are you OK?' I asked again, tentatively placing my hand on her arm. 'Um – has someone died?'

She shook her head and shrugged her shoulders, wept some more. All I could do was unclick my seat belt and squidge myself between the gearstick and steering wheel to hug her, reasoning that's what I would want. I sensed her tears diluting her spirit, I felt bone where there should have been flesh and I wondered whether to call for help but who would hear? Inside my house, Terry and Mum were immersed in their work, dead to the world. Next door in the cemetery, my friends were dead to the world too.

Eventually, Sandrine pulled away from me, sat herself upright, unconvincingly tall. She gazed at me sorrowfully, hauntingly beautiful in her distress, and I wondered what it was she wanted from me. She placed her finger against my lips.

'Please,' she whispered, 'tell no one.'

As I left the black car and walked towards my house, everything seemed the wrong way round. It had all gone topsy-turvy. Children should be the ones to cry, adults the ones to comfort. Grown-ups shouldn't tell kids to keep their secrets. It's kids who should have secrets from grown-ups; lots of secrets, written in code in notebooks hidden under mattresses, or disguised under a compendium of fibs.

I was hugely worried about everything that night. Quietly in my room, struggling with the maths homework I'd overlooked in favour of a history essay, I thought of Mr Swift and his wise-owl eyebrows. How I missed the safe embrace of my little primary school and of being in single figures, when the world barely reached beyond the end of the road.

Mr Walker left his family soon after that evening. He moved to Bristol with a woman called Geraldine. I don't know what part of Celeste he took with him but for a while afterwards she didn't even want to play netball or run her races. She didn't invite me or Josh back to her house, nor did she want to come to ours. We tried suggesting we go to the Shop and help out but she just said no to everything. The only thing she said yes to was each time I asked her if she was OK.

Every now and then for some time after, I snuck a glance at Mum, at Terry. Would it happen to them? Would they divorce at some point? I tried to imagine our front room never again having both of them in it and I thought if ever that happened, the entire house would collapse.

'Will you have to move?'
Celeste didn't know.
'Will you emigrate to France?'
She didn't know.
'Will you have to spend half your time with your dad?'
She just didn't know.

The divorce changed Celeste.
It changed Sandrine.
It changed the feel of their house and the way they were with each other.
It even changed their car which lost its shine and wore dusty smears like an embarrassment. There was a dent in the boot as if it had been kicked up the bum and it seemed to skulk, not slink, along the roads of Parkwin Garden City.

* * *

By the time we were all turning thirteen, I was fed up with Josh being Jewish and with Celeste having parents who'd divorced. Or maybe I envied them – often it was difficult to tell which emotions were which and whether they were caused by incident, fact or hormones. What I did know was that both my best friends frequently had things to do at weekends which didn't include me. I spent a lot of Saturday mornings flumped in the available space on our sofa tracing its monotonous faded pattern with my fingertip while my parents worked. Terry in the corner scurrying his biro on page after page, his breath whistling through his nose. Mum over there doing that thing with her face while she waited for a rhyme; peering over the top of her specs, her mouth an O of concentration while her nose twitched to stop her glasses slipping off. Josh was at synagogue – *again* – doing all his learning-to-be-a-man stuff for his bar mitzvah and Celeste was in bloody Bristol staying with bloody Mr Walker and stupid Geraldine. This left me with nothing to do but slump into our sofa, fidget and huff to elicit any response from either parent.

'Go and see the new arrivals next door, Eadie,' said my mum on one such Saturday. 'It's a been a busy week for the dead.'

'Amy Rogers, fifty-two. No age, no age at all.'

'John Forsyth, seventy-eight. Ross played him out. Good turnout for a bachelor. Very good indeed.'

Terry and Mum rattled off a list.

'I want to spend my weekends with people my own age? People who are actually *alive*?' I spelled it out to them, as if my parents were dense.

'Well, how about you go for a nice stroll then?'

It was posed as the perfect solution, despite it being an activity alien to both of them.

'God!' I huffed as if everything was actually His fault. I couldn't work out my moods at all so it was far easier to blame everyone else for them. 'I'll go for a stupid walk, then.'

The problem was I had no idea where to go. I was utterly without direction. I left the house and just put one foot in front of the other, scuffing along and noticing for the millionth time how Yew Lane was so much shorter than it used to be. A long time ago, I was little Eadie Browne in an oversized blazer walking to Three Magnets Primary on her own, knee-length socks crumpling around her ankles by the end of the street. Now, I was in baseball boots, a ra-ra skirt, stripy top and a pair of braces which served no purpose and my thatchy hair was naturally very Bananarama and quite cool for the first time in my life. It struck me that my younger self, hampered by little legs and a thumping great satchel, still walked with more purpose and covered more ground than the current me. So I decided I'd follow those footsteps, tracking her all the way back to Three Magnets.

But the gates were locked and the playground was deserted apart from a lone football positioned right in the middle, waiting for Monday and a good kicking. Across the playground the main building sat quietly, as if taking a breather, as if having a little peace and quiet from the scamper and flurry of all those farty kids. I gave the gates a rattle but they really were locked and I rested my forehead against them while I clung on, like a monkey staring out at a zoo devoid of visitors. My little school, how I had missed it.

I mooched away and headed for the park that wasn't really a park, just an area of green, edged with shrubs and flower beds, keeping two roads apart. There I found a bench and sat while dappled light pestered my eyes. Nearby, a little old lady fed the pigeons. She was stooped and wizened and her white hair was clipped back to either side with colourful hairgrips; not unlike how I tamed my hair when I was little. And I wondered, would I ever really be as old as her? I'd never known my grandparents but I often thought how nice it would have been to have an old-fashioned granny just like this one. I thought about going over to talk to her, perhaps to ask if she knew how long pigeons live for. I wondered if any of these particular birds recognized me from the playground, whether that's what they were cooing about – look! the funny kid with the Unfortunate Hair! Look how she's grown! And I thought how, if Josh or Celeste were with me now, I'd've said all of that out loud. Your brain is weird, Josh would say. And Celeste would hit the back of his head and tell him to shut up.

As I geared up to say hello, the little old lady left and once again I was the only person in my Saturday. Josh was in his synagogue waiting for the service to end and the Nosh Up in the hall to begin. Celeste was Bristoling with her father which meant he'd be taking her to the shops to buy back her love. I left my bench and walked slowly through light and shade. The pigeons scattered. I ate the apple I'd brought with me and chucked the core into the bushes. As I walked away, I wondered whether I'd just planted an apple tree. Maybe I would visit this little park when I was a grown-up and find a tree grown tall and laden with fruit.

9 a.m. 15th June 1999

'Actually, I think *that* was the last time I smoked a pipe.'

'Huh? What?'

There's traffic where usually there isn't and it's stressing my husband which means he's irritated with me.

I think, I'll just carry on blithely. It's either that or silence or station-surfing the van's radio and run the risk of finding nothing but crackle or a song one of us likes but the other loathes.

'I think he saw,' I say. It's upset me. 'I think he saw.'

'Who saw? Who saw what? Eadie – what are you *talking* about?'

'When I found out Celeste's parents were splitting up – I went to the cemetery. I just sat at the graves of Cecil and Nora Bamburgh because they'd been married for seventy years.'

I pause. Seventy years – imagine that. I haven't yet been married for three.

'And Michael found me and I was upset and he offered me his pipe. I told him I'd stopped smoking and then I told him what had happened to Celeste.' Just now, I recall Michael saying how Celeste's parents divorcing was probably the most grown-up thing I'd've encountered.

'Michael said, it's not easy when you discover parents are only human – and flawed at that.'

The traffic has shifted and so has my husband's mood. 'Was Michael married?'

'He told me that day how he was twice divorced and that divorce was worse than death. It seemed a disrespectful thing to say in earshot of the graves. He offered me his pipe again and this time I took it. But I wiped it. I used the tails of my school shirt and I wiped at the stem again and again – and he saw me do this and I think I hurt his feelings.'

'What an odd kid you were,' my husband says.

'I couldn't get my head around the concept that Michael even existed outside the cemetery. Back then, life as I knew it was contained in that place.'

I listen to the friendly tock of the van's indicator; the turn-off for the motorway is in a mile. I said to Michael that day, I said how I wished I could have stayed eight years old, six even, for ever. *For ever*, I said to him, but he and his three nuns puffed on that and then he said to me, no you don't. He said, it's all about growing up. You'll be leaving us before long, Eadie. You'll be leaving home and making your own life out there in the wider world, he said. I thought he was talking utter rubbish. The pipe smoke was sickly and his concept was cloying and that's when I decided I'd never smoke again or take any further notice of what Michael might have to say.

'I couldn't believe I'd ever leave Parkwin Garden City,' I say.

And my husband glances in the wing mirror and joins the slip road onto the motorway southbound.

'Three and a half hours,' he says. 'And you'll be back.'

The sound of the van's engine. The growl of tarmac under tyres. The hiss and whoosh of cars as we pass them, the thundering shudder of lorries we overtake, there's aggression out here on the motorway. I feel jittery now the journey is truly under way, the funeral looming, and I glance at my husband every now and then. Each time I do, he freshens his grip on the steering wheel, as if he needs to concentrate on the road ahead instead of listening to me witter on.

I turn on the radio and go forward and backward through channels. I don't want to listen to this. Or that. Or that. And suddenly my husband's hand is over mine, stilling it, because I've inadvertently found a random station that is playing its way through the early 1980s. And it's Dexys Midnight Runners and we both *too-ra-loo-ra, too-ra-loo-rye-ay* to ourselves. He starts drumming the crescendo on the steering wheel. Come on Eileen!

'One of the ultimate teenage love songs,' he muses. 'Though to us, back then, it was just the music—'

'—and wearing peasanty pinafore dresses and dungarees with one strap unclipped, staggered that my terrible hair was actually trendy.' Shyly, I check his face. He used to love my reminiscences. 'At school, kids would ask me how much of that green gloopy *Country Born* hair gel I used, but actually my hair just went that way.'

He's starting to chant *Come on!* and I'd be happy to have this song on repeat all the way to Parkwin, so I join in. Here in the cab Kevin Rowland is singing about *endearing young chums* as I think back to mine.

'Have you ever thought how the pace at which we go through life changes so drastically – you can age yourself by it?' I say. 'When you stop scampering, when you start to loll and loaf about instead?'

It's just the sort of topic the two of us might chew over and enjoy while the motorway stretches ahead, but 'Blue Monday' is playing now and it's one of my husband's all-time favourite songs and he's turned the volume up and I'm alone with my thoughts again but it's not such a bad place to be. As we pass by farmland and under bridges, weaving between middle and fast lanes, I think back to when Josh, Celeste and I were closer than siblings, an invincible tribe of three. I'm smiling remembering us scuttling and zigzagging our way through primary school as fast as we could; racing each other to the Shop, running from school to mine, zooming from the top of Celeste's house to the basement, from any A to any B at a rate of knots. Stairs simply there to be charged up then bounced down on our bums, shiny floors for us to skid over in our socks, a straight run of pavement or a stretch of grass laid out expressly for us to belt along for all we were worth. Run, jump, swing and spring. Looking back now, I see the three of us slowing down. It wasn't a conscious decision – just that, in our teens, we eventually stopped speeding our way around our time together because lolling and mooching became our rhythm.

That's probably why I hadn't clocked how much taller than me Celeste had grown, because so much of our time together was spent sprawled on each other's beds, chatting, listening to music, worrying about the world, about nuclear war and the famine in Ethiopia and this terrible new plague called AIDS, dissecting divorce, whispering about Sandrine, about Mr Walker, about my mum, my dad, Thatcher in general and wondering how we would ever get to meet The Teardrop Explodes. With Josh, though, the difference was extreme because we didn't see him every day. He was still our Josh despite the darkening fur on his upper lip, his ever-growing limbs and, sometimes, that strange musky smell. Josh looked at our boobs but he probably didn't even realize he was doing so. I liked to think he was just lost in thought figuring out when we'd all stopped being the same height and shape. It was as if we'd each shed one skin and we were growing into another, as yet unsure how to button it up correctly, uncertain if it was going to be a good fit.

'The cure,' my husband interrupts my thoughts.

'Huh?'

'The *Cure*.'

He turns the volume up on 'Just Like Heaven'

You

Soft and only

You

Lost and lonely

You

'*You're just like a dream*,' I sing quietly as we overtake a coach. '*You're just like a dream*.'

All of it is – it's so long ago that I can't quite believe that once it was real. Now we're heading back to where it all started, but for a funeral.

The pastel strips of plastic at the back of the Shop began to fade without us really noticing. And though we would have done anything for Reuben, gone was the excitement we used to feel in that storeroom. It was no longer a world within the world, it was cramped and a bit dingy. Some of the stacking and re-stacking now seemed pointless and there were only so many times that bottles of ketchup could be counted. And Reuben's stories, well, they went on and on and on.

'The thing is,' Josh explained to Reuben while Celeste fiddled with the price-tag gun and I stacked jars of capers wondering what those things were exactly. 'The thing is that our grey matter is put under such *duress* at school.' Josh scratched his head for emphasis. He was taller than his grandfather now. '*Such* duress,' he said. 'Really, the point of school holidays is to *rest* it.'

Reuben looked from Josh to Celeste to me. He marvelled at my tower of pickle jars before gently taking the label machine from Celeste. He nodded with a small shrug and he ran his hand over Josh's cheek and smiled.

'Ach—' he brushed at the air as if at an invisible fly. 'The Shop is not so busy anyway. More and more folk are going to the supermarket these days. And you know for me, the unpacking and lifting, reaching, bending and carrying – it's my exercise. Keeps me young.'

He gave us a demonstration that made us giggle, but my heart creaked too because perhaps we knew he was saying all of this to release us and perhaps we knew that a little of our help would have gone a long way. But we were teenagers and, by default, self-centred, so we took his words at face value without too much thought. We turned our back on the Shop.

Frankie might have gone to Hollywood but we had town. Oh, Town! The centre of Parkwin became our stamping ground and we loved it. We sang very loudly as we tightrope-walked our way along the rim of the fountain. We ate jam doughnuts and salt-and-vinegar Ringos for lunch, commandeering one of the many benches edging the elegant greensward running between the two shopping streets. There, with a jumbo bottle of cola between us, we almost died laughing as we attempted to out-burp each other while ignoring the tutting and disapproval of passers-by. It was summer and before things became a whole lot more serious at school, we loafed and larked our way through the holidays and we talked utter nonsense for hours on end.

All those projects at Three Magnets when we had drawn maps and just coloured in a block at the centre and simply labelled it TOWN. Town, now, was an education in its own right and we studied hard. Soundz Recordz became the epicentre of our world and we spent hours inside listening, watching, noting. Flipping through the racks of vinyl, we found our tribe and learned the music, the hairstyles, the fashion and lingo. We bought 7" singles with a deep belief that we were instrumental in catapulting the song into the charts. I bought records even though I didn't have a turntable. Just tilting the vinyl to the light and running my eyes along the little grooves could make the music play.

Parkwin Stores, on three levels, had little for teenagers to buy but we tried on a lot of make-up and hats, squished pillows and tested out all the sofas for sale. Opposite it, the boutique Pour Toi had nothing for teenagers either but provided excellent entertainment on account of the old-fashioned mannequins with slipped wigs, strangely double-jointed arms and appalling clothes. However, Oxfam and the hospice shop did very well out of us. We kitted Josh out top to toe. An old pinstripe waistcoat, a collarless shirt whose sleeves we rolled up to the elbow, suit trousers ten sizes too big on purpose and six inches too short by accident, kept in place with bright tartan braces, a shabby overcoat that smelled of pineapple and had a mysterious key in the pocket. Celeste and I hunted for old party dresses and petticoats and we chopped into the hems so we could look part urchin, part Cyndi Lauper. We added fishnet tights in neon green teamed with ankle socks. Granny cardies. Plastic jelly shoes, black fabric Chinese slippers, our beloved Kickers. Various straggles of material in our hair. The occasional beret or trilby. Lots and lots of bangles and beads. Everyone now envied me my hair, imagine that.

We adapted our names. I experimented with being Eddie, Josh swapped his J for a Y, Celeste went the whole hog and decided she'd be Virgine. We liked calling these out over a shop floor, across the park, on the bus. It was a thrill to answer, as if yeah – that's my name. We tried them out when we telephoned each other, with limited success – because parents are boring, parents are no fun. Even Sandrine was nonplussed with Celeste looking like Madonna and acting like a Virgine. But Sandrine was nonplussed at most things these days and she no longer made us platters of nibbles when we went over, nor did she bring us fancy mocktails. Food didn't seem as important to her as wine. Sometimes she didn't appear to be in the house at all. Oh, she'll be asleep, Celeste would say, waving dismissively at her mother's closed door and the three of us would play records as loud as we liked and stay up later than late.

But we fed Celeste, Josh and I. Josh's mum would make proper dinners for us with a soup, a sensible main course and a dessert and Celeste and I would sit at their table absorbed and in love with a family who could sit and chat, debate, tease, challenge, long after the food had gone. I'd make Celeste whatever she wanted when she was at 41 Yew Lane. It became a common occurrence for me to make supper for four. Terry and Mum loved it when she joined us. I think they loved it because there was two-way conversation for them to listen to. I'd catch my mum looking at Celeste, bestowing on her all the maternal concern my friend could ever need. I wondered if a time would come when I'd need it too. I wondered if my mother might have used it all up by then.

Throughout, the cemetery remained my own private sanctuary and it was there that I could be any age or no age, where I could simply be myself. It was there, with my back to the gravestone of Walter Vickers (*peace perfect peace*) and his wife Betty (*together again*), that I sat with the envelope containing my official exam results. The good thing about this grave was that no one could see me sitting around the back of it, not even Michael. And the good thing about Terry and Mum was that they didn't even notice that first post had arrived and they weren't even aware it was results day.

Well, I said to Betty and Walter. I said to them, now's as good a time as any. And Walter said, Eadie, that envelope isn't going to open itself while Betty said, good luck, dear. So the Vickerses were the first people to know how well I'd done at everything apart from maths which I failed spectacularly. I then skipped through the graves telling everyone my results, explaining that I couldn't stay because I had to get ready for the party. By the time I was home I was bored with talking about my results so I handed my parents the slip of paper and watched in horror as they wiped away tears and shook my hand as if I was a dignitary, but I wriggled out of their grasp.

The squashed grey housing of the Newfield Estate didn't feel part of Parkwin Garden City. At Three Magnets, in those maps we'd drawn of the town we knew, we'd been told to cross-hatch this area as if the bulbous 1960s addition to the south was best seen through a veil. Michaela from Netball lived here. Neither Josh nor I knew Michaela from Netball but Celeste talked about her all the time. Where Michaela lived, the buildings seemed to jostle against each other while ignoring each other at the same time. Front gardens strewn with the accoutrements of small children butted up against scratchy paved yards knotted with rubbish, while a lovingly tended lawn and rose bushes shared a low fence with next door's massive chained dog who, it appeared, had only a limited area to shit and shit he most certainly had.

Michaela's house was heaving. There was cider in bottles and beer in cans and wine in boxes. There were red light bulbs and incense sticks and the glorious cacophony of three different boom boxes belting out the mix-tapes. Bowie and Jagger were dancing in the street while Madonna was getting people into the groove and Dead or Alive were spinning them right round, baby, right round. People oozed in and out of the rooms and Josh and I exchanged a look that silently said sink or swim and it all felt slightly scary and slightly thrilling.

Neither Terry nor my mum drank at all, apart from Baileys at Christmas which made me gag. Really, the only alcohol I'd ever tried was the Alberts' sweet syrupy kosher wine and that was just a sip or two from a silver beaker at Friday Night Dinner.

'Shall we get a drink, then?'

I looked at Josh. 'Do you think we can just take what we want?'

'Let's go for whatever there's the most of,' he said and we made as nonchalant a path as we could to the table with bottles and cans in varying degrees of emptiness. 'I'm going for cider,' Josh said.

'OK, I'll try the wine.'

'Where's Celeste?'

'Netballing, probably.'

We hadn't seen her since we arrived.

'Never heard *netballing* used as a verb,' Josh said. 'But you got an A in English so I believe you.'

I filled a plastic cup from a box of white wine. 'You got A's in *everything*,' I said and we proceeded to toast every single result we'd achieved. Eighteen of them between the two of us, with ten A's for Josh. That's a lot of glugging.

Celeste was nowhere to be seen but we toasted all of her results too and we took it in turns to sashay up to the table and refill our cups.

'This white wine is actually gross,' I said. 'I don't think it should be so warm.'

'Here, swap. The cider's too fizzy for me anyway.' Josh belched to prove his point and a girl high-fived him. Seen Celeste? he asked her but she hadn't.

'She's netting,' I reminded him and I didn't know where the ball had gone.

'You're pissed,' he said.

'*You're* pissed,' I said.

Actually, we were both pissed and we'd been at the party all of an hour. The house was hot and noisy. The floor was sticky and there were smells I didn't like and people I wanted to know and others who were faintly terrifying and everything about everything cascaded.

'This is the best!' I said.

'This is fucking ace,' Josh said.

'Yes siree.'

'Yes siree – shall we cadge a fag?'

'You sound so stupid.'

Josh lifted his shoulders to his ears and pulled a face at himself.

'I love you really,' I said. On a small table next to me I found a cup half full of some booze or other which, just then, seemed to be a fine result. I gulped and grimaced and passed it to Josh, whose reaction was the same.

'Awesome!'

'Ace!'

We tipped the contents into our wine and cider.

''Scuse me, mate – can I cadge a smoke off you?'

I started laughing hysterically at Josh's dumbed-down accent and stupid lingo but it worked and we took the cigarette and shared it between us.

'Gross,' I said. 'I prefer a pipe.'

'I forgot you smoke a pipe,' said Josh. 'Weirdo.'

I gave him a playful nudge and he swayed and almost fell over while I lost my footing and held onto the wall for dear life.

'You are so mullered, Eads.'

'I know!'

'I am too.'

'This is so cool.'

'This is *so* cool.'

'It's so cool we were even invited.'

'It's so cool that we're about to go into the sixth form.'

'I love being pissed with you and cadging fags.'

'I love you, Eads.'

'Love you too, Yosh.'

'Let's go and find Celeste.'

'Brilliant idea.'

At least I think that's how the conversation went.

Josh and I staggered this way and that, holding on to each other as we hauled our way over bodies and upturned furniture, scaling mountainous stairs and stopping for a rest every few steps. At the top, when our legs felt like they belonged to other people's bodies, we sat down on the landing and forgot we were searching for Celeste. My head. My head my head my head. The carpet beneath us felt like a waterbed as Celeste swayed and morphed into two of her.

'Oh my God, you guys – are you pissed?'

'Completely.'

'I think Eadie needs some fresh air.'

But Celeste didn't say this to me and nor did she suggest it to Josh. She said it to her netballers as an excuse to turn away from us.

I think I slid down the stairs on my bum. Just like I used to do on Celeste's grand staircases when I was a kid.

The fresh air – or as fresh as it could be on the Newfield Estate – hit us hard, detaching our heads from our bodies and taking the bones from our legs. Josh and I made it to a low wall and kept each other steady. We sat as still as we could and took deep breaths, focusing as hard as we could on objects that we knew couldn't be moving. We burped and sighed and giggled forlornly every now and then.

'Let's promise never to drink again,' said Josh.

'I swear on my own life,' I said.

I put my head on his shoulder and leant into his arm. There we stayed, with 'Kayleigh' by Marillion soundtracking us while we prayed for the still point of the turning world, until at last we stopped spinning quite so fast and the thumping in our heads finally subsided.

'I seriously thought I was going to puke.'

'Me too.'

'I think I'm fine now.'

'Me too – but let's not move for a bit though.'

'Yeah. Let's just drink coke from now on—'

'—but let's just stay completely still for the time being.'

'Josh,' I said. 'What's going to happen after our A levels? Where will we all *go*?'

'We don't need to worry about that just yet,' he said patiently, as if appeasing a child.

'But promise that we'll all go to the same uni? We need to start thinking about that.'

'But not right now.'

'We mustn't be apart. We *need* each other.'

'We'll always have each other – wherever we end up.'

And I wondered, if I hadn't been able to walk through the door of Michaela's party without Josh, how was I going to make it to a lecture, let alone a party, at uni without him, without Celeste?

'Do you think Celeste's OK in there?'

He didn't have to answer that, really. We both knew Celeste was more than OK in there, with all her friends who didn't know us. But Josh and I were together and there we stayed, nice and steady, willing the alcohol to magically leave us without any effort on our part. Our arms were linked and we were holding hands and perhaps that's why we were clinging together – not because we were pissed and reeling, but because one of us was missing.

Was that why I turned to Josh and raised my face and found his lips and kissed them and kissed them until he kissed me back? Mouths sour, tongues rasp-dry from crap wine and cheap cider and whatever else was in those cups that we'd filched from one windowsill or other. I had no idea until our mouths were together that this was what I wanted. Kissing Josh. My first unforgettable kiss which, by the next day, I was told I had to promise not to remember.

'It was just because we were drunk.'

Those were Josh's opening words when he called me the following evening. I took the phone from the sitting room out into the hallway, looping the telephone wire under the door while my mum tutted and told me I'd break it.

'We were *well* drunk, Eads, absolutely bladdered,' he said, and I detected mortification in his voice. 'We were so pissed we – you know. We – you know – *snogged*. Because we were so completely rat-arsed.'

But I hadn't thought of it as snogging; to me it was kissing.

'Nutters!!' said Josh, ridiculing it all with audible exclamation marks while various responses pinged against my aching head like hail at a window.

'Nutters maximus,' I said reluctantly.

'Nutteramus Giganticus! Anyway – let's just forget it ever happened? Eadie? Yeah?'

'Yeah,' I said, thinking no.

'Definitely don't tell Celeste.'

'Yeah,' I said.

'I am never drinking again,' Josh said. 'Feels like my head is on back to front.'

'Yeah,' I said.

And I slid down the wall and took the receiver from my ear and held it against my chest while Josh's voice squeezed out in a tinny trickle from the handset. I heard myself promise him that we'd forget it ever happened. I heard myself muster a laugh to match his. I listened to the deafening click reverberate through my skull as he hung up and, against the soundtrack of the dialling tone, my head clanged with the hell that is a hangover and somewhere, rattling about in the hollow I'd become, my heart creaked.

'I just can't stop thinking about it.'

Celeste repeated this as she tightened her grasp on my hand. We were lolling on her bed one afternoon soon after, concentrating hard on the ceiling as if the answers to everything might materialize up there, amongst the glow-in-the-dark constellations and the mini-chandelier with two bulbs that needed replacing. There was quite a lot in Celeste's house that had needed replacing for some time.

'Neither can I,' I said.

'It's freaking me out – I'm losing sleep over it. Seriously.'

'Me too,' I said.

I squeezed her hand. She was referring to nuclear war. I wasn't.

'Each SS20 missile has a range of over 5,000 kilometres, Eadie. The Soviets have over 600 of them and each one carries three nuclear warheads and each one of those is ten times as powerful as the Hiroshima bomb.' She started to hyperventilate. 'Ten times Hiroshima – times three – times over 600. We're fucked, Eads!'

'The thing is I snogged Josh at Michaela's party.'

Though Josh had told me to forget about it and not to tell Celeste, I hadn't been able to and just then I reasoned it would take Celeste's mind off the heat of the Cold War and the obliteration of the world.

'You *what?*'

My bombshell, it seemed, had immediately usurped the USSR's.

'At that Netball party,' I said darkly, awaiting her horror. I craved her sympathy. I needed her to tell me what to do, how to feel. The relief, the relief that I'd said it out loud. 'On the wall outside the Netball house,' I said. 'That's where it happened.'

For a moment, silence hung loaded as a gun before she broke it with explosive laughter. Celeste, curled embryonically, contorted with what could only be described as joyous hysterics.

'That's the most idiotic thing I've ever heard!' Tears seeped from her eyes while she snorted with delight. 'Brilliant,' she said. 'Pissheads,' she said. 'Oh my God what possessed you?'

'Don't say anything to Josh, though,' I rushed. 'He wants to forget all about it.'

'I bet he does,' she snorted. 'God,' she said, 'that's like snogging our *brother*. Gross!' She laughed some more. 'Ew!'

I fixed a grin on my face and said yeah and I did some synchronized laughing. But that's how I stopped feeling upset about what had happened. I saw it through Celeste's eyes. I just wanted my brother back.

And so, life went on and we entered the sixth form feeling jaded already. As we grew so Parkwin shrank. Town appeared smaller and felt increasingly limited and dull. Celeste and I, both taking English A level, used words like *parochial* and *insular* quite frequently to belittle it. Josh just called it crap. Recently, we couldn't even get a bench at the weekends, on account of noisy, annoying younger kids commandeering them all. We found it impossible to remember that, not so long ago, we'd been just like them. Only better dressed. It had been months since the charity shops had anything worth buying and McDonald's had been denied a permit for the second time.

Celeste said, 'I mean, what are we meant to *EAT???*'

And I said, 'I reckon Edweard Fairbetter would have designated a specific place for Maccy D's for Parkwin if he'd had the pleasure of a Quarter Pounder with Cheese back when he'd laid out the town.'

And Josh said, 'Such a fine takeaway establishment corroborates Fairbetter's call for commercial enterprise pursuant to the ethos of leisure for a Garden City community.'

We asked him to repeat that. We thought it was brilliant but we also called him a tosser. Ultimately, we made do with toasties from the café at weekends and, during the week, I just put my head down and ploughed on with life in sixth form, which I spent mostly backstage or on the sidelines cheering Celeste on at some netball match or other.

When we joined the school two seconds ago, hadn't we whispered to each other, *sixth form block* as if was inhabited by a superior and terrifying alien race? Yet here we were at the top of the school now, with our own Common Room and privileges and all our teachers suddenly becoming more human which we found simultaneously beguiling yet untrustworthy. I charged myself to smile at the minuscule first years; to say hello, to say are you OK? are you lost? do you know where you are going? And then I thought, if someone asked me if I knew where I was going what would I say? Would I say Leeds University or would I say Manchester? Or would I just say I don't know I don't know

I don't *know?* Secondary school, it seemed, was bookended by overwhelmed kids who had no clue what anything meant.

Our teachers fed us the Future, and Opportunity, and University, and Careers, like a sumptuous banquet of plastic food. It was all unreal. Though Parkwin had begun to feel like a favourite old belt worn too tight, could I truly loosen the ties and actually function anywhere else? The concept was faintly terrifying to me but Josh said he was just looking forward to Something New and Celeste said she just wanted to get The Fuck Out of Here. But could I really be happy, would I feel safe, anywhere other than Parkwin?

In the end, I put Manchester University down as my first choice. I weighed it all up with my back to Walter and Betty Vickers' headstone. I told them Celeste hadn't consulted me about Edinburgh and Josh was already accepted by Cambridge. And I asked the Vickerses, is this when it starts? I asked them, is this the beginning of us making our own lives? Does making our own lives mean going different ways? And I asked them, what does being separated do to friendship? I listened very hard but neither Walter nor Betty had answers that day. Ross would have said something sage but it seemed no one of Scottish descent had died in quite some time as I hadn't seen nor heard him in a long while. And Michael simply packed tobacco into his pipe and said what ho, Eadie, what ho.

10.20 a.m. 15th June 1999, the motorway south

We left the 1980s some miles back, just an echo of bunnymen before the signal went. Now we're on a stretch of road where I can't seem to tune the radio to anything. I try again. The crackles and whooshing and sporadic voices and snatches of music sound like the operations room of a secret HQ in a war movie.

'Eadie! God's sake!' He pulls my hand away from the dial and switches off the radio. 'Just leave it.'

'You should have brought your own music then,' I retort and I shift my shoulders away from him, immediately as irritated by myself as I am by him. My husband swears under his breath but directs it at the traffic. According to him, no one's got eyes. No one can fucking drive any more. He thumps at the horn but hits the wipers instead which scrape and judder until he blasts screenwash against the glass. The blades wipe away the dust and dead flies. It makes a surprising difference but does nothing to clear the mood inside the cab.

And I think how I should put my hand on his knee and give a gentle squeeze. An easy gesture, but my arm is like a lead weight. Or I could just say thank you for driving. For taking the day off work. For being here for me. Simple words if only I could find my voice. I could tell him that I love him – he could probably do with hearing that – but the road just rushes away, taking my words under the wheels of the van. And then out of nowhere, a hidden voice proclaims something I had no idea I even knew by heart.

> *The weight of this sad time we must obey*
> *Speak what we feel, not what we ought to say.*

Where's that come from, all of a sudden, crystal clear and out of the blue? Well, over and above it coming from *King Lear*, from Edgar? I quote it again to myself and it strikes me that, if I was brave, I'd do as Edgar says. I task myself with saying what I feel, to be open and genuine. But I don't utter a word. It was never mine to say. I only ever heard it from the wings, all those years ago, while the action played out on the stage three nights in a row. It was our upper sixth performance of *King Lear* when our A level exams were done and school was almost out for ever.

'Can't believe you got off with Edgar!'

Celeste was delighted. Previously she'd told me it was pretty lame that I hadn't snogged anyone in the entire two years of sixth form.

'His actual name is *Ben*,' I said and I covered my face with my hands in mortification. 'I can't believe I did that.' In my mind, I'd got off with Edgar, not Ben.

'He's fit though.'

'He's a knob,' I said.

It was late. We were walking arm in arm away from the King Lear after-show party back to Celeste's. She was wearing a skirt that could pass for a belt whereas I was still in stage blacks, wearing my T-shirt emblazoned with CREW. We'd walked from school, past the half-built leisure centre and on through the deserted town centre. Around our ankles, Saturday night takeaway cartons and chip paper scumbled along the pavement while cans and bottles loitered in the gutter. Overseeing everything, Margaret Thatcher defiant on the poster we'd all ripped into over the last week. But she had won her third term in office and now a single word had been graffitied blood red over her face. *Despair*.

In a shadowy doorway, a man was slumped motionless, his left shoe cast asunder like it had had an argument with his foot. He resembled a badly made Guy on Fireworks Night.

'Do you think he's all right?'

'Should we call the police or something?' I said.

'I'm not sure,' said Celeste. 'We should check if he's breathing.'

'Oh my God, do you think he's *dead*? Oh my *God*.'

We'd done first aid in school, last year, after our exams. We couldn't remember a thing.

'There's a phone box,' I said. 'Maybe we should call Josh?'

Celeste inched closer to the man but I was concreted to the pavement.

I called over. 'Can you see him breathing?'

'I don't know,' she said. 'I'm not sure. HELLO? ARE YOU ALL RIGHT? DO YOU NEED HELP?'

Slowly, I tiptoed towards them. 'DO YOU NEED YOUR SHOE?' At that moment, it seemed important, like a crucial scene from a twisted adaptation of *Cinderella*.

We hovered closer still, calling out to the man, and when he started to burble and shout incoherently, we were triumphant.

'He's alive!' said Celeste.

'Here's YOUR SHOE!' I kicked his shoe towards him. He reminded me of someone but I couldn't think who. It was dark and he was still contorted and actually I was cold and tired. This past month: our final A level exams. This week: hardly any time to prepare *King Lear* with all those set changes and excitable actors to control. Tonight: the euphoria of the last performance, the after-show party, snogging Ben, or Edgar. First thing tomorrow: back to school to dismantle the set and sort out the prop cupboard. Just now though, my priority was hot chocolate and marshmallows and Celeste's vast and bouncy bed awaiting us like an expansive, benevolent hug.

'Seedy,' the man slurred as he began to draw himself upright.

'Here's your shoe,' I called over again, nudging it closer with my foot. It was a large shoe and incongruously shiny.

'Easy,' he mumbled, his bowed head lolling as if it was attached to his neck by skin alone. 'Seedy? Eeshy!'

And Celeste was kneeling down, tying his laces as he straightened himself upright, his hand somewhat alarmingly on her head as if he was blessing her. And then I saw who it was. I saw who it was. I understood *easy* and *seedy* and even *eeshy*. He thought he was saying Eadie.

It was Ross.

It was Ross in grubby dad jeans and weirdly shiny shoes and a dishevelled shirt with what might have been blood on it. This was Ross and this was not Ross. *My* Ross was all about soul and stature, the kilt and the swagger and the towering build. My Ross was about uprightness and not downtroddenness. My Ross was the voice of reason I'd revered my whole life. I trusted every word he'd ever said, even when I didn't like what I heard. My Ross was the Ross of stirring bagpipes and astute philosophy, who guided me through what to do and how not to feel. He was my escort from graves to gate, he was my sage and sensible friend and I looked up to him. Even now, at eighteen years old, I still looked up to him, all the way up his six-foot-four-inch frame to the man whose rolling voice had only ever dispensed wisdom and comfort.

That was Ross.

This, though, was *not* Ross. Could not be. I would not have it.

This Ross couldn't even say my name. This Ross stank and was filthy and repellently pissed. This Ross had a dark rancid stain on his jeans and I just wanted to be gone.

'Are you sure you're OK, sir?' I heard Celeste say.

I turned away. 'Celeste, come *on*. He's fine now – he's alive. Let's *go*.'

'Eadie.'

He said it perfectly and it reverberated around the deserted town centre. 'Eadie Browne? Wee Eadie, aye?'

'Eadie?' Celeste said. Eadie Eadie Eadie everywhere and I didn't want to answer to any.

'Just pretend it's not me. *Please*.'

'But Eadie— '

'Oh *God*,' I grabbed her arm and pulled her away. 'I just want to go.'

And we were slaloming our way through Saturday night's detritus to the central boulevard that dear Mr Fairbetter had envisaged as an elegant swathe of lawn for the gentle folk of Parkin Garden City to promenade. But the fountain had been off for weeks and now rubbish floated on the surface. Around it, the grass was patchy grey and the litter bins overflowed. To either side, the long line of trees appeared to stand in tired judgement.

'He's just the bagpiper bloke who's sometimes at the cemetery,' I said. 'He's creepy.' Celeste winced and I recoiled from my words. 'I don't really know him,' I said. 'I don't really know him at all.'

I wanted Celeste to stop talking about him and to stop thanking me for marching her away. I didn't want to think about Ross. I hoped never to see him again. I felt betrayed and repulsed and, down a cul-de-sac of my conscience, I felt ashamed at myself too. I didn't like the sensation of any of these emotions.

'God, Parkwin's become a dump.'

'It's always been a shitpit, Eadles,' Celeste said. 'Thank God we're leaving.'

'Let the countdown commence,' I heard myself say, thinking how strange that those words should come from my mouth. But I felt done with my home town just then. Oh Parkwin.

Celeste's micro skirt had rucked up. I could see a bit of her bum. I stepped up the pace, craving the comfort of hot chocolate bobbled with mini marshmallows and the billowing safety of her bed.

Celeste fell asleep in her clothes on top of the duvet. I pulled the covers over me and wondered how I could be so tired yet so awake. A thought struck me so hard it became a pounding in my head.

People often aren't who they seem.

Ross's words. Ben who I didn't much like, wasn't really Edgar who I did like. But hang on – was Ross really Ross? I thought just then of Ross, kilted to perfection, playing his bagpipes over the years for all those Scots who, for one unfathomable reason or another, had forsaken their majestic mountainous land of castles and eagles and mournful glens for a life and death in our bland Garden City. People often aren't who they seem. Ross himself had said this to me a long time ago. He'd said it about Patrick Semple from Three Magnets Primary School. But Ross? Well, he was just the hired piper at the cemetery next door to where I lived. I didn't really know him, I didn't really know him at all because people often aren't who they seem.

I thought how the problem with being a teenager was that sometimes I almost buckled under the weight of the adult world on my shoulders but other times I still felt like a child, and there was never any warning of either feeling until I was right in the very fug of it when it was most hard to surface.

The early-morning light had started to peer in through the gap between Celeste's curtains as if in disbelief that I was still wide awake. People often aren't who they seem. I took those words Ross had given me all those years ago and I tossed them aside. And just before I went to sleep I said to myself, be careful, Eadie, be careful.

Terry's birthday fell the day before our A level results and I bought him a leather-look notebook from the new and slightly improved Gifts department at Parkwin Stores. It was navy blue, debossed with *GREAT IDEAS* in gold. My father, Terry Browne, the man with years and years of great ideas that still no one wanted. I hoped that my gift would inspire and not dishearten him.

My parents were ensconced in their worlds at their desks while I opened tins and chopped up salad for a birthday supper. As I gave the ketchup bottle a good whack before balancing it upside down, I realized I hadn't stopped to consider what life would be like for Terry and Mum when I left home. My lovely little indoor parents, living as they felt best. And I wondered, what had possessed me to choose a university so far away? They'd both used the word *remarkable* about my offer from Manchester University but just then I thought how simply getting on that coach would be remarkable enough for me. Suddenly, I didn't want to go. I didn't want to leave. What could I have been thinking? Oh, Parkwin! With the meal half prepared, I went to my bedroom and flipped through every gold-edged empty page of the birthday notebook in which my father could labour his great thoughts.

'I'll come back for your birthday, Mum,' I said when finally we sat down for supper. But as we ate our fish fingers and pressed the peas against the backs of our forks, we all quietly considered how I'd be a hundred and fifty miles away, over four hours by coach. Glancing from my mother to my father, I could see how they had already let that hope go. Terry's birthday celebrations didn't extend much beyond 8 p.m. as he had to go to work. I had made him a Victoria sponge that sloped to one side like laughter ebbing away.

I'd persuaded myself that I was too busy to dwell on the fact that my last summer at home before university had been spent working at the café while Celeste was mostly on a sun lounger at her grandparents' in France and Josh was hiking in Israel. But I had missed them and their postcards had only exacerbated the distance between us. Not just the physical distance but the fiscal disparity too, something I'd never really thought about before. As young children, we'd employed a genial and natural bluntness, which learned manners and honed tact overruled in later years. When we first became friends at Three Magnets, we discussed the vagaries of wealth as if it was a fact as immutable as the colour of our eyes or our surnames. It was just who we were. We're well off – but not rich, Celeste had said. We're comfortable – but not well off, Josh had said. I don't think we're actually poor, I had told them, but we have to be careful. At that age, we put neither price tag nor judgement on things; Celeste loved my magic polyester dressing gown which could light up with static just as much as I loved the springiness of thick woollen carpet in her house. Josh was obsessed with the scent of the potpourri in the little dish in our sitting room and Celeste and I coveted the wholesale boxes of confectionary that Josh had access to. But the truth was that the summer after we finished school, when we had only two months before going our separate ways, I resented my best friends for fucking off on lovely long holidays which I could in no way afford.

Josh came back from the kibbutz with a ponytail, or a risible attempt at one, but he wore it with aplomb anyway. There were strips of knotted leather around his wrists and a necklace that looked like it was made of plum stones. He'd cut the arms off all his T-shirts and wore frayed denim shorts and baseball boots, his legs tanned and lean and fuzzed with wiry blonde hairs. His skin had turned mud brown, his teeth gleamed and his eyes sparkled. He had lots of new expressions, hummed songs we didn't know and smoked cigarettes called Time until he ran out of Time and decided to quit anyway because he said he couldn't study medicine *and* smoke, as if it was a dilemma he'd given great thought to.

Celeste arrived home the colour of honey and her hair chopped into an elfin crop. Her was heart brimming with the holiday fling she'd had with someone called Lois who, from a photo, looked a bit like a girl. I was as pale as when they'd left; making toasted sandwiches at the café was hot work but never gave me a tan.

Next summer, I said, let's all go away together. We could go interrailing, I said. Sleep on a beach in Greece. Work on a kibbutz for board and lodging. Stay at Celeste's grandparents' for free.

'But next summer is *aeons* away,' Celeste said.

'A lot can happen in a year,' said Josh and then he paused. 'Cambridge,' he said, holding out his hands for Celeste and me to take.

'Edinburgh.'

'Manchester.'

We let the names of our new homes linger in the stale air of our current one.

'This is it!' Celeste said.

'This,' said Josh, 'is *it*.'

'This is terrifying,' I said.

And they looked at me and I realized they weren't terrified at all.

I'd taken my leave of Mildred Robinson, of Joy Trimble and Noel Ellington. Ruth Birch. Thomas Jefferey. I'd spent a long time with Walter and Betty Vickers. Now I stood at the grave of Alfred Pennyfeather and, for the umpteenth time, I wondered about his Appellex Modern Tynogrille and what it did and whether it was still in use. Michael was next to me. I'd been helping him sweep as I listened intently to the companionable silence we'd crafted over the years.

'I'm going to Manchester University tomorrow,' I said quietly.

It took a while for him to answer. 'Little Eadie Browne,' he said softly to himself. 'All growed up.'

As we stood side by side, these days shoulder to shoulder, we both conjured Eadie at four years old singing her tuneless songs on that bench over there. And look – there she is, a little older and absorbed in her colouring-in books. Cartwheeling on the undug expanse when no one is around. Standing quietly a little way off when visitors come to contemplate and grieve. Busying herself up and down the rows, using her second-hand school blazer sleeve to sweep catkins from headstones. She's over there, hiding behind headstones to avoid homework, finding respite from that mean boy at school. And there she is, slumping glum amongst the graves as she shoulders the weight of adolescent moods. Old enough to use the secateurs, big enough to push the wheelbarrow. Tea and cake and a puff of a pipe.

'I'll be back all the time,' I told Michael. He looked confused.

'Why would you want to do that?' he said and off he pottered with a what ho, Eadie, what ho.

Back at 41 Yew Lane I listened from my bedroom to Terry and Mum talking to each other in their secret language of soft half-sentences. Every now and then a little light laugh adding melody to their gentle chatter and easy silences. And I thought to myself, I thought how wrong I'd been to worry how they'd fare without me here, with me 150 miles away Up North. I realized that they'd be just fine. It was irrelevant whether I was here or not. The two of them, in their world at number 41, shuffling along as they knew best, absolutely fine in their enclosed togetherness. And I thought – it's not them I need worry about when I leave home. It's me.

* * *

Eighteen years old with three A levels under my hat and a coach ticket in my hand to take me away from Parkwin. I put the ticket down and look around my bedroom wondering how I'll ever fall asleep tomorrow night, in halls of residence in a place called Rusholme. Rush home. You bet I will. All the time.

Drinking in the details of everything, taking snapshots with my mind's eye, ignoring the two suitcases on my floor gaping wide, their interiors gulping up all that's coming with me to Manchester. Will my clothes fit – not just into my luggage, but in Manchester? I take some stuff out and return it to the cupboard, to shelf and windowsill. I don't want to empty my room of me. I don't want to disappear from this house.

Over my clothes I arrange an entire layer of mix-tapes – Josh, Celeste and I have spent hours making these for each other. Terry and Mum bought me a tape-to-tape ghetto blaster as a leaving present, as a moving-in present. A well-done present. A good-luck present. A we're-so-proud-of-you present.

With great care I pack my teddy, the one whose paw wiped away my childhood tears and dabbed the knocks and grazes on my knees when I was little. I prise off the Blu Tack and roll up some of my posters: David Bowie, Kate Bush, Tears for Fears and the naked torso of some man holding a baby. They are all coming with me even though they've left blunt rectangles on the wall like blanked-out windows. But I can't find my Che Guevara beret and suddenly it's crucial that I have it in Manchester with me. I used to feel so strong when I wore it, like a revolutionary. I'll need it up there in the Grim North when I trade my soft little Garden City for a vast Victorian one.

Under my bed is the crate stuffed with important things from over the years. I drag it out and sift for the beret, distracted by old scrapbooks and copies of *Smash Hits* and a bottle of patchouli oil that has dripped over an envelope addressed to *Mr and Mrs T Browne / By hand: Eadie Browne.*

I know that writing but for a moment I can't place it. It's confident and loopy and then I remember – it's Mr Swift's, beloved headmaster of my primary school. And vaguely, vaguely I recall being given an envelope to take home to my parents when I was a little girl. It appears that I omitted to do this. I remember now hiding it in various places and I'm racing through memories, galloping back through time. I turn the envelope over and over, wondering about its contents. It's not addressed to me but I dither on that only momentarily.

Dear Mr and Mrs Browne

It has come to my attention that recently Eadie has been the target of unkindness from a child in her class. I wish to assure you that my staff are keeping a close eye on the situation. However, Eadie is dealing with the matter in her own inimitable way and her plucky approach is to be commended. I would add that, should she wish for her teachers – or indeed I, her headmaster – to be involved, she must not hesitate to ask. Here at Three Magnets we teach our pupils that the world is made up of many different types of person and that, at all times, we should strive to be the best version of ourselves. Your daughter is exploring this notion admirably.

My best wishes
James Swift

Images and sounds of so long ago march into my room. I don't know how long I'm kept hostage by times and people I'd forgotten but suddenly Terry is standing in the doorway with an awkward smile. He appears not to notice the chaos, the deconstruction of my eighteen years, the distillation of myself into two old but rarely used suitcases.

'Mum'll be off to work soon,' he says.
'I'll make supper in a minute.'

'Eadie,' he says, 'a little advice if I may.' And Terry tells me to make sure I befriend students studying medicine, law, accountancy and dentistry. 'The friends you make at university, they will be friends for life – so you may as well ensure that they're a useful bunch,' he says.

'But all I can give them in return is a historian – what use will I be to any of them?' I say.

'They'll *never* have met an Eadie Browne before,' my father tells me. 'Mark my words on *that*.'

I roll my eyes at him. 'I can't find my special beret.'

'Oh, it'll be somewhere,' he says. 'In this house, everything is somewhere and nothing disappears.'

He tells me he'll look for it in the sitting room and off he goes. 'The hunt for the beret is *on*!' he calls out to my mum.

'Which beret?' I hear her say.

'Eadie Guevara's.'

'Oh, I know where that is.'

I put Mr Swift's letter back into the envelope and place it carefully into the crate with all the other souvenirs from my life thus far. As I head to the kitchen and prepare the last supper, I decide that when Mum has left for work and Terry is once again toiling over his words, I'll slip out to the grounds one final time. The living will have long since left, back to their homes until tomorrow by which time I will have gone. And the dead – well, they're dead to the world. Mostly.

Part II

10.55 a.m. 15th June 1999, the motorway

'Shit fuck what *what*?!'

I must have dozed off but I'm startled awake at the sound of my husband honking the horn of the van.

'Sorry!' He's cheerful, tooting merrily at a car that's nipped in front of us. There are Manchester City scarves billowing out of their windows and my husband is delighted, my husband is now chanting football songs.

I always think of him as an outsized schoolboy when he rejoices in his favourite football team. It makes me peculiarly happy, not irritated in the slightest, not even when he's sitting in front of the TV shouting at the ref for being blind, or berating the players animatedly. And when he goes off to matches with his bobble hat and scarf and his cheeks flushed with excitement, anticipation, pride; I tie his scarf and give him a kiss and I tell him *if I had the wings of a sparrow, if I had the arse of a cow, I'd fly over Old Trafford tomorrow and shit on the bastards below*. I quote it very seriously. He always laughs and says wish me luck as if it's him about to play.

Now his joy makes me happy and I start to hum the tune to 'Blue Moon' and it's not long before he joins in and the two of us are singing the Man City anthem. He takes my hand in his and pumps it up and down as he leads the way through various chants. City were at Wembley two weeks ago in the Second Division play-off final. Two–nil down, smashing Gillingham in extra time to gain promotion to the First Division. The fans are still celebrating.

'Best day of your life, I reckon,' I say to him.

'Best day of my life will be the boys making the Premier League,' he says.

We've stopped singing and the car with the scarves is way ahead now; we've watched it zip in and out of the lanes, undertaking and overtaking and generally driving like a knob. But they support Man City so my husband is giving them special dispensation. He puts both hands back on the steering wheel and I return my focus to the hard shoulder blurring by at 65 miles per hour.

'Actually – the best day of my life was marrying you,' he says quietly, too softly for me to detect whether that's fondness or regret in his voice.

Say something, Eadie. Say something now. Say it back to him.

But I just tiptoe my fingers shyly along his forearm, take his hand from the steering wheel and hold it as I hum his club's anthem.

Blue Moon
You saw me standing alone
Without a dream in my heart
Without a love of my own

Eadie Browne. Room D1 – 12, Hulme Hall, Rusholme. Eadie Browne. University of Manchester, Department of History.

That's Eadie with an 'a' and Browne with an 'e'. A first-year student called Eadie Browne. Me.

Take her as you find her. She's in room 12 on the first floor of D Block; a single room with teak-look cupboard, shelves, desk and bed, a basin, drab green curtains and a view out over the roofs of red-brick terraces all the way to the floodlights of Manchester City Football Club's Maine Road stadium a little way off. Like everyone on this corridor, Eadie Browne has her name on her door and under it hangs a small notebook with a pencil, secured with a big blodge of Blu Tack. You can leave her a note, if you like; she's drawn a small flower with a smiling face in the corner of the first blank page. She's in her room, rearranging posters and postcards yet again to make the place hers, eating crisps to avoid the shove and din of the dining hall. You've probably passed by her a dozen times already and you wouldn't know that she has the one quirky dimple because she hasn't done all that much smiling these first few days.

There's a single payphone for D block and it's on the second floor but there's always a queue. There's invariably a student commandeering the phone with a leaning tower of ten-pence pieces being fed sorrowfully into the slot as if solace can be paid for. But Eadie's in room 12 on the floor below and, out of sight in her bedroom, she's wondering if she was mad to come here, wondering if her best friends are feeling the same in their distant worlds of Edinburgh and Cambridge. There's no way of knowing. Cheery Eric in the Porters' Lodge checks the pigeonholes every day for her. She stood there this morning and also mid-afternoon after second post had come, but once again there was no post for Eadie with an 'a' and Browne with an 'e'.

Knock on her door, why don't you. Knock and check that she's OK. D1. Room 12. Eadie Browne. Me.

*Dear Josh
Hi how are you?*

I spent a long time wondering what to write next before scrunching up the paper and chucking it on the floor. I got no further with a letter to Celeste starting with exactly the same wording.

I tried again.

*Yoshwah!
How's it going? How's Cambridge? Have you even unpacked yet? Well, I made it here but today I missed my first lecture because I literally couldn't find where it was!! Nightmare!!!*

All those exclamation marks were dishonest. Rip it up and start again.

Hey Josh – everything in Manchester is so vast and noisy and busy – it's such a different world and I can't figure out where I belong or how I might fit. In fact, I can hear people outside my room right this second having a laugh but it seems I've forgotten the word for HELLO or which way the door knob turns to open.

So I haven't made any friends yet – have you??? And I've been surviving on crisps and chocolate. Anyway, this is the number of the payphone on my block – can you maybe call me on Friday evening at 7.30??? Write to me before then to confirm and I'll go up there and hover???

Eadie
xxx
PS how's Cambridge???
PPS at Freshers' I joined J Soc – I just told them I am Jew-ish.
PPPS write soon????

That letter made it into an envelope. Then I reread it, cringed at the multiple question marks and decided I sounded a bit wet. Josh would only answer with his sensible advice. He'd use words like *discombobulated* and he'd never in a million years advise that I pack it all in and return home. So I tore the page in two and busied myself trying to prise the stamp off the envelope.

Darlingest Slest

How's Edinburgh? Manchester is massive and there are so many people. Everyone else seems to know each other, everyone else seems to be having the best time ever – IT'S INTIMIDATING!!! And also – Hulme Hall only went mixed a couple of years ago so there are about 70 women to 300 men and don't say lucky you because all the blokes are twats. And don't say they can't all be twats – because they can and they are.

Freshers' Week was – bizarre – this girl called Luna glued herself to me and made me join all these clubs I'm never going to go to. Like the Winnie-the-Pooh club. What even is that? I did join the Film

Society. Also J Soc (you just tell them you're Jewish – it's not like they ask for proof). My reading list is insane. Write soon – promise? Also here's the number for the payphone upstairs – but write to me to let me know when you might phone because there's always a queue.

Love and miss you – I even miss small boring Parkwin!! Hey! shall I try and transfer to Edinburgh?!?!?!?

Eadles
xXx
PS write and tell me when you're phoning.

I folded the letter and put it in an envelope and then I carefully soaked off the Josh stamp and glued that on to it. *Celeste Walker*, I wrote in my most flouncy calligraphy. And then I realized I didn't yet have her address. She was meant to write first.

I was probably driving poor Eric in the Porters' Lodge mad asking if there were any letters for Eadie-with-an-'a' Browne-with-an-'e'.

Hi Mum, hi Terry

Ten days in, everything's fine. My course has started now and it's A LOT of work. Please write to me – also here's the number of the payphone in my block (but write first and tell me when you can call??).

Love
Eadie x

And that was the letter I sent.

I took to writing fake messages on the notebook I'd hung outside my door so I didn't appear to be such a no-mates loser. The little flower I'd drawn was still beaming out hopefully above all the white nothingness it was planted in. I wrote *I'm in the Library!!!* underneath it and, the next day, I put a line through that and scribbled *Popped out – back soon!!!* even though I was in my room, sitting on my bed with a pile of unopened books ganging up against me. It wasn't like I expected anyone to take much notice of the messages I left on my door, I just didn't want the page to look so pathetically blank to everyone who passed by. But it seemed I was not the only one.

Tea and 2x sugars!!!

The notepad on that door belonged to someone called Fiona G and I caught sight of it as I walked down the corridor to the women's showers. Avoiding an argument of hairs worming around on the cubicle floor, I thought about Fiona G and two sugars in her tea as I showered and I wondered how many people had made her a cuppa on the strength of that message. I thought that perhaps I'd write something similar on my pad. After all, I'd managed to get my coffee drinking down to two sugars; I could write *Mine's a coffee!!!* and I could draw a picture of a steaming mug. Or I could just write *Coffee??* and then someone might knock and say yes please. But what if that person was Weird Lawrence who had the room next door to mine? I'd been avoiding him. The walls were paper-thin and I'd heard him making strange noises; chirps and squeaks and sometimes a chant: *no no no no no*. He looked odd too: tall and lopey and very pale with darting disconcerting eyes, trousers that were just a little too short and mismatched shoes. A few times he'd knocked softly at my door very late at night and called out in a murdery wavery voice. *Edith! Edith!*

But I'm not Edith, I'd say to myself pulling the pillow over my head.

I'm *Eadie*.

Browne.

And I'd just pretend to be asleep.

After my shower, I slowed right down outside Fiona's door because Kate Bush was cloudbusting in there and it was my favourite of all her songs. At that very moment, she was singing that she just knew that something good was going to happen, and she gave me the confidence to knock.

'I can make you a tea with two sugars,' I said in a rush and the girl, sitting on the bed surrounded by a menacing stack of books, looked at me, delighted.

'Sod the tea,' she said, jumping up and reaching for a bottle on her shelf. 'Fancy a tipple?'

It was port and the bottle looked like something pillaged from a pirate ship. I said yes please, thank you very much and, with my damp towel slung over her chair and my Wash & Go plonked on her desk, I accepted a mug decorated with sausage dogs and filled with port. And as I sipped and Fiona asked me questions, something struck me. No one here knew me at all. I doubted they'd even heard of Parwin Garden City. Certainly, they'd never shopped at Reuben's and they weren't aware that I used to have Unfortunate Hair. They hadn't met Josh or Celeste, they didn't know of my indoor parents or a single soul who lay at rest in the cemetery next door to my childhood home. And just then I thought how easy it would be to make stuff up; backstories to rival those I'd told at Three Magnets Primary School. I could assume any identity I fancied because no one here, on the first floor of D Block at Hulme Hall in Rusholme, Manchester, had a clue who I was. I really thought about that as I sipped at the port.

'The mysterious Eadie Browne,' Fiona marvelled, chinking her mug against mine.

'Huh?'

'You're never in – according to your notepad!'

I could be anyone I wanted to be, anyone at all. I could reinvent the past, rewrite my history, spin the most intricate of yarns and wrap them around Fiona. Just then though, Ross of all people marched across my mind's eye. I heard him say quite clearly, as if he was standing in the doorway of Fiona's room, how people often aren't who they seem. In that instant I knew for sure I didn't want to be one of them. I looked at the door, there was nobody there. I glanced at Fiona and took a bolstering sip from the mug with the dancing dachshunds.

'I just write that,' I admitted. 'But actually, the fact is I've been in my room mostly.' My reflection was wavering murkily on the surface of the port. 'I was just sitting in my room pretending I was out.' There was a sticky silence and I looked up at Fiona. 'The thing is, I've found it all a bit – much – and the truth is, I've been really homesick.'

Fiona closed her eyes and tipped her face to the ceiling, sighing loudly. 'Yeah, tell me about it,' she said. 'Worst pain imaginable. I only put that tea message up yesterday. I was going to take it down tomorrow. Cups of tea – zero. Till you knocked.'

'I've felt such a failure – like I've made the stupidest decision.'

'I've been feeling too pathetic to tell a soul.'

'I thought everyone but me was having the best time.'

'Snap. Do you think there are others like us, then?'

'I don't know – maybe?'

Our friendship started there and then. I heard myself being the real me and it seemed Fiona liked the sound of that just fine.

I'd come to university, to Manchester, with no expectation of making friends – and this I said out loud. I confessed that I'd assumed term-time was to be endured, a stumbling block of weeks keeping me from my real home and my true friends. And Fiona told me how she'd phoned home earlier that very evening but when her mum answered she'd had to hang up, too choked to speak. We chinked our mugs and she topped up the port.

I liked Fiona; I liked what she wore, what she had on her walls and what was in her tape recorder. I liked that she was easy to talk to, open and honest. And best of all, I was comforted that she missed her mum too, that she didn't know where to start with an essay either. And an unexpected thought struck me: what if it's going to be OK here? And I thought, what if it might turn out to be more than OK?

Back in my room, I stood and looked around. I was pleased with the way I'd displayed my posters, my postcards, but my desk could do with a tidy and my clothes were piled on my chair like a creature who'd been vaporized. I winced at the books I should have read by now, the pristine pad of lined paper taunting me for words. But actually, it was OK. It was all just day-to-day uni life and I wasn't alone. I'd have a sort-out and a clean tomorrow so that my room was homely for Fiona, for whomever. I'd buy fresh milk because the bottle I was keeping on the ledge outside my window was becoming cream cheese and the orange juice next to it had gone fizzy. I'd buy biscuits too and challenge myself not to scoff the whole pack in lieu of supper, to put on my brave pants and join the rest of Hulme Hall in the dining room instead. Next door, Lawrence started up with his moaning and his chanting and I couldn't decide whether to thump on the wall to make him stop or pull on my joggers and go and see if he was all right. Instead, with the help of all that port, I fell asleep.

A week or so later, Cheery Eric called to me through the hatch of the Porters' Lodge as Fiona and I headed up to the dining room for breakfast with Karen and Ade and Bob Blenkinsop, Dan and Paul and Rosie and Bill.

'Your *post*, Eadie-with-an-"a",' he chuckled and handed me a small bundle of letters accrued over the previous days. I'd completely forgotten to check if anyone had written to me.

Term rampaged along after that and my education wasn't confined to my course; it extended beyond the lectures I snoozed through, the seminars I panicked over and my boa constrictor of a reading list. But what of it? I'd learned to make snakebite and green meanies, lager top and black velvets, Babycham with brandy and Blue Bols with lemonade whilst working behind the Hulme Hall bar with Karen. I also successfully trained myself to go out at the time I'd previously gone to bed and, though I had lost a lot of sleep, I discovered that the lightness brought by my burgeoning social life perfectly balanced the weight of essays and the huge tomes I had to lug from the library to my room. I learned a lot about the wider world from all the late-night philosophizing which took place in one room or other over mugs of booze or tea and a constant supply of biscuits. Bloody Margaret Thatcher. There was a lot to boycott; from anything connected with South Africa to the coaches which had ferried miners over the picket lines. We needed to free Mandela and plug the hole in the ozone layer and rally for the hostages in Lebanon. I wrote to John McCarthy. I told no one I'd done so and I had nowhere to send it, but it was important to me that I wrote.

In early November, I weighed the merits of returning home for a weekend to coincide with Josh, against staying put and joining my new friends at Maine Road stadium. I made the right call, witnessing Manchester City trounce Huddersfield Town 10–1. Fiona then helped me move Kate Bush from one wall to the other to establish a shrine of newspaper cuttings featuring Tony Adcock, Paul Stewart and Dave White.

'I've never had a favourite football team before,' I said.

'Me neither.'

'But will we ever understand the offside rule?'

'That's not the point,' Fiona said and I knew she was right. We sucked our Strepsils happily, proud of our sore throats from all that cheering and chanting and, though we were exhausted and it was already late, we crowded into Karen's room where we pooled our make-up before heading out to the Cellar disco in the bowels of the Students' Union. My overdue essay could wait. There were far more important things in life. Like trying curry for the first time.

Colour.
    Sound.
        Scent.
            Taste.
                Feeling.

For a girl who'd spent her life in steady Parkwin, Rusholme was to me the most exotic and energized place with its multicoloured pyramids in the Indian sweet merchants, the dazzle and gleam of the jewellery shops and silken rainbows of saris, the grocers selling okra and gnarls of ginger and bunches of coriander and fenugreek, the bright lights and the traffic and the car horns and throngs of people shouting singing laughing. Wafts of spice and drifts of music and everything, everywhere, open and lively late late late.

Manchester. Maybe I still didn't really have a clue where I was but this was no longer unnerving. The city was big, the buildings huge, the traffic non-stop. It was noisy. It was a new world of colourful accents, different backgrounds and people who weren't just white. I'd never known anywhere like it but here I was in this new city of mine joining in the ceilidhs at the Clarence around the corner, the singalongs with the old rocker at the Bowling Green pub on Grafton Street, dancing at the Owens Park bop while dodging the scuffles between pissed students. Here I was scoffing down a madras at 2 a.m., bunking off lectures to catch the bus into town to blow more of my grant money at the hip stalls and quirky boutiques of the indie traders in Afflecks Palace, treating myself to coffee and cake in the Royal Exchange, sneaking a spritz of all the expensive perfumes at Lewis's, mooching around the Arndale wondering if I'd ever get out. I loved it.

Wasn't it meant to be grim up North? 'Strangeways, Here We Come' – according to Morrissey and heaven knows he was miserable now, not least because the Smiths had split up just before I arrived. Wasn't it meant to rain all the time here? A pall of grey gloomy concrete and overbearing Victorian red brick? But I experienced none of this as I came to know the city. Instead, I was blown away by colour, sound, scent, taste, feeling. Nothing had prepared me for Manchester to be such an amplification of all these things. And it hadn't even rained – or if it had, I never noticed.

Now the notion that back home, or in Cambridge or in Edinburgh, no one knew where I was or what I was doing at any given moment was no longer alienating. I felt liberated, not isolated, by it. I was finding my way. I was walking my own path. In Parkwin, Josh, Celeste and I had clung together for being different. Here, in Manchester, my new friends and I rejoiced in being the same and we discovered a fascination about the newness of people we felt we'd known for ever. We were exotic to each other and we were comfortingly familiar. If the Oxford Road was the spine, the backbone of our student body and the university buildings ribbed out from it, then we were the blood coursing through it all, we were Student Life.

We skipped breakfast and ate too much white bread and chocolate. We hoovered up curry rice and chips on polystyrene trays from the Mandarin takeaway at a ridiculous yet magical hour and pizza from Amigo's was tastier when cold and rubbery the next morning. We piled in to Abdul's or the Al Noor late at night for mountains of poppadoms. And, much like I'd trained myself to drink coffee when I was younger, now I could drink pints of home-brewed 42 at the Lass o' Gowrie and Marston's Pedigree at the Whitty, without grimacing. We all drank like fish at the Hulme Hall bar and at the Students' Union, because alcohol was subsidized. We took Pro Plus to pull all-nighters to finish overdue essays and, predictably, we all got ill. As the weeks rolled by, we amassed zits and colds and headaches and upset stomachs and never had we looked worse or felt better. Quietly, I experienced a growing sense of just how large this new world would figure in my life. I was exhausted – but there was plenty of time to sleep when you're dead; this I knew better than most.

Further into term, a few of us sought respite at a club we discovered which was a short bus ride from the university, or a good walk if we were feeling either energetic or skint. One Thursday afternoon, Fiona and I met a man on a staircase in the multicoloured warren at Afflecks Palace. He looked a bit like a professor in his sweeping greatcoat but he told us he owned a nightclub and he invited us along. Fiona recognized him. That was Tony Wilson, she said, from the telly. He was also the founder of Factory Records. Joy Division! New Order! and wow! he was letting us in to his club for *free*!

It was called the Haçienda and it didn't look like a nightclub at all. It was at the desolate end of Whitworth Street West, a grand, curved, crenellated building that had once been a yacht showroom. We couldn't find it at first; there were no lights, no doormen and it appeared that there was no one there. We had to go through various doors, up and down stairs, past a large framed portrait of Tony Wilson and through a heavy plastic curtain like at a butcher's shop. But then – we were in.

Thursdays at the Haçienda became sacred to us; those nights were called *Temperance*, which we thought was suitably symbolic after our excesses further down Oxford Road. Dave the DJ played all the indie music we loved and sometimes there was a free bus back to the halls of residence. But best of all, it was never crowded at the Haçienda. The soaring glazed ceiling made it feel airy and open after all our subterranean partying and it didn't matter that the roof leaked or that it was cold. The quirky interior of traffic bollards and warning chevrons in black, yellow and red demarcating the pillars and the dance floor and the podiums and the stage added a stylish industrial edginess entirely lacking in our university stamping grounds. It was like we'd come across a super-cool place under wraps. Occasionally, we'd spot members of New Order in there and a couple of times Tony Wilson too. We loved the Gay Traitor bar in the basement and we all adored Ang the manager. We discovered probably the best hotdogs in the world from a stall outside which we'd devour in ecstasy on the long trudge back to Hall.

The Haçienda was a breath of fresh air. On the last Thursday before we all went home for Christmas, we said to each other we should come here more often.

And the next term we did.

And it could have killed us.

'But you've only just arrived!'

I looked at Terry and then I looked at the clock, confused. Actually, I'd been home for long enough to unpack and sling a suitcase full of laundry into the washing machine and hang it out to dry over all the radiators in the house. It seemed reasonable to me that I should want to head out and find Josh and Celeste, but Terry looked crestfallen.

'I thought we'd have a family supper – to welcome you home, to hear all your news. I was going to cook,' he said.

Mum glanced up from her work and smiled distractedly. I thought how tired she looked, but the build-up to Christmas was always a busy time and her night-time cleaning meant she was often knee-deep in the debris and waste of office parties. You don't want to know what I come across, she used to tell us, which always made Terry and me desperate for details. Today, she looked older than when I'd left and I wondered if the steel-grey threads snaking through her curls like frayed wire were new. Apart from the papers and files now overflowing his desk to the floor, Terry hadn't changed at all and nor had the fact that he hadn't sold a word.

'Give them a call first, Eadie,' Terry cajoled with a cheery voice and sad eyes. 'In case – you know – their families have plans too.' He tipped his head and gave me that look I remembered from when I was young, when he would come over all contemplative and emotional and ask where has my little girl gone and I would look around and wonder who he was talking about and how we could find her. Back then, I liked to imagine I had an invisible little sister. Now I was taken aback that my parents hadn't noticed all the monumental changes in me.

'OK,' I sighed with an eye roll. 'I'll lay the table in a bit but first I'm going to pop next door and it's hardly as if I can phone any of *them*.'

It was December teatime, cold and dark, and the cemetery was shut to everyone but 41 Yew Lane. I went in through the gate in our wall and felt a wave of calm wash over me. Everything was the same, everyone was here. Hello, Mr Pennyfeather. And hello, Mildred Robinson. How are you, Thomas Jefferey? And season's greetings to you, Joy Trimble. It's almost Christmas, Mr and Mrs Vickers! A sense of calm coursed through me for the first time in weeks. It had been ages since I'd stood by someone's grave, since I'd just stopped, stopped awhile to simply stand quietly and be still. My God, I was tired.

'I've discovered curry,' I announced over our predictable fish fingers and peas. Had my parents ever heard of ladies' fingers? No, they had not. Did they know that brinjal was another word for aubergine? No, they did not. Had they ever tasted paneer? No, they never had. I discoursed on the names of dishes in their ascending scales of heat as I painted a picture of Rusholme versus Parkwin that made my home town appear blandly monochrome in comparison. I gave a glimpse into the quirks of life at Hulme Hall, the wonders of Afflecks, the vastness of the Arndale Centre, the monumental beauty and echoing hush of the Central Library. Imagine if you worked from *there*, I said to Terry as I glanced at his corner of the room. By the time the Viennetta came out, my parents were under no illusion that as they hadn't been to Manchester they hadn't really lived. Politely, they hung on my every word.

Celeste looked thin, Josh looked dog-tired, I looked fat. The three of us stared at each other, as if seeing our current selves through someone else's eyes for the first time. We lolled on Celeste's bed and laughed and said oh my *God* a lot. We were wearing clothes we'd never seen each other in and soon enough we were talking about people and parties and music unknown to the others. We all sighed and sighed again and looked at each other and marvelled at the fact that actually, we'd survived all those weeks in foreign climes. In Edinburgh, Celeste was living in a self-catering block with six others with names like Mazza and Fitzo and Digger and Kags. I was in a catered Halls of Residence where we all wore black scholar's gowns at mealtimes. Josh, it transpired, was living in a staircase.

'It's what Cambridge colleges call the accommodation,' he told us. 'Also, I have a *bedder.*'

'A what?'

'A bedder called Mrs Peterson, but some of the students just call her Peters.' He looked embarrassed. 'She cleans our rooms, changes our sheets. I'm not sure I like it.'

Celeste roared. 'Well, I'll take her off your hands – our flat is an absolute sty.' She sounded so delighted, so proud. 'Christ,' she said. 'Wait until I tell Mercedes.'

'Who names their kid after a car?' I said.

'My neighbour is called Jolyon,' said Josh. 'I think his family actually owns Somerset. His father bought him a walnut drinks cabinet – fully stocked – as a moving-in present.' Celeste and I loved the sound of this. 'He was at boarding school from seven years old,' said Josh.

'Very *Brideshead Revisited*,' I laughed.

'More Brideshead Right Now,' said Celeste.

'I don't like him much,' Josh said quietly.

'Well, my neighbour is a psycho called Lawrence and he knocks on my door at stupid o'clock, wailing *Edith! Edith!*'

'God,' Celeste sighed, 'I can't believe we have literally a month cooped up in this dump.'

'God – me too,' I grimaced and the other two looked at me staggered, as if they couldn't believe what they'd just heard.

Josh walked me home later. We struck a slow saunter and chose a circuitous route, pointing out old haunts like we hadn't seen them in years. We hung on to the railings at Three Magnets and peered into the dark playground where I glimpsed Little Me and she seemed like someone else entirely.

'Another life,' said Josh wistfully.

'But you're happy, Joshy? You've made friends?'

'Yeah, but—'

'—just no one as amazing as me?'

He laughed. 'Yes, Eads – no one as amazing as you.'

'Or Celeste.'

'Or Celeste.'

'Shall I come and visit you next term?'

'My room is tiny.'

'Don't worry – I can sleep on your fabled staircase,' I said. 'Or in Jolly Squire's drinks cabinet.'

Josh laughed and linked his arm through mine and we walked on. 'Got a boyfriend?'

'No?' The concept that I'd have one was odd enough – but the thought that I wouldn't have told Josh was even odder. The streetlight caught his features and, from nowhere, I remembered kissing him once.

We walked up Yew Lane in our easy companionable silence. The Electricity Building lumbered in its shadowy growl and I pointed to it and Josh nodded and smiled.

'But you know, Eadie,' he said as if we'd been mid-conversation. 'If that neighbour of yours – Lawrence – if he knocks. Well, I know you don't want to answer at stupid o'clock ... What I'm saying is – perhaps say hello, just every now and then.'

I heard Josh and I didn't hear Josh.

'Lawrence is *weird*,' I laughed. 'When you come and visit me, *you* can knock for him. I dare you.'

At Celeste's, Sandrine opened the door to me. It was only then that I realized I hadn't seen her though I'd been over to the house often already. She looked like she hadn't slept and yet she also looked like she'd just woken up though it was almost suppertime. Without saying a word she clasped me in a bony hug and kissed me three times, cupping my face in her hands as if drinking in the very sight of me was nourishment enough. She was almost disastrously thin. Dominating her trademark fragrance of Chanel came the sour rasp of stale wine and cigarettes. She was crumpled all over, her mascara was smudged and her hair thatched this way and that, but she was beautiful as ever. She just didn't smell so good today.

'Is Celeste in?'

She glanced up the staircase and then back to me. It was as if she didn't know the answer or, if she did, it was like she wanted to keep me to herself for a little longer. I felt suddenly uncomfortable and I edged past her singing out Celeste's name while taking the stairs two at a time.

In her bedroom, Celeste was busy writing a letter which she hurriedly folded and pushed under a pile of books on her desk, turning to me as if she'd been sitting just watching the door all the while.

'Here,' I said and presented her with a small present. 'I think you'll love it. Who were you writing to?'

'No one,' she said and she sounded about seven years old. She took the gift and shook it.

'It's a mix-tape, silly,' I laughed. 'You can't play it by shaking it.'

'I didn't get you anything.'

'I don't care about that.'

'I know – but.'

'Buy me a super-huge birthday present instead,' I said. 'Anyway, who were you writing to? Secret lover?'

We both looked at the pile of books concealing the letter.

'No one,' she said again.

'Does *no one* go by any other name?'

I was anticipating a Zippo or a Tonks or a Bomber or whomever else she hung out with up in Edinburgh.

'Alicia,' she said and I watched her face redden.

'Alicia?'

'Think I'm a bit in love, to be honest, Eadles,' she mumbled.

'But Alicia is a girl's name!' I laughed. 'Your friends are *mad.*'

'Because Alicia *is* a girl?' She gave me a quizzical smile, as if I was dense, and she watched me and waited for the penny to drop.

Before my brain reached my body, I could feel my nose wrinkle and I laughed like I'd just got the joke. 'Don't be stupid,' I said. And I said Celeste! And then I said but what about poor Lois in France?

And then she said Lois was a girl too.

Again I laughed. I said don't be *stupid!* 'You're not a lezzer,' I said, not bothering to stop, to hear, to think. 'You can have any boy you want!'

And I tickled her and called her bonkers and I said come on – let's go to Josh's. I said it's Hannukah there – let's go and eat potato latkes and doughnuts and all their other festive yumminess.

And Celeste said OK, Eadie, OK.

Peripherally, I may have noticed how my friend suddenly looked very tired, almost as tired as her mother. But I didn't dwell on it. I fetched her jacket and her trainers and I gave her another hug, a kiss on her cheek, and I said come on, Celeste, come on.

'You're probably just tired,' I said.

So Christmas came and went and the break passed in a flash, for that I was grateful. Mum and Terry asked me oddly considered questions every day, like I was a foreigner whose strange world they couldn't comprehend nor had any desire to visit. I talked at them about people they didn't know and places they couldn't imagine and sometimes I saw them switch off.

I'd done all my washing, caught up on sleep and an essay I'd completely forgotten about. I'd come across Michael a couple of times and regaled him with details of My New Life, relishing the amazement on his face. But I didn't see Ross and I didn't ask after him. I'd gone jogging every day around the streets and parks I'd known my whole life and now my jeans didn't feel so tight and once again my belt buckled in as it should.

I'd hung out with my very best friends and listened politely to all the details of their new lives while really only wanting to talk about my own. But I missed my new friends and I missed the clamour and pace of university life and most of all I missed my great big new gritty Northern city. I longed to get back to living a life in which, at any given minute, no one at home knew where I was or what I was doing. Now here I was once again, in bland lower-middle-class white Middle England. 41 Yew Lane got on my nerves, the front room irritated me. All my parents' stuff, pages and pages of writing going nowhere.

'How can you just *sit* there?' I laughed at them one day.

'Because it's a sitting room,' my mother said and it was the first time in my life that I heard cold iron in her voice. 'Don't they have those in Manchester?'

I caught Terry's look travel wordlessly over to her. His eyes were deep with affection and something else. Shared bewilderment, maybe. Disappointment, even. I glanced away.

Celeste was the first to leave.

I was next, taking the coach to Nottingham on New Year's Eve to stay with Karen and the offer of a lift back to Manchester from her parents.

I wasn't entirely sure when Josh returned to Cambridge.

What happens once you've hugged everyone hello again, admired their new clothes and whatever else they received at Christmas, had a couple of lairy nights out, missed a seminar and received only 52 per cent for an essay you thought was top-marks potential? You wander around feeling low, that's what happens. Low and a bit anxious too, because returning to the reality of a place soon quashes all the fanciful and distorted recollections and expectations. I'd heaped so much hope and emphasis on Manchester being my city of dreams for my return, but Manchester in January was noisy and dirty and wet and dark early and appeared not to have missed me at all, nor noticed that I was back. I started loitering at the Porters' Lodge again, asking Cheery Eric twice a day to see if there was any post for me.

It didn't help that one of my courses was taught by a professor whose accent I found impossible, while another was taught by a woman who obviously hated me because she always talked over whatever I was saying. My grant cheque was late coming through, I had less money in my account than I thought and a couple of times I didn't go out with the gang, I stayed in. Motionless at my desk, I sat intending to work but stared at the wall instead, groaning and sighing and knocking my forehead against the desk wondering what use a history degree was going to be anyway. I probably sounded like Lawrence through those thin walls but actually I hadn't heard him since I'd returned; I wasn't even sure if he was back.

It was on one such Friday night, while I was being penniless indoors, that everyone went to the Haçienda and came back calling it the *Haç* and saying they'd had the best night of their lives.

'It was *rammed*,' Fiona told me the next day. 'It was amazing.'

'*Our* Haçienda?' I asked, because all those times we'd gone together on Thursday nights for the indie music it had never been crowded and that's why we liked it.

'It's like a different place,' she said.

'And the *music*,' said Bill, shaking his head in disbelief. 'The *music*, Eadie. It was . . .' and he looked around the dining hall as if seeing the world with new eyes.

'You've never heard anything like it,' Karen said. 'I don't even know what it's called. But next week you're coming.'

We weren't there right at the beginning, but we were pretty near to the start. Acid House soon became our world and the Haçienda our temple, our sanctuary, our home. The newness of the music was intoxicating; it wasn't on the radio, it certainly wasn't on *Top of the Pops*, we didn't know where to buy it or even what to ask for. Instead, it rampaged into our lives via the bags of records that the DJs brought to the club. Whatever they played we danced to, we were helpless not to. Not just my little gang but soon enough hundreds of others. Hundreds and hundreds of *Us*. There was an excitement to the music not just because it was fundamentally new, but because it was swirly and squelchy and synthesized with a driving thumping bass and a hypnotic, blood-pumping beat. It was happy music, funky and brain-befuddling, a little psychedelic but faster, so much faster. It was unknown. It was astonishing. And alongside the music was the visual torrent projected onto the screens at the Haçienda. Weird, clashing, incongruous, rude, hilarious, shocking mash-ups of film clips and imagery. In that old yacht showroom, decked out to look like a construction site, we were teleported into an immersive and multi-sensory world. None of us had experienced anything like it. We were here. It was now. We were ready.

We didn't know what the bands were called let alone what they looked like, what race or nation they were; we didn't even know how they danced to their own music, so we had to make it up. The music swept us up and we bounced and bobbed and jerked as our hearts and limbs raced to keep time to the beat. We danced on the tables. We danced on the stage. We crowded onto the podiums and danced there. We danced in the alcoves and in the queue for the rancid loos. We danced and we danced. And we loved the DJs, how we loved the DJs. We put our hands in the air to show these DJs how much we loved their music. They didn't talk at us or over the music, they didn't play 'one for the ladies', they didn't play any songs we knew but we lapped up everything they gave us. To us, the DJs were the alchemists who mixed it all together to give us the best of times and that's why we applauded them though we could hardly even see them up there in the gallery in their odd little booth.

At the Haçienda, as spring 1988 gently nudged winter away, we were simply a happy sweaty mass of cheerful, like-minded people at the inception of a counter-world around which our lives would soon revolve. We were united. We wished we could dance all night. And then Ecstasy came along and we discovered how we could do precisely that.

11.24 a.m. 15th June 1999, the motorway

I sense my husband looking at me.

'Theme from S'Express' by S'Express is playing wholly unexpectedly on the radio and I haven't heard it for so long. One of the first acid house records to hit the mainstream, go to number 1, rendering everyone who heard it helpless not to dance and chant. Even now, all these years later, I dance maniacally to this song, I shimmy and swirl around my delighted husband while blasting out the chorus at him: *I've got the hots for you boop boop bup d'bup bup*. This song was everybody's anthem, but he and I always felt it belonged to the two of us. The hours we must have spent boop-booping bup-de-bupping at each other. The number of times I have sung at him *I've got the hots for you*. Sung it like I've truly meant it.

I know my husband is looking at me.

Boop b-boop b-boop.

I'm tempted to say eyes on the road but I don't know whether he'll hear it the wrong way. Neither of us seems to have had much control over tone of voice recently. There have been many times when I've wanted my words to flow like the comfort of a gentle breeze licking through harsh heat, but I find I'm unable to say what I mean and invariably what I have said comes out all wrong. Edged in ice, spiked with irritation. Sometimes I don't even listen. Sometimes he can't be bothered to answer. My husband and I have been skirting around the issues and obstacles between us in a slalom of stuttering words and swallowed conversation that slip off the surface. We're like nervous swimmers, him and me, treading water and avoiding the deep end. Stevie Smith said not waving but drowning. Julian Cope said not raving but drowning. We're not drowning, not quite yet, but we've both been reaching for the lifebuoy, too shy too proud too stupid too stubborn to ask each other for help.

Just now I can't even sing. Our song finishes. Some crap comes on instead.

'How much longer, do you think?' I ask. We're both looking at the road ahead where the traffic has slowed down for no visible reason.

'I can't go any faster, Eadie.'

And there you have it. There's my opening to bark back, to bite.

'Stop being so defensive. *God.* I was only asking – not criticizing.'

He's not wasting energy to parry back. I bunch up my sweatshirt and pillow it between my head and the window. Close my eyes. Give a loaded sigh. Wonder if he's glanced at me again. Wonder if he might reach for me in a moment or two, wonder whether I should extend my hand to him. He knows I can't sleep in a car, but he drives on as if he believes me to be out for the count.

It's the oddest, saddest, sensation when tears smart behind closed eyes.

Manchester Piccadilly and Josh's train was late. I knew he had to change twice so I assumed he'd been delayed or missed a connection. I had no way of knowing where in the country he was and what time he'd arrive but I was fizzing with excitement at the thought of having him here for my birthday weekend, to proudly present him with a ticket to my world. *Eadie Bee*, I'd been imagining him marvel, *look at you knowing this big old Northern city like the back of your hand.*

Trains pulled in and disgorged swarms of passengers but Josh wasn't amongst them so I stood there, hopping from foot to foot in the station concourse, glancing intermittently at the arrivals board. And then, at last, I spied the top of his head bobbing along, before his big smiley Joshface appeared and we were hugging and laughing and oh-my-Godding and neither of us could quite believe that he was here.

'Welcome to Manchester!' I linked arms with my old pal, marching him out of the station and into my city. 'Best birthday present *ever.*'

Up and down the corridor, in and out of the rooms of my various friends, over the lawn and through the arch of the old ivy-clad buildings, over the quad to the bar, the dining hall and wolfing down food and back to the bar and out to the pub till closing time and off for a curry and home again into Dan's room because he had a bottle of vodka and then to Fiona's room because she was still up – just a regular Friday night with my new gang and best of all, with Josh too. It's like we've known him for ever, everyone said. Top bloke, they said. And I basked in a reflected glory Josh wasn't aware he radiated. He slept on my floor in his sleeping bag. I woke long before him and listened to his breathing, watched the soft rise and fall of his back, his Garfield T-shirt smooth over his shoulder blades and rucked in between. He turned over and I looked at his face and wondered what he was dreaming, what went on in that head of his. It was hard to tell; sleep's mask is fashioned from such peaceful ambiguity. I lay back in my bed and started to grin. It was my nineteenth birthday. What a brilliant age to be.

'Huh?' Josh yawned and stretched.

'I'm nineteen,' I whispered. 'Best age *ever*.'

'You've only been in it for two seconds.' Josh propped himself up on his arm.

'But it just feels like it's going to be – unforgettable.'

Josh kindly waited for my thought process to go through its stages, it was something he'd honed over the years.

'Nineteen shrugs off the restraints of being a teenager,' I said. 'But without all that grown-upness that real adults have to cope with.'

'Eadie,' he said and he yawned again which set me off. 'Enough with the philosofuckizing – where's breakfast? I'm starving.'

* * *

Karen gave me a giant Toblerone for my birthday.

There was a package from Edinburgh which contained Celeste's old Wham T-shirt that I'd always coveted and would be proud to wear, all these years later, in a non-ironic way.

Bill bought me a card with an *I Am 3* badge on it which I put on immediately.

Rosie gave me a pack of playing cards with naked men on the backs.

Paul and Ade gave me a poster of a banana by Andy Warhol.

Fiona gave me a massive cuddle and apologized for being skint.

Bob Blenkinsop gave me a bottle of Babycham. Everyone sang *n-n-n-n-n-nineteen* whenever they passed me.

Josh had made a flip photo album of madcap photos from our past which my present friends pored over with affectionate incredulity.

Jordan said he'd give me his gift later, at the Haçienda. And he said that it was going to blow my mind.

S ound.
      Colour.
          Scent.
              Taste.
                  Feeling.
             All of it amplified.
          Everything heightened.
       Mesmerically dazzling.
Love writ large.
      What a beautiful, beautiful feeling.
          That tiny little bitter pill supercharged
             everything I'd ever felt.

It was just a small, pretty, colourful tablet with a cute dove debossed into it. It was Jordan's birthday present to me. One for you, one for me, he said. The others paid for theirs.

'But is it *drugs*?' I asked him, unnerved. 'I threw up after a joint, once. I don't *do* drugs. And nor does my friend.'

Jordan laughed at me and gave me a cuddle. 'No, silly – it's not *drugs* – it's Ecstasy.'

I looked around the Haçienda, at the crowd of beaming people; happy and energized, so welcoming and warm. Everyone dancing with abandon, friendship and togetherness beaming across their collective face. Josh was inspecting his pill, holding it between thumb and forefinger like it was an uncut gem which, at that time, I suppose it was. And I said to myself, I said this. Eadie, I said, if Josh is OK with this, then so are you. He's studying medicine after all. He knows everything. I watched him dither for a second before he shrugged at me and we grinned at each other and we swallowed our pills at the same time.

I did wonder if we'd just been incredibly stupid. But where could be the harm in something so little and innocuous-looking? I did think that it'd better be worth it because Josh's cost him £20. But then I stopped thinking because I was too busy feeling.

Initially it was overwhelming, frightening even; a supercharged rush of euphoria settling finally into an acute clarity of the beauty in everything. *Everything.* All that was around us to see to hear to feel; every beat, every note, every face, every movement of every limb of every beautiful human being there. Clean and crystal clear. I was flying, floating, soaring, surfing the rush of pure whipped-up happiness.

Suddenly, music wasn't merely to dance to. It slid through our ears and pulsed in our brains and throbbed through our veins and energized our limbs and liquefied over our skin and oxygenated our blood; the music became a life force. We danced non-stop: crazy dancing, trance-like and abandoned while the music soundtracked the sensation. I'd never seen Josh so elated and it filled me with a floating joy that kept me aloft, high above the messed-up floor in the overflowing toilets, beyond the skank and scuzz of the club emptying out in the early hours.

It was a perfect night out in an extraordinary world. Happy Nineteenth Birthday to me.

'Jesus.'

Josh kept saying Jesus over and over again as we walked home, like he'd truly had some kind of religious experience which, actually, we were still having. He held my hand, he held Bill's hand, I linked arms with Karen who linked arms with Ade. Paul and Rosie and Fiona were wrapped around each other necessitating a sideways gait. No one was on their own and, as we walked all the way home, we felt that our world was a very beautiful place. Sleepy Rusholme, with the curry house lights now off and takeaway detritus strewn around, beer cans and bottles slung aside, the occasional bus – everything oblivious to our return. The deserted quad and the sleeping corridors back at Hulme Hall – unaware of the magical world that we'd just found.

We whispered *night night* to each other, hugged close, waved as we went to our respective rooms. Josh and I stood just inside my door, blinking at the reminders of when we'd left a million years ago. The open jumbo packet of crisps. The jeans I'd decided not to wear. The *Guardian* newspaper we'd bought but not read. Josh's sleeping bag bunched at the end of my bed like it was sound asleep. I'd left the little light on above my basin. I hadn't closed my cupboard door. I'd forgotten to shut the curtains and now dawn was simpering in through the inky sky. I didn't want it to be a new day. I drew the curtains and turned to Josh and grinned.

'Bloody hell – the state of you!' I said.

'Pot, kettle, black,' he laughed.

Our hair was plastered against our heads, faces, necks, in unappealing kinks and splats. Our shoes were filthy and the hems of our jeans bore a creeping tidemark of God knows what. All that frenetic dancing and sweating had soaked our clothes and now we were in the warm we realized they were cold, clammy and stained.

'I bet we stink,' Josh said.

I went up to him and sniffed, twitching my nose like a rabbit.

'Yep.' I smelled my armpits and my T-shirt. 'Jesus.'

'That's *my* word,' Josh laughed. Then he fell quiet, tipped his head to one side and gazed at me. 'Fucking hell, Eadie.'

But I knew it had nothing to do with Jesus or our clothing or the way we looked or smelled. I nodded and wondered if his eyes had always been so large.

'I *know*.'

'You're shivering,' he said.

I hadn't realized. My top was damp and my arms prickled goosebumps which seemed to fascinate Josh. He lifted my wrist and squinted in the fuzzed light at the tiny hairs doing their job in a protective waft over my skin. 'Never noticed,' he said but I think it was to himself. 'You should get out of those clothes,' he said. 'You'll catch cold.'

So I did. I didn't want to touch my filthy trainers so I kicked my feet out of them, wincing at my once pale-blue socks now the colour of puddle. Unbuttoned my jeans and stripped off my top and went to the basin to brush my teeth. A glance in the mirror – Josh stock-still.

'What?' I said, my mouth full of toothbrush. 'What?' Oh come on, Josh, I thought, you've seen me in my underwear plenty over the years.

'Nothing,' he said and he came and stood next to me, squeezed out an ooze of toothpaste which missed the bristles and slid over his hand. He sucked it into his mouth and started brushing. I clambered into bed and, with my head against my pillow, I listened in to the amazing sound of my eardrums thrumming. I watched Josh take off his top, sniff it gingerly and chuck it to the end of the room before putting on the T-shirt he slept in last night. From my eyeline, anything Josh said now appeared to be coming out of Garfield's mouth and it made me giggle. He whoomphed the sleeping bag and laid it neatly before getting in.

'Yosh.'

'Eadles.'

I looked down at him lying on my floor, stuck my arm out and he reached up his hand for mine. We gazed at each other through the half-light that hung so quietly in the room.

'I'm so exhausted but I don't want to sleep,' I said. 'I don't want to wake up and tonight become yesterday.'

I want my birthday to last for ever, I said.

I know what you mean, he said.

'Josh,' I whispered. 'Did we do something stupid, something bad?'

He kept hold of my hand but moved onto his back and exhaled deeply. 'I don't think so,' he said. 'Everyone was on it, it seems. Not just us.'

'Everyone was so happy. Really lovely. So *friendly*! But are we idiots? What even *was* that pill?' To me, Josh was already a doctor and I'd go with what he said.

'It's called Ecstasy, according to Jordan – which is a fair description, I'd say,' he said.

'I haven't heard of that one,' I said. 'Have you?'

'No. But if you think about it, it's probably better for you than gallons of alcohol and packets of fags.'

And then we lay there and listed all the illegal substances we could, trying to sound as nonchalant as possible. Drugs had never been our scene and there were lengthy silences as we wondered if we'd left any out, if smack was the same as heroin and was acid actually LSD? And where, amongst them all, did this Ecstasy stuff fit?

'Really, we were just dancing and drinking water,' Josh decided. 'It's not like I thought I could fly or speak to trees.'

'Yeah – and I didn't see giant pink frogs or hear any talking walls,' I said.

I was giggling when, without warning, I started to cry. The tears came from somewhere so deep, wave after wave, and I had to let go of Josh's hand, turn my face to the wall just to breathe. I wasn't sad, I was far from sad, yet I was sobbing from the very pit of me, emotion surging through me. Overwhelmed. Nineteen.

I felt a blooming of cold air as Josh lifted my duvet and then I felt the warmth of his body spooning against me.

He made comforting whispers into the top of my head, his mouth and his nose against my sweat-soaked hair.

'I don't know why I'm crying.'

'You're just emotional,' said Josh.

'Of course I'm emotional – I'm crying.'

'I mean, it's not like you're crying because you're actually in pain, or because you've been hurt – you're emotional. It's only a feeling. It's not real.'

My super-bright friend, studying medicine at Cambridge, talking utter bollocks. *Only* a feeling. I thought, he doesn't have a clue.

'What are you laughing about?' My very stupid friend nudged me and then attempted to tickle the answer out of me.

'You,' I said at length, and we could both hear the absolute fondness in my voice.

Together we lay while the swimming warmth of the drug still expanded everything we felt and thought about. We talked deeply philosophical bullshit while time stood miraculously still. Josh's hand was lolling on my waist and I took it and pulled it around me snuggly like a shawl. Moments later, he moved his mouth from my hair to my neck and, as his lips touched my skin, my whole body buzzed. His hand beneath mine came to life. The crashing disconnect between thought and feeling, between reason and madness. I thought to myself, this is probably not a good idea at all. But this was overridden by what I was feeling; the tingling of my skin and the immediate yearning of my body.

'Um – shit,' Josh whispered but by then we were both acutely aware of his erection. I liked knowing it was there, I liked feeling the mass of his body, the prickling stubble of his cheek against my shoulder, the warmth of him. We wriggled to face each other, rubbed noses, kissed quickly on the lips. He stroked up my arms and over my T-shirt, down my waist and along my thigh, up across my knickers and, as gentle as his hands were, his cock was unapologetically stiff. It appeared to have an arrogance at odds with Josh's personality.

'Have you done it?' I asked, though I was pretty sure he'd've told me if he had. 'You know – *it?*'

'No,' Josh said. 'You?'

I shook my head. I travelled my fingertips quickly, self-consciously over his chest, his stomach, missing out his groin entirely as if it didn't exist, picking up again at his legs. Our foreheads were together and in the drip of slim light, we gazed downwards at our bodies.

'You know, we could—'

'—yeah, OK.'

'I mean – we could sort of like—'

'—get it over with?'

'Just do it?'

'Because you know – together.'

'Yeah, it would be good.'

'Safe – because we—'

'—go back for ever.'

'Exactly.'

'I mean – if you want to?'

'Do you want to?'

'Um – yes.'

'Yes. Um – me too.'

I scrambled over him and went to rummage in the drawer of my desk.

'Eads? You're meant to be losing your virginity not writing an essay.'

'Dick!' I laughed. 'I'm looking for – here.' And I tripped over Josh's bedroll and back to him in my single bed. Nestling against his chest, I brandished a condom. 'They gave them out for free during Freshers'.'

They were called Mates.

'*For mates who mate*,' Josh mused, like Voiceover-Man, as he opened the packet.

'Am I meant to put it on?' My mind scampered back to awkward biology lessons at school and larking about with bananas at Celeste's with a condom she'd found in her dad's bathroom in Bristol. But while I was busy thinking, Josh had armoured himself against AIDS and unwanted pregnancy and everything else that we'd been told sex is riddled with.

I wanted to keep my T-shirt on but Josh really wanted it off. I wanted to keep my knickers on too, just for a little while longer. I think I was more excited about the concept of doing it than the imminence of the act. We writhed around for a while and I had to stop myself from giggling at Josh's involuntary throaty noises.

'Are you ready, do you think?' he asked and it was only when he put his hand between my legs that I realized he meant physically. I watched how the feel of me made his eyes close. 'I think you're ready,' he said.

And I said, OK.

I whispered, okey-dokey.

And Josh drew me close, pulled himself over me, into me and I thought, bloody hell. And then I thought – fuck – ouch – ow.

Oh.

Oh. OK. OK.

I'm OK.

And I wondered, is he all the way in? I wondered how long should this last? And I wondered if it would soon feel gorgeous and swoony like in films. And then I thought how it didn't sound like Josh at all, that groan he just made.

Though it didn't really feel that big a deal to me, by the sounds of Josh it was obviously monumental for him. I kept my arms around him and my face turned slightly to one side to avoid his sticky nightclub hair. He was panting and grunting and gasping that he was coming, he was coming, fuck fuck he was coming.

Then it was done. In four or five minutes – no, three or four – oh, I don't know, perhaps it was just one or two. In the time that it took, I gave him my virginity and he gave me his.

'Eads,' he rasped. 'Fuck.'

Almost immediately he was sound asleep. I tried to nod off but it was all too sweaty and oozing and cramped so I slipped away and into his sleeping bag instead. There I lay with my head skipping from thought to thought and my blood pumping hard through my body until morning was in full flow with students chattering and banging up and down the corridor and Lawrence rat-a-tat-tatting at my door with his Edith! Edith! and it was only then that finally I slept. I simply conked out, waking mid-afternoon in a dreamy reverie ending in an almighty jolt. Josh was right there, fully clothed. He'd been out to the shops at some point because on my desk there was a carton of orange juice and a bar of Dairy Milk.

'You OK?' he asked and I sat up confused because his tone suggested that I was ill, that some accident had befallen me. I decided not to tell him that I felt a little sore, that my forehead had surely cracked from side to side.

'Yep – you?'

'Good,' he said. 'Tired – and also, I need to go soon, I can't miss my train.'

As I struggled out of his sleeping bag, I noticed that he glanced away from me. And I thought to myself how strange this was – that he'd been right inside me yet now he couldn't look at the outside of me.

'You don't have to come with me to the station,' he said. 'If you just want to go back to sleep or something.' He was now diligently rolling up his sleeping bag which was still warm from me.

'Of course I'll come with you,' I said. I grabbed my towel and my Wash & Go and I headed down the corridor to the showers saying a cheery hello to someone's parents who were visiting. They regarded me with a certain resignation.

Josh hardly said a word on the bus, he stared out of the window like a tourist. At Piccadilly we stood in silence analysing the departures board. His train had yet to be displayed but he didn't want to go for a coffee. He didn't want to go to WHSmith. So we just stood there watching and waiting for his platform to ping up.

'That's me.'

We looked at each other awkwardly. Something had changed, something was different but it was hard to define what.

'Josh?'

'Hmm?'

'Um – are we OK?'

He smiled in the direction of my eyebrows and said of course we're OK. He gave me a quick hard hug. 'Thanks for, you know, everything – but – I've got to go.'

His train didn't leave for ten minutes.

'Write?' I called after him; he turned briefly and gave me the thumbs-up.

I thought how just two days before I'd stood in this very concourse waiting for him to arrive, not knowing where he could be. And now I was standing here again, even less sure of where he was.

I skipped high tea in the dining room. Nor did I feel like any of Josh's orange juice or chocolate. I lay on my bed; my body ached from all that dancing, my body was sore from all that other stuff. I couldn't move but I couldn't stop my mind haring around a tumbling recall of my birthday. It was the best of times, it was the worst of times; my nineteenth birthday when I took drugs and lost my virginity wearing socks the colour of puddle.

Dear Josh
Hope you're OK. It was amazing seeing you at the weekend, thank you for coming. I hope you had fun. Hope your journey back was OK too. Anyway – so I

No. That's terrible. Screw the paper into a ball and start again.

Dear Josh
Hope you're OK.

I stared at the words for a long time wondering how to continue; wondering if he was wondering if I was OK.

Dear Josh
Hope you're OK. I tried to call – twice – but thought I'd write because I'm a bit freaked out and I think you are too.

But what if he wasn't remotely freaked out? What if he was actually disgusted? Worse – what if he didn't care?

Start again.

Dear Josh
Hope you're OK. And I just wanted you to know that everything's cool and I'm fine about everything — about the weekend and all that happened so don't feel that I'm not because I am.

But I wasn't. That was a lie. Tear the paper up and try again.

Dear Josh
Are we OK? Because you were really off when you left and I haven't heard from you and I have to admit, that's freaking me out. I've tried to phone — I hope my messages have been passed on??? It's OK, by me, that we did what we did — it sort of happened in the moment and I think that awesome experience at the Haçienda had a lot to do with it. I don't regret it but I sense that you do and that makes me feel a bit crap about everything. Can't we just accept it happened full stop — and maybe not read into it? I'm completely happy to do that.

Love
Your best friend
Eadles
Xxx
Ps — Ecstasy! Oh my Godddddddd! Jordan said it was actually invented decades ago for couples with marriage problems — is it magic or WHAT???!!!

I went as far as folding the page in half, ready to put in an envelope, but I didn't, I put it in the bin.

Dear Celeste
I've tried to call but you're never in — I hope you're having a blast . . .
    Oh God — Celeste. The weirdest thing and it's really screwing with my head — but Josh and I had sex. I know I know I KNOW.

It was when he came here for my birthday (I so wish you'd been able to come). Anyway, we talked about it (the doing 'it') just before (we did 'it') – but afterwards not only would he not say a word but he left as soon as he could. I felt like he couldn't bare to even look at me (bear? – but bare seems better in this context).

I don't know what to think – but what do you think?

Also – we took drugs that night – well, I don't think you'd call it 'drugs' drugs, not in a scuzzy illegal way – just a tiny little pill called Ecstasy. If you have it in Edinburgh then all I can say is DO IT! It's the most amazing thing which makes the entire world seem beautiful and it's totally safe (it's actually a medicine for blood clotting or thinning – and used in marriage guidance counselling too).

<u>But what do I do about Josh?</u>

Only – promise me PROMISE ME that you won't let on to him that you know. You HAVE to PROMISE ME. He'd be mortified. But this is the thing – why <u>is</u> he so mortified??? (x1000 ???s) Makes me feel totally shit about what happened. And about myself. When he went I felt like he was saying (without saying a word) that it was me who'd done something wrong.

Love you
Eads xx

But I didn't send it. I didn't send it because I didn't want it out there, in the open. What I'd done and how I felt. What had been done to me. And how that felt. I ripped up the letter and sprinkled it over the frustrated scrunches of paper already in the bin, as if spreading salt to thaw a dangerously icy path, as if putting salt on a wound.

'Anything for me?'

'All OK, Eadie-with-an-"a"?' Eric kindly checked the staringly empty cubbyhole and returned with an apologetic smile and a gaze that held me for that extra moment. 'All OK, our kid?'

I nodded. 'I was just passing,' I said.

'Stamp's probably fallen off,' he said. 'I'm sure I read something about problems with the stuff that makes them stick.'

I took that.

Conveniently, I forgot about hearing Eric tell other letterless students how he was sure he'd read something about possible postal strikes or that his friend had told him about counterfeit stamp scandals and that hadn't it been on the news about those postmen pilfering the mail?

'Here.' He gave me a bar of chocolate. 'You'd be doing me a favour,' he said, patting his stomach.

Eric and his chocolate. Michael and his pipe. Fiona and her port. Reuben and his everything. I couldn't speak just then. It was Celeste I missed most of all, the world of Celeste and me on her bed, comfortable and safe to say anything we wanted, soundproofed by all her cushions and pillows and our lifetime of knowing each other. I longed for her so deeply it ached. I trudged back up the Oxford Road to a lecture I hoped to fall asleep in.

Later, I took a tower of ten-pence pieces to the payphone on the floor above and dialled Cambridge, changing my mind and redirecting the call hundreds of miles north. But Celeste wasn't in, her flatmate told me. She's out with Mazza and Zed and just then I didn't like her for hanging out with people with such annoying names. I didn't like whichever flatmate this was for not even knowing that it was me, Eadie, Celeste's oldest and closest and *real* friend who was phoning. They'd most likely misspell my name if they could even be bothered to leave a note saying I'd called. I had all these coins left and no one to speak to. There was a queue now behind me and I felt pathetic walking away with all that stupid loose change.

So so tired. A different sort of tired. I rested my head against my door and, with my eyes shut, I rootled around in my pocket for my key and fumbled it into the lock.

'Edith?'

Oh God, not Lawrence. Lawrence with a takeaway from the Mandarin whose white paper bag had more colour than he did.

'Are you all right?'

The question was simple enough and Lawrence tilted his head, waiting for my yes or no answer so we could leave it at that and he could be in his room, eating his food.

'I don't know, really.'

I really didn't know why I'd said that.

'Oh deary dear,' Lawrence said. He sounded like a kindly grandpa, he looked a little like one too: his suit trousers were held up by a pair of braces, a sensible shirt, old-fashioned shoes, even though they were not a matching pair. I remembered Josh at Christmas telling me I ought to say hello to Lawrence. I didn't want to think about Josh just then.

'Do you want to come in, Edith? I have a huge portion of chips and gravy – you can have some, if you like?'

'It's OK. I'm not hungry.'

'Come in anyway.' He paused, as if thinking how to extend the conversation. 'I don't bite.'

I looked over to him. He had soft violet eyes under slender, expressive eyebrows, but I'd never noticed. He took my faltering shrug as a positive sign.

'Come on in, Edith,' he said.

Lawrence's room, identically laid out to mine, was disconcerting in how different it was. It was tidy, for a start. He'd covered his walls with posters and postcards of cubist paintings and it was like being in a strange and beautiful fractured world of muted tones. I sat on his desk, my feet on his chair, and watched as he tipped his takeaway onto a plate and took a proper cloth napkin from the drawer.

'Do you only ever wear odd shoes?' I asked. His shoes were exactly the same style but one was blue and the other was brown.

He had a mouthful of food but he was so eager to converse he resembled a scrawny bird as he tried to swallow it down.

'Always,' he said. 'Drives my parents mad.'

'Why, though?'

'Because it drives my parents mad?'

I liked his answer, I liked the way he was eating chips and gravy so daintily; knife and fork and a dab dab of the napkin at the corners of his mouth.

'No,' I said. 'But really?'

Lawrence shrugged. 'I like all my shoes. Sometimes I know that what feels like being brown in the morning could well feel blue by the afternoon.'

I regarded him and I then looked at the artwork on his walls and it struck me that actually he resembled a cubist painting himself and I got it, I got it. I realized that Lawrence, weirdo creepy Lawrence with the wavery murdery voice, was actually self-assured in his oddness, he was funny and thoughtful.

'You know my name is actually Eadie?'

'Yep.'

'So why do you always call me Edith?'

He shrugged. 'Who doesn't love a nickname?'

'Shall I call you Lorry, then?'

'I'd like that,' he said. 'That's what my little sister calls me.'

I realized just then that I'd never stopped to consider that he was someone's son, someone's older brother, that he'd come from a home and a place to be here at Hulme Hall. I slumped under the aspersions I'd cast.

'Pardon me but you seem a bit – *burdened*,' he said. His plate was empty and he washed it properly at the sink, he had Fairy Liquid and a sponge. In my room, I used soap and my fingers to clean my mugs.

It was the perfect word. I did feel burdened.

'Want to talk about it?'

I shook my head.

'You sure?' he said.

I wasn't sure. I wasn't sure about anything. I stretched my legs out in front of me and thought how dull and boring my matching shoes were. I looked up and he was regarding me with a gentle curiosity.

'It's just about my friend.'
'The boy – the one who stayed?'
I nodded. 'My best friend.'
'Oh deary dear,' he said.
'It's fine, it's fine,' I said. 'I had sex with my best friend.'
'That's very *not* fine.'
'—and now he appears to hate me.'
We both took a beat to consider sex and hate.
'Edith,' Lawrence said without deliberation. 'I doubt very much that he hates you – I'd hazard a guess that actually he hates himself.'
I didn't really understand.
'*And* it was my first time.'
'There's always a first time,' he said. 'For everything. I did something similar. Not with an Edith but with a Steven.' And Lawrence's violet eyes darkened as he gave me a long look that said go on, ask me. Just ask.
And so I did.
'Steven as in a boy?'
'Yes, Edith – Steven as in a boy.'
Celeste shot across my mind's eye but she was out of sight before I could catch up with her.
'Lawrence March,' he stuck out his hand. 'Your brand new gay best friend.'
It crossed my mind that I already had one of those, not brand new but my oldest, truest friend.
His hand was as slim and soft as a Victorian glove and I shook it gently. 'Eadie Browne,' I said, 'Edith to you.' I really looked at him. 'Thank you.'
'Just remember – it was only sex.'

'Only sex,' I repeated, to see if it made sense. It didn't really.

'Did you use protection?'

I nodded.

'One of the Mates freebies dished out at Freshers' Week?'

'How did you know?'

'Oh, Edith – up and down the country, there will be hundreds of people just like you and him doing what you did.' He took my hands in his. 'Some feel jubilant, some feel appalled and some feel nothing at all. Just be glad you're not the latter. It's better to feel something than to be numb.'

'But I need to tell you about Josh,' I said.

'Oh, I want to know *everything*, girlfriend,' he said, making a big show of getting himself comfortable.

'And Celeste too,' I said.

'Celeste,' said Lawrence, wrapping his tongue around her name. 'It wasn't a threesome, was it?' and he fanned himself dramatically which made me giggle.

'They are my closest friends and she sort of said something about being gay,' I mumbled. 'I didn't believe her.'

'Didn't? Don't? Don't want to?'

'I mean, I really don't think she's properly gay – not like you.'

This made him roar with laughter. He patted next to him on the bed and I left my perch on his desk and sat beside him. I took him for a tour of Parkwin, walked him all the way back through my life and, in return, he led me through his. We talked until the early hours by which time I thought, I can tell this boy anything. And I thought, I will know this boy for the rest of my life.

When I was about to leave, I looked from my shoes to his.

'I'm really sorry,' I said. 'Sorry for being—' And I thought to myself that I could just say, *never in*. Or I could say, *so busy*. But both would be wrong. I shrugged up at my new pal. My goodness, he was tall. 'I'm really sorry that I haven't been that friendly,' I said.

We listened to that, for a beat or two.

'Uni is full of potential weirdos,' Lawrence said sagely while his sensible hands raised the slump of my shoulders. 'I just had a hunch you weren't one of them.'

It took me a moment to unravel that. I gave him a little punch and a long hug which I truly meant.

'Sorry, Lorry.'

'You are forgiven, Edith.'

He held his door open for me and just as I was about to leave, I stopped.

'But I've heard you moan and groan and bang about,' I said. 'And I never asked if you were all right. And I'm sorry.'

Lorry just laughed. 'My course is unrelenting brain-fuckery and sometimes it drives me to the verge of insanity.'

'But – all those times you knocked at my door?'

He gave a quizzical frown, shrugged, because to him the answer was simple. 'I just wanted to check you were OK,' he said. 'That's all.'

I loved him very quickly. And soon enough, Lorry came out. Literally. He was instantly a much-loved member of our gang and, sensing safety in numbers, he liberated his campness and charm which he confided he'd spent years keeping hidden at the back of his closet at home. If we were out and he was teased or insulted or shoved or recoiled from, we were there for him. It was at the Haçienda, however, where Lorry felt safest and accepted. We all did because there was a powerful and beautiful sense of togetherness in the club. Nothing bad could happen at the Haç because everyone was there with the same purpose: to experience the physical swell of absolute happiness and unity, to dance together in one expansive loved-up family and forget about the greyness and worry of outside, of Thatcher and AIDS and the nuclear threat. We all believed we'd discovered a new world, that we'd been let in on a secret which came in the form of a £20 heart-expanding elixir which, it seemed, so nobody outside the Haçienda actually knew about.

'Oh, I shouldn't really,' Lorry would say to the pill, like someone on a half-hearted diet being presented with a huge slice of cake. But of course he did. We all did.

I also should have said *oh, I shouldn't really*. I had masses of reading to catch up on and two essays I'd already begged extensions for and dwindling money in the bank. But I thought to myself that perhaps getting off my face, dancing till I dropped and sweating Josh out of my system was a good idea – some kind of crazy musical sauna for the troubled mind. At the Haçienda, heart and soul were freely given and lapped up. There, I swam and floated and danced with unbridled joy to sublime music. Ecstasy appeared to be the answer to everything. I loved everyone and everyone loved me and feeling that blissed out was an easy trade-off for the utter exhaustion that followed it.

And what of Josh? I decided not to think about him or what had happened or the fact that he hadn't written and he hadn't called. If Lorry asked, anything from Josh? I just shrugged *no* – knowing that Lorry would come out with a withering aside that always made me feel better. But I didn't write and I didn't call because I still didn't know what I wanted to say.

And what of Celeste? When we all went to the International II that May, for a benefit gig for the North West Campaign for

Lesbian and Gay Equality against Clause 28, I thought about her. I thought about Lois in France and Alicia in Edinburgh and I wondered if Celeste really was 100 per cent gay. I wondered how long she'd felt that way and how I could not have known. And if it was so, why hadn't she told me sooner? Why had she hidden it from me? I was angry about that. Lorry asked me what kind of friend that made me – and I said her *best* friend but I mulled over his question later and felt a creeping bewilderment tinged with some kind of shame that was too onerous to think about just then. At the International II that night, though some people were dressed like Frankie Goes to Bronski Beat, mostly I couldn't tell who was gay and who was straight and I knew it didn't matter. I looked around, wondering who was here for the music and who was here for the cause, but that didn't matter either. So I left thoughts of Celeste at the bar as I wriggled my way to the front where this new band, the Stone Roses, blew us away.

And what of Terry and Mum? Banal letters travelled up and down the M6 every couple of weeks or so. Sometimes I felt my words to them were a waste of a stamp.

The truth was that I no longer missed any of them really, because my life had neither the space nor the time to do so, my life was now devoted to Manchester. Cheery Eric often had to tap on the glass of the Porters' Lodge to tell me there was post because I kept forgetting to check.

Life at university was a warm and exhilarating tidal bore, sweeping me along as it surged through the year and, in my excitement, I stopped checking time and I overlooked everything left in its wake.

'Home!' said Lorry, standing behind me, his hands on my shoulders as we looked at the unremarkable late-Victorian terraced house in sunset-red brick. I had four sets of front door keys in my hand. Exams were over and our tenancy at our beloved Hulme Hall was ending and so it was that Lorry, Bill, Fiona and I had walked our possessions the short distance from Hall to our next home in Manchester.

That it began with an H sold it to me in an instant and I told the others it was surely a sign. It's auspicious, I said. I said, everything with an H is Holy with a capital H. Hulme Hall. The Haçienda. And now, Hathersage Road. But they just said Eadie, what are you *like*! For my housemates, the main factor was the price and the proximity to everything we needed.

In the house on Hathersage Road, there was no central heating, only wall-mounted gas fires that our landlord proudly proclaimed safe-as-houses. His word was good enough for us and what did we care anyway – the weather was hot and summer wasn't yet in full force. The carpet swirled browns and beiges throughout the house hiding a multitude of sins, while the curtains were the same in every room, inappropriately diaphanous with a soft floral print. It didn't bother us that the toilet cistern would only refill if the lid was lifted off and the gubbins within was jiggled in a specific rhythm. Our first joint purchase was a removable rubber contraption in pig-pink which sucked on to the taps of the bath like a cow being milked, but it gave us a shower head.

We didn't mind the unnerving dip in the lino floor near the noisy fridge, nor the violence of the gas grill and the smell of singed hair when we lit it to make toast. From the kitchen, the back door opened onto a humble patch of yard with an old coal alcove, a high wall at the end with a rickety gate to a grimy alleyway between terraces, and we hatched elaborate plans for outside seating and tomato plants and summer barbecues. Over the road, resplendent in brickwork striped like a giant humbug, were the magnificent Victoria Baths. In addition to the pools, we soon discovered there were private baths to hire there. To do so was far cheaper than turning on the immersion at our house and, with all the wondrous stained glass and glossy green tiling and mosaic floors, a whole lot more glamorous too. Soon enough we were crossing the road in our towels with our shampoo and a good book tucked under our arms.

My bedroom became my haven and had everything I needed. There was a tall thin bookcase, a small desk positioned under the window and an ancient wardrobe that could have led to Narnia. The bed was tucked under the slope of the staircase which led up to Bill's room in the attic and, at night, it felt like I was in a ship's cabin or a train's bunk or an old-fashioned wagon and I don't know why but I never once bumped my head.

At Hathersage Road, we wanted for nothing. We had our own telephone, we hired a TV and video player and the four of us ate together as a family each night, adapting basic ratatouille for most meals and sharing cold pizza or yesterday's curry for the rest. We took each other cups of tea in the mornings and stayed up late just talking talking talking. We consumed lots of biscuits. We ate cornflakes at midnight. We called out hi honey, I'm home! when we opened the front door. Soon enough we ceased to notice the cloying scent of air freshener mixed with the forgotten history of other students, which rose like musty ghosts from the old brown velvet sofa every time it was sat upon. It was inconceivable that anyone other than us had ever lived there. It was built for us, surely. It was our home.

Our house came complete with the best next-door neighbour too. I'd grown up with the Electricity Building on one side and rows of dead people on the other. Now I had Iris. At eighty-two, she was a gorgeous small cube of a woman; a picture-perfect granny in a children's book come to life, with her little legs and lace-up shoes and a hairdo not unlike the Queen's. On the day we moved in she came over with a Battenberg cake and wanted to know if we liked rock 'n' roll because she didn't much like rock 'n' roll at all and the previous students had played it too often too loudly. She asked us not to break bottles in our yard, as if it was a pastime she feared all students enjoyed. And she made us promise not to feed her cat Sparky because he was too fat. Too fat, Iris said, but not too fat to jump through an open window and gobble up student food which, in her experience, was left on plates on various cat-friendly surfaces. Last year, some students had locked Sparky in, Iris told us. She could hear Sparky yowling all day, she said, but by the time those students had returned, he'd had a good shit on their beds the clever little bastard. Do your washing-up, Iris instructed, and don't forget bin day. We promised. And come in for a brew, any time you like, she said. You too, we said. Iris made a note of all our birthdays – and I wrote down when it was hers.

I felt wrapped up in warmth. Within the shortest time, the house on Hathersage Road became more fundamentally home than 41 Yew Lane and I felt blessed to share it with some of my favourite people in the world. I was paying rent here, where I lived with my tribe, so what was the point of leaving for the summer because what was the point of Parkwin? That previously unbreakable triumvirate of Celeste, Josh and I was now disconnected with an out-of-order tone too loud to talk over. Celeste was probably staying in Edinburgh anyway, I told myself. And I also told myself not to waste time wondering where Josh was spending the summer.

I phoned my old home and asked Terry to tell Mum that I might not be back at all.

He said he understood though I wasn't sure that he did.

I wrote down the length of the call in the notepad we kept by the phone: *1 minute 27 seconds*. Then I took the stairs two at a time and skipped into my room.

The weather became blisteringly hot. The sun dazzled day after day in cloudless skies which hazed with pressure each afternoon; pavements were dusty and the grass in the parks dried out and crinkled. Everyone walked more slowly. As I ambled around Manchester in my bright checked pinafore dress or baggy dungarees over a ubiquitous white T-shirt, my arms went pink, my nose peeled and my hair frizzed. I didn't mind and no one remarked and I don't think I'd ever felt happier. I looked for a job and found employment behind the bar at the Rampant Lion pub around the corner. There was no more studying and every reason to rejoice and the best place to celebrate was the Haçienda. Despite the growing queues to get in, the grimly hazardous overflowing loos and everyone blowing ear-blistering plastic whistles over the music for no apparent reason, the club still held our hearts. What we were experiencing in Whitworth Street West remained new and the world had yet to catch on.

We always called it the Haç. This was a club where there was never a jam for the bar because no one drank booze with their Ecstasy, just water. There were no fights. No beery breath. No pissheads reeling around. Women didn't need to dance protectively together around a handbag to ward off creeps. There were no creeps. No one was on the pull, there was no leeriness. None of that. It was a purely unisex and unpredatory community. It was a club in every sense of the word, we were drawn there to be together, to share in the experience. We all dressed the same, dressed for comfort, spent our money at the indie stalls in Afflecks Palace on anything baggy, anything with a great big acid-yellow smiley-face logo. We sported bandanas to stop the sweat dripping in our eyes and sometimes I just wore a sports bra with shorts to the Haç because it was practical. All we wanted to do was dance and grin and give and take all this energized loving joy.

Ecstasy was magical, that's what it was. It raised our heart rate and matched it to the 120 beats per minute of the transcendental music. Those little pills were expansive, creating love and goodwill which overflowed and wrapped around everyone, friends or strangers. Ecstasy lifted us up and, as we had no lectures to go to, no essays to write, we could come down gently without a bump. Everyone shared the one loved-up smile;

hugs and hand-holding were freely given and the euphoria was contagious. People were beautiful, being alive was epic and this new music, on these trancey dancey nights, affirmed everything that the pill magnified.

That Ecstasy was illegal didn't cross our minds, nor did we stop to wonder what we were taking. How could anything that created such sweet happiness be bad for you? we asked each other, we told each other, time and again. We were safe in the embrace and benevolence of our bountiful Haçienda. The collective purpose was to be happy and friendly and how could that be breaking the law? We felt lucky, we felt blessed.

'E can change the world,' Lorry declared one night. 'It could save lives.'

'It should be compulsory for all governments,' said Bill.

'Especially those with nuclear capability,' said Fiona.

'Thatcher should take it.'

'Thatcher, Reagan *and* Gorby.'

'There would be no war.'

'No hate.'

'People would understand the power of love,' I said.

We truly believed the potential in those nine sentences to solve the problems of the world.

It would come to be known as the Second Summer of Love – though in 1988 we weren't concerned with having a title for it, in fact we weren't aware that it was happening, that it was even a thing; certainly not that it would make the national news and before long incite the predictable backlash. Back then, at the time, we were simply living in the now, leaping aboard for the ride wherever that was going to take us.

As the Haçienda became increasingly popular and as summer broadened, so the atmosphere at the club became rapturous. The place, the people, the music, the dancing, the E. For a while, the balance was perfect. For a short and wonderful period in our lives. Until it wasn't.

Peace, love and euphoria – I never wanted it to end. It was the best summer of my life; I was living with my contemporaries, my compatriots, my Hathersage Road family. There was sunshine and nightlife to enjoy, the peace and the Ecstasy. I made friends with my fellow bar staff at the Rampant Lion where I was earning good tips now that pubs could stay open all day. But then, bewilderingly, my housemates began to leave. They started drifting off to what they called their real homes, to spend their time with their other families.

'Don't you bugger off and leave me,' I implored Lorry when it was just us two left. We were sucking brightly coloured ice pops in a welcome patch of dusty shade in Whitworth Park.

'But I *want* to go and see my family, Edith – my little sis, my granny.' He paused and tapped my knee with his ice pop. 'You should go home too,' he said.

'This *is* my home,' I said quietly.

Lorry took a thoughtful beat. When he sucked his ice pop, any ounce of fat disappeared from his face and I could clearly see the outline of his beautiful skull. 'You could go back for a little while,' he said. 'Hopefully see Josh and Celeste and you know – make things right.'

We regarded each other, our hot open faces, our cold stained mouths. Lorry looked like he was wearing orange lipstick. My tongue was deep blue.

'But I haven't done anything wrong,' I said.

I could see Lorry wanted to say something but I watched him choose not to and I was grateful for that. We sat in silence for a while focusing on how the grass, tough and spiky brown, crimped imprints onto our skin.

So they all left but I stayed. For the first time in my life, I was truly on my own and I didn't venture far, I didn't even go into town. It was too hot and anyway, my new home was enough and I never once felt lonely. I read, I cleaned, I hummed and sometimes I just went up the stairs and down again. I'd choose a step and just sit there, daydreaming through the small stained-glass window next to our front door. Hello little house, I'd say as I trailed my fingertips over the banister, the woodchip walls, the furniture. I put out the rubbish and hoovered, adjusted the Blu Tack so our posters hung straight, plumped the cushions and scruffled up £2.24 in loose change from down the sides of the sofa. I swept the yard and tried to make a barbecue out of some random bricks I found in the coal shed; I made it into a small seat instead. I didn't know where to buy tomato plants but I spent an afternoon trying to separate the seeds from a fresh one, dried them out for days on a piece of toilet paper before planting them with hope in a mug. I went over the road and swam in the pool daily and my hair developed a green tinge from the chlorine. I visited Iris frequently for cups of slightly sour tea while Sparky sat on my lap and sprang his claws into my bare legs.

On evenings when I wasn't working at the Rampant Lion, I'd sit in the back yard just to listen. I listened in on the silence in the empty student house next door and I tuned in to Iris's television. I eavesdropped on the animated Punjabi chattering of the extended family who lived in consecutive houses along Olney Street. I heard Sparky fighting. And, if I really focused, I could sense the Haçienda not so far away thrumming with life and love. But I never went there on my own. Though the doormen knew me – and the dance floor would be awash with welcome – the point of the Haç was experiencing it with my friends and they'd all gone.

When the Rampant Lion closed for maintenance, begrudgingly I returned to Parkwin, where Terry needed a haircut and my mum appeared smaller and their papers and notes now flowed across the sofa and congregated on the table. I wondered if they had to eat standing up. In the fridge, the cucumber and the lettuce and the tomatoes were exactly where I expected to find them and, in the cupboards, the tins of tuna and beans and sweetcorn were stacked as usual. But there was a dusty silence to my room and the garden appeared enervated and parched. It was the hottest summer for more than a century. It was even hotter here than in Manchester and I rarely took off the huge blue-rimmed sunglasses I'd bought at the Students' Union market. Everywhere, flowers were wilting and leaves were curling and dog shit was dehydrating and turning white. It sounded like it was an effort for the birds to sing, and the bees and bugs droned a tired octave lower. It felt as though the life in everything was being desiccated.

Terry and I watched the funerals again from our sitting-room window.

I said to Terry, what a time to die. 'It's too hot to be buried,' I said. 'It's too hot to have to wear black.'

'Alan Thorpe,' Terry observed, as we watched the hearse pass. 'Eighty-seven years old.'

'Good age,' I said. 'A good innings.'

Silently, we counted the cars in Alan Thorpe's cortège.

'A fine turnout.'

'Family flowers only. Donations to the British Heart Foundation.'

'How ever do they dig six feet down?' I said. 'The ground is baked rock hard.'

It was so hot you could almost hear it as a sound, a muzzed, headachy hum constant throughout the fug-heavy days and airless nights. Early evening, when 41 Yew Lane seemed to pulsate with all the leftover heat of the day and opening the windows only drew in flies, the cemetery was a fraction cooler. The dead were quiet as ever in their graves and there was respite to be found where weather was of no consequence or conversation. I did my rounds, visiting all the people I'd ever known over the years whilst making my acquaintance with those who'd arrived since I'd left. There were quite a number of them and it surprised me because I'd taken to assuming how Parkwin life – and death – would be somehow on hold whilst I was away. Tidying as I walked those familiar rows, I remarked to myself how well Michael was doing without me and I imagined him noticing tomorrow how I'd refilled the vases and brought the flowers back to life. When I was a little girl, Michael told me that he had green fingers but that mine had magic powers. I remembered how I wanted to believe him, but his fingers were flesh-coloured and muddy so I'd suspected he'd lied.

I saw Michael just the once. He greeted me with his what ho which made me tearful and fractious and I was grateful that my enormous sunglasses concealed this from him.

'Look at you!' he said and he stilled his secateurs and had a long long look, as if someone else was masquerading as me.

'It's just me,' I said to him.

We did a little deadheading together and, at a bench by a Shrubbery of Sympathy, he motioned for me to sit. He always liked this spot – it overlooked the Fletcher family. There were six graves between eleven of them, always well tended, and the carving of the headstones was perhaps the most beautiful in the grounds. Michael took out his pipe, packed in the tobacco, lit it and puffed, re-lit it and puffed and offered it to me.

'Michael,' I said, 'I haven't smoked for *years*, you know that.'

'Safer than all those drugs,' he said. 'I read about drugs in the papers,' he said. 'All the kids. Doing the drugs.' He sucked at the pipe thoughtfully. 'Not you though, Eadie – you don't even smoke these days.' It was doubtful that Michael would even notice how I'd suddenly reddened because everyone that summer looked utterly broiled. I hid behind my sunglasses all the same and changed the subject.

'We're always talking about *you-plural* in the Shop,' my mum said softly, handing me money and her foldable tartan trolley bag. 'We're always wondering how *you-plural* are faring, all the way in Manchester, in Cambridge, in Edinburgh.'

I flinched from the pride and wonder in her voice and headed off into the heat haze to collect our order. I'd offered to run the errand because, finally, I wanted to see Josh. I really did. I had no idea what I'd say but I just hoped he might be there. If I could see his face and he could see mine, it would work itself out, we would be fine.

Though we grew up in a landlocked county, there was an impressive if incongruous display of seaside buckets and spades outside the Shop and cheap sunglasses pierced into a long roll of card. Reuben, ever-enterprising, always thought up revenue streams to take advantage of the weather and claw back custom from the supermarket. Snow shovels and strange spikes to strap to one's shoes for sale in the winter, chestnuts by the handful in the autumn and, in the spring, little pots of daffodils that he'd planted up and nurtured on windowsills for months.

In the welcome coolness of the Shop's interior, from behind my sunglasses I watched incognito before tipping them up on top of my head when Reuben turned to regard me.

'Kitzeleh! Shefeleh!' He rushed over and bathed me with more Yiddish names for baby animals. 'But you've come for Josh?' He seemed surprised.

'Actually, I've come for the 41 Yew Lane shopping?'

'Of course, Eadie-leh, of course,' he said, tapping his forehead as if he was nuts. 'You of all people would know that Josh is away.'

I nodded behind a fixed grin while my sunglasses slipped back down onto my nose and hid the confusion in my eyes which said no, Reuben, I did not know.

'You've met her?' he asked casually over his shoulder as he disappeared through the waft of pastel plastic strips to the back of the Shop. 'Lisa?'

Who?

'The girlfriend?' He reappeared with our shopping.

I kept my smile in place. 'Not yet,' I chimed.

Reuben made much of tipping his head from side to side, pursing his lips into a skewed smile. I knew that gesture. It meant he wasn't all that impressed.

'You know, your job is open – if you feel like working here,' he said. 'It's nice and cool in the back.'

I think I must have looked horrified but Reuben smiled and gave my cheek a little pinch.

'I understand – you're resting your grey matter,' he said and gave me a pineapple and an elastic bracelet made of sweets. 'A history degree!' he marvelled, with his full-face glinty smile.

How I wanted to say what the heck am I going to do with a history degree, Reuben? It was a question I frequently asked myself.

As I walked home, I thought about Josh not being there. I was relieved, wasn't I? I had dreaded him being there, hadn't I? Because I wouldn't have known what to say, would I, even after all these months. What if my lifelong friend had nothing to say to me, what if he had no sunglasses to shield me from the horror or distaste in his eyes? Thank God he hadn't been there, right? Maybe now was the time to write to him, to say what needed to be said. Or maybe it wasn't. Walking home I couldn't help but feel like I was the old banger he'd learned to drive in so that he could zoom off in a fancy new set of wheels called Lisa.

I put the shopping away and spent some time just staring at the phone before calling myself a twat and dialling Celeste. Sandrine picked up. Celeste is in France, she told me, confused that I wouldn't know that. In France with her friends, Sandrine said. At her grandparents', she said. And she wondered out loud why I wasn't there and I wondered if Celeste had told her that I would be. I hung up and slunk into my bedroom, weighed down by my thoughts and the debilitating heat. Maybe it was time to write to Celeste, to apologize. But why hadn't she told me sooner? And why had she gone away without telling me, too? I remembered how, this time last year, I'd begged my friends that this summer we'd holiday together. Israel or Interrail or Grandparents in Grasse. We don't know where we'll be in twelve months' time, they had laughed. Was that only a year ago? Felt like a lifetime. But here I was, back in Parkwin, resenting all the hot bloody sunshine sucking me dry. What was I even doing here? There was nothing to keep me here. My life was up North now. I thought longingly of Hathersage Road, envisaged the old house ready and waiting for me.

And that's how the summer of 1988 rolled on for me. While up and down the country, long snaking convoys streamed into top-secret fields and disused warehouses and derelict factories for the birth of Rave, I mooched and moped and overheated within the restrictive perimeter of the Garden City I'd grown up in. Nagging at the base of my thoughts every day was that something was severely out of kilter. Josh, Celeste and I had completed our first year at university and that fact alone was momentous. We should have been chewing it over together, marvelling at each other's stories, sharing secrets of our recent history, confiding and talking to a depth we had yet to reach with our uni friends. We should have done so lolling on Celeste's capacious bed or in my back garden on the rickety deckchairs, we should have done so sitting on the boxes at the back of the Shop, or strolling into town throwing peanuts and pennies into the fountain. Instead, we were miles and miles apart; the distance between us growing rapidly beyond the confines of geography. Never had a twelve-month period put such a divide between the present and the past.

D ust. And also the smell of burned toast and baked beans. I shut the front door quietly, stood in the hallway of Hathersage Road and breathed it all in.

'Hi honeys – I'm home!'

I'm *home*.

Summer was done but that was OK; we were skipping with unbridled joy into the first term of our second year at Manchester University. Fiona was nut brown while Lorry was paler than ever and Bill had a black eye with a tall tale to go with it. The dip in the kitchen floor was deeper and the lino there had developed a crack. In the time I'd been gone, a mouse had moved in so we set a trap with a shoebox and a brick which didn't work and we took to sellotaping the kitchen cabinets shut instead. Still, we nicknamed the mouse Klaus and wondered if Iris would let us borrow Sparky for a while.

The Oxford Road once again surged with the chatter and scrum of students running late for lectures. The freshers looked so young and, now that we were jaded second years, we were entitled to think them annoying. I renewed my membership of Film Soc and J Soc but let all those other clubs slide. Two people had dropped out of my course, the

Cellar disco had had a facelift, Rosie had cut off all her hair and Paul's ear was pierced, twice. Lorry was at least five inches taller and Iris had surely shrunk. I walked past Hulme Hall and wondered who was in my room, promised myself I'd pop in to see Eric because I never really said goodbye last year. Last year which was actually July. Only three months ago. Can you believe that?

My course was now dense with study; essays had to be longer, deeper, broader, and the reading list was onerous and dry.

I continued to worry that I'd chosen the wrong degree.

I knew it was too late to change.

I didn't feel I could tell anyone this.

There was just so much work.

My housemates assumed I was beavering away behind the closed door of the bedroom I loved so much, but I was just sitting on the floor with my back to the bed, daydreaming at the licking flames of the gas fire while tracing the swirls in my carpet.

Jordan and that lot moved into a huge draughty place on Daisy Bank Road which smelled bad and Karen and Paul and Dan and that lot crammed into a nice little house on Banff Road but wherever I was I couldn't wait to hurry home to Hathersage Road. Sometimes I turned down going out because I was just so happy and cosy at home. No one else referred to their houses as home and I thought that was very odd.

The Haçienda continued to be our harbour but, as the weeks passed, it began to feel ever so slightly different. The new revellers wouldn't have noticed, but we did; it was the same but it wasn't the same, something had gone and something else had arrived. By the end of term the club was absolutely packed, with huge queues running right around the building and doormen we didn't recognize. Inside, there was sometimes a feeling of tension too – like a belt worn a notch too tight, like cold slicking its way through a crack in a window frame that summer had concealed. Change was afoot at our Haç; gone were the halcyon days when everyone knew everyone, when nobody knew anything and we'd all felt everything. However, none of us wanted to acknowledge it out loud; it was akin to saying your best friend wasn't as much fun any more, that your best friend had changed and you weren't sure whether you were on the same wavelength now, whether you wanted to hang out that much.

I had two essays due by the end of term and instead of asking for extensions I just avoided the department altogether. I reasoned that no professor in their right mind would be marking essays over the Christmas holidays anyway, so they wouldn't miss mine. I stayed at Hathersage Road right up until Christmas Eve, working busy shifts at the Rampant Lion and feeding Sparky for Iris who was visiting her relatives. I was on my own when I heard about the Pan Am aeroplane exploding over Lockerbie and I knew Iris wouldn't mind that I took Sparky with me to bed. The cat and I spent a lot of time together. I had both houses to myself and if I wasn't working behind the bar or staring at blank pages willing an essay to appear, I was happy with Sparky on my lap in one sitting room or the other. One day, I told the cat, I'd like to buy both these houses. I'll knock them through into one and I'll want for nothing. I'll bash down the top of the wall into the kitchen and create a breakfast bar. I'll treat the bathroom to new tiles and a proper shower unit. I'll live like you, Sparky, I said. Two fine houses as one happy home.

I did a lot of cleaning, right up until Christmas Eve.
But most of all I did sitting.

I was determined to study over the break and sneak my essays in to the tutors' pigeonholes before term started so I went back to Parkwin for just four days and hardly left my room though I barely wrote beyond the opening paragraphs. I slipped out just twice to visit the grounds but I never saw Michael, I never saw a living soul. I looked around at all those dead people and wondered what was the point of worrying so much about unfinished essays. It wasn't a matter of life and death. My gravestone would not give space to whether or not I flunked uni. It was never going to read *Eadie Browne, Distinguished Historian*, because I didn't want to be a distinguished historian. Though I didn't know what I wanted to be, I knew I didn't want to be here in Parkwin so, with my essays only half planned and those opening paragraphs scrapped, I told my parents I was heading back to Manchester early. Because of the libraries up there, I explained. The resources. The atmosphere.

I can't work here, I told them, it's just not *conducive*. I watched confusion striate their faces and hurt dull their eyes as they glanced at each other and looked around our sitting room. In this room, their melting pot of ideas produced a peaceable and fertile atmosphere of creativity for them; their desks, books, the paper trails, the pots of pens, the hive of productivity: 41 Yew Lane, renowned for dedicated study and quiet creativity but not good enough for Eadie Browne.

'I mean – why do you two *never* finish anything you write?' I said to my parents. My tone of voice clearly said what's the point. All those stories and ideas and pamphlets and novellas and poems uncompleted, without purpose.

Terry didn't look up. 'Sometimes you really don't need to tell the whole story,' he said.

And Mum said, 'If you paint a picture vivid enough, finishing touches are not necessary.'

I thought it was all complete nonsense and I turned on my heels and went to my room to pack.

Though I was desperate to be gone, the morning I was due to leave I stood quietly in the centre of the sitting room while my parents beavered away and I returned the sad little smiles they sent over to me. And then I happened to notice that on top of a pile of papers on Terry's desk was one of my cassettes. In felt-tip pen and elaborate squirly letters, I'd written *Fave Choons 4* on the label. Though Terry was busy writing, without lifting his head from his work or taking his pen from the page he slid a sheet of paper to conceal the tape.

'That's mine!' I snatched away the paper and pointed at the tape. 'That's *mine*.'

'Oh,' said Terry, 'is it?' And that had to be the stupidest thing he'd ever said.

'Yes, it *is*,' I said and I grabbed it with a huff. 'God! Don't go in my room – don't touch my *things*.'

There followed a panicked chorus of silent excuses from my parents before either actually spoke.

'Sometimes we just like to play your music, Eadie,' Terry said eventually. He wrote for a few moments more. 'We like to listen to the songs we used to hear coming from your room,' he said. 'And the garden.'

'The songs you'd sing with Celeste and Josh,' my Mum said evenly. 'The music brings you back to us – when you're not here. That's all.'

And Terry buffed his glasses with the tattered hem of his jumper, placed them back on his nose and looked over to my mum for one of her smiles. I had a beat to decide what to do with the cassette in my hand and the mood in my mind. I took the tape back to my room in a huff. I put it in my drawer and piled jumpers on top.

Later, as the coach rattled up the M6, I pestered myself with drifts of music from *Fave Choons 4*, with fleeting images of my parents at their desks, of 41 Yew Lane empty of me. If I could have stopped the coach and crossed the motorway and hitch-hiked all the way back to Parkwin I would have, and yet the fact that I could not spun a little sad relief through me. Mile after mile was taking me away from one version of me and back to another. I let my head judder against the window as hidden tears stung my conscience. I tortured myself envisaging Terry – or perhaps Mum – padding into my room and taking my tape, then the two of them singing along to a tune they'd've heard so often, playing the music so they could imagine me in the room with them. Suddenly the freedom I had experienced in Manchester, when realizing that no one back home knew where I was or what I was doing at any given moment, was turned on its head. Now I wondered where had *I* been when Terry and Mum pressed play? When *was* that? And also – what were they doing *right now*? I didn't know.

It hurt my head, the notion that Terry and Mum actually missed me, the two of them not liking 41 Yew Lane with no Eadie in it. Eadie who they could conjure in essence through the music she used to play. A little of their daughter, contained within the cassettes that hadn't made the collection taken up to Manchester. Eadie who rarely wrote. Eadie who mostly shook her head and put her finger to her lips if one of her housemates answered the phone to her parents.

I whispered to the coach window, *my tapes are in the second drawer under the itchy blue polo neck*. My fractured reflection stared back and, just then, mirrored precisely how I felt. I closed my eyes and willed my parents to find my tapes. You can play any of them, all of them. You can keep them in the sitting room. I didn't mean to shut my door nor keep you out. I didn't mean to cold-shoulder the house where I grew up. A tear stung my skin as it oozed out. I didn't know what to do with these thoughts, I didn't like the feelings they brought so I turned away from them. I brushed my sleeve against my eyes and I twisted away from the coach window, from the sight of me. I stared instead at the knees of the woman sitting next to me as I concentrated as best I could on the essays I had yet to write.

Then I was home. Hathersage Road home. The others wouldn't be back for another week or so. Sparky wasn't there. Iris wasn't in. The Victoria Baths were closed over the festive period. I shut the front door behind me and thought how cold the old house felt. How quiet it was. And dark.

'Last time I went to the Haç, they was all off their tits, sweating cobs.'

Denny, who wasn't that much older than me, was my boss at the Rampant Lion and he always helped me cash up. February had been a lucrative month at the pub and March was off to a good start. Denny, whose surname I still didn't know, whose Mancunian twang was melodious and warm. Denny who called the pensioners who came into the pub *love*. Denny with the earlobe with the bit missing because he said that he'd been a right cabbage when he was young. Mad as toast, Denny told me. Denny whose rhymes and phrases were daft and lovely and repeated ad nauseam. Eadie Browne – best in town. Sound as a pound. Kippered. Mithered. Peppered.

'They all looked like a bunch of knob'eads when I was last there – in the Haç,' he said and he gurned and danced in pretty good approximation and had me in stitches.

'Come with me tonight – my mates are already there,' I said.

But Denny was now holding his head in his hands. 'Eadie – your maths isn't even maths,' he sighed wearily, taking the ledger and the calculator from me and doing it all properly while I sat on a bar stool and ate peanuts.

'It has changed a bit,' I admitted. 'This thing happened last weekend.' It was something we hadn't talked about at home, something we'd left at the Haç hoping it would be swept away and binned. 'It was absolutely rammed and all these new bouncers suddenly charged through us on the dance floor with pool cues, and they started bashing this group of lads.'

Denny kept his finger in place on a column of figures and looked at me. 'The *fook*? Who were they?'

'I don't know – we'd never seen them before. They weren't really like us lot.'

He moved his finger down a few rows and looked over to me again. 'Were you all right, our kid?'

I nodded. 'We all just bolted to the sides, into the alcoves, while those lads legged it with the bouncers chasing.' It had only lasted a few minutes but I'd spent hours thinking about it. 'Then the DJ – God love him – he played 'Good Life' by Inner City and suddenly everyone's just dancing again.' I brightened my tone because I didn't want Denny to pass comment or judge, he was unnervingly wise for a twenty-three-year-old who'd left school without a single qualification. Often I'd sought his counsel but today I didn't want it. The truth was I wasn't sure what I'd witnessed on the dance floor last week and though the DJ soon made us all feel happy and safe again, that ours really was a good life, I hadn't fully believed him.

Bill had said bloody hell – crazy or what! Fiona had cuddled me and said nothing bad could ever happen to us in the Haç. Lorry had said they were just scallies. Jordan had said do another E. Yet Lorry kept glancing this way and that and Fiona stayed very close and Bill wasn't really dancing, just standing there looking around, and Jordan was different this term anyway. He didn't seem like one of us any more and it was hard to pinpoint why. He'd moved out of his student digs and in with people we didn't know.

I had tried to dance again but the floor seemed too hard and my legs felt wrong. I didn't let my eyes close or allow the music to fully flood me and I left early with Bill, drawn by the very thought of our front door and all that lay behind it. The toast and the warmth and my room and my bed.

Now, I felt Denny watching me. He'd finished cashing up and he closed the ledger, locked the till. 'You're shit at maths, our Eadie,' he said, 'but surely even you can work out that drugs equals money equals gangs. Gangs plus gangs is – shite.'

'Yes, Dad,' I said.

'Drugs change everything.'

'Only if you let it.'

'You do know you've no control over that?'

Maybe I did. Maybe I didn't want to listen just then.

'You don't even know what you might be taking.'

True enough, it wasn't uncommon for people to pass out in the Haçienda. It was so crowded and hot in there now and usually fresh air and a bottle of water revived them. But I wasn't going to tell Denny how Bill and Lorry had been really ill a couple of weeks ago. Violent stomach kicks and a weird rash and they'd puked down to black bile and perhaps we should have taken them to hospital. I'd told Denny about the fracas with the bouncers and those lads last weekend, but not about the lairy groups of men who regularly jumped the queue and barged to the front at the bar, who had started to commandeer the alcoves and who moved through the crowd on the prowl. No way was I going to tell him that once or twice I'd felt uncomfortable, convinced that someone was watching me, eyeing me, standing too close. I hadn't told anyone at all about that because I'd persuaded myself I'd imagined it.

'Just—' I watched Denny dig around for what to say. 'Just – keep your eyes open, our kid. It *is* about the drugs and it's *not* about the drugs – it's about them that's behind the drugs.'

'Yes Dad no Dad anything you say Dad.'

And Denny looked at me exasperated, concerned.

When the good times roll it's easy to overlook how they will inevitably pick up speed and start to tumble out of control. But I felt proud, we all did, proud and privileged because Manny was our city and we'd been happily strolling in time to its beat long before the bandwagon rolled into town and deposited hyped-up partygoers at the doors of our club. The beauty of this time and place was its inclusivity and everyone felt it. We had said come in! come in! with our arms open. Students, locals, tourists and visitors, hairdressers, lawyers and those on the dole; whoever they were, wherever they were from, together we surfed the tides of benevolence and energy governed by the magnetic pull of Ecstasy with the Haçienda providing the sound, the time and the place.

The media vacillated between lauding our city as cutting edge, Manchester being the epicentre of everything cool – and denigrating it a Northern den of iniquity. When the tabloids published articles on the *Evils of Ecstasy* and the complicity of the acid house scene, we ridiculed the headlines, cut them out and stuck them on the fridge door. In front of the fridge, the split in the lino had now ripped and the dip had become a hole. You would think that if there's a hole right there in front of you, one that you see every day, you wouldn't fall into it. That's what you'd think.

That night, Denny's words reverberated in my head as I walked home. My clothes smelled of spilt beer and my hair reeked of fag smoke and it was raining. I boiled the kettle and brewed tea until it was the colour of caramel, plonking myself down into the brown velvet sofa which had started to groan when we sat on it, as if after all these years of service it had grown tired of supporting students. Perhaps I wouldn't go out tonight. I added more sugar than usual, I blew and I sipped and I thought of Terry proclaiming that Tea was his Drug of Choice. Drugs – the word itself has an uncomfortable sound, mucky and dark. We rarely used it, we never said *let's do drugs*.

E.

Even the sound of just the letter itself was floaty and like a peal of delight. But there was our Lorry and Bill sick as dogs and scared. There was the aggression on the door and the violence on the floor and now there was Denny tonight saying that drugs change everything. I knew he was right. Drugs = money = gangs + gangs = shite. His equation was irritatingly simple and even with my risible arithmetic, I could compute it.

Perhaps I wouldn't go out tonight. Hathersage Road was quiet. Opposite, the Victoria Baths lumbered in the shadows and the shops were shut, shoulder to shoulder in a sleepy line. It had stopped raining. Outside, the tarmac glistened under the streetlights. In our sitting room, the dusty old paper lantern gave a warm glow. Next door, the muffled chatter of Iris's TV. It was all comforting. I loved where I lived, I could have a perfectly happy evening staying right here.

Only – should I go out? Friday night after all. Friday night, Eadie. I gulped down my tea and went upstairs to my room where I looked from my bed to my wardrobe to my bed to my wardrobe while I decided what to do.

The queue at the Haçienda was ridiculous, longer than I'd ever known. Nearer the front, people were chanting, singing, blowing their bloody whistles as they pumped from foot to foot in anticipation of entry. Further along, there was excited chatter and laughter as groups of friends made new groups of friends. On from there, people stood mostly motionless as if, by blocking it out, time might speed up and move them forward faster. Where was my lot, though? I expected to find them in a babble near the front of the queue but they weren't there. Perhaps they were inside already. I didn't recognize any of the door staff and this lot didn't look like they'd be amenable to my lengthy descriptions of Fiona and Bill and Lorry, nor care that I was a regular, so I mooched up and down the line again. The hotdog man was setting up, I gave him a wave and he sent back a toothsome smile and, for a split-second, I considered simply buying one, two even, and just heading home. Yes, actually, maybe that was a good—

But then.

Screeching brakes, the roar of engines, a barrage of car horns and a lot of shouting
too sudden to know what was happening. Happening too fast to even spin to locate it
and someone was grabbing my arm

yanking me from the crowd
marching me away
I couldn't see who – they were pushing at my back and I
stumbled and tripped
and couldn't shout
couldn't stop myself from being dragged off
think think think – but I couldn't
say something – can't.
shout – no voice
pull back – no strength
run – legs not working.

The world was now topsy-turvy but on Whitworth Street West I still knew the right direction from wrong. It was dark around the back, near the canal. So dark and eerie it distorted time and I couldn't tell the difference between a moment and an hour. I managed a strangled sound which I feared only I could hear but I summoned energy from deep in my stomach and, from the back of my ribs, I howled out NO NO NO.

A gloved hand was slapped over my entire face, leaving only a tiny porthole for part of my right eye. It was too small for me to see my life flash by.

'Fookin' shut it, all right?'

Friday Friday not a day to die day. Not in the Rochdale Canal.

The hand came briefly away from my face in time for me to see a van. The back door was being wrested open while my upper arm was in a vice-like grip. I was shoved inside. The man jumped in after me and clanked the door shut.

Then there was only dark dread silence.

No – there was my hyperventilating, disembodied whimpering. I was told again to fookin' shut it, man – but I couldn't breathe slower and I couldn't make it quieter. I begged in a whisper just one word – *please*. I couldn't tell where in the van he was. The terror.

'Please,' I said, 'I've got my period.' Maybe I should have said gonorrhoea. I twisted my legs and clamped my hands between them and I sat there and shook in spasms. Just breathe, I told myself. Just. Keep. Breathing. In. And out. And in. Out. Good girl, Eadie, good girl.

I couldn't tell where he was. The darkness was like sludge. It was also strangely warm and smelled faintly of earth. I padded my hands in a small circle around me with some vague hope of finding something heavy or sharp to wield about myself. There was nothing. Nothing at all. The nothingness was suffocating and I pressed my back hard against the steel side of the van hoping it might yield or absorb me. I closed my eyes against the unrelenting darkness and I prayed. I really prayed. I prayed like we used to do at Three Magnets, the Lord's Prayer. I prayed the Alberts' Hebrew blessings they said on Friday nights. I made deals with all the gods who might be listening.

And then, a sound. A ratcheting snap snap snap. It was a lighter. In the dim glow, the doom-dark mass of the man approached like a malevolent monkey. I started to kick out with all my might and with everything I had I screamed, but immediately the gloved hand smacked over my face again. Greasy, hairy, thick. Wool on my tongue. I gagged. The flame sputtered out.

And then—

'Eadie.'

* * *

Huh?

I am known?

Who was this skank of a person who knew my name? How could *they* know *me*?

'Fook's sake. I'm not going to hurt you – but you've got to be dead quiet, yeah?'

The lighter flicked on and the lighter flicked off. The lighter was told it was a fookin' piece of shit. With one hand pressed against my shoulder to pin me to the spot, the man reached for a bag which I now saw had been so nearly in my grasp. Things in the bag clanked and jangled and then something was being drawn out and brandished.

I'm done for.

I started to cry little girl lonely sobs.

I was shaking uncontrollably.

There was a fizzing feeling under my entire skin. So hot. So cold. My skull was shrinking hard against my brain, squeezing out only what had true meaning. An image of my bedroom – not Hathersage Road but Yew Lane. The feeling of stepping into our garden, bare feet on warm patio slabs. The sound of Ross's bagpipes. The taste of Viennetta. The scent of Terry's jumper – the red one that had turned brown over the years. Three Nuns tobacco. The playground at Three Magnets. The shelves at the back of the Shop. The funny mannequins at Pour Toi. Josh. And Celeste. My mum bunny-twitching her nose so her specs stay on. I was loved. I was loved.

A dim light.

It was a *torch*, that thing from the clanking bag.

'Eadie – not going to hurt you. Fook's sake.'

Who *was* this arsehole who knew my name? 'Fuck you!'

'Keep it down, yeah?' His voice had softened and his grip on me loosened as he sat down heavily, right beside me, shoulder to shoulder, our legs touching – his still while mine jerked.

'Don't remember me?' He sighed a little, as if his feelings were hurt.

Of course I didn't remember him. I thought, I'm not even going to dignify that with an answer. I thought, I must be very very quiet and think think think.

Then the gloves were off. It was the pad of his warm fingertip that touched me next, tap-tapping on my cheek. Gently. Right at my dimple.

'It's Patrick, yeah?' he said. 'When you were little, right, we was in the same school.'

        What

   the...

      but I mean

         ...what the actual

     ?

'It's *Patrick*,' he said again, with a strange and delicate hope simpering through the gloom of the van. 'Patrick *Semple*. From Three Magnets Primary? Best school in the world, that. I were about seven or eight when me family moved from Parkwin up here.'

He didn't sound anything like horrible Patrick who'd made my life a misery, whose burial plot I had earmarked in the cemetery a lifetime ago. This Patrick spoke with an accent even more twangy than Denny's. He sounded like someone taking the piss out of someone like him, a caricature of a Manc scally.

'I swear I'm not going to hurt you, Eadie,' he was saying. 'Just needed you to be quiet, yeah? See – I seen you, in the 'Ass a few times. And things were going to kick off a bit tonight in there, in the 'Ass, know what I mean? And you were there and I wanted you out the way so you'd not be *in* the way – yeah?'

Too much information ricocheted around my head at breakneck speed. My mind ran circles around the fact that Patrick Semple had abducted me, shoved me in the back of a van and was only now claiming to be my rescuer. Fibres from his revolting glove were in my mouth making me retch as we sat, shoulders touching, at the back of my beloved club, inches from the inky trudge of the Rochdale canal.

Though he was mumbling an apology for giving me such a shock, and though I slowly sensed there might not be malice in the van, still my legs trembled sporadically, as if zapped by a weak electrical charge. The torch gave out a bloom of soft light and I could sense Patrick's eyes on my face. It felt like there was a hole where his finger had pressed into my cheek and I wasn't sure whether my skin felt frozen or burned. Once again, Patrick Semple had touched me uninvited. But today, there was no Josh to come to my rescue.

I wondered, what did he look like when we were at Three Magnets? I sped through racks of memories, but could only pull up generic images of grubby little schoolboys.

'Eadie?'

These days he pronounced it *E-deh*.

Finally I turned to face him and found some random young man staring back. I'd never have known it was him. I didn't recognize the dragged-down face with gaunt eyes and pocked skin but I did know that his nose back then looked nothing like it did now, all kinked and flattened. I looked at him, shining my horror and disbelief into his torchlight. While gaze held gaze, the face of this known stranger started to reveal a shy and curious sadness. It struck me then that this Patrick was more broken than his nose.

I hate you I hate you I hate you. I hated you then and I hate you now.

'I'm dead sorry if I scared you,' he said and he fumbled around in his back pocket while I gasped and flinched. 'It's all right, our E-deh,' he said, stopping what he was doing, laying his hand on my arm. 'Not going to hurt you – just getting me chuddy. Want some?' He offered me chewing gum and I sensed then that he wasn't going to kill me; he wasn't ready to let me go but he wasn't going to harm me. And so it was that Patrick Semple and I yomped on sticks of chewing gum, both of us quietly chumbling over the facts of the moment while memories of such a long time ago slid in from the shadows.

But I just wanted to go home. Hathersage home, hearing Iris's telly through the wall. I wanted to be switching on the immersion heater to have a long hot bath. I'd change my bed linen. Light the gas fire in my room. Eat a packet of Jaffa Cakes in bed and listen to Hipsway or The Waterboys. No – the *Birdy* soundtrack. Yes. 'Under Lock and Key'. And 'Close Up'; with its exquisite melody lasting less than a minute which I'd been playing on a loop since being blown away by it at Film Soc last week.

I thought, I just want to listen to Peter Gabriel.

I thought, I want toast – I want to be sitting on the brown velvet sofa eating toast. I didn't know what was going on outside. I didn't know what was happening in the Haç. Where were my friends and were they OK? Would Patrick's people want to know where he was? Would they start hammering on the van door? Was he really keeping me from danger – or throwing me right into its path? And why didn't he seem interested in any of this?

I thought, I don't want to be talking to Patrick Semple.

And then I thought how actually, I did a bit.

'But Patrick—'

'Yeah. Mad, innit.'

It was.

'You a student then?' he asked.

'Yes, second year, history – are you?'

He laughed a short sad ridicule to that.

'But this is where you moved from Parkwin? To Manchester?'

'Well, Stockport, but I left home at fifteen, didn't I? Fell out with the family, yeah? We don't – you know – *speak*.'

'Where do you live?' I needed to know so I could be sure never to be anywhere near there.

'Hulme,' he said and he chuckled morosely. 'In the Crescents. I know I know – Hulme – ninety per cent unemployment and all that.' He exhaled loudly through his nose, as if he found himself pathetic. 'But I do all right, as it goes.' He waved the torch around the van. 'Got a job. This is my family now – know what I mean?'

I didn't.

'I do all right, me,' he said proudly. 'And I seen you in there, E-deh – in the 'Aciendoor – giving it large with your dancing. You and your mates – on the old Es all of you, yeah? So I've been keepin' a lookout – checking you're, you know, OK.'

Hang on hang on hang on.

Rapidly, I recalled the times recently when I'd felt watched. But wait – that was *Patrick*, taking it upon himself to set himself up as my own personal bodyguard? Those eyes I'd felt slither over me, making my skin crawl – that was *him*? Well, he can sod right off if he thinks I'm going to thank him. I shuddered.

It was a stupid question to ask because I knew the answer. 'Do you work at the Haçienda?'

He gave a snort. 'You could say the 'Ass works for us.' He waited for my response but I had none. 'You all right?'

And I thought no, I'm not all right, I'm bloody furious. 'The Haç has changed since you lot showed up.' I filled my voice with spite and added even more. 'You lot have spoilt *everything*.'

'Us lot?'

'Bloody drug dealers. Fucking gangs.'

'E-deh,' he chuckled softly, as if the answer was simple and I was dense, as if I was a kid and he was the grown-up. 'Don't be naive, yeah? There's money in drugs, and you know it.'

And it struck me full force that I'd heard that before. I'd heard it this very evening from lovely Denny, a million years ago, thousands of miles away at the Rampant Lion. Patrick gave a little sigh, like a teacher with a child who just can't grasp a concept. I thought of Bill and Lorry puking their guts up. I thought of the times that I swam in the air and floated on floods of love. I thought of the days when I felt so tired, my body and my mind wasted, that I'd sworn to myself never to do any of that again. I thought of all that happiness and empathy and joy shared with a family of strangers while the magic of the music morphed into colour and light. And I thought of the growing unease, the fights and the shoving, the previously loved-up atmosphere getting stamped on and trodden into the filthy floor.

'It's not rocket science. We control the doors, that's all,' Patrick was saying. 'When you control the doors, yeah, then you control the supply and that way you keep it all *ordered*.' It was as if he was giving a job description.

'But the Haçienda is not yours to control,' I remonstrated. 'It's Tony Wilson's, it's *his* brainchild. *The Hacienda Must Be Built* – he built it for people like *me*, not the likes of *you*.' I moved a few definitive inches away from him. 'The Haçienda is owned by Factory Records and New Order,' I growled. 'It's *their* club, it's *my* club – not yours. You can't just come in and take it.'

He gave that some thought – I don't think he knew who owned the club, I don't think he'd heard of any of them. 'That lot might own it – but that's not what it's about.'

I was cross about this, about Patrick and his hideous fake family, these gangsters sailing in and wreaking havoc in our harbour. 'Yes, it *is* and you lot have totally ruined it,' I hissed. 'You have no right. We all *hate* you for it.' And I really laboured that word and I felt triumphant in the ensuing silence.

'You don't hate cheaper Es though, do you,' Patrick said calmly into the gloom and he snatched the silence back into his court with that. 'Supply and demand, E-deh,' he said. 'That's what it amounts to.'

I recalled Denny's maths; it was correct. 'Oh, fuck off,' was all I could say. I wanted Patrick just to feel small and shit and hated and I just really wanted to go home. The chewing gum had lost its taste. There was glove fibre in it anyway.

'Cellavy,' he sighed and then he spelled it out. 'Say. Lar. Vee.'

Out of nowhere I suddenly remembered beautiful Sandrine and how she tried to support me all those years ago, driving me home in the slinky black car and referring to Patrick as *the little sheet*. Her gorgeous French and her equally gorgeous Franglais. All these years later and finally it made sense – little *shit*! I laughed, just then.

'What's so funny?'

'Nothing,' I said. 'Nothing. I was just—'

'You can go now,' Patrick butted in, his voice flattened. 'Just go.'

Thank Christ for that.

An image of Celeste's oversized kitchen rushed in. The banquets that Sandrine would prepare. Colour and flavour and opulence on any given day. Warmth and safety. I took the chewing gum and flicked it into the shadows. Patrick waved the torchlight in the direction of the door and I scrambled to my feet, nervous and unsteady, as if I might hit my head, trip, fall, never actually make it out of there.

'By the way,' he said. 'How's that Josh, then? And Celeste? Josh and Celeste.'

I stopped. 'You remember them?'

'I remember it all,' Patrick said. In the murk, he was looking up at me and I was looking down on him. He sounded old and tired, nostalgic, he sounded sad and young. 'E-deh,' he said sorrowfully and he took a beat. 'I know I were a proper little cunt – but I were dead happy back then,' he said. 'Just being little.'

I shouted at myself to go. Just go. Go right now. Go to the Haç, go to Hathersage. Go and find your tribe. Go to the embrace of the loveliest people in the world. Instead, resigned, I sat back down.

'See,' Patrick said proudly, pulling up his sleeve and showing me a tattoo on his arm. It was of three magnets, with his own name in the centre. Ebenezer Howard's Three Magnets design. Our primary school's emblem. 'Best school in the world,' he said. 'They say school days are the best in your life,' he said. 'But no one told me that.'

I thought then of my friend Josh. I remembered that day with the biro, Patrick pinning him down. And I thought of Reuben and the numbers tattooed on his arm. I remembered Celeste and I going to Mr Swift's office, how I felt I was protecting yet betraying Josh. I remembered Reuben coming in to our assembly at Three Magnets and how we learned about the Holocaust. I recalled, too, how I dreaded school, anticipating pain from pinching and punches and, worse, the relentless slash of name-calling. I remembered how I feared the park in case Patrick was there; how I couldn't slide down the slide quick enough and how once he twisted and twisted the swing I was on, the thump of his shoe at the base of my back. Sometimes, I'd just wait for the hit, the shove, the nastiness, because it seemed futile to run away as I'd only make it worse, he'd always catch me. Those were meant to be safe times – when kids could skip down to the park to play together with no need for helicopter parents. Our parents simply told us to be home for tea. Come back before it gets dark, they said. Come back when you're hungry. I never told. I never told.

'You made my life a misery.' My voice wasn't working too well. 'I was *scared* of you, Patrick Semple,' I said. 'You bullied me. All the scratching and pinching and tripping me up. Chinese burns. And the names. Hurting. Humiliating. And I couldn't tell anyone,' I said. 'You *hated* me and I felt it. I *felt* what it was like to be hated. I never knew what you were going to do next – I was frightened every day. I was just a little girl and you battered me with your hate.'

In the murk of the van, silence hung long and loaded.

'Well, I hate *you*,' I whispered and I heard him wince.

'I'm sorry, E-deh,' Patrick whispered back. 'Dead dead sorry.'

I heard his apology. I knew I could accept it quick and be out of there or I could pointedly not acknowledge it and still be out of there; yet something kept me sitting right next to him.

'We're all friends you know. Still. To this day. Best best friends. Josh and Celeste and me.'

For a while, Patrick said nothing. When he did, his voice had cracks in it, as if he was under an iced-over puddle and I'd stamped down on it with the heel of my shoe. You're nothing, we're everything, was what I was saying. Patrick and I, sitting in the dark side by side, listening.

'That's mint, that is,' he said quietly.

'*So* amazing. All of us.' I boasted about how well we'd done, how amazing we were, universities begging to have us.

But Patrick agreed. In fact, he marvelled. And then, after a loaded beat he said, E-deh – it wasn't ever about you. 'I can't explain, really,' he said. 'But back then, when I were a kid, it wasn't about *you*. And now – it's not about you either,' he said. 'In there, in the 'Ass. On the door and the floor with the drugs and that. It's not about *you* – it's us, protecting our interests.'

I was tempted to bang on about Tony Wilson and Factory Records again, but suddenly I thought of my tribe. The Haçienda was ours – it was where we gathered and partied. It was our space to feel safe and happy and high and I was furious that Patrick felt he had a right to barge in and take that away. We were a good and lovely lot. He wasn't. We belonged there. He didn't.

'Know what I mean?'

'No, Patrick – I don't. And also – I don't forgive you for then or for now.'

I rolled my neck around my tired tired shoulders and I stood, making my way through the dimness to the van door.

'I will never forgive you.'

'I *am* sorry, E-deh. I'm dead sorry,' Patrick called from the slump I'd left him in. 'I swear it. Believe me?'

I could no longer be bothered to listen. I wanted to find my friends whose faces weren't fucked up, who had promising futures and wholesome, worthwhile lives. My people, my tribe, who lived with hope and by a moral code and with a zest for it all; who lived in happy homes like Hathersage Road which were warm with chatter and laughter and searching conversations and meaningful goals and hot buttered toast and digestive biscuits and values.

I didn't look back into the van. I slammed the door shut and I kicked it for good measure, encasing Patrick in rusting gloom as I stepped out into the cold, cold night. Then I ran. I turned into Whitworth Street and, magically, a taxi was right there. I cried all the way back to Hathersage Road where I paid for the cab with the money I'd've bought Ecstasy with.

11.55 a.m. 15th June 1999, the motorway

Out of the window, the Midlands pass by in a blur of fields and cooling towers and radio masts. People ride horses over the motorway bridges and monstrous construction vehicles churn up the land. It's a strange stretch of road.

'Do you think we can stop? At the next services?' I ask.

'Bloody hell – she lives!'

'Huh?'

'You've been in another world,' my husband says.

He's right, I was miles away travelling at speed on a parallel motorway through memories.

'Was it last year or the year before that the Haçienda finally closed?'

'Where's that come from?' But he has a think about it. 'Must be a couple of years ago now?'

'I think you're right,' I say.

'You know they're going to demolish the old building?' he says. 'They're going to rip it down and redevelop it into flats for yuppies.'

That makes me sad even though it makes sense.

'Apparently, they're going to auction it off,' he says. 'The bricks. The bogs. The bollards,' he laughs. 'You could literally own the dance floor.'

'Best hotdogs in the world,' I reminisce. I'm really hungry. 'Can we stop at the next services?' I say again. 'Do we have time?'

I remember, now, my friend the hotdog seller. What was his name? He knew my name – why couldn't I remember his? 'They beat him up, you know.'

This startles my husband. 'Who?'

What *was* his name?

'Eadie – *who*?'

'Outside the Haç one night – bastards from one of the gangs. They trashed his stall and beat him up. Back when Manchester was becoming Gunchester.'

'Is that where you've been these last miles? Back there and then?' There's tenderness to his voice. He says hey. He says hey sweetheart hey, though I wasn't aware of my tears.

'That's where I've been,' I say, wiping my eyes and blowing my nose. 'Back there in the past.' Perhaps we don't have time to stop. We really can't be late. Not today.

'I could do with a coffee,' my husband says and he changes lane and heads for the services.

'Thank you.'

There's peace between us, a quiet relief for the time being.

'Strange, really,' he muses. 'I love the music of the Madchester scene – The Mondays, The Roses, The Charlatans still amongst my all-time favourite bands – but the Haçienda? I hated that place.'

'I know you did,' I say. 'I get it. I do. But just for a while there – for me—'

He's indicating to come off at the services. '—for a while it was so special to you,' he says. 'I know,' he muses. 'I know.'

'It's so long ago,' I say. 'It was another life, a former me. An unformed me.'

Lorry and Bill told me to go to the police.

You have a name, my friends said.

You know where he lives, they said.

You know what he does – *because he actually told you* – they said. It was as if they believed I could bring the gangs down.

Fiona though, Fiona said poor bastard – what a messed-up life he must have. I was determined not to agree with her. Just then, I felt Patrick deserved such a life, that he should be punished for it and for everything he'd ever done to me.

I almost did as the boys told me. A couple of days later, I picked up the phone and I so nearly dialled but then I decided it would be better to go to the police station in person instead. And I was on my way there, over half the way there actually, when I stopped and turned away. I missed my seminar and sat with Iris for the afternoon instead.

I lied to my friends when they asked about how it went. I told them I'd filed a report and I said that the police were looking into it. They'll do sod all, Fiona said darkly. There's sod all they can do, I said.

The truth was, I hated Patrick more than ever for making me feel so utterly, utterly compromised. I'd lied to those I trusted most because of him. He was filling my head so that there was no room for studying. He'd been the bane of my childhood and now he'd slithered his way into my life again, affecting not just me but the people and the places and the things I cared about so much.

So why – why – was I suddenly feeling this stupid, fucked-up conflict between turning him in and letting him go? And why couldn't I speak to anyone about this?

He just wouldn't leave me alone. I was constantly on high alert, as if he was loitering on every corner. He barged through my thoughts during the day and stole into my sleep every night.

Just go away, I said.

Leave me alone, I said.

But I also said—

—where exactly are you? This very minute – where *are* you, Patrick?

At 41 Yew Lane, when I was a child, I'd startle myself awake in the small hours terrified that the parent who'd gone to work wasn't home, would never return. Now, in Hathersage Road I dreaded the drift into sleep because it was then that Patrick would appear from the shadows, his face leering through the wall, his voice hissing through the gas fire, his gloved hand touching my face, my entire room becoming the inside of his van. Sleep now terrified me and I avoided it, attending lectures expressly for the chance to doze safely in a warm dark auditorium with the raised hands of the super-keen affording me a privacy screen. I had essays in a logjam I could no longer look at.

My housemates remained none the wiser. As far as they knew, the police were after Patrick and I was in my room either working or tired or I had a headache, my period or an early lecture. Above me, Bill creaked over the floorboards while he paced as he revised. Downstairs, Lorry's music played while Fiona's voice sang through lengthy phone calls. I had only to open my door an inch and call out and one of them would come; I could walk into any of their rooms at any time for company. I could make toast or a brew, or simply sit on the brown sofa for a few moments and someone was bound to join me. But I didn't tell them how frightened I felt, that there were now two ghosts hounding me. In addition to Patrick, the odd little girl I'd been at Three Magnets was shadowing my every move.

I tried phoning Celeste. I tried mornings, evenings, but she was never in and I didn't believe her flatmates were passing on my messages.

How I wanted to speak to Josh, the Josh that I hadn't had sex with, the Josh I hadn't seen or spoken to for a year, the Josh I'd loved so much and who'd protected me from Patrick from the age of six. I did try. I knew he'd stayed a second year on his staircase at Cambridge and I phoned twice. He answered the second time. I closed my eyes and just drank in his voice while he said hello? hello? hello? He hung up with a sigh, as if calls were never for him anyway, while all I could do was whisper Josh, Josh, into the dead line. I attempted letters to both of them but I couldn't stop Patrick reading over my shoulder.

It was almost two weeks since that night with Patrick. I was heading to the Central Library, determined to write one essay and plan out another. Iris was locking her front door as I was closing ours. She was dressed very smartly from top to toe; her best shoes that were just a little too big at the back, a rigid handbag like the Queen's and a summer hat nesting on her candyfloss hair which had recently been rinsed the colour of Parma violets.

'Off to the library,' I announced, patting my satchel.

'Off to see the husband,' she said, all proud.

'But Iris—'

She gave me a benevolent smile. 'I know, love, don't worry, I know. He's dead. I might forget a lot these days, but I always remember that Sid is dead.'

I gave her hand a little squeeze.

'I go to the cemetery – the last Thursday of each month, Eadie,' she said. 'We have a date, me and my Sid. Makes good sense to me of all this time I have left without him.'

The strap of my satchel, heavy with all the work I needed to do, nagged at my neck. I absolutely was going to go to the library. But. Lovely Iris all dolled up for her monthly date with dead Sid. I absolutely wasn't going to let go of her hand.

'You know I grew up next to a cemetery?' I said. Of course she did. She knew almost everything about me after our hours of chats over gallons of tea. I paused to consider how, in all my time in Manchester, I hadn't noticed if I'd passed a graveyard, let alone a cemetery. 'May I come with you?' I heard myself say as I hid my satchel behind our bins before she could answer.

So off we walked up Hathersage Road, Iris in her finery and me in my jeans, to take the bus down to the Southern Cemetery. Iris was bubbly, she was going to see her Sid. In Parkwin, I used to note how some folk would rush to the graveside as if they had exciting news to share whilst others would approach slowly knowing that, when they poured out their hearts, sometimes they just couldn't stop. Dear Iris, who spent so much of her life from cup of tea to cup of tea just waiting; but here today with a spring in her step and a flush to her cheek because it was the last Thursday in the month.

Sidney Glennon
1900–1979
Doting son of the late Betty and Fred
Cherished husband of Iris
Beloved father and grandad

To live in the hearts of those we love is not to die

I knew very well how to afford a mourner time and privacy at the graveside so I went over to a nearby bench, dedicated to the memory of Peter Banuckle. I was pleased for Iris to take all the time she needed because just then, there amongst the graves, finally I felt calm.

'He was a good man, my husband,' said Iris who'd sat herself down next to me. 'Ten years this autumn and I don't want it to be officially a decade. That's too long.'

I stared at the Queen's handbag in Iris's lap as the maths of it all confronted me. A decade ago I was just reaching double figures and in ten years' time I'd be turning thirty. Right now I didn't know if I felt like a child or an adult.

'I was married by your age,' Iris said, unaware I was having an existential crisis right beside her. 'Our Sid – swept me off my feet at a dance when I was seventeen and they hardly touched the ground till the day he was buried.'

'I'm sorry you didn't have him for longer,' I told her because when I was little, an elderly woman at her husband's graveside told me that until her dying day her sole regret was that she didn't have him for longer.

'You're a good girl, you are,' said Iris and she took a hankie from her pocket to dab at her nose, press against her eyes.

'Why don't we go for a little wander,' I said, linking my arm through hers. 'It's what I call *doing the rounds* – then we can come back and see Sid again.'

I'd forgotten how comforting it was to be among the dead during daylight and that night I fell easily into a cosy sleep.

Wake up, Eadie, said Patrick. *We need to get out of here.*

I woke and sat up and looked at him and it didn't seem strange that he should be in my bedroom. Patrick in Three Magnets uniform, pulling at my duvet telling me to come, come quick, come *on*.

Then, in front of my eyes, his seven-year-old face started to wither and twist and his skin began to drip Dali-like from his skull. *We need to get out of here*, he was crying and his lips were disappearing. He pulled at me, pulled me from my bed with hands which felt like wet rope but looked like blackened rubber.

I'm dead sorry, E-deh.

Let go of me!

Come with me – I'm dead dead sorry, E-deh.

Get off get off get off.

Dead dead decaying Patrick clawing and pleading at me. I told myself to wake up but found I was already wide awake, immobilized. And then I woke a second time, drenched with sweat, my bloodied heartbeat filling my mouth. I was breathing too fast and my hands were clenched tight, my legs shaking too hard for me to move. I just had to wait it out in the dark.

Go away, Patrick.

Leave me alone.

I had to see him.

Really, I should have been furious with Patrick. He might have said that he was dead sorry, and this might have alleviated his conscience but he'd shifted the weight from his shoulders straight onto mine. He'd abducted me in real life and then stolen my sleep and robbed me of my capacity to think of little else ever since. And so it was another day, another missed class, but I wanted my life back and I thought I knew where to find it. I called out to my household that I was going to the library and I left before all of them.

The only place I actually knew in Hulme was the PSV club which I loved for the varied music and less frenetic vibe than the Haç. Some said the club was originally for the drivers of Public Service Vehicles, while others called it the Russell Club or the Caribbean Club. In daylight that morning, its brightly painted signage with the beach and the palm trees was a welcome surprise, I hadn't noticed it on the nights I'd gone there, I'd been too eager to get inside. It was one of those benign spring days when the promise of summer puts everyone in a good mood, even gangsters surely. There was hardly anyone about and I laughed at myself: stupid Eadie – what were you expecting? a Mancunian Al Capone to come out of the shadows? The Northern Krays? The scariest thing was the Dobermann guard dogs kept on the roof at the nearby Henry Royce pub; they made me jump out of my skin.

I'd heard a lot about the infamous Hulme Crescents from Denny. Four vast mass-housing blocks of glowering grey concrete which had been built in 1972 to house 13,000 people and replace the district's overcrowded Victorian terracing. How, almost immediately, the Crescents had failed due to shoddy construction, leaks, damp, an inadequate sewage system, cockroaches and mice. Within three years, most of the residents wanted to leave, Denny's family included. Now the Crescents were mostly empty and the council no longer charged rent to those who'd stayed.

Robert Adam. John Nash. Charles Barry. William Kent. Each block had been given the name of Britain's finest classical architects. They were all seven storeys high, constructed from lumbering and relentless concrete which somehow made even the grass in front seem flat grey. And now here I was looking for a boy who lived somewhere in one of these crumbling behemoths. Though most of the flats were derelict these days, it didn't make my search for Patrick any easier. I looked around me; layer upon layer of grimness stretching far, like a wide yawn of rotten teeth. I thought of Edweard Fairbetter, of Ebenezer Howard; they'd be turning in their graves. *Hulme Garden City* I tried quietly under my breath. I'd never been anywhere so relentlessly grim-grey and downtrodden.

Do not obey – shoplift!

The graffiti was like a call to arms but I could see no shops, there was nothing. A lad with a football appeared from a stairwell, blinking at the brightness of the day as if he'd emerged from subterranea and he nodded at me. I nodded back, found my voice and commandeered a rubbish Northern accent. I hid Eadie behind it to masquerade instead as Patrick's old mate E-deh. I said the first thing that came to mind.

'Seen Patrick, then?'

'Y'what?'

'The Semple kid, yeah?' I sounded ridiculous and the boy shook his head and mooched off, dribbling the ball as he went.

Patrick, where are you, where do you live, which one is yours? I spoke under my breath as I climbed a stairwell to the first raised walkway. Everything appeared to be chipped and crumbling and cold, as though the structure itself was just dog-tired of having to stand there in all its desolate ugliness. Many doors and windows were boarded up though an eerie silence seeped through. I went up another floor, walked along another walkway detecting sounds of life behind some of the doors, and I looked out at the other Crescents wondering how ever would I find him.

'Patrick,' I said conversationally, as if he was just ahead of me. And then I said it louder, with a question mark. Then I called his name at the top of my voice as if he was being a little shit ignoring me. A door opened behind me.

Not Patrick.

A woman, a beautiful African woman wearing a brightly patterned robe, her head crowned by a complex swathe of extraordinary coloured fabric knotted and fanned like impassioned applause. Dazzling against the interminable grey, she took my breath away.

'Hello,' I said, dropping my stupid accent and, I think, curtseying instead. 'Um – do you know Patrick Semple?'

She regarded me shyly, tipped her head to one side and gave me a gentle, sweet smile. 'Hello,' she said. She wore orange plastic sandals and her toenails were shiny gold.

'Hello,' I said again.

'How are you?'

'I'm very well, thank you, how are you?'

She nodded and nodded. 'How is your day?'

'Yes,' I said. 'Fine,' I said.

She waited.

'Um – how is *your* day?' I asked.

'Very good, thank you,' she said. I think she was practising her English.

'I am looking for Patrick Semple,' I said and I made much of looking around me with lots of shrugging. 'Patrick Semple? He's my age,' I said. 'He has – bad skin and a broken nose.' She was regarding me, steadily. 'Patrick,' I said. 'Pat, maybe?'

But she shook her head though she kept her smile. Kept shaking her head as she backed into her flat, closing the door, keeping all that beauty from the world.

I was so tempted to knock, to ask to sit awhile with her, but I just shuffled on. I called myself stupid, stupid, stupid for thinking I could find him. It struck me only then that perhaps Patrick didn't want to be found. What was I even going to say to him? I had no idea, no idea at all. My pace turned into a trudge. It was horribly quiet and the air seemed stagnant. Where was everybody? Everyone in my life was miles away and no one knew I was here. And I asked myself – why *was* I here? Was I stupid or something? I wanted to turn and go back and find that amazing woman and just stand safe in all the colour and light that she radiated – but I couldn't remember which was her door. The brutalist monotony had swallowed her down.

I tried the next Crescent, erroneously named after John Nash and, after walking about trying to look like I lived there in case anyone was watching, I just stopped. I was tired and fed up and as I looked over the second-floor balcony and down onto what was little more than wasteland, my home on Hathersage Road seemed desperately distant. The warmth of its red brick and the chatter and spirit within. The pretty mosaic fish swimming joyfully through the Baths, our humble corner shop, the takeaway, the clang and whirr of the launderette. Perhaps Bill was home making endless cups of tea as usual, Fiona singing above the drone of her hairdryer, Lorry putting out the rubbish tutting and muttering at us all. Right at this moment, Iris in her overheated front room keeping company with no end of stories from the old days. And then I thought of my other home with my mum and my dad. As I clung to the blade-grey balcony I closed my eyes and conjured my faraway land; all the greenery and the trees and the thoughtful planning of Parkwin, everything plotted so philanthropically by Fairbetter. I walked my mind from Yew Lane to town, into the café to sit with a frothy coffee and a toasted teacake before returning to the bungalow of my birth where my indoor parents were sitting and working, content with their lives.

A noise snapped my eyes open and stripped me of my dreaming, plunging me back to the uncompromising here and now of Hulme.

'You all right, chuck?'

A woman had stuck her head out of a window. Purple hair and lots of piercings and fierce make-up, but everything about her was softened by Cat Stevens playing in the background leaping and hopping on his moon shadow. She regarded me suspiciously.

'Looking for our Patrick.' I'd put my accent back on, pulling it over the real me like a balaclava. 'D'you know him?'

'Patrick Who?'

'Semple.'

She shrugged. 'Can't say I do.'

I described him, she shrugged again and laughed. 'A lot of them look like that round here.'

'I knew him a long time ago,' I said. 'He said he lived here.'

'Try a couple of floors up, some young divvies up there.'

'Nice one – *sound*,' I said and cringed at myself. I paused. 'Um, I love Cat Stevens.'

'He's the absolute bollocks,' she grinned and blew a huge bubble with her gum which took ages to burst gently against her face. She closed the window with a shrug and a wave.

I climbed two more floors and meandered this way and that way along the walkways, calling out Patrick! every now and then. I chose a random door and knocked. No answer. It was so eerily quiet here, an emptiness that felt morose. I thought how soon enough, just a couple of miles away, students would be flowing into the Students' Union for cheap sandwiches and the lunchtime episode of *Neighbours*, singing the theme tune en masse. That's when neighbours become good friends. But not here where people apparently lived in self-contained isolation.

'Patrick!'

I walked.

'Patrick!'

I called.

'Fucksake,' I said under my breath.

I tried the crescent named after Robert Adam. Walked a bit, climbed the stairs, looked left and right and walked some more. I had surely been walking for miles, my sense of direction and time skewed. I could be doing this for days, walking and never getting anywhere, looking and never finding, calling out into a pall-heavy silence. Patrick Patrick Patrick. I conjured Lorry skipping up the stairs to plonk himself on my bed and natter his happy nothings. I imagined Fiona in our kitchen, dodging the hole in the floor, making tea for us all. She was terrible at tea and little better at coffee but we all drank it regardless. How I could do with a steaming mug of either right now. And a Hobnob. Take them over to the cuddle of the brown velvet sofa.

'Patrick,' I called out. 'Patrickpatrickpatrick.' Goosebumps prickled over my arms, as if the seasons were different here. I felt cold.

'You wanting young Paddy?'

A man was suddenly right beside me and in an instant I didn't like him. He was standing too close. He stank of stale beer and too many fags and wore trainers that belonged in the bin.

'Young Paddy,' I said with a nonchalant shrug and my crap accent. Perhaps that's how Patrick's people knew him. 'Yeah.'

He beckoned with his head and mooched off. I followed behind, studying his jeans which almost glowed with grease. Every fibre of my being said just leave, doesn't matter, you tried, now go, but one tiny cell hiding somewhere told me to follow or I'd never know.

We climbed another floor up, scuffed along another walkway. There was a clagging silence perforated by our footsteps.

Cat Stevens and the beautiful Queen of Africa, the dogs on the pub roof and the boy with the football; from up here on this Crescent even they seemed miles away which made Hathersage Road and the warmth of my home impossibly distant. Eventually, we came to a door that was ajar and the man nudged it open with his foot.

'Paddy,' the man called out. 'Lass here to see you.' He shrugged at me and left.

I peered inside. There was newspaper everywhere and polystyrene takeaway boxes with beige caked-on food, cans of Special Brew tipped on their sides. Dirt. However much I wanted to find Patrick and however much I hated him, I realized instantly that I didn't want him to live right here, like this.

'Pat— ddy?' I decided on my proper Eadie voice as I picked my way over the detritus and along the rank corridor and through to the room at the end. 'Patrick?' A mattress on the floor. A dead mouse. A pile of clothes at the other end which suddenly shuddered, roared up and collapsed and roared up once more.

I knew in an instant that the man was not Patrick. I thought, I have to get out of here *now* and fast.

'Sorry,' I mumbled. 'Sorry – wrong guy.'

This person was so very wrong, off his face on God knows what. Couldn't speak, only grumble and growl; could no more stand than he could sit, as if whatever substance he was on was slowly dissolving his bones. An acrid smell I didn't know, terrible and vaporous. A cockroach scuttled along the wall and bellyflopped onto the floor and I had never actually seen one until now. Like a real-life zombie, the man was up on his feet with a stagger and a lurch while my legs were encased in concrete. He crumpled down again and started to crawl.

Eadie. You *have* to go. Just – *go*.

He grabbed my ankle, looked up at me. More red than white in his eyes. I didn't know what that was coming out of his mouth. A sort of foam.

Eadie, Josh shouted. Get *out*.

Run, Eads, Celeste yelled at me.

I jerked my leg to free myself, making contact with his body which felt like it shattered on impact. The floor appeared to absorb him and I bolted, panic rising as bile in my throat. The door was still ajar and finally I was back out in the decaying labyrinth, running and tripping and stumbling down the stairs two, three, at a time.

No one was around. I could hear nothing. Cat Stevens wasn't singing any more. Sunlight on the grass, fag butts between the blades, a floating plastic bag caught in a sort of flamenco, as if trying to antagonize a nearby bin. The day was warm and bright, yet I was shivering as I spun around and around while my internal compass failed and a disembodied sobbing turned out to be mine. There's no place like Hulme. There's no place like Hulme.

I blew money on a train fare and, some hours later after a protracted journey, I opened the door to 41 Yew Lane and Mum said darling! And Terry said, darling! what a lovely *lovely* surprise! My parents seemed so genuinely happy, as if I was the greatest unexpected gift. Boundless love danced in their eyes. I sank to my knees by Terry's desk, placed my head in his lap and I cried and I cried while he patted my shoulders and stroked my hair and he said there there darling there there. It's OK, Eadie, it's OK.

My mum said to my dad perhaps it was boy trouble; from my bedroom I could hear their voices, soft and worried. In some ways it *was* boy trouble but I couldn't tell my parents about Patrick because I never had. It occurred to me that I could no more tell Terry and Mum about having been bullied as a child than I could tell them I'd been bundled into a van against my will the other week. As a little girl, I had felt compelled to keep Patrick secret and he was going to have to continue to be. I didn't want to talk about it, I didn't even want to talk.

I had brought nothing with me and, as seemed to be a habit, I'd told no one where I was going. I phoned Hathersage Road later that night and Lorry laughed. I thought you were here up in your room, Edith, he said. You've been spending so much time in there, he said. Then he paused and said but are you OK? And I told him yes, no, I don't know. Oh Edith, he said, you know I'll *always* be here for you. And after the call I thought about the words *here* and *always* because the horrible truth was that Lorry — all of us — were living in Hathersage Road only temporarily and that was a far shorter time than *always*. It hit me hard: when you are a student, there is a beautiful permanence only in the moment. The things you think will last for ever actually might not.

For two days I barely left my room and there was a fuzziness in my head which distorted the passing of time. I shuffled out for food but the constant sensation of heaviness pressing hard on my chest took away my appetite and ate at the strength of my voice, too. I cried as quietly as I could but the effort of it made my throat sore. I wasn't even sure of the provenance of my tears and I certainly didn't want to have to explain it to my parents.

Terry and Mum, however, gave me space and time and kept a quiet, gentle distance from me. It was as if they feared that coming too close might make me evaporate in front of their eyes, that asking a direct question might cause silence to swallow me up. Instead, they sent over a lot of nodding and smiling whenever they caught my gaze, and they laid a place for me at mealtimes whether or not I sat myself at the table or ate more than a few bites. I watched them work but mostly I spent the next few days curled up on my bed while my eyes darted as if umpiring a tennis match between colliding thoughts.

I couldn't tell them about Patrick. Or Paddy. Or any of it. I absolutely couldn't tell them that I was failing my course, that I felt aimless and cynical about what any of it was worth. However, for the first time in my life, as I watched them I saw how their work ethic was exemplary; that they laboured and toiled without vanity, with no need for an end result. I used to think what an epic and ridiculous waste of time it was that they wrote thousands of words that were going nowhere, but now I understood how their work sustained them. Mine was sapping my soul and that's why I couldn't tell them. I felt desperately alone and held hard by heart-racing exhaustion. I wanted someone else to tell me what to do, but who? Then, in the lonely early hours, one person sprang to mind though it would take me another day to muster the energy to go to them.

In the playground it was breaktime at Three Magnets Primary School and very small children skittered and romped while their thin pure voices carried like violins, none tuned with the other. It seemed to me that all these children were so much smaller than we'd been at their age. They were all so – *young*. Just a joyful scamper of very little chaps. As they rampaged around the playground with abandon, I detected no discord, no malevolence. I watched carefully but could not see a single Patrick amongst them. Or maybe there was. Perhaps that was a bully's insidious skill – the hunter hidden, the grown-ups unsuspecting, the victim pretending to be fine. I tuned in to the rustle and shake of leaves in the trees that stood along the perimeter of the little playground like benevolent minders. I'd forgotten about that sound, I used to think it was applause.

I was so busy with my memories that Mr Swift made me jump.

'Is this an Eadie Browne I see before me?'

The bell sounded for the end of break.

'Come on,' he called over his shoulder. 'Chop chop.'

I looked around his office noting what hadn't changed and what had. The tub chairs (old) and slatted blinds (new). The painting of a cellist (old) and a small radio-cassette player on a stand beside the desk (new). An entire set of the Encyclopædia Britannica (new) and that beautiful run of leather-bound books (old) on the wooden shelves. Dickens. I don't think I ever knew until now that it was Dickens. When I was little I probably thought they were just ancient tomes on headmastering. Quite suddenly the strangest notion made total sense and I looked at Mr Swift in amazement.

'I want to work *here*!' I told him. 'This is where I should *be*!' I sat back triumphant, as a rush of heat fizzed through my cells. 'Can I have a job, please?'

Slowly, Mr Swift picked up his fountain pen, took the lid off and put it back on again, then rolled the stem between his thumb and fingers, as if he was writing his response in his mind. He tipped his head to one side and fixed me with his owl gaze. One of his many particular and unforgettable skills; how those eyes of his could elicit confessions and apologies and secrets and draw the truth from anyone held in their thrall. He didn't have to say a word.

'I don't like my course,' I said. 'I'm really behind but don't want to catch up. I've missed so much. I panic when I realize how much I need to do simply to scrape a pass, but even that's not enough to make me tackle any of it.'

Mr Swift put his pen down, his index fingers remaining at either end. 'You say you'd like to work here?'

'Yes! Please! I could teach! Anything really – apart from maths. Even art or PE. But definitely reading and writing. I'd love to, Mr Swift – here is totally where I'm meant to be.'

He nodded sagely at a point beyond my shoulder.

'Eadie,' he said. 'A question, if I may. You'd like to *teach* – or you'd like to teach *here*?'

Of course I'd given scant thought to this. I hadn't even thought about careers or what I'd do after university, what my world would look like when I stopped being a student, where I'd live if I didn't live in Manchester.

'I don't really know,' I admitted, because one always told the truth to Mr Swift. 'But I would like to work here. I could do something else if there are no teaching jobs.'

'You want to come back to Three Magnets,' he mused. 'But you're not sure if you want to be a teacher.' He hummed as if it was a conundrum. 'So – let's think about why?'

I tried to think about why, but it made me feel tired and emotional. I shrugged like a six-year-old might, or any seven-, eight-, nine-year-old who sat in this very chair in front of the headmaster.

'I don't like it,' I said quietly. I was too tired to define 'it'.

'When we go out into the world it is wider than we ever imagined,' Mr Swift said measuredly. 'And we feel underprepared for our journey so we retreat back to a time when the thinking was done for us.'

I just sat with those words for I don't know how long.

'Eadie.'

'Yes, Mr Swift.'

'Is there something I can help you with?'

He waited. I thought to myself I don't want to tell tales. I thought, I hate you, Patrick. But then I thought how I didn't want Patrick to get into trouble. I realized how I had no idea what to do with all that had happened back at this school, or in the back of the van or in darkest Hulme and it took some time to collate any of it into words and even longer for my voice to work.

'Do you remember a boy here – he was in my class – but he left,' I began. 'I think he left in Junior 2. I don't know or maybe Junior 3. I'm not sure. It's a long time ago. Anyway. Do you remember Patrick Semple?' I sighed, struck by the irony of someone who was a little shit not worthy of being remembered.

Mr Swift, though, was already nodding. 'I do indeed.'

'You do?'

Everything. It all came out. My Hulme Hall, my Haçienda, my Hathersage. Patrick and his Haçienda and the inside of the van. A Three Magnets tattoo and a broken nose. E-deh. And Paddy. Iris and Sparky and a dead mouse in grimly failed housing.

Ecstasy.

And my agony.

I talked and I talked and I talked. Sometimes I looked at Mr Swift directly, at other times I spoke to the faded print behind him, Constable's *Hay Wain* with the chipped gilt frame. I talked to the spines of the books on the shelves, to the swirls in the patterned rug, to where woodgrain met leather inlay on Mr Swift's grand old desk. And I talked to his softly clasped hands.

I understood, finally, that I wasn't getting someone else into trouble, not at all. I was the one in trouble. I needed to tell someone all about me.

'Eadie,' Mr Swift said with tenderness. 'I'm so terribly – *terribly* – sorry to hear of this. Any of this. All of this.'

I waited for my job offer.

'But I don't think that teaching is the answer,' he said. His words stole my oxygen and I felt myself deflate. 'The industry would certainly benefit from someone like you but not here. And not now.' He sat back and observed me over the top of his glasses. 'I know you don't want to hear this – I can't make you finish your course, but I can only advise that you do.'

Perhaps I'd known that he'd say that. Even if I'd said all I'd ever wanted was to teach, he'd've still said that. Of course he would. But I just sat there and wished that he hadn't.

'You will no more find Patrick Semple here in Parkwin than you can hide from him here, in Parkwin,' Mr Swift said. 'If you ask me – and I do believe you came here to do just that – I would say that Parkwin is not the place for you to be.'

'But it's home,' I said quietly.

'Is it?'

I looked at him, startled.

'Certainly it is the town in which your parents live,' he said. 'The place where you were born. But is this *really* where you've *grown* – not in age, but in breadth, in depth?' He raised his eyebrows at me whilst slowly shaking his head, magically eliciting the mirror response from me.

'I do believe that it's the falls we take when we are far from the place where we grew up which make us robust, Eadie, which equip us for the world. I do believe it's when we can get back on our feet and haul ourselves upright, miles away from where we perceive the safety of our childhood to be, that we become adults, that we are prepared for life.'

I listened. How I listened. Everything about this man was so wise, so reassuring. How many years would it take, I wondered, before I could feel this way about the world?

'But Patrick?' I said. 'I can't forget him.'

'Nor should you,' said Mr Swift. 'But you can forgive him.'

I doubted very much that I'd ever want to do that.

'My advice?' said Mr Swift, mind-reading. 'Let him go. Let him inhabit his world and you crack on with yours, Eadie. Let him go from the front of your mind and just tuck him into the furthest reaches of your memories. He has, in so many ways, contributed to making you the fine young woman that you are today.'

'But it's all so *grim* – his life.'

'The way he lives his life is no business of yours,' Mr Swift said. 'When you can forgive him – that's when it ends.'

'Maybe,' I mumbled, for Mr Swift's sake. 'I never want to see him again.' I thought about that. I thought some more. 'But what if I never see him again?' I was making no sense and I knew it.

'You can still forgive him.'

'But why did I go looking for him?'

'I think you went looking for him to see if it was really hatred that you felt. And I don't think it is hate, Eadie Browne. I think it is compassion.' Mr Swift paused. 'And I believe you can stop looking for him now.'

Twice there had been a knock at the door and someone had popped a head around to be politely dismissed with a wave from Mr Swift. I had heard the bell go and I couldn't remember if that had been five minutes or an hour ago. The bell sounded again. I didn't want to leave. I didn't feel ready. If I could just stay here then I could learn more about life and the human condition from Mr Swift than ever I would from studying history at university.

'You'll be OK, Eadie,' Mr Swift said, rising from his chair. 'You are already OK.'

We walked back down the corridor where, behind all those half-glazed doors, afternoon lessons were in full swing. I glanced into each classroom as we passed. I recognized none of these teachers. My school had moved on without me. In the playground, Mr Swift automatically walked me to the exit I'd always used.

'I shan't say goodbye,' he said. 'I shall say farewell. Fare *well* as you navigate all these exciting times unfurling right in front of you. Open your eyes, Eadie Browne, and you'll see it all in glorious detail – blink and you'll miss it.' He extended his hand and we had a long shake. 'And when you come to a crossroads, as invariably you will, pause for as long as you need before you decide which is the right direction for you to take. But it is never behind you.'

I thought of something. 'But you – *you* live here,' I said. 'You live here in Parkwin, Mr Swift. You work here at Three Magnets.'

'Ah,' he said with a friendly wag of his finger. 'I *moved* to Parkwin when I was twenty-eight years old. I am fifty-nine now. But I grew up near Dover, Eadie, not here.'

And a notion struck me while Mr Swift held the gate open. It was Manchester where I'd actually grown up and, as I walked home from school, I experienced such a pang for my city in the North. Manny – where I'd experienced everything from excruciating loneliness to ultimate togetherness, where I'd lost my head and found my feet, where I'd felt vulnerable and invincible, where I'd experienced love, joy and fear in unimaginable degrees. Maybe I'd finish my course, perhaps I wouldn't, but I did need to return if only to decide which direction to take. I had outgrown Parkwin, of course I had; I knew that.

I picked up my pace from a trudge to a stroll and it was a sense of gratitude for both places which propelled me forward. But I couldn't go back to Yew Lane just yet.

The great big black car had turned quite grey with dust and the front tyre was completely flat. Its windows had a thick film of stickiness, of pollen, leaves and dust. It was as if the car had closed in on itself, hoping no one would notice as it was slowly absorbed into its surroundings. I walked all the way around it before going to the front door, whacking the knocker against the wood because the bell wasn't working. Sandrine opened it and gasped.

'Eadie?'

She looked like a distant cousin of Brigitte Bardot, long after the buxom years when beauty had been easy and life was a breeze. Sandrine's hair was in a careless higgle clipped haphazardly to the top of her head; tendrils ribboned around, partially hiding her eyes and catching in the corners of her mouth. She was wearing a navy blue top with a scooped neck, a pair of jeans which I was pretty sure were Celeste's and yellow flip-flops. She was effortlessly stunning, she was a mess.

Sandrine kissed me three times, held me at arm's length so she could drink in the sight of me, then kissed me again. She murmured in French and I don't know what she said, only that the words hurt her throat. She led me by the hand through to the kitchen where suddenly I was tiny because none of its vastness had diminished and I was pleased about that. There are some things that one depends on staying exactly the same when one treads a careful path down memory lane.

'Coffee?'

'Yes, please – but Sandrine, the *car*? *Ce qui s'est passé?*'

'Pffft!' she said, swatting at the air. 'It's too expensive to fix.'

We were looking through the window at it.

'It seems so forlorn and forsaken,' I said.

'It's a *car*,' Sandrine laughed. 'It has no feelings.'

'I guess I have feelings still left on the back seat though,' I said.

'Eadie,' she tutted. 'You are too romantic. I have another car – a petite Renault. It's red and in the garage. I love it!'

We sat and drank our coffee and I answered all her questions about Manchester and university, all those questions I expected adults to ask me. And perhaps it had something to do with the smudged eyeliner she still wore from yesterday, or the heavy quiet I sensed would curtain the house again when I left, or that the newspaper open on the counter was four days old but, for the first time in my life, I wondered about her. I really wondered about Sandrine, not as Celeste's mother, but as *her*.

'How are you, Sandrine?' I asked. 'How are *you*?' She baulked with bewilderment. 'All that time,' I said sadly. 'All that time you were on your own after Celeste's dad left – we sort of ignored you and we shouldn't've. We should've tried – and we didn't.'

She frowned and smiled simultaneously.

'I think we all knew you weren't OK,' I said quietly. 'But we never asked why. And I'm sorry that we didn't.'

'It's certainly not the job of a kid to take on board something like that,' she said lightly, busy washing a couple of mugs which were already clean and on the draining board.

'But we *knew*. We could *see*. We turned *away*. And I want to say that I'm sorry. It wasn't that we didn't care, it was that we didn't want to *think* because we wouldn't have known what to do.'

She stroked my face. 'There is no apology needed.'

'But Sandrine – I know now how loneliness feels – and so it's only now that I see how we turned away from yours.'

'My love – your eyes aren't fully developed at that age, they lack depth,' she said. 'With good reason. They are protected from seeing ugliness. It's OK, Eadie. It's OK.'

I looked into my coffee and watched my reflection waver in the soft milky ripples. 'Well, I can see stuff now,' I said. 'So when I look back, things are clear. And I am sorry if we – if we didn't—'

She put her finger against my lip and hushed. I sat there quietly while she looked steadily at me. I glanced away.

'I hardly speak to Celeste any more,' I confessed. 'I don't know why – perhaps we're too wrapped up in our separate lives.'

'I hardly speak to her also,' said Sandrine, 'if it makes you feel better.'

'Not really,' I said and I took a beat. 'The truth is I haven't been a good friend to her. I haven't listened.'

'So you will talk and she will hear because your friendship is true – it is as deep as it is long.' Then she smiled and took my chin between her finger and thumb. 'No matter how old you are, still you grow. You walk forwards and you grow. You walk away and you grow. You fall down, you grow taller as you get up. And also this: I have a man now, so enough of you feeling sorry for me.'

'You do?'

'Don't sound so surprised!'

'It's delighted surprise.'

I watched a blush rise from her neck to her cheeks. I saw then how her face was radiant. And her hair wasn't unkempt, it was gorgeous.

'That's very very cool!' I said. 'And God you deserve it because Celeste's dad was such a—'

'Sheet,' Sandrine said.

'*Such* a sheet,' I laughed. 'Does Celeste know?'

Sandrine said of course while her gaze drank me in as I struggled with my words.

'Is Celeste – you know – still with—'

'With Alicia?' said Sandrine. '*Non.*'

'Is she OK?' A rush of shame and regret hammered at my heart.

'She will be. It is usual for first love to be the worst heartbreak.'

'I didn't believe her,' I whispered. 'I said *don't be stupid.*'

'She needs people who believe her,' Sandrine said. 'She needs you.'

If I could have run all the way to Edinburgh right then, in my knackered old trainers, I would have done so – but I couldn't leave Parkwin just yet.

Reuben didn't notice me, he was behind the counter, standing on the low stepladder with his back to the Shop, putting the sweet jars which he'd refilled back on the shelves. I wanted to help. I used to love that job because we were given a sweet from each jar as payment. I had a quick and surreptitious look around. He'd splashed Day-Glo cardboard stars around the Shop which proclaimed the prices of certain items. He was clever that way. A good salesman encourages a customer to buy something they didn't know they want at a price they assume is good. That's what he used to tell us. He said a bright cardboard shape could save him a whole lot of spiel – the prices were exactly the same but the star and an exclamation mark made the customer think they were getting a very special offer.

How I wanted to say hello.

I very much wanted to see his eyes light up and hear his voice again, all the Yiddish pet names he always had in store for me. I wanted to hear him say that Josh was mishugas – nuts. I wanted him to be angry with Josh. Perhaps Reuben knew, perhaps he did not. Perhaps he no longer wanted to talk to me anyway, much like his grandson, with whom his loyalty lay. I wanted to say hello, how I wanted to say hello, but I wasn't sure where hello might lead nor whether I yet had the words to follow it. So I just backed out of the Shop silently and walked home. I wondered how business was doing now that the supermarket had expanded, how long Reuben could keep his shop going. I thought about unfinished business, wondered what its lifespan was, whether it could simply be cancelled out in time like a minor debt or whether it would always remain.

That night I ate with Terry and Mum. For the first time since I'd been back, I cooked our usual and we had Viennetta for pudding. I was pleased to find one already opened in the freezer, imagining that once in a while one parent might say to the other, shall we treat ourselves tonight, dear? I liked to think that perhaps they talked about me over a slice of Viennetta, musing about my life, hoping I'd be in for a change when they phoned Hathersage Road.

Manchester and Parkwin, the two magnets of my life; one here, one there, both vying for me. But the pull of Manchester was stronger. I was ready to go yet my heart felt heavy about it. I wanted to be chatty and upbeat for my parents but I didn't trust my voice not to quiver. When either looked at me in that way they had – a blend of charmed curiosity and kindness – my eyes stung and my throat closed. Mr Swift said that my future wasn't here and deep down I knew that to be true but to me just then it was as burdensome as it was liberating. I was tired of all the thinking, it was using up my energy and my grey matter, both of which I needed for my horrendously overdue studies.

'You should come and visit me,' I said, despite correctly anticipating that Terry and Mum would simply nod and hum politely and say ooh yes; while we all knew it was never going to happen. I could say, *please* come and visit me, but what a terrible situation that would put them in whether they lied or told the truth. We don't want to. We can't. We can't tell you why because we don't really know. Perhaps the old Eadie might have challenged them but not now. 'Maybe in a few weeks,' I said and they nodded enthusiastically. My lovely indoor parents, seeing no point in exploring beyond a world that contained everything for them.

Just before Terry headed out for his shift later that evening, I went into our sitting room.

'Here,' I said to my parents. 'These are for you. I think you'll really like them. I've underlined my favourites in red.'

You would have thought I'd given them the crown jewels as they passed my mix-tapes between them.

Before I left the next morning I let myself into the grounds very early, too early for Michael, for anyone living. I walked amongst the graves saying hello and goodbye to all the dead people who'd known me my whole life and I continued on to one of the furthest lines, to the plot I'd earmarked for Patrick Semple when I was a little girl. But there were new graves beyond it now. The nettles had gone, the ground was good, someone else was there.

Mary Livingstone
1900–1988
Beloved wife of Paul 'Yorky' Livingstone
Mother of Gemma and Abigail
Adored Nana to Sam, Tracey and Tom.

Time Passes Love Remains

Time passes, love remains.

I thought about that as the coach trundled me back North. I hoped it was as true of life as it was of death.

I could never have anticipated the drama that greeted me on my return to the house on Hathersage Road. My housemates sat me down almost as soon as I was home, as if I'd been no further than the chip shop and away for only an hour. Our Hathersage family always had the best meetings where all the important things in life were discussed around the table with a bowl of crisps, tea or beer or both. Let's call a cab and go to Asda's in Longsight. The Stone Roses are playing the International again and someone knows someone who can put us on the guest list. Happy Mondays are at Band on the Wall, let's get tickets. The electricity bill isn't as big as we thought – we can spend the difference at the Lass o' Gowrie. Shall we throw a party at the weekend? Who's going to phone the landlord about the hole? Klaus the mouse is dead – he's in the corner of the kitchen – let's give him a proper funeral. We were a tight little cuddle of democratic togetherness.

I'd been gone only a week but I came home to such disruption that I wondered if some type of time warp had occurred.

'Some professor came here – from your course, Eadie – he actually came *here* to the house. Left this letter for you,' Fiona said.

'I got my placement for my year abroad. Madrid. It just came through,' said Lorry and whilst he contrived a reluctant edge to his voice, I saw how his eyes glinted. 'I leave. Mid-July. For a year.'

'Also we really need to think what to do about *here*, about the house,' said Bill. 'The landlord came over to look at the hole and he wants to know if we're extending our lease for next year.'

I didn't understand any of it. This was more than a house, it was our home and I'd sooner my parents sold 41 Yew Lane than I moved out of Hathersage Road. Why did Lorry want to go away for a whole year? And what was this letter for me that had been delivered in person? I looked at my name, written in Professor Blakemore's unmistakable hard, scratchy letters as if he wrote with tightly pursed lips. It seemed that my housemates had already tried to open it.

'What did the landlord say about the hole?' I asked, placing the letter on the table.

'He just did that shrugging thing of his,' said Bill.

'He'll only fix it if new students move in,' said Lorry. 'He'll just leave it if we stay.'

'But you're *not* staying,' I said pointedly. 'You're leaving.'

Lorry concentrated on Professor Blakemore's envelope.

'I'm thinking of going back into Hall for third year,' Fiona announced sheepishly. 'You know – have my meals cooked for me. Knuckle down to my thesis.'

'But Hall food is—' I couldn't think of the word. 'And we cook delicious meals here.' In my head I screamed at both of them – what are you talking about? Don't leave don't leave don't leave! I shot Bill a look to implore him to say something but his face was open without a wrinkle of worry.

'Bill?'

He shrugged. 'I'm pretty tempted to move back to Hall, to be honest. Why don't you too?'

'They'd give us neighbouring rooms,' said Fiona sweetly.

'Is it a summons?' Lorry interrupted.

'Huh?'

'The letter,' he said. 'From your professor.'

I opened the envelope and slid out a single sheet of paper, skim-read the contents.

'It is,' I said and we all sat at our table with the crisps untouched and tea gone cold. We sat quietly, contemplating the enormity of all that had just been said. It was hard to unravel the complexities of our future while the muffled fuzz from Iris's telly coursed through the walls.

I loitered outside Professor Blakemore's office. The teaching day was in full swing. I had no idea what lectures or seminars I should have been at but other students seemed puzzled by my presence, as if I was back from the dead.

'Ms Browne,' the professor said, opening the door. 'Come.'

When Professor Blakemore called a student Miss or Mr, it was never a good thing. He wasn't the friendliest of tutors, he never added a comment to a good essay but had plenty to say, quite snidely too, when dishing out low grades. It struck me that Ms was possibly worse than Miss, so there I stood, like a bit of a lemon, an uneasy half-smile on my face which I hoped was somehow appeasing. It was a hard expression to keep fixed.

'Take a seat, Miss Browne.'

He fixed me with emotionless eyes and drummed his fingers against a brown paper folder on his desk that had a white label with my name on it, while I ducked away from his gaze and stared at his ancient and bashed leather bag instead, its strap curling up like a desiccated snake.

'Sorry,' I said, trying to pre-empt.

'You cannot afford to fail this course, Ms Browne.'

Back to Ms. In the awkward silence, I vigorously nodded as if his words had sunk in and made perfect sense. I wondered if I could leave now.

'I've spoken to Dr Finbow and Dr Mann and we are willing to give you a ten-day extension for the overdue essays, Eadie.'

And in that moment, I think I was more grateful that he used my Christian name than I was for the adjusted deadline. He was shuffling his papers gently and rhythmically, like he loved them very much. Just then, he reminded me of Terry and I dipped into thoughts of what Professor Blakemore's home looked like. A desk similar to my father's, I imagined, but with everything on it already in print or at least eminently publishable.

'Anything else?' he asked and I sensed he was about to use *Ms* again. I longed to be out of that office but my voice, disembodied, had other plans for me.

'The thing is,' I heard myself say, 'I've decided to – I don't know what the official term is – *opt out*.'

Professor Blakemore snapped his eyes to mine.

I tried again. 'Leave? Resign? Um – *stop*?'

He sat back in his chair and held the silence like a weapon.

'Drop out? Give up?' he said levelly. 'Quit?' He took a beat so that the insinuations of failure could reverberate around the room.

'Yes,' I said, determined. 'I'm quitting and giving up.'

'You are quitting and giving up.'

'I am.'

'Eadie.' It was with unexpected deflated sorrow that he spoke my name. He gazed down sadly at the file that said *Eadie Browne* on the label as if he was laying it to rest. 'You are – were – a promising historian,' he said. 'It thus begs the question – *why?*'

Before I could moderate my answer, it tumbled out as clear as it could ever be. 'I don't want to learn of the past any more, Professor Blakemore,' I said. 'It's not good for me. We have to stop making such a big deal out of what *happened*. I don't want to revisit it. I don't want to look over my shoulder. None of this is good for me. I want to be gone from it. The past – it's *done.*'

He had a think about that.

'Good Lord, Eadie,' he said. 'The Tudors weren't that bad a bunch, surely?'

It was the closest he could come to making a joke and I wanted to roll my eyes and groan like I did when Terry came out with an equivalent.

'It's just not where I want to be, it's not what I want to do,' I rambled. 'I can't be in the *past*. I don't want that.'

He had a think about that. 'What *do* you want to do?'

'I dunno!' I knew I sounded like a recalcitrant teenager. 'I'm not sure, Professor. I just know I do not want to be going over and over and over stuff that *happened*. Times that I can't change.'

He had a think about that.

'The Tudors?'

But he knew this wasn't about the Tudors. His voice was soft and his kindness confronted me. I shook my head and forbade myself to cry but failed almost immediately.

'Not the Tudors,' my voice came in hacking great sobs. 'But pretty much everything that came after.'

He had a think about that, too.

'Is everything all right on Planet Browne?' he asked, with such unexpected sensitivity that I looked up with a jolt to his steady smile. 'There are people you can talk to, my dear,' he said. 'The student counselling service. It's there for you.'

'I'm fine,' I said. 'Just – you know.' But how could he know? He was at least one hundred and eight. And I didn't know about the student counselling service and I doubted they could help anyway; they didn't even know me. Was this one of the crossroads Mr Swift had spoken of? Which direction should I take?

'Oh, *Eadie*.' He nudged a box of tissues towards the edge of the desk with his pen.

'I'm fine,' I said again and this time I fooled myself that I was. I left the history department and trudged back to Hathersage Road, detouring to the Rampant Lion where Denny gave me a pint, a hug and some peanuts but said there were no staff vacancies.

Nightmares continued to invade my sleep. One morning soon after I'd returned, I woke with my mind filled once again with the towering glum greyness of the Hulme Crescents where Patrick might well live. The weight of all that concrete lay heavy on my mind but scrunching my eyes shut hoping for sleep was futile. I pulled the covers over my head like I used to when I was small, creating a soft wigwam world where I could block everything out, but soon enough staring at the weave of my sheets became boring. I sat on the edge of my bed, sighing every now and then, at a loss for what to do. The house was quiet. The others would be in lectures, in the library, in the Students' Union. I went over the road for a bath after which, smelling faintly of Dettol, I had a bowl of cornflakes, using up all of the milk and half a pound of sugar.

Someone had done all the washing-up.
The post came but there was nothing for me.
I had nothing to take to the laundrette.
The house today was too clean, too quiet.
Next door, Iris wasn't in.

I didn't know where she was but, standing on her doorstep, I suddenly thought where I could go, where I needed to be; somewhere that seemed to be waiting for me.

Three days in a row I went, for hours on end, but I told no one. In that time, the Southern Cemetery became something of a sanctuary for me, a world where I was welcome, one which I understood. I felt so much more myself surrounded by the dead. And so on the fourth day, when everyone assumed I was in the library being industrious, I took the bus in the opposite direction and meandered once again along the paths at the cemetery, between the plots, returning to graves I'd come across belonging to people who I didn't know but who offered silent support and friendship nonetheless. I wondered what Michael would say about the planting at these grounds; I imagined he'd be quite taken with the size of the place and the layout. I thought he'd like the fact that the main paths were named after trees. Lime. Hawthorn. Acacia. Holly right at the centre. Horse Chestnut and Yew curving to meet at the two chapels. He'd have something to say about older headstones being askew and graves disturbed by tree roots. He'd want more litter bins. He'd devote a lot of time tenderly making sure the Baby Garden hadn't a blade of grass out of place.

A flag of cellophane flapped on the ground like a dying bird and I picked it up. I straightened the plastic flowers for Seamus O'Leary who was dead and buried almost a decade and had an unopened bottle of whisky propped against his headstone. With the back of my sleeve, I brushed away the bird shit that had crusted on the grave of Charles Edward Arnold who was only twelve when he died in 1880. I gathered a few pebbles and placed them on the Jewish plots and the neighbouring Muslim graves too. I tidied as I went and I felt useful; I had purpose, I knew what I was doing in a place like this where the past was calm and steady. For everyone who was at rest here, their future was known.

Some of the paths at the Southern Cemetery were tarmac, some were grass and avenues of trees sheltered them. It made me think that back at Parkwin this is what we needed. Shrubberies of Sympathy are all very well, but our cemetery could do with the grandeur, the life force, of great big trees and the practical support they could provide. I knew that though the catkins or conkers or acorns or leaves or blossom would drive Michael mad no doubt, so too would they keep him gainfully employed. But then I thought how any trees planted now would take years and years to grow and the notion depressed me. The dead had all the time in the world to watch and wait but their mourners in Parkwin were getting wet and windswept in the meanwhile.

Macey Darling Griffiths. I hadn't come across her on my previous visits but felt drawn to stand and contemplate such a beautiful name. Her plot was well tended, her headstone creamy white with beautifully engraved lettering. It was her name, however, which compelled me to stop. I imagined how all her life she'd have heard Macey Darling this, Macey Darling that. Even when she was in trouble as a kid – Macey Darling. Her husband, their whole married life, even when they were arguing – Macey Darling. I wondered if he'd called her Macey Darling, darling. Had he written love letters to Darling Macey Darling?

'Macey Darling,' I said quietly, as if she was dozing. I read that she'd left a daughter and two sons, also five grandchildren and one great-granddaughter. Macey Darling's bunch of fresh flowers had fallen right out of the vase and I was glad to rearrange it for her, pinching off a bent stem and pulling away leaves that had been in the water too long. Seventy-eight when she died. Beloved wife of the late Owen Griffiths. Where was he buried, I wondered, why wasn't he here? Loving mother, adored nana and great-granny. I bet not a day had gone by these last five years when the family hadn't thought of Macey Darling.

I Will Be In The Wind That Moves By You

I thought I knew pretty much every phrase, quotation, saying, psalm, poem and quip which could find its way onto a headstone, but this one was new to me. *I will be in the wind that moves by you.* And just then the breeze that had been gently whispering its way with me along the paths and between the plots upgraded to a sudden gust against me which whipped my hair into my face and stung dust into my eye like a rebuke. I thought Macey Darling, why did you do that? And then I called myself stupid because Macey Darling was of course very dead. I sat cross-legged and muttered at myself, Eadie Browne, what the *fuck* are you doing? Why are you even *here*? It was one of those horrible moments of clarity when I saw myself as others might, perhaps as the whole world saw me. An aimless young woman traipsing around a cemetery stopping by the graves of people she never knew, feeling too much.

I told myself I wasn't normal. I called myself a stupid cow. I asked out loud what the fuck I was going to *do*. But there I continued to sit and rock, miles away from lectures and from the red-brick terrace house I loved so much but might have to leave, further still from the home I'd grown up in where my indoor parents, this very moment, were contentedly toiling at their desks.

'Oh, Macey Darling!'

My words caught in a rasp of tears stripping my throat. It struck me how I had no idea where I should be, no sense of where to go. The wind was moving by me and all I could do was just sit right there, my head in my hands, while the flowers someone had left for Macey Darling brought colour and life into this dark dead world.

'Did you know her?'

It was a man's voice, right behind me, and it was gently enquiring. I didn't turn. I felt embarrassed, stupid, wondering how long he'd observed me lost in my fug. This hadn't happened to me before, this would *never* have happened in

Parkwin's Multi-Faith Cemetery. There, I had always been granted invisibility.

'Yeah,' I decided to say over my shoulder in a bid to appear less odd. 'I did.'

'Oh?'

'We were really close,' I said. 'So so close.' The man didn't move off so I elaborated. 'I loved her so much and I miss her to this day.' I'd hoped he'd now leave me alone to grieve. 'I still can't believe she's gone,' I said for good measure with a long and heartfelt sigh.

But still he was there. 'That's beautiful,' he said. 'I'm sorry for your loss,' he said. 'And how did you know her?'

Oh, won't you just sod off and leave me and Macey Darling alone? But I chomped down on the words, reading again her headstone, imagining she was in the wind blowing by me.

'I'm one of Macey Darling's five grandchildren,' I said.

'Oh?'

'Yeah.'

'Which one?'

And I thought well this man is an idiot.

'Her *granddaughter*,' I said as if to a small child. I could hardly be mistaken for a grandson, I was wearing my dungaree dress, pink socks and hi-top trainers and I'd bunched up my hair with a polka-dot scrunchy. I put my head in my hands.

Unbelievably, the man sat himself beside me, cross-legged too, just on the outer reaches of my personal space. I glanced at him, he was perhaps a little older than I. He appeared to be reading all about Macey Darling. He didn't look like a nutter but all the same I wished he'd get up and go. I was here first. I felt I had a right to stay and I returned my head to my hands hoping he'd take the hint and leave me to mourn my new grandma in peace.

But no. He spoke.

'Amazing,' he said. 'Because I'm her grandson and I've never seen you in my life.'

I scrambled upright so fast that I tripped over my own feet and fell down hard. I think I heard him laughing. I think he was laughing and saying oh shit oh shit are you OK? I wasn't OK at all. My knee had taken the brunt and it bloody hurt. As I blundered away mortified, disorientated, I think I heard him calling after me wait! wait!

No way. I limped and hopped as fast as I was able. Where was the exit, where had it gone? Yew, the row where Macey Darling lay ridiculing me with her real grandson, was the second avenue closest to the way out but somehow I'd bolted all the way over to the war memorial. From a light drizzle, raindrops became hard oily splats and some of the paths were immediately slippery. God, my knee hurt. I would like to have staggered around a bit moaning, but I kept soldiering on, head bowed and eyes fixedly down like a child believing that if she can see no one, then no one can see her. Finally I was back at the West Chapel, now having to weave my way through mourners filing in; people with every right to be there, unlike me. I dinked down the side paths and finally I was out on Barlow Moor Road.

The rain was sheeting down now. It does that in Manchester. Drizzle, mean and irritating one minute, becoming staggering blasts of fast fat wetness the next. By the time I reached the bus stop I was drenched, my socks squeaking in my trainers and rubbing my heels, my hair a slither of eels sucking at my neck. There was no telling how long I'd have to wait for a bus because graffiti obliterated the timetable. I parked my bum on the annoyingly angled plastic plank that certainly wasn't a bench and had a good look at my knee. The graze, hot and sore and almost perfectly rectangular, was right on top of my kneecap which was creaking inside. There was tarmac grit and graveside dirt caught deep in the raw scratchings which no amount of rain was going to wash away. Once upon such a long time ago, I'd had a teddy whose paw I'd use to make things better. He'd wipe away tears, dab at a graze, pat at my cheek. At this very moment, he was still in my bedroom all the way down the country at 41 Yew Lane where I imagined it was sunny and peaceful, where I could see so clearly my mum teasing out rhymes and Terry tap tap tapping a biro gently against his teeth while words and concepts danced over the blank pages in front of him.

In the here and now came the swish and fizz of traffic on tarmac running with water. Headlights on in the early afternoon. The rumble of something larger – just a lorry, not a bus. A cyclist pedalling past me saying fuck this shit as he went. A car pulling up right in the bus stop – the moron – but still no bus in sight.

And then: Hey. *Hey*. You OK?

And again: Hey, *You*! You OK?

And in the car obstructing the bus stop, stretching over the passenger seat and winding the window fully down, was Macey Darling's Bloody Grandson.

'It's absolutely pissing down,' he said and I thought to myself wow, you should be on *Brain of Britain*. And then I thought

I'll just pretend not to hear, and I absolutely won't look. So I scoured the distance for a bus.

'Listen – are you OK?' he called over. 'You went down pretty hard – I kind of felt it in my own knee, you know?'

And I did know. I remember Celeste shutting the door of the big black car on her finger and it made me bend double, clutching my hand between my thighs as I gasped for breath because I too could feel it. But I couldn't figure out why this bloke would stop his car in a bus stop in the rain to tell me I'd made his knee hurt.

'I'm fine,' I snapped. 'I'm *fine* – my bus is coming.'

I don't know why he didn't drive off immediately but I kept my gaze focused on the progress of my non-existent bus and breathed a sigh of relief when finally the car pulled away. But there was no bus, the rain was still at it and I was just as wet in the bus shelter so I thought I'd walk along to the next stop.

I kept going, marching over to Palatine Road, stepping into puddles because I was so wet that it made no difference. The traffic hissed along angrily, as if Greater Manchester as a whole was pissed off with the weather. Not a single bus passed in either direction and, in my own sopping world, I gave up on the bloody 143 and 142 and the sodding 41 and just kept slogging along through Withington towards Fallowfield, bolstered by the thought of the bag of chips I'd treat myself to.

'There is no bus.'

A hand gently at my elbow which made me jump all the same. It was him. *Again.* My Macey Darling's other grandchild.

'Look,' he said. '*Please.*' He gave me a little tug to stop; I snatched my arm away. 'I was driving,' he said, 'and there you were, trudging along. I've pulled in just up there on the left and I came to say that—'

'You came to say *that*?'

'—I came to say that I'll give you a lift. There's no shitting buses anyway. That's all.'

The 41 bus hurtled past us, splashing grey kerb-water against this man's jeans.

'God! And now I've just missed my bus,' I said, exasperated, as if it was all his fault.

'So I *have* to give you a lift now,' he said, as if it was all his fault.

'I'm not getting in your car.'

'I'm not an axe murderer.'

'Well, that's what all axe murderers say.'

'Look – just tell me where you live.'

'I'm not bloody telling you where I live. And stop following me!'

'I'm not following you – you're going my way – my car's just up there. It's that blue Mini.'

'And there goes the 143. Jesus!'

'And a 42,' he said as another bus grumbled past. 'So I really do *have* to give you a lift – because you wait ages for a bus then three come all at once. Which means now you'll be waiting ages again.'

'I'm happy walking.' Actually, my heels were stung sore from the rub of soaked sock against sodden trainer.

He sighed and tried to start a sentence. 'Look,' he said. 'Look. I just also really wanted to know why you were at my nan's grave, why you want her to be yours.'

And that, I knew, was the truth of it. Entirely reasonable. His chivalry with the Mini wasn't the driving force, nor was my bashed knee in any way his fault either. In fact, it was he who should've been weirded out by me, not the other way around. I did owe him an explanation; but it's not easy to lose face when you're turning twenty years old. It's not easy to turn your face and meet the eyes of a stranger when you know well enough how Manchester downpours turn you into a drowned rat and not Ophelia.

I shrugged at the pavement. 'I live on Hathersage Road.'

'I know Hathersage Road,' he said. 'It's by the hospital, yes? If I give you a lift, will you tell me why you were there?'

I shrugged again. 'All right.'

And so, in silence, we sloshed our way through the rain to his car.

12.12 p.m. 15th June 1999, the motorway

With my head full of then, I look at you now.

We're back on the motorway after the briefest of pit stops and you're concentrating on the road. It's started to rain and you can't decide whether to have your windscreen wipers on or off. You call this type of rain pizzle. Or shizzle. You say you'd rather walk in pouring rain than in pizzle, or sometimes you'll say shizzle. Now you have no choice but to drive through it.

And I look at you and I remember.

I remember that day in the downpour.

I remember asking you whether you had a bag in your car on which I should sit.

That you told me not to worry, that the seats were plastic anyway.

They're leatherette, you said.

Pleather, you said and, quietly, I thought that was clever and funny.

I remember the particular smell of your old Mini.

The radio was tuned to Key 103 and you turned the volume down, not on the music but because you wanted to hear me speak. To listen to what I had to say for myself.

We sat for a while; the engine running and the radio on low, the windows fogging up. I looked determinedly ahead though I could see nothing. You turned towards me but I didn't alter my gaze.

So what's your name? you asked.

I couldn't figure out where my voice had gone, so I traced my name on the steamed-up windscreen with my finger instead.

Eadie, I wrote.

Browne, I added beneath it.

Kip, you wrote.

Turner.

And under that you wrote *Hello*.

That day is so vivid and yet it seems that for a long time I've forgotten to remember it, to rejoice in its significance. For years and years. For a decade.

But that was the day that I met you.

We were going nowhere, slowly. The sky was one big Gatling gun firing rain, and every now and then the traffic ground to a standstill. Kip tapped his fingers against the steering wheel and peered through the wipers going full pelt. The sound they made was strangely comforting, the car was warm and there were Opal Fruits.

'If you're sure you're not my nan's granddaughter – who exactly are you, Eadie Browne?'

I spent a little while just thinking about how to explain because in my head it sounded perfectly reasonable but out loud, pathetic and plain weird. I'm just an oddbod who finds comfort at strangers' gravesides. And I like the green Opal Fruits which any sane person hates.

'Where I live,' I began. 'Where I've lived all my life – is a small house, a bungalow, right next door to a cemetery.'

And Kip said oh I see, as if everything made perfect sense now.

'Have you heard of Garden Cities? I live in one. Not a very good one, really – and these days it's more of a dog-eared small town.'

I decided to witter on about Edweard Fairbetter for a while, continuing with Ebenezer Howard's Three Magnets philosophy, then on to my school, my street and how there was no McDonald's in town. I took him further afield to Welwyn and Letchworth. It surprised me how much I could remember.

'Interesting,' said Kip and I didn't think he was taking the piss. It struck me that I could discourse on Garden Cities far better than anything about the Tudors.

'Parkwin,' he mused as if following a road map in his mind's eye. 'Park-Win.'

'Yes,' I said and continued pompously. 'Named after Parker—'

'—and Unwin,' he said.

I had a green Opal Fruit midway to my mouth and there it stayed.

'You've heard of Parker and Unwin?' It was like discovering we were related.

'Barry Parker and Raymond Unwin – I grew up in Wythenshawe which your boys also planned as a Garden City,' Kip said as he glanced at me and laughed. 'Your gast looks flabbered.'

'But—?'

He tutted at me as if I should know all this. 'Parker and Unwin laid out the design for a neighbourhood up here too, you know, in the 1930s – on undeveloped land south of the city. Working-class housing for industrial Manchester – but along Garden City lines.'

'Hang on. Wait. You lived in a Garden City? Up *here*?'

He snorted. 'Far from it. I mean – Bazza and Ray had a fine idea, but it was the Depression so finances ran out and all sorts of district bullshit followed. Then the Parkway – which they'd envisaged as a wide green gateway to the development – rapidly became a busy thoroughfare tearing right through the middle, slicing and dividing the community into two. All the trees and shrubs went and, by the time we moved there, it was practically the M56. Few shops or amenities or employment. The poorest of families. It was grim. Wythenshawe became the biggest council estate at the time in Europe – a Garden City it was *not*.'

I sat quietly. It was both unifying and yet bizarre to be talking about the Garden City movement with a complete stranger. 'But – how do you know all this *stuff*? Parker *and* Unwin?'

Kip laughed at that, looked at me as if to check that my gast was still flabbered. 'Various school projects,' he said. 'I lived in the heart of the soullessness of it. Slightly different experience to yours, I expect.'

I remembered back to all those school projects we did at Three Magnets with our maps and our timelines and our portraits of Ebenezer Howard and Edweard Fairbetter. We grew up grateful to them, to Raymond Unwin and Barry Parker. Parkwin was a place to be proud of, that's what we were taught and that's how we felt until we outgrew the city limits which is true of any place for any teenager. I thought of the fountain and the greensward promenade and the trees and the benches and the benign residential streets. I thought of the mannequins in the window of Pour Toi, steady and self-confident despite their slipped wigs and terrible clothes and passers-by pointing and laughing. I remembered Ebenezer Howard's quote defining the Garden City as *the peaceful path to real reform*. We'd learned that off by heart at school, like a mantra. The PP to RR. A joyous union of town and country from which will spring a new hope, a new life, a new civilization. Now, in Kip's car, I thought of Messrs Parker and Unwin having their wholesome and visionary design for Wythenshawe defiled.

'Did it ever feel like a Garden City – Wythenshawe?'

'No, the part where we lived was an absolute shithole.'

I wondered if it was as much a shithole as the Crescents in Hulme. The traffic lifted for a few yards then stopped again. 'In Parkwin, my house is at the end of the street and our garden has a gate in the wall directly into the cemetery.'

'This is bollocks,' Kip said and I must have shrunk at that because quickly he turned to me, put his hand fleetingly on my arm. 'I meant the traffic,' he said, 'not you. Sorry – please. You were saying, about the gate? The cemetery?'

'I liked it in there. I didn't mind that the people were dead. I'm an only child and they were great company.'

And then Kip wanted to know – did it ever freak me out?

No, I said, I was never spooked.

Did I imagine ghosts? Did I have nightmares? Did I even manage a wink of sleep as a child?

I don't believe in ghosts, I said.

But you talk to the dead, he said.

That's different, I said.

How so?

I don't know.

'Bet you were teased at school.'

I looked at him sharply. 'How d'you know?'

'Because kids can be little shits.'

I sat in his car and thought about Patrick, the little sheet.

'You all right?' he said.

I nodded. Actually, I felt tearful and sore and tired. Finally, we were in Rusholme but going nowhere fast and grinding to gridlock again. We weren't all that far from Hathersage Road. I really could get out and walk but my heels were blistered and Kip's car was warm and so was he and I had melded comfortably into the seat.

'I was picked on at school too,' Kip said. A muscle flexed in his cheek. 'My dad wasn't around – and my mum worked all the hours. She still does. Nurse – night shifts.'

'My parents work nights too!'

'We lived with my nan – she brought us up really, me and my sisters. She had a limp, walked funny. Making personal remarks against my nan was an idle pastime for some of the kids in my class and practically a religion for others.'

'I was picked on because of my looks – and for my parents being a little eccentric.'

'What's wrong with your looks?' he said. He was regarding me steadily and I felt oddly self-conscious of what the rain must have wreaked on my appearance. I turned away from his confusion and blushed to myself.

'We moved here from Wales,' he was saying. 'So I had the piss taken out of me for that too.'

'Macey Darling was Welsh?'

'Macey Darling had a disability, was Welsh – and also Indonesian.'

'*Indonesian?*' I instantly regretted my tone of voice.

'What of it?' Kip was defensive, the traffic was jerking along and he stalled the car.

'Nothing of it,' I said and I thought how headstones give such scant stories. 'In fact, it sounds enviable, being Welshdonisian.'

He smiled at that. '*Hey, Taffy! Dai! Sheepshagger! Your nan's a spaz, your nan's a Chinky spaz.* My sisters and I never told anyone about the name-calling.'

I stole a look at him. I didn't know what being a quarter Indowelsh looked like but Kip had olive skin smooth over fine features. He was handsome. He didn't have unfortunate hair or an odd dimple.

'Did it stop?' I asked him.

'Once I lost my accent, grew into my body and became good at footie, then yeah, it stopped. By the way – she was just Macey,' Kip told me. 'Darling was her middle name. You look disappointed?'

'I just thought how it was the best name ever,' I sighed, looking out of the window where a bin lorry was holding up the traffic the other way.

'She thought so too,' he said.

Stop start stop start. I was feeling a bit carsick now. Patrick; that was a bit more than teasing too. I found it hard to say *bullied* out loud. Kip had bypassed the word too.

'I was picked on,' I clarified. 'By one particular boy. It was—' But I really didn't want to think about Patrick or talk about him, not just today but any more. 'It was a long time ago.'

We silently agreed about this and then we were turning into Hathersage Road.

'You a student, then?' Kip asked.

I shrugged. 'Not really,' I said. 'I've sort of quit.'

'Why would you do that?' Kip asked bluntly. 'You don't want to do that,' he said.

I looked at him sharply and he obviously felt it.

'Sorry – didn't mean to pry. But trust me, Eadie Browne – the real world's far more of a pain in the arse so I'd stick with your studies and enjoy.'

I needed some air, not a lecture. 'You can drop me anywhere here.'

'Let me take you all the way home.'

'It's fine,' I said. 'I'm just a bit further up, near the Baths. I've got to get milk anyway. I finished it all this morning.'

Kip pulled in and stopped the car and we faced each other full on, for the first time. Older than me, but not by a lot. I quite liked the way he dressed. I quite liked his face. I noticed his forearms, for some reason. Powerful khaki eyes.

'Well,' I said. 'Thanks for the lift.'

'Any time.'

'And thanks for – you know—'

'—for sharing my nan? Any time.'

My cheeks felt hot. 'About that – I'm really not a weirdo. It's just that being there, with *them* – it helps me think.'

I watched him compute that. 'Listen,' Kip said, 'you visit her any time you like. I hadn't been in ages. I had a day off today – she was top of my list. I still miss her.'

I mumbled some more thanks as I peeled myself away from the pleather seats.

Just before I closed the door he said my name.

'Eadie,' he said and I peered back into the car. 'She'd've liked you,' he said. 'My nan would have liked you a lot.'

Lorry was home. He said that mustard powder in a bowl of hot water was a miraculous cure for sore feet and he set about boiling the kettle and rummaging in the kitchen.

'We only have chilli powder,' he called through. 'But I'm sure it'll have the same effect.'

I believed him. I trusted everything Lorry said. The water was a terrible colour, really, and the washing-up bowl could've done with a scrub but I put my feet in anyway. They stung like crazy but whether this was the hot water, or the chilli powder, or just the rawness of my skin, it was hard to tell. Lorry winced for me and it reminded me of Kip and my knee, it reminded me of Celeste and her finger.

'Look at your knee!' he wailed.

'I'm not putting chilli water on that,' I said.

Lorry went into the kitchen and returned with a mug of hot water into which he shook the contents of our salt cellar. We didn't have any cotton wool so he made pads from loo roll. He dabbed as gently as my teddy bear used to do.

'Lorry,' I said to the top of his head. 'About Madrid—'

'—I should have told you sooner,' he said to my leg. 'Workshopped it with you. I'm sorry.'

'I'm sorry too,' I said and then I stumbled over how to say what I truly felt. 'But I just want everything to stay exactly as it is,' I whispered. 'I want time to stop so we can rewind and live it all again.'

Lorry had a long think about that. 'But maybe without the drugs. And the kidnapping.'

We chuckled at that, we sighed.

'Lorry,' I confessed darkly. 'I haven't been to classes for ages. I've done no work at all. I think I'll quit.'

He gave this some thought while he dabbed at my knee again with his salty water. 'Loads of students say that.'

'But I think I mean it.'

'Well, I'm glad you only *think* you mean it.'

'But – what's the point? I'll probably just end up on the dole.'

'Edith,' he said. 'Moroseness doesn't become you. But more to the point – if you haven't been to lectures and stuff, what *have* you been doing? Not the washing-up, that's for sure. It's only me who does it, *ever.*'

'I've been in the cemetery,' I said. 'Every day. I take the bus to Didsbury and spend hours in the cemetery.'

Lorry looked at me. 'Yeah – that's not normal.'

We took a long beat during which we gazed down at my feet in the bowl of rust-coloured chilli water, at Lorry's mismatched socks, at my skinned knee. He called me a nutter and he laughed but I had to bite at my lip to stop myself from crying, which didn't work. Lorry placed the mug against my cheek.

'To catch your tears,' he said, draping his long skinny arm across my shoulders, resting his head against mine. 'To add to the salt water, to make the bits of you that hurt a little bit better.'

Side by side we sat in the humble home that didn't belong to us, staring contemplatively at the TV which wasn't even on. There we stayed companionably still, in the beloved rented house we called our home, hearing the countdown to when we'd have to move out, move apart, move abroad, move on.

12.36 p.m. 15th June 1999, the motorway

'There are so many people I haven't seen,' I say and I rest the side of my head against the window. Kip is a good driver and I find the soft juddering soothing against my temple. 'I haven't seen Fiona for years – she hasn't been back since she moved to California.' I don't want to think about the funeral, I want to cast my mind back instead. It seems Kip does too.

'That day I first met them all,' he remembers.

Though we've been together ten years and married for nearly three, it's still his favourite story to recount, not so much meeting my housemates for the first time, but how he tracked me down again. And now, in traffic on the motorway while the vehicles are gnawing on tarmac, I really hope he'll reminisce.

But Kip says, 'I'm seriously concerned we're going to be late.' And then he says, 'Can you see if there's a road map? Find an A-road or something?'

I search around, reach under my seat and haul the gigantic book onto my lap; squint down the massive index and waft through the pages to figure out an alternative route. It's the sort of thing we usually row about: I'll complain he doesn't know where he's going, he'll claim that he does. Sometimes, if he asks me to read the map I'll just say it makes me feel carsick. But just now I want him to narrate that day, I really want to hear it all again.

'Tell me about that day,' I say while my fingers track A-roads.

'You've heard it a million times.' But it seems Kip is happy enough to recount it. 'It was about a week or so after I first met you—'

'Not a week—'

'—OK, OK, it was exactly ten days.' He laughs a little, I like that. 'I'd thought about you that first night but work was suddenly manic and yet every time there was a lull, you'd pop up in my mind – when I was watching TV on my own, or in the pub with my mates, or listening to my mum on the phone. Putting out the rubbish. Making toast. There you'd be in my mind's eye. At first it amused me and then it irritated the hell out of me because—'

'—because you didn't know why!'

'Exactly. Because I didn't know why,' he says.

'Why?!'

'I couldn't work out why this slightly odd, gobby Southern girl had infiltrated my thoughts and barged into my days.' He pauses – because he always pauses at this bit. 'It pissed me off – that you were all I could think about.'

'It pissed you off that I was all you could think about,' I say.

'But then that day, ten days later, when you should've been driving to a meeting—'

'—that meeting in Stockport. There I was, driving, when I said sod it. I said sod it because there was nothing else I could do. I knew.'

'You knew,' I say. 'You just *knew*.'

'I did. I *knew*. So I made a U-turn and drove to exactly where I'd dropped you off—'

'—ten days before.'

'On Hathersage Road.'

'Oh Hathersage Road.'

'I drove on from where I'd dropped you off but of course I wasn't sure which was your house. Weird how I actually ended up parking practically outside number it.'

Now the news comes on the radio and Kip turns the volume down. We listened to the news an hour ago, nothing will have changed. Dole queues will still be shrinking. Serbian troops are continuing to withdraw from Kosovo. Mbeki is about to become South Africa's second black leader and South Korea has sunk a North Korean torpedo boat which can't be a good thing. Something about Pavarotti and his much younger fiancée but that's not really news. In the world, it's all the same as it was sixty minutes ago yet I sense a shift between Kip and me.

'I parked the car,' Kip continues while he changes lanes. 'All I knew was that you lived opposite the swimming pool. I began knocking on doors to find you. *Does an Eadie live here?* I'd ask. I was invited into one house because they said you did, but it turned out to be a bloke called Eddie. Another neighbour just said bloody students and shut the door in my face. And there really were bloody students next door to him, all stoned. One door was opened by a small child, another by the scariest-looking dude I've ever seen. Eventually, I rang a doorbell and a little old lady answered and said that you lived next door. *My Eadie*, she called you.'

'Lovely Iris, bless her,' I say and I think I must visit her soon. When I next take flowers for Macey Darling, I'll buy a bunch for Iris too. They lie not too far apart, my favourite ladies. 'We never called it the swimming pool – we always called it the Baths.'

'So, finally, I turn up at your house,' Kip says. 'And I know for certain now that it *is* your house. I didn't know if you'd be in but I rang the bell and I said to myself, I said this one's for you, Nan. And you *were* in. There you were – looking extraordinary.'

'That's one word for it!' It's still so vivid, I *love* this feeling!

We really laugh at the memory and I realize sadly how this melodious sound has been a rare visitor in our lives recently.

'But were you nervous?' I ask. 'Just turning up unannounced like some crazy stalker?' I don't think I've ever asked him this.

'Nervous?' Kip takes his eye off the road and looks at me, quizzically. 'No, I wasn't nervous. I just really wanted to find you,' he says quietly. 'I wanted to find you because I kept thinking how lost you'd seemed.' He pauses and smiles wryly. 'Nothing to do with the fact that I fancied the pants off you.'

I look out of the window and my heart is full and my heart is hurting. I've never heard him describe the event thus. Usually he runs through the facts, spends longer on the details of the various neighbours, of Lorry's response when he opened the door, of my expression when I saw him. Of what happened next.

'I looked such a state both times,' I remember.

'No,' he says. 'No, you didn't. Not to me.'

Gently and tentatively, he runs a fingertip down my nose and over my lips. His touch is as unnerving as it is lovely; it is something old that feels new because of its recent absence. Kip only leaves it there a moment, then he faffs with the packet of crisps he bought from the services. The van swerves. Someone honks their horn at us.

'Fucksake,' I hiss as I stamp dramatically on imaginary brakes and though I regret it immediately, I say nothing.

The traffic is moving again.

'Sorry,' I mumble a few minutes later.

'It's OK,' he says quietly. 'It's OK. It's a big day.'

'I'm dreading it,' I say. 'Sorry,' I say again and I steal a look at him and wonder how many sorrys we owe each other and how many our stubbornness and apathy have kept unsaid. And when we say the word out loud do we mean it, do we truly mean it, and does the other person hear it, do they even listen?

'Edith!'
Lorry was yelling up the stairs for me but I only vaguely heard him because Fiona and I were singing along to 'Push It' by Salt-N-Pepa; not singing, caterwauling. We were caterwauling in her room in our swimsuits, holding hairbrushes as microphones, getting ready to go over the road to the Baths. So that's exactly how I appeared at the top of the stairs when Lorry hollered again. Swimsuit and socks and a pair of goggles. Belting out my lungs into Fiona's paddle brush. And, down there looking up at me, one horrified and the other amazed, stood Lorry and Kip.

I like to think I froze for only a split-second but most likely it was a lot longer than that before I bolted back into Fiona's room. She was still in full voice, doing a terrible 'Everyday is Like Sunday', managing to sound even more whiny than Morrissey. I tried simultaneously to mouth and mime my predicament, finally overloading information in a whisper while her eyes scanned my face as if aliens had taken the real me.

'What's he even doing here?' I threw my hands up in despair.

'I think,' she said, 'we should go swimming *right now*.'

'How do we get there?' I whispered. 'How do we even get down the stairs?'

We looked out of the window as if assessing alternative routes from our first floor, but then she turned to me and shrugged. 'The normal way,' she said, and she took my hand and pulled me to the stairs.

Kip regarded me like nothing was amiss. Lorry had his arms crossed and an eyebrow raised.

'Hey, Kip,' I said, squeezing past him while he had to contend with our tangle of bikes.

'Off for a swim?' he asked, casual and deadpan.

'Yep.'

'Mind if I wait for you?'

'Nope.'

And off we went, Fiona and I, in our towels and flip-flops, to the Baths over the road.

We were both dreadful swimmers. During the course of the year, we had morphed our own technique which was breast-stroke arms and crawl legs and sometimes when we were feeling speedy, crawl arms while turning our heads side to side keeping our faces out of the water. I tended to grunt with my stroke and Fiona found it hard to talk as she kept her mouth tight, like a purse with a jammed zip. And that was how she learned about what I'd been doing, about going to the cemetery instead of lectures, about meeting Kip and Macey Darling, about my dither whether to continue with my course. I panted it all out until we reached the deep end where we clung to the ledge, frenetically kicking out our legs.

'What's he doing in our house though?' I asked her.

'Maybe he likes you?'

'I stole his grandma, Fiona, and now he's seen me in my cossie and socks singing into your hairbrush.'

'So maybe now he likes you even more.'

'Don't be stupid.'

'Don't *you* be stupid and leave uni, Eadie,' Fiona said. 'I forbid it.'

I sped up my legs. 'I'll stay – if you stay in the house and don't move out.'

'I'll stay if Lorry decides not to go to Madrid,' she said. And there it was, reverberating off the tiles and washed clean by chlorine – the impossibility of it because of the reality and imminence of our final academic year. We swam around it for a while before leaving the pool, our fingertips pruning.

'Why didn't I bring clothes and a hairdryer? *God!*' I said.

The answer was because we never had. The Baths were an extension of our home, part of our day-to-day on Hathersage Road and now, with hair dripping and with eyes slightly bloodshot, we returned to the house in our towels.

I wonder if he's still there, I thought out loud.

Of course he is, Fiona laughed. God, you're *so* naive, Eadie, she said.

And there he was.

Kip was sitting on the sofa with a mug of coffee, Lorry very close to him and further invading his space with his unflinching gaze.

'Nice swim?' Kip asked.

'Perfect,' I said and then I mumbled something about drying my hair while Fiona, still in her towel with her arms goose-pimpling, sat down and introduced herself.

I disappeared, taking the stairs two at a time. From the doorway to my room I listened to Fiona's interview voice though

I couldn't hear her questions. I didn't actually have a hairdryer and Fiona's had started to spark so I dragged a brush through my hair and bunched it up on top of my head. I struggled damp skin into clothes and wrestled some thoughts into order; neither was easy to do.

Back downstairs and they were all chatting gamely while I stood quietly on the threshold. The periphery had always been a safe spot for me. I observed Fiona holding court and Lorry staring intently at Kip, who looked over to me and grinned a little shrug. He waited for Fiona to pause for breath then he clapped his hands at his knees and stood. Fancy a quick walk, Eadie? he said. I looked at my wrist as if checking the time even though I didn't wear a watch. Just a quick one, I told him.

Not that I had anything else to do; I had so much to think about yet nothing, actually, to do.

We turned right from the house and meandered. The early evening was infused with true spring, with a pleasing freshness and green fragrance. Swinton Park was warmly lit with a rosiness and charm that belied its more usual drabness. We found a bench and sat.

'That's Elizabeth Gaskell's house,' Kip pointed to the edge of the park where two Regency villas in pale cream stone stood a little shabby and forlorn as if they'd time-travelled to the wrong period and place.

'Actually, it's the International Society,' I corrected. 'For the foreign students at uni.'

'It's Elizabeth Gaskell's house,' he stated and I didn't want to let on that I hadn't known this.

'Sometimes I come and sit here for a little breather,' I said. 'For time out from studentsville.'

I told him how I liked the yin and yang of this small park, the forsaken beer cans and the mums with prams, the info boards and occasional graffiti, the teenage scallies on BMX bikes, the elderly and toddlers who fed the birds and the two grand old buildings which these days resembled aged aunts sedately observing the scamper of modern life with both amusement and slight alarm.

'I did *Cranford* for A level,' I said as we noticed a dog take a dump in the middle of the path while its owner turned a blind eye and a woman in a sari in all the colours of sunset had to step around it. We watched a couple of kids share a fag and a can of Tizer. A small girl was being told off by someone surely too young to be her mum. And all the while an elderly lady quietly fed the pigeons and two people much my own age shared a bar of chocolate and a kiss. Someone was playing 'House of the Rising Sun' on guitar, quite well. A drunk had conked out under a tree. 'But Cranford this ain't,' I said.

'I prefer *North and South*,' Kip said, relaxing into the bench. 'You know: spirited Southern girl comes up to Manchester and meets an opinionated Northerner.' He looked at me with a wry smile and I glanced away, giving a light laugh. I wanted to stay on this bench for ever. I wanted to run back to Hathersage Road and hide under my duvet. 'You know Dickens chose the title for her?' Kip carried on. 'Gaskell wanted to call it *Margaret Hale*. He visited her here. Charlotte Brontë too. You know Gaskell's Milton and Dickens's Coketown are both Manchester?'

I was surprised by all of this, by him.

'English degree,' he shrugged. 'Bristol Uni.'

'Brizzle,' I declared. 'My best friend Celeste – her dad moved to Bristol and she told me that it's pronounced *Brizzle*.'

'Is she still there?'

'No, she's in Edinburgh being a lesbian,' I said.

'Right,' said Kip. 'And that doesn't sound homophobic.' But while he laughed it off, an ache for Celeste ran through me, settling just above my chest, and I sat quietly with the pain.

'Far from it,' I said. 'I sort of hate myself for having not realized – and I'm cross with her for having not told me earlier. And again with myself for actually not believing her. I said to her *no, you're not.*' The memory made me shudder. 'It's like time and distance have warped us and we've lost the fit we always had.'

'You'll get it back,' Kip said. 'Have you been? To Bristol? Edinburgh?'

I shook my head. 'Before Manchester, my entire life was Parkwin. I thought Parkwin was the world.' I told him about the fountains and the funerals, about Reuben's Shop and Terry's supermarket. About Sandrine and the huge black car. I painted a picture of the inside of my house and the length of Yew Lane. I even told him about Ross in the kilt and Ross in the piss-stained jeans. About Michael. And smoking a pipe. Mr Swift and Alfred Pennyfeather. Soundz Records, Pour Toi, the Appellex Modern Tynogrille.

'And you call your dad Terry.'

'I call my dad Terry.'

'I didn't have a dad to call Dad – let alone anything else,' Kip said and I said I was sorry about that but he changed the subject. 'Still thinking about quitting your course? Don't quit your course.'

'You said that before.'

'It's none of my business but—'

'—you're going to say you're older and wiser and stuff like that. You're going to tell me I'll regret it. You're going to bang on about education.'

Kip's silence was loud for a beat. 'I wasn't going to say any of that. I was going to say don't quit your course unless you have something else you truly want to do.'

I listened to that.

'Partly,' he said. 'Actually, what I *really* mean is – don't quit your course because I'd like it if you were in Manchester a while longer. So I can see you again. And perhaps again after that.'

His directness was a shock; it zipped a novel feeling through to my stomach and shredded my ability to respond sensibly. I ran through whether to quip about my Unfortunate Hair, or launch into a comparison between my cemetery and Macey Darling's. Shoot the shit about Dickens. Try and remember more about *Cranford*. Describe Celeste. Describe Josh. Perhaps even tell him about Patrick and ask Kip what *he* would do. My mind darted about and I couldn't keep up with any of it.

'I like Dickens too,' I said. 'My hair,' I said. 'Unfortunate.' And then I chirped *what the Dickens!* I groaned at my fumbled nonsense. 'Anyway,' I said. And then I said, 'Anyhoo – what do you do? Where did your English degree get you?'

'I'm in marketing,' he said. 'How wanky does that sound? Obviously I wanted to play guitar in a band but that didn't work out.'

'Got to have a dream,' I said.

'Got to have a guitar more like,' he said and he paused. 'I can't even play guitar.' This made me laugh, really laugh.

I asked him where he lived and he told me he was buying a flat in Salford but at the moment he was at his mum's in Mobberley. I told him I didn't know where that was, so on my leg he drew a map. If Hathersage Road is here, he said, dotting my thigh with his finger, and the Southern Cemetery is here and Wilmslow is here – then Mobberley is *here*. And he tapped at a point near my knee which appeared to turn on a switch and made my stomach flip, made me talk too quickly and too variously again including a tangential discourse about *Jane Eyre*. All the while Kip watched me intently, as if my odd little face was a source of endless fascination, as if listening to me witter on was riveting, as if sitting next to me on this bench in this park right now was exactly where he wanted to be.

That's what I saw and it skittered feelings through me I hadn't known about. I didn't know what to do with them so I stood up and I said I had to go. I said that Fiona was cooking spag bol and that I had to go.

We walked back to the house. Perhaps Kip was hoping I'd ask him in. However, when we reached Iris's, I just gabbled goodbye. I said thank you for visiting and other vague pleasantries like wishing him all the best with his career in marketing and lots of luck with his new flat. Then in I went, shutting the door behind me, pressing my back against it, listening to the sound of a car driving away, wondering if I'd ever see him again. We students believed we were a breed apart, there was an Us and a Them and I'd become used to the divide, the disconnect, between studentsville and the world beyond. Now I had a glimpse into something else, a glimpse into I don't know what.

* * *

It rained a lot after that, so it took a while for me to come across Kip's note in the basket of my bicycle because I was a fair-weather rider. In fact, I'd hardly left the house on foot, let alone bike, but a few days later I found it. It was a quirky caricatured self-portrait in smudged biro which was so accurate that it made me laugh. Beneath it, Kip had also written his telephone number. I didn't know he could draw. I didn't know if I should phone him. I didn't really know who he was, this man from the real world.

'I didn't know you could draw.'

'I didn't know if you'd call.'

'How did you know which was my bike?'

'Because when I gave you a lift home that first day, you told me you had a bike with a basket on the front.'

'I did?'

'Oh, I've hung on your every word, Eadie Browne.'

'Are you taking the piss?'

'Yes, I am.'

'Oh.'

'Yeah – sorry. Anyway.'

'Anyway. Thanks for the drawing.'

'You're welcome. I take commissions.'

'I thought you were in marketing.'

'It's a sideline.'

'Really? Oh – you're joking again.'

'You're quite easy to tease, you know.'

'I get on my own nerves. Don't laugh! Anyway. Hi. So. Did you – you know, go to work today?'

'Of course I went to work – it's just a boring Tuesday for the world at large. What did you do?'

'Well, I went in to the history department.'
'You did?'
'On my bike.'
'And?'
'Oh – you know – there were forms to go through and stuff to sign.'
'Oh. Right. So you've decided? You're definitely—'
'—um, you know Mobberley?'
'Huh?'
'Mobberley, Kip – where you're living at the moment? Is it nice?'
'Well, my mum certainly thinks so.'
'So can I cycle there? From here?'
'On *that* bike?'
'What's wrong with my bike?'
'Eadie – why don't I just come and pick you up.'

In the notepad which we kept under the phone on the milk crate in the hallway, I wrote down the length of the call and ticked the column for local. There were only a few empty pages left. I flipped through the book; Lorry's tall thin writing, Bill's larky squiggle, Fiona's bold hand. In all our time at the house, I'd hardly used the phone.

'This isn't Mobberley,' I said. The place name on the sign spelled it out. 'This *is not* Mobberley.' For a moment that was as sharp as it was short, I panicked. We'd just driven through a small place I'd never heard of. I had no idea where I was. I should have bloody cycled to Mobberley. Mobberley is where I'd told Lorry and Fiona I was going. 'This is *Tintwistle*,' I said. No one knew I was here.

Kip had pulled in just beyond the village. 'Bugger Mobberley,' he said. 'With weather like today, this is where we should be.' There was blue sky and a river and fields and trees. 'Look at where you are – in the High Peak – only twelve miles from your house.'

But *only twelve miles* seemed too far away just then. I could feel him studying my face, wondering about why I was just staring at the dashboard not saying anything.

'Sorry,' he said. 'I didn't mean— We can turn around and go to Mobberley if you'd prefer?'

Eadie Eadie Eadie. I inhaled, I exhaled; inhaled exhaled. 'This is going to sound stupid,' I said. 'I was put in the back of a van once. Not so long ago. Sorry. I just panicked for a moment.'

A clear sky, a freshness.

'Will you tell me about it?' Kip asked evenly.

I shrugged. 'If you really want to know.'

'You tell me what you want but yes, Eadie, I *really* want to know.'

The Three Magnets playground. The van by the Rochdale canal. The Hulme Crescents. Patrick. Kip listened intently and when he was done listening, I watched him struggle for what on earth to say.

He gave a long low thoughtful whistle. 'Bloody hell,' he said. 'I am *so* sorry that happened to you.'

'Bit of an overreaction to Tintwistle, I know. But.'

Kip put his hand gently on my arm and gave it a squeeze as a wry smile broke. 'By the way, Browne, it's pronounced *Tinsl.*'

He'd changed path for me and I gratefully followed. 'Well, I prefer Tintwistle,' I said. 'It sounds more magical.'

'I'll show you magical,' he said. 'Come on.'

We left the car and walked to a series of waterfalls.

'*The Seven Falls of Tintwistle,*' I said. 'How superbly Enid Blyton.'

He laughed. 'Tin*sul.*'

'The seven falls of tinsel is how our Christmas tree at home could be best described,' I said, suddenly wistful for the lopsided Christmases at Yew Lane. The last two years, I'd rushed it all.

Kip found a conveniently square chunk of rock for us to sit on. Heather whispering of its summer livery yet to come. The rocks behind the falls were clad lurid green with moss which was sopping wet and looked refreshing enough to suck. The pools so still and so very clear. I'd never been anywhere like this.

'These are the first actual waterfalls I've ever seen,' I admitted. 'I only know water which can be turned on and off. The fountain in Parkwin is like a shower-head that's fallen downside up – sometimes it goes everywhere.'

Kip was looking at me with that gaze again, like last week on the bench in Swinton Park. Now, as then, it found a route under my skin where it bubbled and I looked away then I looked back at him.

'What?' I said.

'Nothing,' he said. Then he changed his mind. 'Actually, not nothing,' he said. 'But this.'

And Kip leant in and kissed me; just softly, just quickly, on the corner of my mouth, and I had absolutely no idea what to do about what he'd just done.

'Waulkmill,' he murmured and he kissed my cheek. 'Kinder Downfall,' he kissed my nose. 'Middle Black Clough,' he said and he kissed my lips for longer and I didn't care if he'd made these names up, I found his mouth and I kissed him back and my body spun and surged. The day felt so new, the air so clean and all around was water falling falling, crystal clear.

And I thought, so *this* is kissing. Previously, kissing had just been something done, not felt. Now it churned my blood and squeezed my stomach and fluttered its way up between my legs. We kissed for I don't know how long, ignoring everything about anything until the scamper and bounce of young children bombarded our space. Kip stood and held out his hand. I took it and wove my fingers through his.

Come, he said and he smiled at me.

Look at where you are, I told myself. I told myself to really *look*. Look all around, Eadie. Look up. And just stop right here and look at who you're with.

I fell in love with where I was very quickly, charmed and amazed that here we were, so close to Manchester and yet a world away. We walked on while the landscape opened out; pasture plotted and pieced by old drystone walls which had settled into the land over time, forming sturdy spines of mottled grey all the way up to the open heathered hills. On we scrambled through farmland to moor and I don't know how far we walked, or how long for, or what the time was. None of that mattered. At intervals Kip took his hand from mine to pass me a piece of chocolate, an apple, a little carton of juice. I didn't even recall him having the small duffle bag but I was struck that he'd packed it with me in mind, with this walk all planned, and I liked the thought of that. He strode on and I noticed how the rucksack fitted against his back. And I noticed the breadth of his shoulders and the back of his neck and privately I wondered about his legs behind his jeans. I focused on these quite a lot while he led the way. I jogged back to his side.

'Wait,' I said and he turned to me, his features bathed in sunlight. 'This,' I said and I kissed his lovely face, holding it between my hands. Then we just stood still, side by side, entranced by the view while the sky settled gently on our shoulders and the earth was a soft bounce underfoot.

'Tell me more, Eadie,' he said. 'Tell me everything.'

'Everything?'

'Everything.'

And so I did. Josh. Patrick. Everything.

'What'll you do?'

'Nothing,' I said.

'You can't do *nothing*,' Kip said. 'Your rent rebate will stop. So will your student grant.'

It took me a moment. I thought he was referring to Josh, to Patrick, but actually he wasn't because in his mind, they obviously belonged in the past.

'I'm *staying*!' I laughed. 'At uni. In Manchester. In my house.'

He was confused. 'But you told me you'd gone in to sign forms?'

'I did,' I said. 'However, when I looked at that dotted line I realized I absolutely didn't want to.'

I made it sound like a three-minute process but when I'd gone in to the history department I'd stared at that form until the dotted line bounced. I'd looked over to Julia, in the admin office, who could only shrug as she handed me a biro. I watched Professor Blakemore gathering sheaves of essays from his pigeonhole as if he couldn't wait to dive in, and still my pen hovered. I noted people I'd never seen talking to classmates I'd rarely spoken to, and I was waved at by Hilary who'd been in my seminar group and who I'd always thought lovely. And still the dots kept dancing instead of staying straight and still for the signing. I'd imagined Terry and my mum with the news that I'd dropped out – the two of them trying to nod, trying not to let their bewilderment and disappointment show. Much as I knew it was unlikely they'd even attend my graduation, did that really matter? I knew they'd be proud as punch just as they were, in our front room, gazing at a framed photo of me in cap and gown. Mr Swift's sage and craggy face came to mind. Hadn't he told me to open my eyes to exciting times because in a blink, I might miss them? Hadn't I scrunched my eyes shut to all that was on offer, right here? As my resolve slowly settled, so too did the dotted line. I gave Julia back the biro and I walked over to

Professor Blakemore and I touched his sleeve. *I've decided to stay if that's OK.* He'd looked at me gravely. *Dear God but you have a colossal amount of work to catch up on.*

But he didn't call me Ms Browne or Miss.

'Well done, Eadie,' he'd added. 'Well done you.'

'So you're staying,' Kip mused. The wind was up and we were sitting with our backs slowly melding against a run of stone wall, a straggle of sheep staring at us while we had a finger each of Twix.

'I am indeed,' I said and I rested my head against his shoulder and grinned at the grass.

I would try to explain Tintwistle later that night to Lorry. How up there, out there, in the open, it made sense of where I'd been before. What I'd tripped over, what I'd leapt and what I'd skirted around. It was clear to me now how I'd spent so much time unaware of what was right in front of me because I'd been too preoccupied looking over my shoulder or squinting for the horizon.

That day, my first visit to the Peak District, out in the open; the ups and the downs of the landscape mimicked my life. But the land was vast and ancient and, within it, I was small and inconsequential and the order of things struck me as correct. I saw my first waterfalls. I sat for hours on a hillside falling in love with a man called Kip. He had taken this girl out of Manchester – with no need to take Manchester out of this girl. And he'd kissed the real me and I'd felt it. Out there, with him, I had a sudden sense of everything. Sheltered from the wind. Happy. Safe.

So I was staying. I was going to remain in my adoptive city and continue at university and live in my lovely house whether or not the others moved out, and that was that. I decided simply that there was no need to fret about careers and salaries or the meaning of life just yet. I could think about all of that another time. For now, I had to knuckle down and work and, for the first time, I felt inspired to do so.

My housemates went out without me because I was either studying or hiking in the countryside. Kip had a list of days out all planned – rewards, he called them. So I worked, how I worked during the week, to earn them. When I received 69 per cent for an essay, I would have been happy enough to have celebrated at the Rampant Lion and a curry, but Kip took me to Hayfield instead. There we hiked the Kinder Downfall to Brown Knoll trail for almost twelve miles. It was the furthest I'd walked in my life and the most breathtaking place I'd ever been.

'We'll have to come back another time,' he said because without us noticing, evening had slicked its way over the land, flipping the afternoon breeze into a time-to-go chill. 'You need to see the Mermaid's Pool. Jacob's Ladder. Also the Woolpacks,' he was saying, when I interrupted him.

'We could stay the night.'

I was about to add that we could see all these other places tomorrow but I didn't. I wasn't thinking about landscape and more bloody hiking, I was thinking of my body; not my tired feet and aching legs, but how inside and out I was alert and fizzing for him and had been for days now. After a fortnight of kissing in the open air and snogging in his car and making out in my room at Hathersage Road, where the door didn't quite shut and the bed squeaked like it was taking the piss out of us, I knew what I wanted. Kip was looking measuredly into the middle distance with a huge grin on his face. In such a short time I'd grown to love the way he could be lost in thought but remain so solid and present next to me. I slipped my hand into the back pocket of his jeans. 'Let's stay the night,' I said.

He turned towards me. The light and scent of dusk murmured around us. We gazed at each other intently.

'You're ready?' he asked.

'Very,' I said.

It was a straightforward B&B on a farm outside Hayfield. The room was old-fashioned but spotless and it had its own bathroom with a fresh bar of Palmolive soap and towels of a colour to match. On the chest of drawers was a kettle and mugs, coffee and tea, UHT milk in little pots and sugar in sachets. There was also a radio, but the owner said we were welcome to watch TV in the guest lounge though it seemed we were the only ones staying. The bed was bedecked in floral linen topped with a sateen eiderdown, the likes of which I had not seen since I was a child and a turquoise one adorned my parents' bed. The lampshades were bell-shaped, fringed with silky tasselling which Kip and I were helpless not to run our fingers through, as if eliciting the softest of scales. From another part of the house, we could hear the owners' voices, muffled and distorted, compelling us to whisper.

'It's like having parents in the house,' I said. 'Grandparents, even.'

'We'll have to be quiet then,' Kip said, pulling me close. 'If we want to get up to no good.'

The curtains were already drawn but appeared to breathe in the draught; the radiator was on but the room was chilly.

'I'm cold,' I said, burying my face in his chest. I'd thought about this scenario so much but now that it was imminent, the truth was I felt a little shy.

'Does that mean I can't strip you naked?' Kip murmured. 'Can't carry you around the room and roger you senseless on every available surface?'

He was kissing me hard.

'You can if I can keep my socks on,' I murmured into his mouth. Fleetingly I remembered the last time I had sex. The first time. The only time. I'd worn socks then, as well, socks which were damp and dirty. But Kip was sucking at my neck, his hands active and enquiring, pulling at my clothing, finding my skin, making soft throaty moans the very sound of which turned me on. My mind emptied, and that is how it should have been, when I got naked with my boyfriend and made love for the first time in my life. I thought of nothing and I felt everything; hyper-aware of my body and his, the transcendental pleasure, the moment, today, tomorrow, our future.

Kip took me to Hathersage the next day, after a farmhouse breakfast that I was tempted to eat twice over.

'The *real* Hathersage,' he said, and then he laughed. 'And you thought all roads lead to your house.'

I suppose I did. However it was dawning on me, slowly, that my Hathersage might not be the centre of the universe. Perhaps my true path led *away* from the house on Hathersage Road not to it.

On the eastern fringes of the Peak District and guarded by the stern gritstone escarpment of Stanage Edge, the village of Hathersage unfolded between the hills, refreshed by the river Derwent and its brooks. The buildings were built in the local stone, dark cream bloomed with grey like a ferret and when the village petered out, the trees bounced into the dips of the hills crowning the crests before heather and moorland stretched and rolled. This was Brontë country, the setting for *Jane Eyre*, but we didn't walk to the manor house that had inspired Rochester's.

'I'm tired of walking,' I told Kip. 'I walked my legs off yesterday,' I said. 'Twelve *miles*,' I reminded him. 'I'm shagged,' I said.

And he looked at me and I looked at him and we laughed and clasped each other in delight. He rubbed his nose against mine then held me at arm's length before drawing me close against him.

'God, you're gorgeous,' he said.

And strangely, I didn't burst out laughing. I told myself, he's talking about me. He's talking about *me*. I felt beautiful.

So he didn't make me hike. We found the stepping stones instead; Kip taking them easily in his stride whilst I wobbled and, once or twice, became stuck.

'Take my hand,' he said and tentatively I did, and I wondered if he'd always be there for me, hand outstretched, patient with me during times when I might dither and even stop altogether.

As we headed to the car for the journey back to Manchester I said to myself, I said this: Eadie Bee – *anywhere* in the world can be as lovely as Hathersage and any place can be as special as Hathersage Road – if you're with this man. And then I told myself – if this man offers you his hand, you make sure to take it.

Part of the Hope Valley came back with me to Manchester that day.

12.42 p.m. 15th June 1999, the motorway

'Take my hand,' you'd said to me all the way back then.

And I wonder, are you still here for me? Or is it you who now dithers, you who might stop altogether? Because it strikes me very, very hard that perhaps I haven't been there for you. Impatient. Remote. Self-absorbed. Lacking.

Look where we are, where we're going, what you're doing for me today. In my head I am willing you to take my hand and I spend the next motorway mile focusing on telepathy. Your hands, however, stay steady and determined on the steering wheel, while mine lie limply in my lap.

The light was on in Lorry's room when Kip dropped me home and I charged in there, leaping onto his bed where he was facing away from me, curled up on his side listening to music. I laughed and sang out and I said Lorry! I said *now* I know what sex is all about!

'I've been made love to a dozen different ways,' I sighed. 'Who knew! Who *knew*! Lorry?'

He hadn't responded, he hadn't moved. We often snuggled up on one bed or another for heart-to-hearts, general nattery or just to nap. But I sensed he wasn't sleeping.

'Lorry?' I gave him a nudge and he flinched. 'Hey! Don't you want to know all about sexysexy time?'

Very slowly, he started to turn, wincing as he did.

'Don't say anything, please,' he said as he faced me.

My beautiful friend with a blackening half-closed eye, a split lip, his nose lumpy and swollen with a bloodied clod of cotton wool stuffed up one nostril. He put his finger to his lips when I made to speak and I watched a tear slip painfully down his cheek.

'I'm OK,' he croaked. 'So don't do any worrying or gasping or oh-my-Godding or anything like that. I met a bunch of the *loveliest* chaps today, Edith, that's all,' he said. He tried to smile, but it clearly hurt him. 'The loveliest gay-bashing bigotty bastard fascists.' He gave me a brave sorrowful smile. 'Whilst you were shagging in the heather.'

I was distraught. But I feared cuddling him would hurt so I stroked his arm as gently as I could. 'But have you called the police?'

'No.' He attempted to chuckle risibly, but it obviously hurt to do so.

'Well, I'm calling them now,' I said.

'No, you're not.'

'I bloody am! The police need to get them.'

'You're *not* – because they never will. And it's only a black eye,' he said. 'And a thick lip. Maybe a broken nose. A bit of a bruise.' Gingerly, Lorry lifted his T-shirt and I gasped at the rust-brown mottling across his ribs.

'Oh, Lorry.' I slipped my hand into his. 'Shall I get some frozen peas?'

'I already did that,' he said. 'But I felt them cooking – literally. My body was so hot – and not in a good way.'

'*Please* go to the police.'

'What – like you pretended to after you'd been abducted outside the Haç?' he said with a gentle grin at my embarrassment. 'There's no point, Edith. You know that. And anyway, I'm gay which means I'm *swirling around in a cesspool of my own making* – to quote the delightful Chief Constable of our fair city.'

'They're not all like James Anderton,' I said.

'*No police*,' he reiterated. 'Only you.'

'But what can I *do*?' I felt utterly impotent.

'Just stay.'

'Shall I make a bowl of warm water with chilli powder?'

'You shall *not*, Edith,' he said. 'Just stay?' He looked so tired, so afraid. 'I'm scared to go to sleep.' He lowered his voice to a whisper. 'I'm frightened of what I might see there.'

I knew exactly what he meant. I cuddled around him as gently as I could. Eventually, Lorry fell asleep in my arms while I gazed up at his ceiling. As I trailed the cracks in the plaster and the cobwebs in the corner, I thought a lot about love and I thought about hate and then I thought about Celeste.

I stared at our telephone for a long time before dialling Edinburgh. I had spent most of the night wretched and fretful. I was raging on Lorry's behalf, at one point determined to track down his assailants and beat them up myself. I was also furious with myself for the way I'd treated Celeste, even more so for having not yet made amends. Over and over, my mind replayed that distant Christmas. How I'd said no you're not when she'd said yes I am. And how lonely and let down she had looked when I had laughed and ridiculed her revelation away.

Love is love is love – the simplest of concepts. Now I wondered if Celeste had ever been targeted too, attacked like Lorry had? Please no. But how would I know? These days, I was probably the last person she'd turn to and this appalled me.

The call connected and a bloke answered. Probably Digger or Boggins or someone like that.

'Is Celeste there, please?'

'It's six in the morning!'

I gave his remonstration scant attention. 'Well, rise and shine,' I said flatly. 'Can you put Celeste on?'

It took a long time for her to come to the phone and when she did, when I heard her voice, I ran the risk of her hanging up because I found I couldn't speak.

'Who is it?' she mumbled. 'Hello? Who the fuck is this?'

'It's Eadie,' I managed. 'Your friend.' I held the handset to my heart for a moment and closed my eyes. 'And I'm sorry,' I whispered. 'I love you. I *love* you.'

'You *what*?' Celeste said. 'And you *what* what?'

I repeated it all even though I knew she'd heard.

'And you rang me at ridiculous-o'clock to tell me?!'

'Yes,' I said. 'I had to call.'

There was a loaded beat and I prayed she wouldn't hang up. 'Is everything OK, Eads?'

This was my chance to make it so. 'I didn't listen, Celeste,' I said. 'I just didn't *think* – and I was cruel. I didn't mean to be, but I was.' My voice was hollow, I was gripping the telephone hard and my toes curled against the swirly carpet. 'I'm sorry – with everything that I am, I'm so sorry.'

An excruciating silence choked the line but then a gentle half-laugh sang through. 'I suppose it's not every day your best mate tells you she's gay, though.'

'But I didn't *listen*,' I said to her. 'I ridiculed what you were telling me. All those years when you had my back. But then I wasn't there for you, I haven't been there for you and I *hate* myself for it.'

'Eadie. Shut up. Doesn't matter. Don't cry.'

But I couldn't help it and I wailed and burbled and sniffed.

'Idiot drama queen, you daft daft cow,' Celeste said. 'Get a grip, woman. God, I've missed you.'

'I've missed you more.'

We competed over that for a while.

'It's fine – Eadles – it's *fine*, I promise. I understand.'

'But – I didn't *listen*.' And I needed her to listen to this.

'I hid it though – so how were you to know?'

'But then you confided in me and I just rubbished it and I turned away from you. I left you.'

'Will you please just stop it with all the self-flagellation!' Celeste groaned. 'I'm gay – hurrah. And now you're happy about that – double hurrah.'

'But I *love* you and I'm *sorry*.'

'And I forgive you, Browne. And I love you right back. Jesus, can we change the subject, please? Tell me what's been going on down there.'

I was about to launch into the story of Kip, but I stopped. None of this was about me down here, it was about her up there. So I said nothing much, I said nothing much has being going on down here. 'I saw Sandrine not so long ago,' I said. 'And she told me you'd split with Alicia. And I want to know – are you OK?'

'I'm all right,' she said, before sighing theatrically. 'But I've been on an epic rebound ever since, so predictably I'm full of self-loathing at the moment. And zits.' She laughed at herself. 'I guess that's what growing up is all about. Trying to find the best way to figure stuff out.'

Trying to find the best way to figure stuff out. My friend was so wise.

'For the way I reacted, for letting time pass, for being wrapped up in myself and not being there for you – I am truly sorry,' I said sadly. 'I am ashamed. I just had – no idea. I'd never even suspected—'

'—it's OK,' Celeste said, soberly at last. 'I was ashamed too – scared, as well. I'd avoided it and for so long I'd refused to have the conversation with myself, never mind anyone else. For a while I even hoped I might, you know, *change*.' She paused. 'The thing is, Eads – I'd always believed you and me and Josh were exactly the same – then suddenly I was different. I didn't want to lose *you*, you know? I really feared that.'

I'd never thought about it that way. 'I haven't pushed you away, have I?'

'That wouldn't be possible,' Celeste said and I think we both considered the meaning of our friendship in the quiet moments that followed. 'Talking of Josh – have you been in touch much?' she said at length.

'Will you come and stay?' I said. I didn't want to talk about Josh. Nor about what had happened to Lorry. I didn't want even to mention Kip. I just wanted it to be me and her. 'Come and visit me in my lovely little house here? So I can make it up to you in a million different ways?'

'I'd love that,' she said and I think I swooned. 'Hang on – did you say you saw my *mum*?'

'I did,' I said. 'And you'll never *guess* who else I saw.'

'Do you actually want me to guess?'

'You can if you like,' I said. 'But you'll never get there.'

'Who?!' And oh, her voice! 'Who – damn you – *who*?!'

'The Little Sheet,' I said.

In the end, we didn't stay on at Hathersage Road. Oh, how I loved that house – my home. For that single seminal year during which so much had happened, those bricks and that roof kept me safe and supported, brought me comfort and joy – such joy.

Behind that front door lay a beautiful world where life was bathed softly golden from the dim bulbs behind greying paper lanterns, from the lick and flicker of the gas fires which singed our hair but kept us cosy. At that table in our sitting room, we had fed one another. Sometimes the table heaved with bottles and cans and empty boxes of wine, often it was laden with mugs of half-drunk stone-cold tea, and every day that table was the bulletin board for the notes we left for each other. Next to it, the old brown sofa in all its weary velvety glory. Like the fifth member of our household, it was there for us, patiently tolerating the satchels and folders and files and coats flung onto it; crumbs and spillage – so many crumbs and so much spillage. The welcoming snuggle it gave us when we all squidged together to watch TV, the quiet safe space it provided for us to curl up and huddle for heart-to-hearts that lasted into the early hours. This was the sofa onto which we tumbled after a big night out, ravenous for towers of hot buttered toast balanced on its arms and on our knees. The sofa on which we lolled whilst we put the world to rights and the sofa that had, for a while, held me in its dusty cuddle when the others were at lectures and I'd spent day after day wondering what to do about everything. This unremarkable house on Hathersage Road, Manchester M13, had a hole in the kitchen floor and a mouse we'd called Klaus. My bed belonged in a skip, the immersion heater was a health hazard and the swirling carpets were an affront to basic tenets of taste. But the house was so much more than the bricks and mortar of which it was built. It had extended to us a patience, a wise benevolence and, under its watchful eye, we had grown, we had done OK.

In my last few days there, I spent a lot of time walking through the house, soaking up the details, remembering what never to forget. It struck me that when we'd first arrived, scampering in and out of the rooms, putting up posters, stuffing the cupboards with shopping, designating shelves in the fridge, scrubbing the bathroom and vacuuming into corners, it had felt like we were Playing House. But ultimately, it had exemplified Home. We weren't its first students and we wouldn't be its last but we felt as though we'd been special. That was the magic of the house – the feeling that we were its favourite tenants.

So it took me a long time to pack up my room, not that I had many possessions. I kept stopping to just gaze off while Kate Bush and Clint Eastwood regarded me from my walls. I pottered around, picking things up and putting them down again, taking lots of breaks to sit on my bed and quietly look around, to stock-take details to store for posterity. When I did take down my postcards and photos and the pictures torn from magazines which had adorned my walls, I spent ages staring at the patterns made by all the nubs of Blu Tack left in their wake. Without my sheets, the bed looked forlorn; it looked lumpy and saggy and not fit to sleep on, really. But I'd cried on that bed; on that bed I'd daydreamed, read, revised and also confronted night terrors, the recall of which still made me shudder and freeze. In that single bed, tucked under the slope of the stairs climbing to the attic room, I'd embraced the squashed sleep in the arms of the man I was falling in love with. Kip and I explored lovemaking in all its guises; from tender and slow to giggling shags and urgent fucking. I learned about sex in that bed and I came to understand that whatever had happened with Josh in my room at Hulme Hall last year had been as far from making love as getting mashed on Ecstasy had been from genuine happiness.

I daydreamed out of my window for inordinate periods of time when I should have been packing. The warped and overpainted sash frame had never closed properly. In warmer months the air that slicked through was welcome and during the winter I had simply run lengths of masking tape along the gaps to keep out the draught. Instead of sorting my stuff I became readily lost in thought, looking out over our tiny back yard to the alley beyond. The *ginnel*, Iris had called it. She told us that long before students, these had been family homes and the children would spend their entire summers playing out there – decorating the grimy cobbles and the bricks with coloured chalks, hosting dolls' tea parties and football matches. Sometimes they'd all have their tea there too. Iris used to laugh at that – how when you were clempt, other people's barm cakes tasted so much better than your own mam's. It was a good way to make sure everyone ate, she'd told me. Happy days, she said. The best of times.

Oh, Iris.

I'd gone round to visit her daily during my last week. I'd made her promise she'd always call me if she needed anyone to look after Sparky, for any help whatsoever. I swore to her that I'd often be there, on the last Thursday of each month, to catch the bus down to the Southern Cemetery with her when she went to see her Sid. I told her she was my friend and I was hers and I hugged her, inhaling hair lacquer and Nivea face cream and the scent of violets and slightly soured tea, feeling the furred softness of her cheek and the poke of an occasional whisker. She held my hand and told me what a good girl I was. She told me she liked Kip. She said he was a Keeper. She said, he's a Kipper, Eadie – and she chuckled and wheezed at that.

We housemates went into each other's rooms a lot whilst we packed, talking quietly and reflectively, glancing around at how different it looked with all signs of us disappearing.

'You know,' I said to Fiona as I helped her cram her duvet and pillow into a bin bag, 'it doesn't matter how many people live here after us – we're special to this house.'

She looked at me as if I was bonkers.

'No,' I said. I said, 'Really! *Listen* to me.'

'I'm all ears, Eadie,' she laughed and she muttered *nutter* under her breath but I didn't mind. She'd called me worse.

'Wherever we go, wherever we end up, we'll always be able to conjure this house,' I said. 'That it was home and there will be no place quite like it.'

'Yes, Miss Dorothy-with-the-Ruby-Slippers.' Fiona laughed at me and I joined in at my own expense – but privately I knew that I could click my proverbial heels any time I liked and I'd be back here. Fiona took down Kate and Clint and gently rolled them together with Naked Man Cradling Baby into a cardboard tube she had spare. She handed it to me with reverence and it crossed my mind that in a year's time, I just might be receiving a scroll at graduation with similar solemnity.

The landlord came to fix the infamous hole by the fridge for the next students. The Bloody Hole, we'd taken to calling it, but when we went to inspect the new lino we all agreed we much preferred the floor the way we'd known it. The house looked uncomfortable with something so new and pristine. Really, there was no need for house or inhabitants to hide or gloss over a single thing from each other.

It was strange, really, that it should be me who was the first to leave. I'd vacuumed, dusted and cleaned. Everything I had was now out on the street and being loaded into Kip's blue Mini. A suitcase, a rucksack, a box and the cardboard tube. I left one thing in my room on purpose and I didn't go back for it – and that was a significant part of Me. To this day, inside the first bedroom at the top of the stairs, it is still there.

And so it was – with Bill and Lorry and Fiona waving like crazy from the pavement, and with my head out of the car window craning my neck right round so I could soak up the very last glimpse of my beloved home on Hathersage Road – that I left.

* * *

Bill and Fiona were to return to Hulme Hall and Lorry was heading for Spain and I moved in with Kip. It felt right, it felt like we'd been waiting ages to do so though we'd been together only a few months. Sometimes, it happens that way. We didn't question it, we marvelled at it. Finally he had the keys to an apartment in a modern block in Salford, just a short train ride to Manchester Victoria and then an easy walk to the university. The flat was on the fourth floor; it wasn't big but it had square airy rooms, double glazing and heating that came in through ducts. It felt about as far away from bungalow living in Parkwin as it did from Victorian terrace quirks in Rusholme. While in Berlin the Wall came down with a surge of liberation and joy, Kip and I built up our own barrier behind which I discovered a level of safety and self-confidence new to me. I believed in him and he believed in me. Anything was possible.

About a month after leaving Hathersage Road, there was a plan to go to the Haçienda. It was meant to be the last huzzah before we went our separate ways for the rest of the summer before returning in the autumn to the serious business of our final university year. Not Lorry – he was already in Madrid. And not Kip, who said he could think of nothing worse than spending a gorgeous summer's night in a hot and sweaty club surrounded by a bunch of twats off their faces dressed for the beach thinking they could dance. I laughed and called him a grumpy old git and he chased me around the flat and caught me and held me and kissed me.

'Anyway,' I said, 'maybe I can't be bothered to go. I'd much rather stay home with you.' Privately, though, I'd been dithering about it for days.

Kip looked at me and raised an eyebrow. 'I think you're worrying about that Patrick kid being there again, aren't you?'

I was.

'So I think you *should* go,' Kip said.

I didn't understand.

'Because if he's there then I think you'll see how far you've come,' Kip said. 'You'll see just how distinct your lives are. It'll put a final nail in that coffin, Eadie. Give you – what do the Americans call it? – *closure.*'

I shrugged and started to walk off.

'Eadie – stop.' I wasn't sure whether Kip looked exasperated or concerned. 'What would you say if you saw him – if you saw Patrick again?'

I thought not only of all the scathing soliloquies I'd rehearsed in front of the bathroom mirror, but also how I'd imagined sitting on a park bench next to Patrick discussing the paths we'd taken. It was as if I wanted to save his soul and bury him simultaneously.

'Eadie,' Kip said, 'if I accompany you to Hulme and we knock on every door – like I did to find you – if I helped you track Patrick down, if we sat with him having a brew – what would you say to him? What is it you want to know, Eadie – what do you want to hear?'

I shuddered. 'I don't want to see him ever again,' I said to Kip. 'I want to stop thinking about him.'

'Then that's why you need to go tonight,' Kip said. 'So that he no longer exists for you, so he doesn't come between us.'

Still I felt reluctant and apprehensive. I had intended never to go to the Haçienda again, much less touch another drug, and I was certain I didn't want to see Patrick. But I went that night.

It was like meeting up with a friend. An old friend not seen in ages who'd had a haircut which didn't suit them, who didn't look well at all. I realized almost immediately how it wasn't my scene any more. The magic for me had gone.

It was 14th July 1989 and it was the night that someone died in the club, the first Ecstasy-related death in England. Her name was Clare Leighton and she was sixteen years old, I saw her collapse and I watched her being carried out. I'd seen people pass out at the Haç before. On nights when it was particularly hot and crowded in there, when they drank too much water than was good for them, they'd drop like flies. This, though, was horribly different.

I got out of there. I ran to the payphone at the City Road Inn on the corner and called Kip to pick me up. While I willed the friendly headlights of the blue Mini to appear, I stood quietly next to my chum, the hotdog seller. He greeted me warmly and offered me one for free, but I had no appetite. Do you know if the girl is OK? I asked. He said he didn't know but she hadn't looked good, she hadn't looked good at all. And then he said it's not the same any more. And he said that he didn't know why he still came. It's not the same, he said. It's shite.

It struck me then that this really was the last time I'd go to the Haç. It had continued to change and so had I.

* * *

I never returned to the Crescents at Hulme either, despite Kip offering to accompany me. Ultimately, only twenty-five years after being built, they would be razed to the ground. Hulme was to be rebuilt in red-brick terraces once more.

* * *

I thought of the Haçienda occasionally and sometimes wistfully in the years to come, but those days were gone for me. Despite the Haç putting out a plea not to buy or take drugs in the club –

and introducing a dress code of no trainers or shell suits in an attempt to keep the gangs out – by 1991 the violence had become so bad that the club closed for five months, reopening with a metal detector installed. Over the next few years, the original and unique camaraderie, the loved-up pioneering spirit, the ethos and concept of the club, was quashed under the weight of real violence, and the gangs pretty much controlled everything by then. In the end, it was finances which finished the club. It never made money – instead it haemorrhaged it – and, on 28th June 1997, the Haçienda finally closed its doors.

Tony Wilson said it was necessary for any period to build its cathedrals, for any youth culture to have a sense of place, for a city like Manchester to have the facilities that New York and Paris have.

He did that for us. He did that for us.

* * *

I saw Josh just the once. I bumped into him during one of my increasingly rare visits back to Parkwin. He was with a girl and I think they'd been having an argument. We said hello. We remarked how it had been ages. How are things? Good – you? Good, good. Better be going. Me too. Well – see you! Yep – take care! We held eye contact only for a split second and then we turned away from each other and went off in opposite directions.

* * *

And I never saw Patrick again. In fact, with Kip's help, I had successfully trained myself to rarely think about him.

Until. Until. Until.

1 p.m. 15th June 1999, the motorway

'We're not going to be late, are we?'

'We should be fine,' Kip says.

It's so hard not to look at the speedometer – he hates it when I do that. Usually I huff at him to slow down, stop driving like an idiot, *Christ!* Sometimes I might say *like a bloody idiot* – but today I want him to go faster. Before we left we said we'd take it slowly. However, we really cannot be late. Kip's mum sometimes says he'd be late to his own funeral. We absolutely cannot be late to this one.

'Do you think we'll make it back later tonight?'

'Eadie – how many times are you going to ask me that?' Kip says and he's exasperated.

'Well, either later tonight, or first thing tomorrow,' I say convivially, as if for the first time. However annoying it must be for my husband, for me there's been a strange comfort in such repetition.

'We'll play it by ear,' Kip says – the same thing he's told me a number of times already. 'Let's see how things go.'

'See who turns up,' I say, unsure.

'If they come, they come,' he says.

'I hope they do,' I murmur. And then I say *God!* I say God, this is *weird*.

So weird, Kip says. At least we agree on this.

In my bag I rootle around for a packet of Starburst and it takes me back to Kip and his blue Mini a decade ago when they were called Opal Fruits and the sweets themselves were surely bigger. I could cry about that right now. I'm hyper-emotional about everything today.

'Opal Fruit?'

'Red one, please – you can keep the greens.'

For the time being, we're relaxed, we're friends again. This is how it's been recently – navigating the fragility that's between us; treading on eggshells one minute, hurling unkindness or impatience the next while just sometimes, short shy moments of connection resurface. It's been exhausting. We've been too tired to deconstruct, analyse, resolve. It's as if neither of us has been grown-up enough to do that and yet I've turned thirty and Kip is now thirty-four. And to think when I was little I defined old age as starting at thirty; then in my twenties I believed that once I turned thirty I'd feel like an adult and that life would seem clear. These days, I'm not so sure.

'They never used to be so fiddly,' Kip says, giving up on unwrapping the sweet.

I peel off the paper for him and I pop the sweet into his mouth. His lips touch my fingers. He glances at me and I at him. We suck and chew companionably for a while.

'How are we doing for time?' I ask again.

'We're *fine*, Eadie.'

I don't think the symbolism occurs to him. *Are* we fine – will *we* be OK? And I whisper, 'Everything will be fine.' Keep driving. Keep driving. Oh my goodness – what a day this is going to be. 'I *am* nervous actually,' I tell my husband. 'I'm nervous about everything.'

After a while he clears his throat and glances away from the road, to me. 'Not an easy day,' he says. 'I'm not surprised.'

'I guess that's what funerals are all about,' I say. 'Laying something to rest, picking up some of the pieces, burying the remainder; moving on with life.'

'You OK in the back, Patrick?' Kip calls over his shoulder.

Instinctively, I turn around but the back of the van is blocked off from the cab. I look at my husband and note the creeping redness to his ears, over his cheeks and across his neck. This happens when he's anxious or angry or sad; when he's emotional. He doesn't know it, but I do.

'He's OK,' I assure him.

Patrick Semple in the back of the van; in a coffin we've paid for, heading to his funeral that's cost us the deposit on a house, to be buried at the cemetery next door to 41 Yew Lane.

Part III

Three months ago, it was just a regular Thursday in March and I had no expectations of the day, beyond hoping that it would pass quickly so it could be Friday and the gateway to the weekend. Kip and I headed in to work. Really, we were heading out to work because from our flat in Didsbury you were either heading *in* to town or *out* from Manchester, and KATmedia was based in a business park on the outskirts of Wilmslow ten miles away. Kip Alexander Turner – director of his very own company. Kipkat, I liked to call him. He'd done it.

A decade earlier, when I'd dripped over the interior of his blue Mini after appropriating his dead grandmother for my own, Kip had told me that one day he hoped to run his own business to assist young arts-based companies in the North-West find their audience. I didn't really take much notice, I was too busy being a reluctant undergraduate and his ambition sounded so grown-up, so beyond any aspirations I had. At that stage, I didn't even know if I wanted to carry on with my studies, let alone be in that car with a complete stranger; I was far more preoccupied with my throbbing knee that day, my sore feet and mortification in general. But within weeks, love came and walloped the inertia right out of me, presenting me instead with a new version of myself to try on, one which I found to be a very good fit for most of my twenties. And so it was, in our first little flat in Salford, that I discovered a gear I never knew I had for studying which was as unexpected for my tutors as it was for me. All the while, Kip dreamed big and grafted hard and KATmedia was born.

Meanwhile, after graduating, I'd worked all the hours to pay off my student overdraft and fund a part-time master's degree. I'd been a sales assistant at Kendals in homewares, I'd done a Sight-and-Sound typing course and temped as a secretary, I'd waitressed everywhere from Withington to Parrs Wood until I had a bound thesis on the shelves of the history department at Manchester University on *Class Discord and Land Appropriation: The Commercialization of Agriculture in the Late Tudor Period* but no idea what I could do with it. What I did know was that I wanted to work in the present and not the past, but that selling crockery or taking dictation or being covered in other people's food for paltry tips had lost its allure. Anyway, there were no jobs in Greater Manchester for a specialist in Tudor socio-economic history so Kip asked if I might help him in the short term. Almost five years later here I was, still the temporary office manager at KATmedia.

Gratitude and boredom create a dissonance impossible to umpire but I'd kept my soul-sapped exasperation hidden from Kip. I struggled alone with the sensation of my squandered brain shrinking behind my skull, the panic of careening towards thirty still not knowing what I wanted to do, yet also feeling I was in the wrong place. I didn't know how to leave, or if I'd ever be able to. How could I ever resign when I owed everything to the best boss in the world? Who was I to consider a change in career when Kip was in love with his office manager? I called myself an ungrateful cow yet still I hid in our bathroom to scan the careers section in the *Guardian*. It felt like the ultimate act of betrayal, and to linger on an ad and imagine myself in a new role seemed nothing short of adulterous. The temptation of something different, something new; they weren't even dream jobs.

So, three months ago on that nondescript Thursday in March, I had made five copies of KAT's twenty-four-page proposal for a new client and spiral-bound them. There was little else to do all day beyond a stationery order which entailed flipping through a catalogue the size of seventeen telephone directories and assessing the merits of one brand of highlighter pen over another. By eleven o'clock everything was done and there I sat, listening to drifts of Kip on the phone being gregarious and energized. There used to be a time I'd feed off this, now it made me feel withdrawn and deflated. I rested my forehead on the stationery catalogue and stared at the faux woodgrain of the desk, my mind trudging on empty while Time all but ground to a halt.

Then, at midday, Paintz&Snax came in for their meeting and I swooped on the *Manchester Evening News* one of them left on the sofa in the waiting area. It was yesterday's edition, but old news was riveting enough for me, even the classifieds and the sports pages and the crossword that had already been done. I liked the paper. I felt like I knew the people in the stories within its pages; we passed by each other on the street, queued together for fish and chips, they served me at the pub, they sat by me in the cinema, they chatted to me about the weather, we bemoaned the bloody buses together. I felt on the periphery these days languishing at my desk in an office on an undersubscribed business park outside the city. The newspaper reconnected me with Manchester and I pored over its pages.

Man Caught. Someone had been stealing kids' bikes from the shed at their school and four lads from the fifth year had given chase. Look at them! Their young chests puffed up behind their school blazers, standing proud alongside their headmaster and someone important from the police.

Dog Found! A welcome exclamation mark amidst all the conflict and bike thievery going on. I gazed for a long while at the photo of Muffy and her elderly owner, reunited at last.

Man Identified. There wasn't a photograph so I skipped over that story. Anyway, Kip had stuck his head around the door and asked if there was any chance of coffee. He mimed a plunging action to signify that Paint&Snax deserved the cafetière, not instant granules. So I made the coffee, arranged digestive biscuits into a flower pattern and finally, with the dregs and the crumbs for myself, I sat at my desk again and returned to the newspaper, still open at the same page.

> **Man Identified**
>
> The man found dead at a bus stop in Moss Side on 5th March has been identified as Patrick Semple. The 30-year-old, of no fixed abode, died of natural causes, the Coroner found.

I read it again. I read it again. I read it again and again and again.

'It might not be him.'

'It is,' I told Kip. 'I know it – I *feel* it.'

I'd boycotted Kip's afternoon with all of this and now we were home and I could still think and talk of little else.

'Poor sod if it is,' Kip said.

I had the paper spread out on our table, as if we'd invited Patrick to join us for our tea.

'I don't know what to do,' I said.

Kip shrugged and scooped at his noodles. 'There's not a lot you can do – he's dead.'

I couldn't sleep that night and I was a useless office manager the next day and, over the weekend, I wasn't much company when we went walking in the Peak District. I strode next to Kip but I might as well have been at that bus stop in Moss Side. Questions surged and I asked them out loud, but Kip could only say I don't know. I don't know, Eadie – *I don't know.*

Which bus stop?
    How did he die?
        Had he been ill?
            Was it sudden?
                What were the natural causes?
            What time of day?
        Who found him?
    What does no fixed abode actually mean?

And—
—where is he now?
I don't know, Eadie.
—but, what will happen next?
Eadie – I don't *know*.

'Do you think there will be a funeral?'

It was 4 a.m. and I woke Kip up to ask him this.

'Of course there'll be a funeral,' he mumbled. 'Everyone gets a funeral.'

'Do you think I should go?'

I nudged him awake again. 'Should I go?'

'Do you *want* to go?' Kip turned towards me, fumbled for my face in the dark. 'Why would you want to go?' he said. 'After everything?'

There was nothing I hadn't told my husband and he remembered everything.

'Eadie,' Kip said and he patted me sleepily. 'You're breathing funny. Slow down.' He pulled me into his arms and stroked my hair awhile until his hand stilled with sleep. My mind continued to whirr, thoughts and questions colliding in the dark.

What happened to Patrick? What *happened* to him? Dead at thirty. That was my age. Of course it was – we were at school together. I knew him when he was six years old. A man, dead in a bus stop and unidentified for almost a month, had once been a six-year-old boy.

'God only knows what they'll write on his headstone,' I said. I woke Kip again and repeated it.

'You don't believe in God,' he mumbled but I was already wondering who the 'they' could be. Did a *they* even exist for Patrick? When you are of no fixed abode, who looks out for you? Who do you have in your life to look after you in death? Who buys your headstone and chooses what to have engraved on it? Where would Patrick Semple be laid to rest and who would be there to see him on his way?

It was these thoughts that haunted me most just then, disturbed me enough to know that I had to do something. I had to find someone, somewhere, to ask what had happened and what would happen next. Over all these years, whilst Patrick's life had unravelled and then ended, I'd rarely given him a single thought.

I knew there were no meetings at KATmedia that Monday and, however nonplussed he was, Kip agreed to me taking the day off. He reminded me that in the evening we were going over to see the house we were buying and taking our tape measure.

'I only need a couple of hours,' I told him. 'I'll probably be back in the office by lunchtime.'

The *Manchester Evening News* was still on our table, open at Patrick's page. It was like he was staying with us and a silent bone of contention between Kip and me. He was an unwelcome house guest in my husband's eyes, while I was insisting he stayed until I knew where he'd be going next.

I went to the Southern Cemetery hoping to find future funerals listed somewhere, but only those being held that day were on the board. Over by the East Chapel, a caretaker was putting new black bags into the bins. I went over to him, hoping he might be someone like Michael.

'Excuse me – but if someone has died, how do I find out where they're going to be?'

'Go to the office,' he said. 'They'll show you on the map.'

'But he doesn't have a grave,' I said. 'He's only just died. I don't know if he's coming here – or somewhere else. Or when. That's what I'm trying to find out.'

I made as little sense to this man as Patrick's death did to me. He shrugged and gave a half-smile and his whiskers climbed down into his wrinkles. He made to leave and I called Wait!

'If someone has recently died,' I said, 'how do I find them?'

'I'm just the gardener, love,' he said, walking away with his roll of black bags. 'Ask the family.'

There is no family. There is no one. The enormity of this struck me.

'It was in the paper,' I said. 'No fixed abode – found at a bus stop.'

'That's dead grim,' he said. 'Sorry, love.'

I paid a very quick visit to Iris and Sid and then to Macey Darling, just long enough to have a tidy and to apologize that we hadn't been to see her in a while. She had nothing to say, really. I imagined she might feel that her grandson was a saint for putting up with me.

There was a monumental mason's opposite the cemetery but they said it would be too soon for anyone to be thinking about headstones and there were no orders for a Patrick Semple anyway. They suggested I call the newspaper, that possibly I'd find out more information that way. I kicked myself, just then, for not having a mobile phone. Kip had offered to buy me one for my birthday but I'd said I'd have no use for it. I'm always with you, Kip, I'd said. You can just call my name instead of a number.

So I walked to a payphone and riffled through the phone directory for the *Manchester Evening News*. The number was engaged engaged engaged and when I was finally connected I was put on hold by which time my coins ran out. I considered phoning again, reverse charges, but the phone box stank of piss. I might as well just walk home and use the phone in the flat. And it was on the way there that I passed somewhere I'd never noticed before. I'd had no cause to. Doig & Daughters, Funeral Directors.

Inside, it was like I'd stepped into someone's neat front room. It was quiet, very quiet and delicately fragrant. There was a floral display and I wondered if it was left over from a funeral. Michael sometimes took cuttings from the roses in wreaths, he'd potted one up for my parents one Christmas and it had thrived. I took a seat and waited because that's what the little notice told me to do. Other than the flowers, there wasn't really anything to look at, just two pictures of gentle landscapes and a leaflet I didn't want to read. The room, though, was conducive just to sitting quietly. More places should be like this, I thought to myself. People need somewhere to sit and just be.

'Hello.'

She was a little woman and I knew Kip would describe her as cuddlesome which is how he referred to his mum; warmly stout and welcomingly bosomy.

'Hello,' I said.

'Are you here to visit?'

'Visit?' I said and suddenly I felt overwhelmed. I'd grown up next to a cemetery, conversed in depth at gravesides and yet here, right now, in the Doig's building, the newly dead lay between homes and just inches away from me.

'I'm Shirley,' she said and her eyes looked Walt Disney huge and kind behind her glasses.

'I'm Eadie,' I said, 'and I don't know where to begin.'

'And was Patrick a friend of yours?'

I thought how she must be thinking to herself some friend I am if he was of no fixed abode and died in a bus stop.

'No,' I shook my head. 'The truth is, I've hardly given him a moment's thought for years and years.'

She nodded as if she heard this a lot.

'In fact,' I said, 'he was sort of my enemy.'

Shirley was a good listener. I imagined she had to be, in her line of work.

'Well, I'm terribly sorry but he's not here,' she apologized gently, once the whole story had come out. All along I'd known he wouldn't be, yet still I felt deflated. She had her hand gently on my wrist. 'But if you want to find him, I'm sure I can help you. He'll still be at the hospital that the Coroner oversees,' she told me. 'You could go and see him.'

'Patrick?' I baulked. I most certainly did not want to see him dead.

'Not Patrick,' Shirley said. His name. His name kept filling the room. 'The Coroner.'

When someone dies in the way Patrick died, they remain under the Coroner while next of kin, relatives, friends are sought – someone, anyone to claim them. That's what I learned from Shirley that morning.

So I took the bus into the city centre and walked to the Town Hall where the Coroner's office was based. I'd always loved the building, the exterior was like a condensed version of the Houses of Parliament with its own Big Ben at the centre while the interior chorused Gothic splendour which knew no bounds; arches and vaulting and pillars, painted ceilings and statues and busts, gilt and mosaics and coloured tiles, and vast stone staircases offering to sweep one into a fairy tale. That's why I was expecting the Coroner to look like a Dickensian judge, in a voluminous robe and a long wig with a sage, kindly face not unlike Professor Blackmore and Mr Swift. But it was a woman in a light grey suit with a pink silk shirt who led me into a room which had dozens of chairs stacked in towers along the walls. We each wrestled one down and sat at a long table where I tumbled out my reason for being there.

When someone dies in the way Patrick died, every effort is made to find family, next of kin. All leads are followed from various sources. And if no one can be found, then a Public Health Funeral will be held for them. And no one, so far, had been found for Patrick, no one had come forward. That's what I learned from the Coroner's office that afternoon.

'When will the funeral be?' I asked because I wanted to think about Patrick that day, regardless of what I actually thought of him.

'*Are* you family?' she asked.

'No,' I said.

'Friend, then?'

'No,' I said cautiously. 'I read it in the paper. He was someone I once knew a very long time ago.'

'It may not be him then,' she said somewhat wearily. 'There will be more than one Patrick Semple, you know.'

I knew that. But I also knew in my gut that this was my Patrick. We sat there quietly while I flummoxed over ways to say that I felt certain it was him. A flashback to that night ten years ago. The back of a van between the Haçienda and the Rochdale canal. So clear it sent a sharp shiver through me. E-deh.

Why *was* I here? Why did any of this matter? Patrick dead dead sorry. Patrick dead.

'Did he have a tattoo?' I asked. 'Of three magnets?'

She consulted her papers and gave me a gentle and well-practised smile of sympathy.

It really was him. He really was completely dead and gone. I wanted to cry, I didn't know why.

'What is going to happen?'

'Next, the council will take control if no one can be found,' she said. 'They will hold just a very basic cremation, usually first or last thing.'

'How can I find out when that might be?'

'Well, the details are at the discretion of the council,' she said. She glanced at her watch and her lip twitched as if assessing how much more she needed to say. 'I have to tell you, up and down the country – this happens *all* the time,' she said as if it was burdensome. 'Costs the local authorities hundreds of thousands – millions – each year.'

'Will *anyone* be there?'

'Sometimes,' she said with a shrug.

'Only sometimes?' I said quietly.

'They used to call it a Pauper's Funeral,' she told me. 'Nowadays they're known as Public Health Funerals. Someone officiates. Occasionally someone from the council might attend.'

I didn't know what else to ask her because I had answers now. 'It's very sad,' I said.

'It is indeed, love,' she said. 'Bless him.'

That evening, when Kip and I went over to the house we were hoping to buy, I held one end of the tape measure while he ran it along the rooms and wrote down numbers with a pencil he kept tucked behind his ear. He paced out the dimensions of our sofa and our table, jubilant that they'd fit wherever we wanted them. He surreptitiously lifted the edge of the carpet in the living room and gave me a beaming thumbs-up at the floorboards beneath. And upstairs, in the prettiest of the bedrooms, the little one overlooking the garden, he drew me close and kissed me softly on the forehead. I wasn't sure whether it was in sadness for the two miscarriages we'd had or in excitement for the nursery this room might become. God, I love this place, he said. It was indeed our dream home.

Kip sweet-talked the vendors into leaving the curtains and agreed cash for the washing machine. He patiently listened and nodded and jotted down more notes while the couple showed us around the garden and told us about each shrub like they were family members reluctantly being left. I followed behind and any time anyone looked at me I smiled but I could tell Kip was acutely aware that I wasn't fully present. Much as I tried, my vocabulary seemed only to stretch to 'lovely' and 'yes'.

'Did you see the fireplace!'

'Yes.'

'And the shed at the back of the garden – it's so much bigger than I remember. We could actually convert it into a summer house.'

'Lovely,' I said but I wasn't listening, I wasn't looking where I was going. Kip steered me away from walking off the kerb and into the road.

'You could try and be a bit more enthusiastic,' he said. 'We've waited a long time for this.'

'I know – I'm sorry, I'm just tired.'

Actually, I was biting down on questioning the expense, the risk, whether we needed four bedrooms. All our eggs in one basket. Feathering a nest I privately feared might be destined to remain empty. I wanted to veer away from talking about babies because I didn't want to tempt fate, jinx things, with my mind being very much on death at the moment. So we walked home in silence. Sometimes, when Kip and I walked together, whether out in the Peaks or around town, we fell into easy step and convivial silence. Not tonight; our paces didn't match and the wordlessness between us was fog thick.

Kip rarely swore but he swore the next morning. I'd tossed and fretted, keeping us both awake most of the night, exclaiming 'but—' at regular intervals as I veered away from sleep into culs-de-sac of unanswerable questions. Now I was telling him that I couldn't come to work.

'Jesus,' he said. 'Some skanky kid who made your life hell winds up dead. There *is* no story, Eadie.'

'It's just—'

'It's just – *nothing*,' Kip said. 'He led a shit life and had a shit death. It's grim. Let it go. You've *got* the ending. In fact, you had it ten years ago – why are you exhuming all of this?'

I couldn't move for too many half-thoughts that were weighing me down, I couldn't speak because I didn't know how to respond because a small and sorry part of me understood exactly what Kip was saying. He was right – yet neither did I believe I was wholly wrong. I stood in our kitchen and stared at the tiles. It felt like I was being told off.

'You do not need his death in your life, Eadie.'

My life, though, was full of Patrick's death.

'Are you coming?' Kip asked, his voice flat. 'To work?'

I shook my head. Without a kiss, without looking at me, he left.

Taking my seat in Doig & Daughters as I had the day before, I noted that the flowers were different. Perhaps they changed them on Tuesdays. I waited only a short while before Shirley appeared. If she was surprised to see me, she didn't show it and she came to sit beside me.

'They haven't found anyone for him,' I explained. 'No one's come forward.'

'Poor soul. So it'll be the local authority that takes him then,' she said. 'Ten minutes, all done.' She wiped her hands, as if that's what the council would be doing with Patrick.

I looked at my lap and my forehead felt very heavy. 'They used to call it a Pauper's Funeral.'

'They did indeed,' Shirley said. 'Funny word: *poor*. The truest meaning goes way beyond money, really.'

'Do you know how I can find out when and where?'

Shirley made to talk, thought better of it momentarily before continuing. 'I knew a lad who worked at the council – p'raps he still does. But I have to warn you – I remember him saying if people want to come along to a Public Health Funeral, bloody well let them pay for it. His very words.'

The absurdity of it made me laugh. 'I can't pay for Patrick's funeral!'

Kip and I had scraped and saved and everything we had was either tied up in KATmedia or destined for the house we were buying. Our whole purpose, these last few years, was to invest in our future – as a couple, as a family.

'Love, I think you'd be best off having a few quiet thoughts about the poor lad – saying your goodbyes that way,' Shirley said instead. 'Go somewhere special to you. Or significant to him. Send your thoughts out from there.'

The door opened. Three people came in clasping each other and looking ashen. Suddenly it struck me how I had no real business being there. None of it was any of my business, really. As I left, I gave the family who had arrived one of those gentle smiles Terry had taught me when I was little.

People die all the time. The bodies simply stop and the souls disappear. In and out of life they go, every single day. Leaving us behind to stumble along until we can walk steadily ahead without them there, though they remain with us still.

I took the bus back to the Town Hall and I asked for the lady who'd seen me the day before. And I said to her this – I said, if I leave my name and number could she please just keep in touch with me. Because, you know, maybe someone who knew Patrick *will* show up. And if she could then pass my number to them, I'd be grateful, I said. I wrote down my name, address and phone number, but by the way she took the paper from me I suspected my details would soon be as forgotten as Patrick himself.

I walked back down the swooping stone staircase and away from this strange world, out into the daylight and back into my life. In Albert Square, I looked up at the clock tower of the Town Hall. I stood for a while and read the inscription, carved across the stonework above the faces of the mighty clock:

TEACH US TO NUMBER OUR DAYS

WHAT WOULD BRUCE DO?

I hadn't a clue. I didn't really know all that much about Bruce Springsteen. But here, in the corner shop near the station a good mile's walk from the KATmedia office, was a framed picture of The Boss with this question printed onto it in the font used in old Westerns. What would Bruce do about *what*?

The shopkeeper cleared his throat, he was waiting for my money. I paid for a packet of Nice biscuits. They were Kip's favourite and my olive branch. He wasn't expecting me in at work, I'd made the effort and a protracted journey to get there for the remainder of the afternoon. I nodded towards the picture.

'Bruce,' I said.

'Ah!' The shopkeeper was delighted. 'He always has the answer for me too.'

I didn't think of Bruce Springsteen as I walked to the KATmedia office in the business park, but I did think of Celeste and I did think of Josh and I wondered – what would *they* do? I couldn't really answer on their behalf because I had no idea how their minds now worked at the age of thirty. I hadn't spoken to Celeste in so long. We used to write regularly, now it was sporadic and I wasn't sure whose turn it was. As for Josh – he and I had simply disappeared from each other's lives; now he was but a memory bleached of colour like an old photograph. I knew him once. My enduring memory all these years later was how I had loved him.

As I walked to work, it was to their younger selves that I posed the question. What *would* you do? Young Celeste said a defiant RIP, Little Sheet. Josh though, as he had been then, sighed at me kindly and said just let him go EadieBeads – just move on now.

Josh. I smiled sadly as I walked. Actually – bloody Josh, really.

What would Reuben do? I wondered. Oh, he'd combine philosophy, anecdote, examples and a treatise. And how about Terry and how about my mum? How might they counsel when they possessed such limited knowledge of my life, right from when I was young? How ably could they advise, with their scant involvement in the world beyond the threshold of 41 Yew Lane? It wasn't a question I'd even think to ask them, but I realized now that this was OK – I'd achieved a workable harmony with my parents over the years. I must call them, I must remember to do so. It had been a couple of weeks and that was on me.

As I turned into the enclave where KATmedia was based I asked myself, what would Mr Swift do? His voice was still so distinct and I was halfway through his words of wisdom and sensitivity when I arrived at the office. Kip had his back to me, photocopying, doing my job, a resigned slouch to his shoulders. He hated that machine and it seemed to hate him right back.

'I can do that,' I said as the door closed behind me with its little sigh.

'You're here?'

I nodded and pulled the biscuits from my bag.

'Nice,' he said.

'*Nice*,' I said, pronouncing it like the French city.

We'd had this same exchange over these biscuits so often during our years together. Just then, though, something about this made us simply stop and there we stood while we looked at each other; Eadie to Kip to Eadie. It struck me hard how I really hadn't looked at him deeply for a while, how I myself had felt unseen. Just then, though, our eyes suddenly adjusted focus and I felt it once more, flowing through the blood, stilling the mind, energizing the heart, spinning desire.

Kip crossed reception and cupped my face in his hands and he kissed me and as he did my head quietened and my body swam into his embrace. The tingle and surge. I kissed him back, I really kissed my husband back. My arms thrown around his neck, the biscuits gone I don't know where. His hands wresting my top up, fingers at the waistband of my skirt making my skin twitch, my body vibrate at his touch. I grasped the backs of his thighs and pulled him against me, aware of his hunger, his quickened breathing, his cock ridging behind his trousers. He grabbed my upper arm tightly, almost too tightly, and pulled me into the small meeting room next to his office, banging me up against the wall, slamming the door closed with his foot, his tongue in my mouth while he pressed against me. I faffed with the zip of his jeans and he yanked up my skirt; his gravelled exhale as his fingers found me, the sound of my gasp, the urgency with which he pulled my knickers to one side and bucked up into me fast and deep. The room started to reel as we fucked the life back into each other. The room with the flipchart and the round table, the beanbags in the corner, the small fridge with Coke and beer, the vast whiteboard and pens in a thousand different colours, the TV screen and the hi-fi and the posters of logos and clients framing his hard-won success. We don't call it a meeting room. Kip calls it the Thinking Ship.

There wasn't much for me to do that afternoon so I sat in the office, eating the broken biscuits and gazing out at the car park, feeling pensive and peaceful in the post-coital calm. On that day, like persistent sunlight winning through thick winter haze, a steady happiness I hadn't felt in a while filtered through the boredom. I looked down at the biscuit in my hand, it was broken but only at one edge. I stared at that biscuit for quite some time. *Nice*. There's a lesson to be learned right there, I realized.

Over the last few months, Kip and I – we hadn't been nice. I wasn't sure why and I didn't think he knew either. We'd been snappish, sometimes distant or distracted. Often, if one of us was talking then the other didn't really listen. We'd become quick to bicker and slow to make up. We accused each other of trivial things which we'd allowed to assume ridiculous significance. I was impatient with him and I irritated him. It was his fault that I was unhappy at my stupid job. It was my fault that I didn't mirror his energy and drive at work. What had started as a sporadic disconnect had become habit, tightening around us like a lack of oxygen, blocking out the view. But I loved him. Sometimes I'd forgotten the words for it, sometimes my limbs felt too heavy to show it. We were tired, we hadn't been having sex so often over the last year or so. But I loved him. Sometimes, though, we went to sleep without even saying goodnight.

And then there were the miscarriages. We lost our first at nine weeks, our second a few days before our twelve-week scan. Neither pregnancy had been planned, just very happy accidents.

My doctor had said not to worry; that some women wouldn't even have known they were pregnant. That didn't help. Kip had said not to worry too; at least we knew we could get pregnant. But that didn't help either. Just not the right time, he said. Yeah, there's no rush, I said. But privately, in terrible dark silence, I suspect we occasionally levied fault at each other for the miscarriages. Perhaps that's why we weren't discussing it in the clear light of day, why we weren't making appointments with doctors. After our initial togetherness over the loss, we'd then tiptoed around the subject until it just became easier to avoid talking about it at all.

I looked at the biscuit and I propped it against my pen pot instead of eating it. Kip and I, we'd overlooked simply being *nice*. I thought, we've been careless with each other's feelings. And I thought, we mustn't do that. We must talk more, be open, lay ourselves bare and share without fear of judgement. We need to look, to *see* each other again – marvel at the sight of the soulmate with whom we'd chosen to hike through life. We need to shout out our battle cry – that it's us against the world. We must take each other's hands and run with joy back to our still point of the turning world, smug that ours is better and truer than the still points that other couples think they have. I thought, we should make love, have sex, shag, fuck, more often. And I thought, we're really good at all of it – we always had been.

I loved him.

And then I thought how sometimes, he might have wondered whether I actually did.

I don't know why, then, when I was lying awake late late that night while Kip slept soundly after we'd made love, I don't know why I didn't wake him, why I didn't workshop my thoughts with him or ask him directly. Instead, I lay in the darkness and I thought back over my day. I remembered the stony fragrance of the Town Hall and the sugar crystals on the biscuit, I recalled the light slicing around the half-empty car park at work and the sound of the KATmedia photocopier, the smell of it. I thought about the shrine to Bruce Springsteen in the corner shop and I wondered – what *would* Bruce do?

And then I thought what would Kip do?

Now there's a question.

What *would* Kip do?

And I should have asked him but I didn't.

So what would Kip do? I knew what he'd do. He would go to the Town Hall. He would find that woman in the Coroner's Office and he would go into the room with the chairs all stacked up and he'd sit there at one end of the long and empty table and he'd say to her, he'd say to her this:

'I will take responsibility for Patrick Semple.'

That is what Kip Alexander Turner would do.

He would do so because he'd know how it was highly unlikely that anyone else would be turning up to claim Patrick Semple. He would do so because he'd believe it was the right thing to do – because Kip is a truly decent person with a deep conscience and a profoundly big heart.

That's what Kip would do.

So I don't know why I didn't just wake him and ask him.

And what would Eadie do?

She wouldn't talk to her husband about any of it. She'd go back to the Town Hall without telling him. And, once she'd been, she still wouldn't say a word. That's what Eadie would do.

That is what I did.

I went ahead and did what Kip would do. Only Kip, first, would have researched and assessed all that this would entail. He'd have talked to me every step of the way. I, though, didn't give any of that a second thought. I didn't say a word to him beforehand or after. And this time, the dotted line didn't dance before my eyes. The dotted line on all the forms stayed perfectly still and I signed my name, I signed away.

'Robert who?' I mouthed at Kip who was on the telephone. I thought the call had been for him. He'd been on the phone some time, saying 'hmmm' and 'could you repeat that', at regular intervals.

'Robert Dilys,' Kip chirped, as if I'd completely forgotten that the man was our close friend though I knew neither of us knew a Robert Dilys.

'From the hospital – *Mortuary Admin Team.*' Kip stared at me levelly while he laughed and it was a strange laugh because it was underscored with fury not joy. 'He wants to know if you've made the arrangements yet. He wants to know when the Deceased will be taken into our care.'

And then, oh how Kip's eyes, dark with disappointment, unblinking with accusation, blank with disbelief, bore into mine.

'You know,' said Kip, cupping his hand over the receiver theatrically, '*the body.*'

The body – as if Patrick had been a car in for repair and everything was now sorted.

Kip continued to listen to Robert Dilys from the bereavement department at the hospital, then he called over to me, 'Have you picked up the death certificate yet?' like it was next door's post. And then, 'Who's the chosen undertaker, darling?' Kip looked right through me and returned to his conversation with Mr Dilys. 'Ah – I see. Yes, indeed. One moment, please.' He didn't attempt to cover the mouthpiece this time. 'I'm under the impression we're taking up space in the mortuary. Robert really would appreciate a date.' Kip might as well have been asking me when we were free to have a curry with friends. 'Robert, let me put my wife on the phone,' Kip said, not taking his eyes off me. 'She's handling this.'

But I had no answers for Robert Dilys and he obviously found me tiresome – as if I'd bought a huge item on a whim some weeks before and he was stuck with it until I'd figured out whether it would fit through the door. I wished Kip wasn't standing so close, hearing both sides. I wished he wasn't here at all. Why did it have to be Kip who'd answered the phone? I wished it could all just stop and then start again, with everything magically changed.

Why hadn't I just told him? The gravity of the situation sucker-punched me. Patrick Semple was mine now. Not just physically mine, Patrick was now fundamentally in my marriage, standing between me and my husband and I didn't know what to do with him. I had grown up in a place where funerals were a daily occurrence and yet I had no idea how they were actually organized. I suppose I had been expecting someone to inform me when it was to be held, which graveside to turn up at – that I'd be back at my desk by lunchtime and that no one need know. How ridiculously naive. I was appalled at myself – and I wasn't the only one.

I replaced the handset very slowly, as if Kip might not see, but behind my back I could feel the disbelief flooding out of him. I tipped my head to one side and stared straight ahead, as if midway through a profound thought whilst actually I was scurrying around for a single sentence to make any sense to him, even to me. My gaze alighted on my degree certificates. I hadn't wanted to hang them on the wall but Kip had insisted and he had bought incongruously huge and lavish frames for them and I liked the dichotomy of achievement and kitsch. All Patrick had to show for his life was a death certificate and even then I'd overlooked collecting it on his behalf. Slowly, I turned. Kip was regarding me like he knew me and didn't know me, as if he did not want to be in the same room as me, as if I had no business being here. His arms were crossed, redness crept up his neck and a muscle twitched in his cheek.

'The last time I saw Patrick—' I said.

'—he manhandled you into the back of a van owned by his gangster mates,' Kip reminded me. 'Ten *years* ago.'

'He said he did it to keep me out of the way – because he knew things would be kicking off.' I looked down, willing sentences to write themselves onto the floor for me to read out; instead I could only stare gormlessly at my feet and Kip's, at our patterned socks clashing with the rug we'd reluctantly agreed would look out of place in our new home. Perhaps Kip would soon say the same about me.

'They told me he'd be given a—' and I went blank as I scurried through my mind for the phrase both Shirley Doig and the Coroner's Office had used. It was a familiar term, dull and legal-sounding. Without me, Patrick would belong to the council and be all but dumped. What was the *phrase*, though?

'He'd just get a ten-minute state funeral,' I mumbled.

'*A state funeral?*' Kip exclaimed, exasperated.

No – not state. In any other context, in any other situation, we would have laughed ourselves silly at such a blunder.

'A Pauper's Funeral,' I rushed. 'I can't remember the correct term for it these days.'

'So you go and decide you'll take him off the authority's hands?'

I nodded.

'This person who only *ever* made your life hell? What *is* all this?'

I could hear how it didn't really make much sense. It was deafeningly absurd.

'Fucksake,' Kip said hoarsely.

'I was going to tell you—'

'—but you *didn't*.' His hurt and bewilderment made me flinch. I wished he'd just be furious with me.

'Do you know how much this is going to cost?'

I didn't know the answer to that. I hadn't even thought about it.

'Because last year, when Uncle Huw died – I gave my mum two grand towards the funeral.' Kip turned away from me. He sat down wearily, facing all the forms for buying our house which lay in complex piles on our kitchen table.

'Kip—'

'Why couldn't you just *talk* to me?' He didn't look up. 'Jesus, Eadie.'

My voice, when it finally came, sounded as hollow as his. 'I don't know,' I said. 'It's too confusing, all of it – I didn't think.'

'I'll say,' he muttered.

'I can't explain. It's as if this is between just Patrick and me. All along. It's been about me and him.'

We fell silent.

'No,' he said. 'You're wrong, Eadie. It's about you and *me*.'

And there it was, out in the open.

Kip placed his hands on the forms and the documents. It was as if he was suddenly enlightened.

'We're buying a house while we're growing apart.'

The statement staved itself into the room like an estate agent's board.

'Even before all this Patrick stuff – we've been growing apart, Eadie.' Now he looked at me. 'What happened? Where did we go?' Kip paused, trying to find his voice. 'We've gone.' There were tears in his eyes and he shrugged at me, helpless. 'Eadie?'

I did not have an answer for him.

'Why aren't we talking about this?' he said.

'Not *state*,' I said. 'Not *Pauper*. Public! Public Health Funeral – that's what they're called now.'

'Why won't you *listen*?' Kip yelled, standing up, the chair falling. I'd never even heard him so much as raise his voice and this was very different. 'I don't *care* about public state funerals. And I don't care about the person who hated you.' He stared at me as if I'd just come into focus, as if he'd woken up to find a complete stranger had trespassed into his home and was running roughshod through his life. 'I was talking about *us*.' He paced a short tight circle, his hands pulling at his hair. 'Or perhaps there is no Us.'

I couldn't sleep. For two days, we'd hardly spoken; we'd driven to the office with the radio jabbering over our silence and at work we'd functioned perfunctorily as office manager and boss.

In the evenings, we'd eaten ready meals; Kip in front of the TV with the volume up, me at the table where the house particulars still lay. Kip had gone to bed early, apparently not hearing me say goodnight. He'd gone to bed without saying goodnight himself, shutting me out of our bedroom. I'd slept on the sofa and beyond being raggedly tired, I was hollow and lonely and so desperately sorry.

I had to do something, something about everything. Very late on the third night I crossed the room, eased open the door and crept into bed without waking him. There I lay, looking up to where the ceiling should have been though there was no visible surface in the cloying dark of the small hours. My eyes could find only an unhelpful nothingness up there, no answers. I turned onto my side and looked towards Kip who was facing away from me. His lovely shoulders, his breathing just audible, rhythmic and untroubled. I envied him his sleep.

I'm sorry. I'm sorry. I love you.

Well, bloody well say it then.

I shifted over so I was closer to him, traced my fingertips as lightly as I could from under his ear along the curve of his neck, down his bicep to loll my hand on his thigh. I placed my lips at the smooth valley between his shoulder blades, kissed him and brought my body close, fitting myself against him, my hand up and along and over his skin and under the duvet where his body was hot and his body was hard. I knew he was awake. We made love silently, slowly, feeling for each other in the dark.

Afterwards, he trailed his fingers through my hair as I lay in his arms, but still he hadn't spoken.

'The last time I saw Patrick,' I began. 'On that fucked-up night a decade ago, in that hideous van when I feared for my life – believe me, I gave him both barrels. I told him that I hated him. *Hated.* I told him how he'd made me feel. I told him what I thought of him. I let rip. I really did.' I paused. 'He said *sorry* a lot. I said *hate* a lot. I was full of fury and scorn that night. I made it plain that he was as repellent to me as shit on my shoe—'

'Eadie,' Kip interrupted. 'You can't feel bad about what you said just because he's dead.'

'I don't regret it,' I said. 'But what occurs to me now is that in his pathetic way, Patrick was trying to do the right thing.'

I let Kip listen to that for a while.

'But it's not about that – it's not.' I sat up in bed. 'It's not about what he did – either when I was a kid, or that night at the Haç. It's what he *said*. Not about being sorry – his apology was sort of irrelevant – but something else. He said, *I know I were a proper little cunt – but I was dead happy back then. Just being little.*' I paused. I could hear his voice so clearly again. 'And Kip – *that's* what haunts me these days. That's what I can't stop thinking about now. About Patrick being young, when he'd felt happy in his own dead-end helpless and hopeless way.'

The playground at the Three Magnets. From nowhere I remember Patrick standing stock-still watching Josh, Celeste and me scamper over to Sandrine and the panther-sleek car. I could weep for him now. 'He was just a little boy once. A littl'un.'

In the darkness, suddenly the one fundamental fact was neon clear and it lit up the room. 'You see, it's not about me versus Patrick any more. It's about grown-up me, Kip. It's the thirty-year-old me of today – having once known a young kid who didn't stand a chance.'

There was quiet in our bedroom. Perhaps Kip had fallen asleep. It didn't matter.

'Patrick had a horrible life,' I continued. 'He died with nothing, but worse than that he died with no one knowing or caring. So he should at least have a decent funeral. I believe that's important. It's the right thing to do, really.' The room was soundless and still. 'Well – I think so. What's the point having a conscience unless I put it to good use?'

Exhaustion swept over me at God-knows-what-o'clock. I lay back down. So very tired. And then fingertips were tracing up my arm, tucking my hair behind my ear.

'You're beautiful,' Kip whispered.

How could he see me? It was too dark. It took a moment for me to realize that he didn't mean that kind of beautiful. I cried, then. And finally, I slept.

This time I did it the proper way. I phoned Doig & Daughters and made an appointment for Saturday. And I asked Kip whether he might come too. Shirley Doig gave me a cuddle when she came into the waiting room and she shook Kip's hand warmly and said so genuinely that she was sorry for *our* loss. She took us through into another room; it was soundless in there, with soft carpet and a vase of gently fragranced flowers, old-fashioned table lamps giving off a subtle warm light, comfortable armchairs and a sofa on which Kip and I sat side by side.

Shirley asked if I had the death certificate. I did not. She told me how I needed to go to the hospital, to the mortuary department, to collect it. I quaked at that and asked her if she could do that for me, but she said no. You have to do it Eadie, she said, you'll be OK. Meanwhile she would make an appointment for me with the registrar, at which I'd be given a folder for Shirley to enable Doig & Daughters to collect Patrick and bring him to their premises.

'You'll become the Appointed Funerator,' Shirley told me. The title struck me as unnervingly official, so fundamentally grown-up, such a solemn responsibility, and I wondered what I had started. I looked from Shirley to Kip for reassurance. But there was a gentle atmosphere of benevolence and it occurred to me how the business of dying could be so thoughtfully handled, that Robert Twatface who'd phoned us could learn a thing or two from the Doigs. Everything Shirley asked was for Patrick, not me. He was the centre of attention. I liked the way she kept saying his name. What would Patrick want, she asked.

I had to choose a coffin for him.

They were all expensive.

She went through their Professional Services, explained the costs of all the arrangements, what they would need to undertake, being undertakers – and words like embalming were cast into the room, banging off the walls like a dying fly. Sensitively, she explained what was and wasn't necessary. She asked how we'd like Patrick dressed. She suggested that perhaps the clothes he'd been found in might not be appropriate and a plain gown would be best. She told me anything Patrick had had with him at the time would now be handed to me. She asked if there were any items we'd like placed in the coffin. None of this had occurred to me.

'And a burial or a cremation for Patrick?' Shirley asked. 'Obviously, a burial is more expensive,' she said *sotto voce*, lest he should hear. 'I'll contact the crematorium at the Southern Cemetery,' her voice returned. 'See what date we can set for Patrick. I know a lovely celebrant,' she said. I hadn't thought about that. I hadn't thought of headstones or plaques, either, that this would be our responsibility too at some point.

While Shirley had talked through the options, she had jotted down numbers on a pad angled subtly towards us so that we could read them. Even with my terrible maths, whether I inadvertently rounded the numbers up or down, I knew it was going to cost a lot. Kip's maths was excellent. He sat pensive and still. And I think Patrick would have been embarrassed. Or maybe not, perhaps he'd have felt shame, which was different. Or humiliated, which was different again and worse. Or maybe Patrick would simply have been grateful. I had no way of knowing, though – he was too dead to ask. However, there was one thing of which I was sure. Something that Patrick and I would have agreed on.

'I don't want the funeral to be at the Southern Cemetery,' I told Shirley and Kip. 'He didn't have a good life here in Manchester. He died alone. No fixed abode in a bus stop.' I sensed them staring at me as if I were about to suggest we dig a hole in our garden and lower him into that. 'He needs to go back to Parkwin to be buried and not cremated,' I said. 'He was happy there,' I told them. 'When he was little.'

Shirley inhaled sharply, raised her eyebrows and glanced at Kip and down at her notepad. 'I will liaise with the council in Hertfordshire on your behalf,' she said. 'The title deeds will be in your name.' The skin was reddening up Kip's neck, around his ears, over his cheeks. I felt slightly dizzy. The flowers now smelled too strong. Shirley added a new figure to the list. Our deposit for the house would be all but gone. We would have title deeds, but they would be for a grave, not a home.

1.30 p.m. M1 junction 12, Toddington interchange

It feels like we've slowed down drastically now we've come off the motorway but actually the road is clear and Kip is driving at a constant 50 miles per hour. We're about twenty-five minutes away, we're in good time. I was back down in Hertfordshire two weeks ago, meeting the bereavement officer at the council. All these careers I had no idea existed. I want to bury someone, I had said. Don't we all, he had replied with sweet dark humour pitched just right. I'd decided to refer to Patrick as my friend – it was just less complicated that way. I came away with a plot at our cemetery, a date and a time and a further diminished bank account. I'd taken the paperwork to Shirley Doig the next day.

'I don't know what to do,' I told her. 'This is costing a fortune.'

She helped me choose a different coffin and she led me to buy the most basic one available, extolling its qualities without making me feel cheap. Shirley had asked if I'd like him to be buried with anything but when Patrick was found he had no possessions on him, just loose change and chewing gum in his pockets. So those were to go in the coffin with him, along with my old school tie which I'd kept in a memory box all these years.

'You know, Eadie,' Shirley said. 'For us to drive Patrick such a long distance is going to be horribly expensive. Patrick doesn't need a hearse and you don't need a limo. You could take him yourself. Have you thought about that?'

Bless her, she made it sound as though Doig & Daughters were so busy, the hearses in such high demand, that I'd be doing her a favour. Kip had sold his blue Mini many years ago. We had a Toyota now. It was spacious for a hatchback but there was no way a coffin would fit.

'I think Patrick would be perfectly happy – tickled even – if you simply hired a van,' Shirley suggested.

And so that's what we did.

The hire van has bright green decals all over it. Hare Hire Ltd. Predictably, their logo is a giant cartoon bunny leaping along. *Hare for Where You Need to Be.* What a rubbish shout-line; Kip could do so much better for them.

'Thanks for driving,' I say to Kip. Thanks for so much more than driving is what I should say. There's so much more to be said, but we're on the outskirts of Parkwin now. I haven't been here for almost two years; I didn't tell Terry and Mum when I was down a fortnight ago. I chose Patrick's plot from a plan of the grounds at the bereavement office; I know my cemetery off by heart and I made sure he'd be nowhere near those other Semples with all the weeds and nettles that Michael once told me no one ever visited. I didn't even know if they were his relatives anyway.

And now we're on Yew Lane. Kip has slowed down to a respectable funereal pace. Ahead I can see the Electricity Building, blocking number 41 from view for a few yards until the road bends and my childhood home and the cemetery gates come into view.

'When I was little, Terry and I would watch the funeral cortèges pass right by our house. We'd count the cars while Mum told us about whoever was being buried.' I smile at the memory. 'Then we would visit the grave after everyone had left. Check they were settling in OK. *Here lies the meaning of life*, Terry would say. *This is what it's all about*, he told me.'

'What a peculiar childhood you had,' Kip says. 'I used to sit in trees and throw frozen peas and stale bread at people from the branches.'

It makes me giggle.

I wonder what overview Terry would have given watching our cortège from the sitting-room window. What would Terry and Young Eadie have to say about a hearse disguised as a Hare Hire van? How would he have quantified the number of mourners, and Patrick's age, and cause of death? And what gems and random facts might my mum have come out with as Patrick passed by? Seeing 41 Yew Lane lodges a knot of emotion in my throat, but it's not for Patrick. Just now, it's for the little girl and her dad who were once at that window watching and counting and concluding always with compassion and contemplation.

'Do you know,' I say, 'this is the first time that I've been through these gates – I only ever went in via our garden.'

Kip has slowed right down while he figures out where to go. I point and we continue on towards the chapel.

'You OK?' he asks.

I nod. I shake my head. 'But who will be here?' I wonder.

Terry and Mum are there, like they said they'd be.

Oh, Lorry – you came! Bill too!

Sandrine's here and – please – it is! Celeste.

Is that tiny man Reuben? I clock that there's a handful of other people too, but it's time to stop. It's time to start.

Almost six hours ago we collected the van. We drove it to Doig & Daughters, to the back of the premises where their three hearses and two Daimlers were parked like gleaming black horses at rest. Shirley was already there, standing to attention in her funeral blacks: a frock coat, long skirt, top hat with the ribbon and a silver-topped cane. She waited for us to park, she smiled gently at me and then she nodded soberly and out came members of staff with Patrick's coffin.

Though I had chosen it, this morning the coffin startled me when I saw it. I could sense the body inside it and the enormity of the day ahead suddenly confronted me. I gasped and Shirley put a gentle hand to the small of my back. None of us had spoken. Kip opened the van doors. It was pretty much the same size as the one Patrick had bundled me into all those years ago but early this morning, slowly and with reverence, the Doig attendants lifted the coffin with Patrick in it, from the trolley into the back of the van. They rolled the trolley away and then they returned to the van and they all bowed slowly, as if they were bidding farewell, as if they were saying you're in safe hands now, sir. I had bought a bunch of flowers and before I placed it with the coffin, Shirley took from it a single perfect rose and handed it to me. And then, they shut the back doors of the van. Now, almost 200 miles later, we are opening the doors again.

Despite the guy ropes, the coffin has slid and is at an angle but there again, everything about today is a bit askew. Kip steps up into the back of the van and has to climb right over the coffin to give it a push while Terry pulls. Both men are trying hard to make it seem like they're exerting no effort. A trolley is being brought over but a voice suddenly says no, it's OK, there's enough of us. And I know that voice. I know that voice. I know that voice is Josh's.

Who would have thought that, actually, Patrick Semple would have the full quota of six pall-bearers? But that's what he has. There is Kip and Josh and Lorry and Bill, Terry and – oh my goodness, he came! – Mr Swift. They lift Patrick up and onto their shoulders. I follow behind and someone takes my hand and gives it a squeeze and whispers *mad woman*. I turn and of course it's Celeste. Her hair is cropped close and dark red these days; she has a nose piercing and one through her eyebrow and she's wearing what looks like a bus conductor's outfit from the 1980s. And I think to myself how she looks textbook lesbian and although now's not the time to tell her this, I'll be sure to later and she'll be delighted. My oldest friend. We walk into the chapel together, arm in arm, and take a seat at the front. It's so true: nobody should be invited to a funeral – but everyone should come.

The Chapel

I organized Patrick's service over the phone, and now I can't remember what was decided. So it's only when the recorded music starts that I think oh that's right – I asked for our school song from Three Magnets Primary. And I wonder, how is it that I still remember all the words? Celeste obviously does too, she's singing her heart out. I'm suddenly a little worried about the funeral celebrant as I've never met him and he didn't know Patrick and I asked that he just keep any talking to a minimum. I gave much thought to whether I should speak today, but I wasn't comfortable with it. The celebrant, however, is a lot younger than he sounded on the phone and he looks a little uncomfortable. We are gathered here today, he says, to wish Patrick Semple well on his final journey. But his words are slightly over-rehearsed, delivered pedantically with excessive sincerity. I think to myself how Patrick would have had a field day with this poor boy in the school playground.

Oh, but I don't remember the next bit. This isn't what we talked about. I think we should be singing 'Jerusalem' now? Instead, I hear the celebrant say how he's going to hand over to Jim, who knew Patrick well, who'd like to say a few words and

I swivel my head because I don't know a Jim and I'm suddenly gripped by a wholly irrational panic that this might be some crime boss from Moss Side.

But it's Mr Swift. It's only Mr Swift. I can't remember if I even knew his name was Jim.

Mr Swift nods at me, then behind me and to the left of me and I know it's to Josh and Celeste. And then he tips his head to one side for a beat as he focuses on the coffin, as if he's listening carefully to a small child gabbling important things at him. He bows his head at the coffin and I feel a tear slip from my eye which I brush away.

'I knew Patrick Semple only for a short time,' Mr Swift says. 'He wasn't a star student yet neither was he the naughtiest boy I've ever known. He was always chipper. Energetic. Contrary,' he pauses. 'Bit of a mouth on him.' There's chuckling. 'He told me he wanted to be a sheriff or a zookeeper when he grew up. He didn't make it as either – we know that, we know that.' He pauses again. 'Though we are aware of what Patrick did *not* achieve – so too must we remember him for the dreams he *had*. We should do that. We must hope that, wherever he was and at whatever age, there was always a part of him that still held on to his dreams. Rest in peace, Patrick, rest in peace. I hope you find joy rounding up the cowboys to help you herd the elephants, the lions and the giraffes.'

And that's why Mr Swift was the best headmaster in the world.

We walk Patrick out to a rousing rendition of 'Cauliflowers Fluffy' because anyone who has ever sung that song at their primary school remembers it off by heart for the rest of their lives. As we belt it out, we look around, catching each other's eyes, smiling fondly. Celeste has tears streaming down her cheeks and I love her for that.

The apples are ripe, the plums are red, Patrick's sleeping in his blankety bed.

It was very strange choosing a plot for Patrick. In the end, I opted for one where he has company to either side, looking out over the arable land, part of which the cemetery has now expanded into over the years since I've been gone. People don't stop dying.

As we near the grave, the breeze carries a fragrance to me that I haven't smelled for so many years. Nutty and sweet and warm. And there he is, puffing on his pipe packed with Three Nuns tobacco, my old friend Michael who is indeed very old but still gainfully employed right here in the grounds. He doffs his cap and bows his head to the coffin and sends a twinkle-eyed smile over to me and I have to stop myself running to him to watch proceedings together from afar, as so often we did a long, long time ago.

Dust to dust, ashes to ashes, dirt to grave. I hear Reuben's voice low and private off to one side, quietly chanting in Hebrew the Kaddish, the Jewish hymn of mourning. I hear Josh join him. They are wearing matching skullcaps, crocheted in all the colours of summer.

Goodbye, you little bugger I say privately to the coffin and I tip a shovelful of soil down into the grave. Earth on wood six feet down; it's final, it's done. Farewell, Patrick, farewell.

'My wife and I would be very honoured if you'd join us for a cup of tea in the garden,' Terry is saying and for the first time

I notice it's a really lovely afternoon. My father is beckoning us to follow him, leading the way through the graves to the gate in the wall to our garden. I stay at the back and watch and count: not a bad turnout for somebody who had no one.

As I walk, I pass by the plot I'd earmarked for Patrick all those years ago. I'd forgotten about that. Mary Livingstone has it, now I remember. Beloved wife of Paul 'Yorky' Livingstone. Mother of Gemma and Abigail. Adored Nana to Sam, Tracey and Tom.

She's more than ten years dead, these days.

Time passes. Love remains.

The Garden

I don't think my parents have actually catered for anyone, ever. But at some point this morning, they carried the kitchen table out into the garden which will have necessitated a mass clearance of papers, mail and random things from its surface. On the table now there's an oilcloth I remember from my childhood and on top of that appears to be our entire crockery collection, all mismatched and mostly chipped. Plates, cups, saucers, mugs and sugar in a soup bowl with every single one of our teaspoons diving in, like synchronized swimmers. There is a sliced loaf and to the side of that, butter in a dish and three different types of jam. But that's OK, everything's OK, it's a DIY reception for a DIY funeral and there's charm and generosity here in the garden at 41 Yew Lane.

Celeste comes over and cuddles me and then punches Kip on the arm.

'You'd better be looking after her,' she says.

He gives a shrug and says he tries his best. He says, I try my best – but what can you do?! and Celeste thinks it's funny while I know it's true.

'You're looking properly lezzified these days,' I tell her.

Celeste roars with laughter. 'Hallelujah for that – it's only taken me my whole adult life to perfect.' She takes a beat. 'Remember Patrick calling us lezbicans?'

I nod.

'He was right about that after all,' she says. 'Wrong about you, obviously.' And she looks at me intently. 'He was *so* wrong about you, Eads. Look who you've become.' I frown, confused. She cups my face in her hands. 'Look what you've done today.'

What I've done today has cost us the deposit on our house and possibly my marriage.

'I'm a crap friend and I've missed you,' she says.

'I'm a crappier friend and I've missed you more,' I say.

'From one crappy gay friend to another,' Lorry pipes up. 'How are you, Edith?'

'So so pleased to see you,' I whisper to him as I stand on tiptoes, clinging to him while he hums into the top of my head.

'I miss you, Edith.' He squeezes me tightly.

'But Lorry – your *shoes*?' It's a terrible sight to see him in a matching black pair that are very clean and laced correctly.

'Jesus, Edith – I'm a thirty-one-year-old lawyer and I'm at a funeral.' But he inches up his trousers so that I can see that his socks are gloriously odd, one blue, one orange. He turns to Kip. 'Still as handsome as ever, you bastard.'

Kip hands Lorry his glasses. 'Here – you need these.'

Bill saunters over and my favourite boys slip back into a banter it seems they left mid-sentence such a long time ago, now with Celeste joining in too as if we all hung out only yesterday.

But where is Josh? He is over there, standing under the shade of the pear tree with Reuben. They've made themselves jam sandwiches, Reuben is talking, Josh is listening. Josh with a goatee beard and carrying a fair bit of weight – I'd've passed right by him on the street. I catch his eye, lift my hand and he mirrors it back to me.

While Celeste holds court passing anecdotes to Kip, Lorry and Bill like she's dealing cards, I go into the house and step back in time. My parents' desks look the same – strewn and overwhelmed – and the house smells the same – a sort of dusty quiet permeated with sweet tea and self-belief. The clock still doesn't tell the correct time and the windows need a clean and the Silver Jubilee mug stuffed with biros and pencils has lost its handle.

What *is* on all those pages and pages on their desks? What is it that takes up so much of their time – years, decades? I take a look. In the main it's dense and incomprehensible but both my mum and Terry have often added huge exclamation marks and ticks and asterisks double-ringed in the margins and it strikes me now how their work brings them such joy and contentment and purpose. It's more than can be said of mine.

In the bathroom, I wash my hands and breathe in the nostalgia of Imperial Leather soap and I hold the hand towel with the embroidered daisies against my cheek. In my bedroom, the afternoon sunlight slips in soft, gauzy and still. On the walls, all the posters are now long gone; most likely they stayed up until they simply fell off. My bed is made and I sit on it, open the drawer of the small cabinet next to it and rummage: a Bazooka bubble gum from my school days, pens, a mix-tape, a paper-clip necklace and a ball made out of elastic bands.

'I do believe *I* made that.'

It's Josh.

'Catch,' I throw it over to him and he tosses the ball lightly from hand to hand.

'Good to see you,' he says.

'And you,' I say.

'How are you?'

'I'm good – I'm good. You?'

'Yeah – pretty good.'

We do some nodding.

'That's your husband?' Josh points to a vague point beyond the window.

'Yes,' I say. 'Kip.'

'And I'll like him?'

'Everyone likes Kip,' I say while the sudden taste of silent panic coats the thought that maybe I'll lose him.

'I'm happy for you,' Josh smiles. 'Can I keep this?'

'The elastic-band ball? Well – sure.'

'Cheers!'

'Are you married, Josh?'

'No.' I detect derision spike his brief laugh. 'I mean – not now. I was. But now – not.'

'Oh. I'm – I didn't know.'

'Anyway,' he says.

'Yes – anyway.'

We fill the pause with self-conscious smiles and random sighs and shrugs.

'How's Reuben?'

'Just the same – but smaller,' says Josh. 'He's dying to say hello.'

'Not literally, I hope – one funeral is quite enough for the time being, Dr Albert.'

'Dr *Rubenstein*,' Josh corrects me and I'm confused. 'A few years ago, I changed my surname back to Rubenstein.'

'*Back* to?'

'It's Reuben's original surname – but when he came here as a refugee he changed his surname to sound English. So he chose Albert – *like Victoria and Albert*, he likes to say.'

'How could I have not known this?'

'I didn't either. Turns out a lot of displaced Jews chose new surnames – they were ashamed of their Germanic roots but also felt they had to hide their Jewishness. They sought to blend in, you see, to embrace their new country.'

'Wait! His real name is Reuben Rubenstein?'

Josh smiles and takes a beat. 'Actually,' he says, 'his given name was *Josua*.'

The name rings out around us and we listen to it quietly before Josh continues. 'My grandfather lost everyone – *everyone* – in Auschwitz, remember, so he chose Reuben to keep the memory of his entire family alive. I guess I wanted to do something similar for him – hence changing back from Albert to Rubenstein.' Josh pauses, he looks pained. 'I lost my Faith for a while, Eadie, a few years ago,' he says quietly. 'But that's for another time.'

I'm staggered. I look out of the window at the man I know as Reuben, whose kindness and zest for life, whose work ethic and respect for grey matter, whose wisdom and compassion and capacity for forgiveness, brought both joy and crucial gravity to my youth.

People often aren't who they seem. Someone said that to me once.

'Thank you for coming – I'm glad you're here,' I tell Josh and I mean it.

'You did a thing today, Eadie,' Josh says quietly. 'You did quite a thing – you know?'

Others have implied this and it's making me feel awkward. Let's change the subject, let's go back outside. I want to find Kip. As I follow Josh through the house and into the garden, I open the freezer just to check – but there's no Viennetta in there. Nothing to celebrate anyway, not now that I've used up all our house deposit money on Patrick's funeral.

Reuben is eighty-two years old. He sold the Shop when he turned eighty. Nothing to do with the schmucks at the supermarket, he said. Actually, it was down to his arthritis. Is it still called Albert's, I wanted to know? No, he tells me, now it's a pottery painting café. Children paint on plates they then eat off – or their parents give them as gifts to friends to eat off. He thinks this is amazing and not in a good way and he does a lot of tutting. I think of Paintz&Snax and wonder out loud if Kip might be able to assist with the marketing.

'You remember when you were my shop assistants?' Reuben says and Josh and I smile while Reuben takes a spritely gallop through the good old days. And I remember – I remember it all. The multicoloured cram of the shelves, the sound of the bell every time the door opened, Narnia behind a curtain of pastel-coloured plastic strips. The storeroom – our territory. Stacking packets, balancing cans, constructing walls from boxes; the thrill of the trigger of the price-tag gun. So much standing on tiptoes and laughter, always the laughter.

'Slave labour,' I say.

'Chutzpah!' Reuben says. 'You were paid handsomely in rollmops.' We all laugh about that; laugh and sigh and laugh and sigh. So much time has passed in the blink of an eye between those halcyon days and now.

Josh and I glance to and from one another — about to say, about to ask, only to think better of it. It's all so long ago, it doesn't matter, it doesn't matter any more.

'Come and meet Kip,' I say to them. 'He's a mensch.'

Terry comes through from the kitchen with another bag of sliced bread. Never have jam sandwiches tasted so good. I feel proud of him and Mum, grateful too — they read the situation perfectly. Josh and Celeste and I, with Lorry, Bill and Kip in tow, have flocked around Mr Swift, who keeps telling us to call him Jim but none of us ever will. We don't feel our age in his presence — he'll perennially be our headmaster and it seems we all relish the questions he's asking about our lives. Kip, Bill and Lorry chat to him as equals but Josh, Celeste and I stand to attention, as if eagerly awaiting our turn to tell him what we did over the weekend. Celeste talks about the books she's reading, Josh discourses about the NHS and I bang on about the Tudors. And we ask Mr Swift about Three Magnets Primary and he says he'll retire in two years' time and we say you can't do that! you *can't* not be there! the school will fall down, collapse, cease to be!

He laughs. 'Anyone would think you're after extra house points,' he says.

And we're so pleased to hear the house system is still in place. 'Little has changed,' he tells us. 'It's very much the same.'

I gaze at Mr Swift and over to Reuben, to Terry and Mum. I look around the garden at 41 Yew Lane. The back door open into the house. Sandrine in enormous sunglasses, still making smoking look so stylish and cool. I look for Michael but he's gone. He didn't say goodbye but that's OK, that's very Michael. He'll have gone off to tend to a Shrubbery of Sympathy, to mooch up and down the rows straightening flowers on a wilt, brushing twigs from the path, sitting the occasional soft toy upright by a headstone, cursing at cellophane which dances off when he goes to collect it up. I sense that everything in my particular Parkwin remains very much the same and it no longer irritates me; today I feel grateful for it. I think of Edweard Fairbetter – how pleased he'd be. Community – the driving force behind his vision for this second-rate Garden City.

Celeste bustles in on my reflections. 'Anyone fancy a walk?'

The Three Magnets Primary School

'I remember clinging on to the fence like this – but from the inside.'

We are all lined up outside school, our hands monkey-grabbing the chain link as we look in at the playground. Even Kip and Lorry and Bill are doing so and it wasn't even their school.

'It's so small,' says Celeste and she sounds baffled.

'So were we,' I say, wistful.

'Remember how we'd sit, us three, in a circle with legs wide, feet touching?' She sighs.

'Our own force field,' Josh says. 'For the Jew, the Rich Kid and the—' He looks at me, everyone does and we're all wondering – what exactly had I been back then? 'The Jew, the Rich Kid and the—?'

'What *was* I?' I wonder out loud. 'I had crap hair and this,' I point at my solitary dimple. 'I lived next to a cemetery and my parents were slightly odd.'

'The Jew, the Rich Kid and the Oddbod,' Celeste says.

'By the way, what are Centrists exactly?' Josh asks me.

'Huh?'

'You used to say your family were *Centrists*,' he says. 'I've wondered about that sometimes, over the years.'

'Type of Quaker, perhaps?' Celeste says. 'Wasn't the Garden City movement founded by Quakers?'

I think and I think. '*Eccentric*,' I laugh. 'Not Centrists. That's what Terry and Mum would declare if any remarks were made about us. No, darling, we're not poor we're *eccentric*. No, darling, we're not Jewish we're eccentric. We're not vampires – we're eccentric.'

'The Jew, the Rich Kid – and the Eccentric,' Josh muses and we all concur.

'But look at our tiny school,' says Celeste. 'Just look how *small* it is.'

'We had home, we had school,' I say. 'And we all believed the very edge of the world was just beyond.' I wave my hand at a point somewhere behind me.

We shufty along the perimeter and cling to a different part of the fence and everything we say is prefaced with *do you remember* and *I remember* and *remember when*. We haven't forgotten a thing but we realize we just haven't thought to recall much of it over the years until now. Kip and Lorry and Bill are enjoying it – they're peering in through a portal and coming across me back in time. I can't tell whether it's fondness on their faces or whether they're storing details for piss-taking purposes at a later date. I don't mind, though. I remember Little Me with such fondness.

Every now and then my arm brushes by Kip and we look at each other and away. Every now and then Josh and I glance at each other as we take another step along the fence that separates us from the past. The old Hut has gone. There's a new one in the playground, it's very fancy and more of a summer house, really. It's in a completely different location too.

'I hope there's still second-hand uniform in there,' I say. 'I hope this continues to be a school where there's help for kids who need it.'

'Jim,' says Celeste.

'Mr James Swift,' says Josh.

'He'd ensure that it is,' I decide.

'Did you need help?' Celeste asks me, her voice down a key.

'I suppose I must have done – I don't ever remember feeling deprived. What we could or couldn't afford was never a big deal at home.'

'No – I mean did you need *help*, do you think, from the adults?' She pauses. 'About Patrick?'

I think about that. 'I had you and I had Josh,' I say. 'And it wasn't just me, you two were targets as well.'

We consider this quietly.

'Looking back, I think it was worse for you,' says Josh. 'It was unrelenting.'

'But you see I think I took it as a given. I think I thought that was just – life. I'd seen it with my parents – Terry and his horrible line manager at the supermarket. My mum and the unfathomable mess and thankless tasks that greeted her in the offices she cleaned.'

'I wonder – if any of the grown-ups had known, how different might things have been for you?' says Celeste.

'Well, I wouldn't have this scar on my knee,' I say lightly and we all peer at the pucker spidering my skin.

'But you know, if the adults had been involved, I don't think things would have been any different for Patrick,' Josh says.

And we all look at him and know he's absolutely right.

We walk past the gate where Celeste used to be dropped off and picked up. She says she hasn't a clue what happened to the enormous slinky black car. We walk on to the entrance Josh and I used and Celeste says how much she envied us.

'What will it look like in another ten years?' I muse.

We stand awhile and we all wonder about this. We can't expect it to stay the same. It will be a decade into the next millennium by then, and perhaps kids will be taught by droids and never have to feel the indignation of a teacher's stare again. Perhaps there will be no library, only computer files, no need for handwriting because six-year-olds will type faster than any of us. Will spell check do away with the need for spelling tests? Will kids still surreptitiously count on their fingers or will they have calculators hot-wired into their brains by then? Will breaktime still be a raucous scamper or will there be stillness and silence with kids glued to computers? Hopefully not.

We stroll back via Josh's old route. Here is the Shop but it isn't the Shop – it's Café Ceramix. We peer in through the windows. It's impossible to superimpose Albert's onto it, it's changed beyond recognition. Nothing of the old Shop remains, even the door is in the wrong place these days.

'Was Reuben OK about selling it?' I ask.

'It was time,' Josh says. 'We all knew that. And ultimately it was his decision – so.'

'My mum's sold the house,' Celeste tells us. 'She's moving to Norfolk. She has a boyfriend called Leo. A toy boy, if you will. Actually, he's very lovely.'

It's the first time I've heard Celeste's deep fondness for her mother. Tender. Proud.

'If Terry and my mum ever move, it will be only a few yards beyond the garden and six feet under.'

And we all cast a thought to Patrick who's settling into one such spot right now.

We're strolling back to Yew Lane. Lorry, Bill and Kip are flanking Celeste while she fires questions at them and then natters on before they have a chance to answer. Josh and I walk just behind making the politest of conversation about the weather, about the sudden growth in personalized car number plates in this part of the world, that finally there's a McDonald's in Parkwin where Pour Toi used to be. I ask about his job and he tells me pretty much what he told Mr Swift. And then he asks me about mine and he seems so surprised to hear that I do what I do. But aren't you bored, he asks. It's so not you, Eads, he says and I detect just the slightest dip of Kip's head, listening out for my answer.

'We never had recycling bins when we used to live here,' I say and I point up the driveways of Yew Lane as we walk by.

We hug Bill and wave him off. Back in the garden, Sandrine is drinking white wine, sitting alongside my parents and Reuben in the dwindling sunshine, and they greet us as if we've just come home from school, which I suppose we have. Chairs are moved from the shade into the warmth and I sit with everyone and I listen. I just listen. I listen to voices I haven't heard for so long talking about aspects of lives I haven't been party to for ages until Lorry says he has to go. He starts the process of unfolding himself from the chair until he stands before us, still gloriously gangly. He kisses everyone and gives me a long and bony hug.

'We should do this more often,' I say to him.

'Ooh – who shall we bury next?'

'Idiot! You know what I mean.'

'I do – I do. I haven't seen Bill in so long. Just Christmas cards from Fiona these days.'

'Same,' I say.

'Nothing like a death to make one yearn for the living,' he says. 'We must get together. And let's not just talk about it this time – let's make it happen.'

'We could all go to San Francisco and stay with Fiona.'

'What a fabulous idea but do you know, I'd rather gather at yours – gad about Manchester's memory lanes. It's been so long.'

'Perhaps,' I say, wondering where I'll be living when Lorry finally organizes such a reunion. They'd have loved the house we've just lost. They wouldn't all fit in our flat.

Celeste and Sandrine are arguing because Celeste is telling her mother she's drunk far too much to drive and Sandrine is saying nonsense, nonsense, and throwing choice French fulminations into the mix.

'*Tu es beurrée, Maman,*' Celeste says with an enormous tut but I watch her ease Sandrine to her feet, linking arms with her protectively so that it doesn't look like she's keeping her steady, it just looks like they adore each other.

So Celeste drives her buttered mother home and Kip gives Lorry a lift to the station. My parents and Reuben sit themselves back down, happily chatting about the loveliest small things in life, their faces like flowers turning to find the last of the sun. Josh and I listen for a while and then Josh says here – let me help, as I begin to clear the cups and plates, the jammy knives and all the tiny hillocks of squidged teabags. We take them through to the kitchen, then we carry the table back into the sitting room. I wonder whether to transfer back onto it the piles of stuff that are temporarily on the sofa but I decide against that, I don't want to disrupt the order of my parents' chaos. It's also the sort of thing Terry and Mum are happy doing together. I fill the sink with soapy water and begin washing up. Josh takes a tea towel and starts to dry.

'You don't have to,' I say. 'You can just leave things to drain.'

He takes a beat. 'No,' he says. 'That's what I did to our friendship.'

I wash.

Josh dries.

I wash increasingly slowly because as he dries, he talks. Our crockery has never been so clean.

'I know it's over ten years too late,' he says, 'but mind if I say I'm sorry?'

I look at the bubbles in the sink, how en masse they're just foamy white but individually each contains a fragile rainbow on its surface, a world within the world, liable to pop and disappear at any moment.

'I don't mind,' I say.

'Well – I am genuinely sorry. I was a complete dick.'

I'm feeling around under the water for something else to wash up and something to say too.

'You were,' I said. 'But you were young. So was I. And it was a long time ago.'

'I was old enough, by then, to know that I was behaving like a fucking arsehole.'

Swearing has always been so un-Josh and it makes me laugh. 'Do you remember when you went to your secondary school and came back with a complete lexicon of profanity?'

'Yeah,' Josh says but he steers my digression back to what's important and, just like he used to do, he tells me to listen. 'Eads, listen,' he says. 'I need you to hear that I deeply regret the way I treated you and I'm sorry.'

There's nothing left to wash up but I keep my hands under the foam all the same.

'I know at the time I couldn't give you more,' Josh says and there's a rawness now to his voice. 'I loved you too much – and I know that doesn't make sense but nothing made sense to me at that age – and that's why I ran away from it all.'

'But Josh – I didn't *want* more,' I say. 'I just didn't want to lose my best friend – but that's what happened.'

'I know,' he says, 'I know.'

'I never told Celeste.'

'Nor did I,' he says. 'Didn't the world seem complicated back then? Little did we know.'

'We three,' I say wistfully. As I gaze out of the kitchen window at 41 Yew Lane, I can see us, I really can; aged seven in a scamper dodging the garden spray, aged twelve lolling on the grass singing to the radio, aged sixteen at the back of the garden trying to smoke kitchen herbs and figure out the entire universe but especially the Tories. And aged eighteen, simply standing together attempting to fathom what leaving home would actually feel like.

I grasp around for the plug and pull it. Our sink has always sounded like an animal gurgling for breath as the water drains away. My hands are gloved in suds. Josh holds out the towel and

I place them in it. He folds the linen over them and holds my hands in his.

'There's so much of this past decade I really could have done with sharing with you,' he says. 'I am truly so sorry.'

He gives my hands a little rub.

'You are officially forgiven,' I tell him grandly. 'But you know what? I have no regrets – I'm really pleased it was with you.'

'Putting the ecstasy into sex?' he laughs.

'Josh – we had no masterplan. We just fumbled about and did it – because "it" was something we decided to do. All these years later, I'm glad about that.'

He unwraps the towel and lays it on the kitchen counter, then he takes my wrists and places my hands to either side of his face. He lets go but I don't. I keep them where they are. There's the beard now, chubby cheeks, but behind those eyes nothing has changed and I remember now just how comfortable I always felt with this boy.

Love, sex, ecstasy, friendship. But the only person with whom I've ever truly experienced the apotheosis of each is Kip. And here he is, back from taking Lorry. Josh and I watch him standing in the garden chatting amiably with the older generation. My blood is flung through with fear. I've been hurting that man, the person I love most, and I don't know what's to happen next. I don't know what I can do. I don't know if it's too late for me to do anything.

The Cemetery

Kip and I are ready to go. Terry and Mum keep trying to ply us with just one more cup of tea but we need to head off, really. We all stand on the drive and look at the Hare Hire van. Strange to think that it served as a hearse today. I sense how the back of the van is now empty, even behind its closed doors, just as I could sense that the coffin this morning held a body. Sometimes, what seems to be opaque is anything but; just as the barriers we believe to be impenetrable will actually yield with the gentlest touch.

'Give us three rings when you're home,' Mum says.

'You'll be at work, love,' Terry tells her and I want to ask them why they don't synchronize their shifts these days? There's been no child in the house for years. But then I decide that perhaps this is just another quirk of being Centrists.

Mum goes back into the house and brings us an opened bag of Cadbury's Chocolate Eclairs for the journey. Kip says they'll be a nice change from Starburst and Mum says what's Starburst? and Terry tells her Opal Fruits, Jill, *Opal Fruits*. And there's chattery and laughter and we really should be going when suddenly, beyond it all, I hear it. I hear that sound that has always taken my breath away. Travelling straight through our mundane talk comes the lament of the bagpipes.

'I have to—' but I'm already walking away. The pied bagpiper of Parkwin. It may not even be him. 'I can hear— I need to—'

The main gates of the cemetery are closed. They close at 6 p.m., quarter of an hour ago. Five minutes, I say to Kip as I hurry back through the house, across the garden to the gate in our wall and out into the grounds. I walk quickly in between the graves of Mildred Robinson, of Noel Ellington, of Joy Trimble, of Walter and Betty Vickers with time only to send my best wishes to them, my apologies that I can't stay and chat, my assurance that next time I'm visiting I'll spend more time with them but for now, the pipes are calling me. I stop for a moment or two by the grave of Alfred Pennyfeather and I give him a salute before the piper reels me in.

There he is. His back is towards me and I stand alone, just watching and listening while feeling overrides thought. It really is Ross and he is piping at the freshly dug grave of Patrick Semple.

I've always loved this melody. Since I was a little girl it's brought tears to my eyes. Ross is playing 'Amazing Grace' and it bubbles every nerve ending. Slowly, I walk up to him and we stand by the mound of clodding earth under which lies the body of a thirty-year-old man.

Terrible really, I imagine Terry commentating on Patrick's cortège from our sitting-room window. *Far far too young. And just twelve people in attendance.*

The bagpipes wane like a dying breath and the day seems suddenly bereft of sound until I tune in to birdsong, a lawn-mower, a distant car horn.

'Hello,' I say.

'Miss Eadie Browne,' Ross says and I look all the way up and he looks all the way down and from under the roll and twitch of his great moustache, he sends his smile my way.

'It's Mrs Turner now,' I say.

He chuckles. 'You'll always be Eadie Browne,' he says. 'The wee girl who inhabits the soul of this place more than those at eternal rest. I can see her now,' he says, looking around. 'She's always here.'

A faint whiff of alcohol.

But it's OK, today. Grown-up Eadie thinks so. It's sad, but it's OK. And I could say nothing, I could just let things lie, after all Ross probably doesn't remember any of it. We could just say hello, how are you, goodbye. But then I think how Josh, too, could have said nothing – however, he squared up to the past. So I look all the way up and Ross looks all the way down and I say how *are* you, Ross? And he says, can't complain, Eadie, can't complain.

'I have my own teeth,' he says, 'and some of my wits most of the time.'

Patrick's grave draws our attention again and we stand quietly and just look. And I don't take my eyes off the earth when I say I'm sorry.

'I'm sorry, Ross,' I say. 'That time in town – when you called out to me and I didn't come.'

He puts a hand on my shoulder and leaves it there. 'The apology is mine to make – not yours.'

'I'm sorry, though – not just that I didn't come, but that I turned away from you. Worse, that I pretended not to know you.'

There's a heavy silence now and I don't hear birdsong or gardening or traffic.

'I wouldn't want to know me either, on a night like that night,' Ross says and he sighs and again I smell booze. My old pal, the Pie-Eyed Piper of Parkwin. I link my arm through his and then I turn away from Patrick and I raise my face to Ross and give him a smile. From behind his tired eyes and a faint yellowing complexion, he beams one back to me.

'Thank you for playing for Patrick,' I say.

Ross, though, gives an almighty frown and, behind his stacking great whiskers, his lips are moving over silent words. I wonder, then, if he just plays at random graves after hours, if music is the thing, not the deceased.

'It was for you, Eadie,' Ross says. 'I was playing for you.'

I walk back towards our garden gate slowly, stopping at the grave of Thomas Jefferey because despite being a father and a grandfather, he never has any visitors. I take the rose that Shirley Doig gave me from the bunch I'd bought for Patrick, and I lay it at Mr Jefferey's headstone.

'What ho, Eadie.'

Michael, out of nowhere, is right by my side. I'm suddenly so tired.

'I just saw Ross,' I say. 'I didn't realize he still— I thought he'd stopped. I remember there being a new piper before I left.'

'Yes, there is a different piper though he's not so new any more,' Michael chuckles. He lights his pipe and has a thoughtful puff. 'Every now and then, Ross likes to be here – just like you do. I told him about today. Wasn't sure if he'd come. Had to wait and see.'

Michael offers me his pipe. I laugh and decline. 'I gave up smoking a long time ago,' I remind him but I inhale and smile at the nostalgia that the nutty sweet smoke brings, the memories which spin through its scent. I steal a look at Michael, he looks just as old as he always has. We stand a while longer and oh, I could stay here for hours but there's a long journey ahead and I need to go.

'Goodbye, Michael,' I say. 'Be well. See you next time.'

He puffs on his pipe and nods. He, of all people, knows there will always be a next time, however long the gap might be, because a part of both of us lives here. I make my way through the graves and head for the garden gate, saying goodbye goodbye goodbye to all these souls I've known my whole life.

What ho, Eadie. What ho.

The Long Road Home

'I can't believe we have to drive all this way again.'

Immediately I hear how stupid I sound. How else are we going to get home? And it's not *we* – it's Kip driving.

'Sorry,' I mumble, 'I'm just really tired.' But he's the one behind the wheel – he's entitled to be far more tired than I. 'You should've put me on the hire form too,' I say and it sounds like an accusation. I'm truly getting on my own nerves now. Kip, though, doesn't respond. And I wonder if perhaps he's just developed a way of blocking me out.

'Have a sleep, then,' he says, so I bunch up my sweatshirt against the window, fidget my head into it and close my eyes.

'I can't,' I say moments later and I decide to faff with the radio, the temperature knob, I tug at the seat belt. I am so uncomfortable. Jesus bloody Nora, there's a good three hours to go.

'God, Eadie – you're stressing me out. Just – chill.'

When did saying *chill* ever make anyone feel anything other than hot and bothered? I unwrap one of the sweets Mum gave us and bite hard into the toffee to release the chocolate in the middle. I chew on another which all but glues my jaw shut, which is probably no bad thing. I offer one to Kip but he shakes his head. I try with the Starburst instead but he doesn't want one of those either. Lightly, I trail my fingers along his forearm to say sorry without having to say sorry, but he's concentrating on the road. The van grinds through the miles and in the cab there's a heavy quiet.

Kip pulls in to the services at Newport Pagnell.

'I need a coffee,' he says.

'I wish I was on the hire form,' I say again.

'I'm *fine* – I just need a coffee.'

'But you won't sleep if you have coffee now,' I warn him. This much I know.

'Well, I'll fall asleep at the wheel without it.'

I feel I have to defend myself, I don't know why. 'I said I wish I could drive for a bit – it's not my fault I'm not on the form.'

'Well, you're not, so you can't – so I'm just going to mainline caffeine and get us home, OK?' He doesn't want to walk with me into the services. He strides ahead and I dawdle behind.

'I'm just going to the loo,' I tell his back and he nods and heads off to the cafeteria without asking me if I want anything.

I wash my hands and have a good look at myself in the mirror. My skin is bleached out under the strip lighting and there's a darkness around my eyes from the demands of the day. He's just tired, I tell myself. We're both just really tired. It strikes me how full-blown arguments over something of substance are preferable to the snipe and stab of bickering. I think, why didn't I just instigate light chattery? Why haven't I said how much I appreciate everything he's done, everything he has forgone to make today possible? I notice the dispenser oozing little shiny globules of lurid pink soap onto the surface of the basin and I fiddle with it, pulling and pushing, but I just make it worse.

Eventually, I discover gentle coaxing is all that's needed for it to stop. I wipe away the mess I've made. Everything is now super-clean. I think to myself – life lessons from a soap machine. And I think how much I love Kip.

I walk to the cafeteria and I can't see him. I surf my eyes through the queue to pay, over the tables where people sit with their food but I can't find Kip. He's just not there. We stopped because he wanted a coffee and now he's gone. I'm tired and emotional and I don't understand; I don't know where else he'd be. I turn around and around and I hurry back to the car park which is packed and there are so many vans, a cacophony of brightly coloured signage, but not one fluoro-green hare amongst them. I rush back into the services and alternately cry for God and Kip and shit shit shit. Where has he *gone*? Where have I sent him? I turn small circles, my hands in my hair. What have I done? What did I do? He's gone. He's left. I've lost him.

But here he is. Here he is, coming out of WHSmith. Here's Kip, and the look on his face when I burst into tears: confusion and amusement and, threading it all together, love.

'What?!' he says, only he doesn't say it, he laughs it. '*What?!*'

'I didn't know where you were,' I sob. 'You'd gone – but you'd said you were going for coffee only you weren't there and all this pink soap in the loos and so many people everywhere and none were you and hundreds of vans but no hare. And. I thought. You'd left.'

'What?' he says again, in a murmur. 'What?'

I'm pushing my face into his chest while I cry juddering great howls. My breathing is erratic and I'm snotty as a child. And as soon as I feel his arms encircling me with their tender strength, I allow my body to slip, knowing it will be caught.

'Eadie – I only went to buy a paper to read with my coffee,' he says. 'That's all.' He peels me away and looks at me quizzically. 'Why would I leave you at a service station?'

I wipe my nose on my sleeve and he brushes away the smear it's left on my cheek. I remember once how he held back my hair when I threw up everywhere, all over him; he wiped my mouth with his bare hand and kissed me – I was stunned at the time, wondering how can someone love another enough to do that? Could I? I don't know. He's never thrown up all over me.

'Why would I leave you, Eadie, at a motorway services?!'

He has a copy of the *Guardian* tucked under his arm and I think of all the times I've furtively scoured the careers section with a growing sense of hopelessness tinged with shame.

'Because I've lost us the house,' I whisper. 'And I hate my job.'

'You what?'

'The deposit—'

'No – what you said next.'

'My job,' I sigh. I have to tell him. 'I hate it.'

'You hate your job and therefore I'll leave you at a motorway services?'

'No,' I say. 'Not at the motorway services. In real life.'

I drop my shoulders, my head, and I cry quietly, staring at the floor while Kip makes no sound whatsoever.

'Is everything all right?' It's a little old lady – her comfortable shoes come into frame with mine, with Kip's, but I don't look up.

'Everything's all right – it's just been a long day,' Kip tells her. 'Funeral.'

'She needs a nice hot drink and a sit-down,' she says.

'That's exactly what we're going to do,' Kip says and I watch the pair of old lady shoes shuffle off.

My tears have stopped but my breathing is still stammering.

'Why would I leave you, Eadie,' Kip says. 'Here – or anywhere else?'

With his arm around me, Kip leads me away from the concourse.

'Stay here,' he says, all but plonking me down on a seat at a table in the eating area. 'Don't move.'

Finally he gets to buy himself that cup of coffee. And for a few minutes there's just me and the newspaper and a melamine table that could do with a better wipe-down. Kip's bought me a hot chocolate which I hold on to as if my hands are freezing. I sense him watching me as he sips his drink.

'I didn't realize you were so unhappy at work,' he says with a sigh. 'Why didn't you say something? Why didn't you just talk to me?'

I'm grasping to remember all those carefully plotted conversations I've rehearsed in my head for so long, even just a sentence or two to start me off, but it seems my mind is empty.

'I'm not going to leave you just because you don't like your job,' he says and I look up to see him looking at me as if I'm the most curious creature.

'But – and also – I took the deposit for the house,' I say. 'And spent nearly all of it on the funeral of a little shit I once knew.'

'I am not going to leave you because of money,' Kip says.

'But you loved that house,' I say. '*West Didsbury*.'

He shrugs. 'Yeah,' he says. 'I did.'

And I look at him full on, because if not now, then when. 'What's happened to us, Kip?' I whisper. 'All this bickering and cold-shouldering and eggshells everywhere?'

He looks deep into his cup for a long beat. It appears the murk of crap coffee doesn't hold the answers that tea leaves might. 'I don't know.'

'How did we let it happen?' I say sadly. 'It just crept in and took hold – like the damp in the back wall of the kitchen.'

Kip swirls the liquid in his cup and sips at it distractedly. It must be cold by now. It must taste awful. I'm waiting for him to say something.

'I don't like the way we are,' I say sorrowfully into his silence.

'I don't either. But I am *not* leaving Us,' Kip says and his eyes are dark and ablaze and steady. 'Are you, Eadie?'

It's difficult to hold hands when the driver needs to change gear – but once the motorway is ribboning ahead, I take my husband's hand and I keep it. I'm going to hold on tight until I know exactly where we are.

The nine o'clock news

I finally let go of Kip's hand when he exits for the M6. I turn on the radio because he fancies some music. There's either crackle or just stations playing only our personal All-Time Worst Songs Ever, but then I tune in to the news. Kip and I say *nine o'clock? bloody hell.*

Since we last listened this morning, it seems nothing much has happened in the world on the day that Patrick Semple was buried. The bulletin is followed with a segment looking back on this day in history.

The fifteenth of June.

Kip and I look at each other. Today is the fifteenth of June. We both forgot to remember. It's three years to the day when I nearly lost him.

I was twenty-seven and Kip was thirty-one and we had decided to start playing the grown-up game seriously. We had a joint bank account and now both our names on a mortgage and we lived in a lovely garden flat on an excellent street in Didsbury. Finally I had my master's degree and, alongside working at KATmedia, I took on occasional research for Professor Blakemore – which I really needed to work on that particular Saturday. But the kids next door were apparently garrotting each other in their garden and it was impossible to concentrate.

'Want a lift to the Central Ref?' Kip asked, placing a cup of coffee next to me and a kiss to the back of my neck.

'Yeah, OK,' I said – and those two words ricocheted off our walls and made us grin like idiots, ameliorating my bad mood instantly. Those two words. Some couples have a special song, a sacred place, a favourite wine, a rhyming couplet, a private look – Kip and I had those two words: *yeah, OK.*

Oh, I so loved my boy. The previous week, a momentous thing had happened which now shone the brightest light on our future together. It had been our seventh anniversary and Kip had bought me a bottle of calamine wrapped in fancy paper, tied with a bow, nestling in a golden gift bag frothing with tissue paper.

'Calamine?!' I had rummaged around the bag but there wasn't anything else.

'In case you get the seven-year itch,' Kip had said and I'd flung my arms around his neck crying never never never! And then I'd proposed to him, just like that.

'Marry me, Mr Turner, marry me!' I'd said and, without missing a beat, he'd said *yeah, OK* – with a shrug so nonchalant I might as well have asked him if he'd give me a lift to the library.

'Yeah, OK,' he had said. 'Yeah, OK – I'll marry you, Eadie Browne.'

I love you I love you I love you. We'd sung it, we'd whispered it, we'd yelled it to one another over and over as we'd kissed and kissed each other's flush-happy faces.

Now, a week later, Kip was saying come on. 'Come on, Eads – I'll run you up to the Central Ref and I'll go shopping while you're there.'

'You hate shopping!'

He smiled wryly, taking my hand. 'There's stuff I need. Boxer shorts. Maybe a T-shirt or two. A book, perhaps. Might treat myself to a Mars Bar.'

I knew he was teasing me. I'd been wearing a red elastic band doubled over on my ring finger since I'd proposed and now he was pinging it against my skin.

'Might wander over to Afflecks when I'm done at the Arndale,' he said. 'See if there's a cheap ring there.'

We drove through Rusholme, passing Victoria Place and Hulme Hall, then Hathersage Road, and I kept forgetting to turn my head.

'You know, I miss your blue Mini,' I said.

'It died, Eadie,' he said soberly. 'It was very dead. You have to come to terms with that – or go to grief counselling.'

I giggled. I had really loved that car even though I'd been highly resistant to getting into it that rainy day when we'd first met.

'Want to meet at the Royal Exchange for lunch?' I asked.

'I'll probably head to the pub,' he said. 'Watch the footie.' It was Euro '96 and England were playing Scotland.

A car behind was beeping at us. I hurried off. I didn't kiss Kip, not even on the cheek. I didn't look at him, I don't think. I just made for the library with my head full of footnotes. I settled into my favourite spot in the mighty circular reading room. It was just gone 9.15 a.m.

And then, at 11.17 on that Saturday morning, 15th June 1996, the IRA bombed Manchester detonating the largest bomb in Great Britain since the Second World War.

9.10 p.m. 15th June 1999, M6 near Coventry

'I didn't know if you were alive, Kip – I had no way of knowing.'

'I was desperate to let you know I was OK.'

Gently, I ease up his shirtsleeve and look tenderly at the scars puckering his left forearm. They form a wonky noughts-and-crosses board of sorts. When finally he'd come home that day three years ago, it was his face which had upset me most, not his arm because that was bandaged from view. But his hair was matted with dust and debris, his lovely face was scratched and spattered, the blood – some his own, some belonging to strangers – was now black as ants. It didn't look real. It looked like fancy dress, like Jackson Pollock on Halloween.

'I had no way of contacting you,' I croak, even though we have recounted this so many times. 'I didn't know how to find you because they evacuated the library and we weren't allowed anywhere near the city centre.'

'Three years ago and we thought mobile phones were a fad we weren't buying into,' Kip laughs but then he falls quiet.

'I couldn't contact you.' The desolate panic of that remains vivid. I could only head home praying he'd be there. He wasn't and I dropped to the bedroom floor, closed my eyes and whispered Kip Kip Kip, willing his name to traverse the ether and find him.

'I was OK.'

'But I didn't *know* that. I didn't know if you were dead – I had no way of knowing.'

'No one died – it was a bloody miracle.'

'But I didn't know that.'

'When the explosion happened,' Kip starts, pauses, starts again. 'There was this millisecond lull that came after it, like a strange vacuum where time and movement, light and dark, just ceased to exist. Like a heightened peace with everything known suspended. And then the next second, it's shattered and glass is raining down. Glass and everything else.' He pauses while he remembers and I wonder again what those seconds must have been like for him. 'I thought I was going to die,' he says quietly.

'I sat rocking on the floor, feeling so sick,' I say. 'So grateful for the cacophony of next door's kids, everything as it was, all normal for a Saturday. There was no way you were going to be dead when life all around was continuing. I was adamant about that. I just sat there and stared at the phone willing it to ring, didn't dare call anyone just in case you were trying to get through.'

'I had no change for the payphone at the hospital. A nurse gave me 10p. I think I was more grateful for that kindness than for all the medical care I received. God bless the NHS.'

'I prayed. I sat on the floor and I really prayed.'

I slip back through my tears and the years to that day. My heartbeat all but drowning out the sound of our phone ringing. Lifting the handset; the taste of adrenaline and panic taking away my voice. I held the receiver to my ear, cupped my hand over the mouthpiece and forced out just the one word. I whispered *Kip*.

'Hello you,' he'd replied.

He was OK. He was alive. He was coming home.

'Three years to the day,' and Kip marvels at the fact that we'd both forgotten.

'It's quite something that we didn't realize until now,' I say and I wonder if we've somehow been careless.

'I guess I decided that I'd never let it be a defining point in my life,' he says.

'You went back into town far sooner than I could.' It had taken me months.

Just now I recall the aftermath, the days that followed. I was in shock, I was in bits; night terrors the likes of which I hadn't experienced in years returned. What if what if what if.

'You saw it so simply,' I say. 'You were insanely philosophical about it.'

'About the bomb?' He really has let it go. We're a good few miles further on. 'I felt almost euphoric for a few days. Just so lucky. We all were. No one died.'

'Three whole years ago,' I marvel. 'And today, we plain forgot.'

'Major triumph,' Kip says. 'By *not* remembering it was today – we *win*.' His voice is soft. Kip is the strongest person I will ever know.

'I *really* love you,' I tell him and I can feel my heart breathing out the words.

He doesn't answer. I note how he's swallowing and a muscle is flickering at the edge of his cheek. He nods. He nods again. I gaze in and out of my ghostly reflection in the passenger window while Kip drives us home. I hope he heard me. I hope he believes me.

Bed. At last. I'm almost too tired to sleep. The day replays across my mind's eye. Josh with the beard. And Celeste with red hair and piercings. Both of them the same, really. I love them. I love them so. Michael and Mr Swift and elderly Reuben. Pipe smoke and bagpipes. Teaspoons in the sugar bowl. Sliced white and strawberry jam. Cauliflowers fluffy. 41 Yew Lane stacked high with sameness. I think of Ross and I think how Adult Me feels so differently about who he is, than who I felt he was back when I was a teenager. Finally I understand why I was repulsed as a teenager – I was scared by the stark fallibility, the imperfection, of a grown-up. Now, though, I feel only tenderness and a little sorrow for Ross.

I think of the bright green cartoon bunny leaping along the side of the van which is parked right outside our flat and how this morning, when we collected it, was a lifetime ago. We collected it empty, then it was full, now it is empty again. I think of the chain-link fence at Three Magnets Primary School. I think of Lorry's shiny shoes and Sandrine's huge sunglasses and the fact that she has a younger boyfriend called Leo and they're moving away from Parkwin. And I think of my hands in a tea towel wrapped up and held tightly by Josh and I stay with that memory for a while; all that we said, all that we were.

Oh! And Patrick! How can I almost forget to think of Patrick?

In the serene darkness of my bedroom, I can recall again what he looked like at Three Magnets. He was impish, the skin around his bitten nails was always dirty, as if neither parent noticed or told him to wash his hands before supper. His tie was never straight, his shoes were scuffed at the toe, he ate fast, really fast. He could pinch and scratch and shove and his singing voice was sweet and pure. But I can't quite remember how he looked when I saw him ten years ago, when he called me E-deh and told me that he was dead dead sorry.

I lie in bed exhausted but still waiting for sleep and I think how it was Patrick's day today, really. And what a day.

'I'm glad people came for Patrick,' I say out loud.

Kip turns over; if I just woke him he doesn't say so.

'No,' he says. 'They came because of you, Eadie.' He finds my face. 'They came for you.'

Epilogue

Kip calls me into his office. And by that I mean he actually telephones from his desk to mine and summons me. I'd been sitting at my desk idly watching staff from one of the other companies having a cigarette on the grassy bank that borders the car park. I've observed these two every day for a couple of months. Initially, they'd come out with others for a smoke but gradually they've manufactured a time for just the two of them. I spin yarns about them to myself; I like to think they're seeing each other, that it's clandestine and a grand passion. Who knows, though – maybe there's nothing to it and the others in the office have simply given up the fags.

And then the phone on my desk rings – it's the short tone which signals an internal call. Kip, just a few feet away in the next room, is phoning through. I wheel back on my chair and lean – his door is open and I can actually see him with the receiver to his ear, but he's not looking my way. I propel myself back to my desk and pick up the phone.

'Er – hello?'

'Hi,' he says. 'Can you come in for a meeting at noon, please?'

I look at my watch. That's in twenty-two minutes.

'But I'm—'

'Thank you,' he says and the call goes dead. I hear him walk across his office and then he shuts the door.

Daft bugger, I think. I check his diary – he has a meeting in Buxton at two o'clock and it'll take him around forty minutes from here. It's a lovely route if he takes the quieter road past Lyme which doesn't add much time. I note that it's gone very quiet in his office.

At one minute to midday I leave my desk and less than ten seconds later I give a little jaunty rap on Kip's door and in I go.

'Hi,' he says.

'Hi,' I grin but his face is straight and he motions for me to sit. 'Don't forget you've got Buxton at 2 p.m. – and you wanted to go to the bank as well,' I say. 'But I can do that and also get you a sandwich or a salad if you like?'

'This is your appraisal,' he says.

'Huh?'

He looks down at a folder opened on his desk, sits back in his chair and regards me levelly. 'You've worked here four years and five months.'

'God – is it really!' And then it strikes me that he doesn't expect me to comment.

'Yes. So an appraisal is long overdue. Right,' he says and he leafs through some papers and suddenly I'm transported back to Professor Blakemore in his office when I went in to say I was quitting my course.

'I want to thank you for your hard work and input at KAT-media,' Kip is saying. 'However, you're actually not very good at what you do.' He looks at me straight. 'You spend too much time daydreaming, you leave early, you've taken more than your entitlement of holiday allowance, you slope off for longer than an hour at lunchtime and it takes you far too long to do simple tasks like photocopying or going to the post office.' He looks at the folder again. 'Oh,' he says, 'also you *still* can't keep paper straight when you staple pages together.'

Trying to absorb all this is like chugging a drink that's too fizzy, I can neither swallow nor can I gulp for air. I'm expecting him to pull a wry smile across his face, make a paper aeroplane and fly it over, swivel in his chair, throw half of that chocolate bar to me, discuss what we're having for supper. Something. Anything. But Kip just sits there, quietly observing me, waiting for me to respond.

'I need someone who has a burning desire to be an office manager,' he explains sternly and he clasps his hands and places them on the desk with a thump. 'I need someone who is passionate about managing an office, assisting the business, negotiating deals for stationery.' Kip closes the folder in front of him and gives me a quick courteous smile. 'So, I'm interviewing next week.'

'Sorry?'

'You are rubbish at your job.'

'*Sorry?*'

'You're completely crap,' he says. 'At your job.'

I am really – but still.

'And don't say *sorry* again,' Kip says. 'It's too late for an apology.'

'Are you sacking me?'

'Yes. You are officially one hundred per cent fired.' And then he continues to sit as he is, contemplating his dumbstruck wife and her gormless jaw-drop while her brain scurries to catch up with his words. 'That's all,' he says. 'Thank you.'

I sit there and stare at the clock: four surreal minutes, that's all it's been.

'You can go now,' Kip says. 'I need to make a call.' He picks up the phone and jabs a load of numbers, starts chatting away and, even though I can clearly hear the dialling tone, I leave his office and go back to my desk where I sit very still. In front of me, a letter to type, envelopes to stamp, a proposal to staple together. Outside, no one is smoking or flirting.

When Kip goes off to Buxton for his meeting, I'm still lost for words but he takes my chin between thumb and finger and gently closes my gawping mouth. That afternoon I tidy up a bit, change the cartridges in the printer and give the small fridge in the Thinking Ship a well-placed shove to stop it humming. There's nothing else to do, I don't think. Or at least nothing that can't wait until Monday. I may as well head home early for the weekend.

I trudge off to the station with my eyebrows knitting and knotting in bewilderment. Kip has sacked me. Why would he sack me? What sort of a husband would do that?

And then I stand stock-still on the platform as my thoughts unravel back to the journey home from Patrick's funeral ten days ago.

Kip has fired me from the job I told him I hate.

It's the most beautiful thing he has ever done for me.

We're on one of our walks, Kip and I. My entire life before I met Kip, walking was something which simply took me from A to B. When I was little I'd trip and scuff my way to and from school in my buckle shoes. When I was a teenager I'd mooch along with Josh and Celeste to the fountain or Soundz Recordz or the café or the charity shop, wearing trainers or my monkey boots or my black velvet Chinese slippers. At university, in ballet pumps or baseball boots, I'd join the bleary shuffle of students to lectures then hurry home to Hathersage Road and, with my clan, we'd skiddle our way to the Clarence for a sing-song, to the Haçienda for a dance, to Whitworth Park or Platt Fields for a loll. But then I met Kip and he took me to a new land called the Countryside; a place of uneven ground, of mud and rock and waterfalls, stepping stones and scree slopes, the suck of spongy heather and the twist of tussocks; up high peak and down Derbyshire dale. I had to forsake my fashion trainers for robust walking boots and I'm on at least my fifth pair. Most weekends we go and it's the perfect antidote to the working week. There is no A-to-B necessity, we just ramble and hike for the joy of it. It's not about the destination and it's not about time, it's about the being there.

And here we are, clambering the Black Hill loop at Crowden.

I haven't said it yet but I'm thinking about it now because up here, with the sunshine glinting off the grass and the air sweet, I am infused with energy and hope. I slip my hand into his and I pull, but for a few steps he hauls me along, as if he'd assumed I'd been asking for help. I tug him until he stops.

'Thank you,' I say. 'Thank you.'

At first, he appears not to know what I'm talking about. Then he makes to brush it away, like it's a gnat.

'No, Kip,' I say. '*Listen* to me. *Thank you.*' I hold his face and kiss him. 'Thank you for firing me.'

He grins; it's clear he enjoyed every minute of it. 'I just want you to do what you love.' He's serious now. 'You sparkle when you're energized.' He looks out across the moors. A skylark is belting out its song and Kip shields his eyes as he tries to locate it some three hundred metres above us. 'I just want to see that sparkle again – and for you to feel it.'

I know he's saying that it's been missing. And I know this is true.

'It's what I fell in love with,' he tells me. 'Well, that and your stroppiness and the whole weird graveyard thing.' He pauses. 'And your boobs.'

I'm looking for the skylark too. The birdsong is so clear and pure and joyous. I squint up and scour the sky but I just see so much blue and dreamy wisps of white. I could gaze for hours. Sometimes it's not necessary to pinpoint beauty for its power to be present.

'I'm sorry for so much,' I tell him, my arms tightly around him. 'And I'm grateful for so much.'

'I know you are,' he says into the top of my head.

'Are we OK?' I whisper, looking up to him. 'Are we going to be OK?'

'Yes, we are,' he says.

'How do you know?'

'Because we are. I don't have a neat answer, Eadie – I just have the determination.'

'But we're not as we were.'

'We're still pretty damn good.'

I think about this. 'It's just so bloody boring bickering about bollocks and bullshit.'

'And that,' says Kip, 'is an alliteration of pure genius.'

I laugh. 'I think we should have it on a fridge magnet.'

'But you've nailed it, Eadie,' Kip says. 'In the main, it's just mundane nonsense we react to. It's OK – it's neither reflection nor renouncement of what I feel for you. I can show you my stupid side, I can show you my ugliness because I trust you to see beyond momentary lapses and surface details.'

'Of course I do,' I say softly, hoping he's never doubted it but fearing that he may have. 'But also – the last three years – there's been big stuff,' I say. 'The bomb. Your business. Loans and mortgages. We bought our first flat, we lost our dream house because Patrick died. Life got serious.'

'Two miscarriages,' he says, slipping his arm around me.

I lean against him.

'I'd really like us to see someone about that,' I say. 'I feel it's time.'

Kip agrees. 'I've been thinking about that too. It struck me hard at the funeral – the death–life continuum.'

'I'm sure everything's fine – with me, with you,' I say, 'but it would be wise to seek advice. I'm keen, now, to do that.'

On we walk and I unzip the pocket of his trusty old rucksack which is slung between his shoulders like he's giving a tired child a piggyback. I wonder what he's popped in there for today's sustenance. I find two Flake bars and a carton of Um Bongo. Perfect.

'Sometimes I find it overwhelming that I'm actually thirty now. Other times I laugh because I can't quite believe it. When I was young, that's the age I used when defining people as *old*. I mean, I remember my parents' thirtieth birthdays – and they seemed like proper grown-ups. Sensible. Annoying.'

Kip laughs at that.

'And we're heading for a new millennium,' I say. 'Everything suddenly feels huge – and serious. And, if I'm honest, I'm a bit stressed by it all.'

'The year two thousand,' Kit muses.

'But Kip,' I say quietly. I stop and turn from him and let the view soothe my eyes. 'What if there's another miscarriage?'

'What if there isn't.'

'What if I'm a terrible mother?'

'That, Eadie, is as unlikely as you being a fantastic office manager.'

I look away from the day and my fears of the future to rest my head against my husband's chest, closing my eyes to stay as I am in this very moment with him. His arms around me. The sound of his heartbeat. This beautiful place.

'Was I really dreadful at my job?'

He laughs. 'Not dreadful,' he says. 'Just utterly crap.'

I think I must look a bit glum because Kip kisses me.

'You were amazing when I set up KAT – remember that?'

I do. I do. Working from our kitchen table, working all the hours. Hitting the phones. Hand-delivering leaflets. Brainstorming at silly o'clock. Standing in the new empty office role-playing while we imagined the business thriving. Finding the mini-fridge in the sale and saying Kip! we need this! we can fill it with Coke and beer and chocolate – it'll be cool!

'Teamwork made my dream work,' he says in an overdone American accent before continuing thoughtfully. 'But really, your work was done – quite early on.'

'Did you keep me on because you felt sorry for me? Because you worry about me?'

He thinks about that. 'Maybe I did a bit.'

I don't know whether to feel touched or insulted so I say nothing for a while. 'I felt if I told you I wasn't happy at work, I'd be letting you down, that I'd hurt your feelings.'

He considers this. 'It hurts more that you felt you couldn't tell me,' he says.

'I am so sorry.' I really am.

'I know marketing and media isn't your dream,' he says. 'But I don't actually know what your dream is – and you have to have one, Eadie. Because however fanciful it is, you can make it happen.'

We clamber over a wall in whose drystone shadow some sheep are nestled. They stagger up and away, bleating indignantly.

'What *is* it you'd most like to do, Eadie?' Kip asks. 'Put it another way – when and where were you happiest?'

'With you, Kip – with you.' I worry it's a trick question.

'No – I mean outside of me – beyond me. Think about it – *think*.'

Recently, a thought has been popping up which I've skipped over because it seems so – odd. Daft almost.

'I can hear you thinking,' Kip says. 'I can see you biting back on what you might say.' He laughs. 'I know you, Eadie. I know you off by heart.'

I stop and look around. I've grown to truly love this part of the Peak District. It's beautiful and peaceful and it's also wild and feels so remote. I can see for miles. I'm near waterfalls and rivers and heather-clad moorland overseen by a vast and ever-changing sky yet I'm not that far from my beloved Manchester.

'I love it out here – the space, the openness, the drama. Nature's theatre,' I say and I don't really care how corny that sounds. I breathe in, I breathe out. I know I can answer Kip. 'I'm a history graduate with two degrees. I can type at break-neck speed and I can carry four plates on one arm. But what I'd really like to do is to be there – with words – for the dead and for the living. What I want to do is assist with people's history.' I regard Kip who is rapidly attempting to compute all this. 'Because I have the words, Kip. I've had them since I was very small, thanks to Mum and Terry.'

'Eadie?'

'Probably just a pipe dream,' I mumble, then I tell myself to buck up. Perhaps it is indeed the pipe part – the conduit – for an idea that is, in fact, potent and attainable.

'You want to run a *funeral parlour*? Like Shirley Doig?'

He's struggling with that notion and I laugh. 'No – I couldn't do what she does. That's very special. I want to be a celebrant, Kip. That's what I'd like to do. And not just deaths. Marriages too. I loved the lady we had at the registry office for our wedding – but I felt the chap at Patrick's funeral lacked – *something*.'

I'm now nervous for Kip's response. A Master's degree in history hasn't actually led to this point. Or perhaps it has.

'This is *exactly* what you should do,' Kip says thoughtfully. 'It's your calling, Eadie. Just ask Macey Darling.'

I walk on a little way.

'I already have,' I tell him.

I told Iris and Sid too, when I visited their graves on my rounds at the Southern Cemetery after I got home from work yesterday, while Kip was making his way back from Buxton.

We hike a long circuitous route back. Kip suggests a very late lunch at the Bull's Head in Tintwistle, just down the road. Cheese sarnies never tasted so good. We meander around the village afterwards and then head back to Didsbury, to our flat which is on the market again. I have a long bath and then pad through to the sitting room in bare feet and a towelling robe. I snuggle up to watch Saturday-night telly but Kip keeps turning his head and looking towards the window. I follow his gaze but I can't see what he's looking at. He takes the remote control and switches the TV off and turns to me.

'Just don't say anything, OK? Don't react,' he says and he places his index finger gently at my lips for emphasis. 'Please – allow what I'm going to say to float and flit for a while, let's just see how it might settle.'

He has narrowed his eyes as if the thought – whatever it is – is still forming for him.

'How would you feel about looking further afield?'

My first thought is that he actually does want me to run a funeral parlour.

'This afternoon we walked by a house in Tintwistle,' he's saying, 'with a *For Sale* sign outside. I don't know how much, I don't know anything other than I saw it was for sale. That's all.' He pauses. 'But what do you think, Eadie? Fancy a change? Shall we do something different, something new? For the millennium – for us?'

In the ensuing silence, it feels like there are fireflies darting around my head as my mind scoots this way and that, as my imagination spins myriad images of a homely cottage kitchen and a wonky staircase, an open fire and walking to the hills right from our back door. I think of 41 Yew Lane; of the driveway and the porch and the gate from our garden to the cemetery, my bedroom and my parents' desks, a bowl of potpourri, tinned tuna in the kitchen cupboard and, occasionally, Viennetta in the freezer. I think of the corridors at Hulme Hall and all the little notepads hanging hopeful on the doors, Cheery Eric in the Porters' Lodge and how I kept my milk on the ledge outside my window. I think of the house on Hathersage Road; the comfort found in our sitting room and all of us squashed onto the brown velvet sofa, the warmth of the gas fires, the safety of my bedroom with the view to the ginnel, the alley. Sparky the cat, Klaus the mouse, Iris with her telly next door and the splendour of the Victoria Baths opposite. I think of Kip's modern flat in Salford and the double bed that was our first joint purchase and then I think of Kip hoicking me into a fireman's lift and carrying me over the threshold of this small, expensive flat in Didsbury. I think of the house down the road which he loved and I recently lost for us, with the fancy shed and the good floorboards on such a desirable street. And I wonder, now, what awaits.

I conjure Edweard Fairbetter standing in the playground in Parkwin Garden City's little Three Magnets Primary School, having a wry nod to himself knowing that all of this makes sense. I recall Ebenezer Howard's Three Magnets design from our many projects at school and from the tattoo on Patrick's arm.

    Town.
        Country.
            Town-Country.
                And, at the centre, with the will to choose: Me.

In my life, two of the magnets have had their pull and now the third is luring me.

'First thing Monday morning,' I say, 'I'll make some calls.' And I pause and turn to my husband. 'If I'm still allowed back into the office, that is.'

Then we look at each other, Kip and I. We truly see down deep to a place where we're able to read every word of each other's racketing thoughts. And now I know, I know exactly what will always keep us safe and steady – it is that we're happy for each other to have separate dreams but actually, we'll always end up sharing them.

Acknowledgements

In addition to rummaging through boxes of photos and letters in the loft, the research for this novel required me to sit very quietly, challenging myself to *really remember*. It's over thirty years since I left Manchester and, as I focused on my memories, I realized how little I had forgotten – it was all still there, vivid as ever it had been – it's just that I'd overlooked thinking about that period in my life for a long time. But, with my son Felix at university, his first year blighted by Covid restrictions and his third year cruelly wrecked by the marking strike, it struck me how privileged I was to have been at university in the late 1980s – and how lucky I was to have lived in Manchester at that time. The past is indeed a foreign country and certainly we did things differently there - it's been both nostalgic and cathartic to revisit it and write this book. Leaving home is leaving home, it's emotional and that will never change and I owe a debt of beaming gratitude to Greater Manchester for looking after me so well.

All of Eadie's teachers are fictitious. However, I want to take a moment to salute those teachers in my life who educated me way beyond the parameters of any syllabus. At school, Robert Hardy and Fanny Balcombe – I *loved* your lessons and am inspired by your teaching to this day. You were always interested in me, you motivated my self-belief and I am so pleased that we're still in touch. Whilst at Manchester University, my enduring thanks to Professor Richard Thomson as well as to the late Professor Andrew Causey and to the late, and unquantifiably great, Professor Paul Crossley. At the Courtauld Institute, my thanks go to Dr Margaret Garlake who, in the early 1990s when I'd completed my MA, gave me the go ahead to put my PhD on hold so I could write my first novel instead.

During my research for Eadie & co., I wrote to a house. I wrote a letter to the house on Hathersage Road, Manchester, in which I'd lived as a student. The next day, I had a reply. All these years later it is *still* a student house. In February 2022, I knocked at my old front door and five gorgeous grinning faces appeared and welcomed me in. These days, the house has central heating, two bathrooms and no hole in the kitchen floor but the heart and the soul and the character of the house is intact. My love and thanks to Issy Fairham, Ryan Higgins, Lucy Perryman, Alfie Ross and Georgia Taft. They have all graduated now, from Manchester's superb Arden School of Theatre – so look out for them; they are a talented bunch and thoroughly wonderful people and it's a joy to have befriended them.

Early in 2020, before the world collapsed in on itself, my children Felix (then 18) and Georgia (then 16) had roles in *The City of Tomorrow* - a play by Glyn Maxwell for the Barn Theatre in Welwyn Garden City, near to where we live. The play was commissioned to celebrate the centenary of Welwyn Garden City. Then Covid came and the theatres went dark. Undeterred, the cast gave innovative, arresting performances on Zoom. I realized I hadn't known much about Ebenezer Howard and his visionary Garden City movement and I was as captivated by the subject matter as by Glyn Maxwell's beautiful play. Thank you to Glyn and also to Danny Swanson.

To my beloved university pals Dan Lubman, Adrian and Karen Watts, Paul and Rosie Taverner, Al Dury, Fiona Glennon, Bob

Blenkinsop, Simon Mellor and Mark Ballin – thank you for so many fond and colourful memories and for enduring friendship. We will never need to put a number on how many reunions we can have.

Behind the scenes, my sincere thanks to all at Curtis Brown, Mountain Leopard Press, Headline and EDPR for your support, enthusiasm, hard work and guidance. Special mention for Mary Chamberlain: after all these years and all due credit to you, copy editing is no longer quite so hair-tearingly frustrating ... Thank you to my very lovely and empathetic author pals Tasmina Perry, Lucy Atkins, Alexandra Potter, Chrissie Manby, Lisa Jewell, Mike Gayle and Cathy Kelly. I know I speak for all of us when I say how grateful I am for the vibrant community of book bloggers across social media who provide such valuable support for authors and readers alike.

I'm extremely grateful to Peter Burke for his photo of the Haçienda and to Chris Hughes for sending me his last DVD of his wonderful documentary *Do You Own the Dancefloor*.

On the home front, the Groucho Cycling Club, the Cucumber Girls and the Tuesday Night Potters continue to keep me both sane *and* in paroxysms of laughter. For ensuring I feel steady and happy and wrapped up with love, my heartfelt gratitude goes to my beautiful friends: Lucy S, Mel, Simon and Mo, Amanda and Jonathan, Sian and John, Nick and Cheryl, Sue V, Lucy F, the real Shirley Doig and Emma o'R.

Saving the very, very best until last: Ma, Pa, Fee 'n' Gee and Anto - thank you thank you thank you.

in loving memory
Liz Berney 1968-2005
Hannah Berry 1983-2013
Jonny Zucker 1966-2016

Further Reading

MANCHESTER

Mostly, the research for this novel was done from my own memories of Manchester in the late 1980s so forgive me for any erroneous details . . . The following books served as an invaluable and thoroughly enjoyable aide-mémoire.

Sonic Youth Slept on My Floor: Music, Manchester and More, a Memoir – Dave Haslam

The Haçienda: How Not to Run a Club – Peter Hook

From Manchester with Love: The Life and Opinions of Tony Wilson – Paul Morley

The End-Of-The-Century Party: Youth, Pop and the Rise of Madchester – Steve Redhead

Tony Wilson: You're Entitled to an Opinion – David Nolan

GARDEN CITIES

English Garden Cities: An introduction (Informed Conservation) – Mervyn Miller

Garden Cities – Sarah Rutherford

Garden Cities of To-Morrow – Ebenezer Howard

City of Tomorrow – Glyn Maxwell

Read on for an extract of Freya North's novel, *Little Wing*...

1969. Florence Lawson, a 16-year-old schoolgirl who dreams of being an artist, finds herself pregnant and banished to one of the most remote parts of the UK.

1986. Dougie Munro, searching for adventure, leaves the Isle of Harris – the island of his birth – for art college and a career in London as a photographer.

2005. Nell Hartley, content with her life managing a care-in-the-community cafe in Colchester, discovers a shocking truth about her family.

Between the sprawl of London, suburban Essex, and the wild, unpredictable Outer Hebrides, three lives collide and interweave as questions are asked and secrets surface. What happened to Florence? Why is Dougie now so reluctant to return home? How can Nell make peace with the lies she's been told?

Somewhere far away the answers are hidden.

Prologue

Colchester, February 1969

Nothing will ever be the same again.
This I've known these past long weeks as the waves sweep through me in rushes and ripples, pulling me under, lifting me up.

Wave after wave after wave on a tide that only ever comes in; ribboning through me with pitching fear but wonder too; excitement cresting on the surges of dread. Elation roiling with loneliness and curiosity undulating with panic.

But there is the swell of love. There is the flow of contentment.

How is that? That I love you?
You. Little tiny nonsensical you.
The flutter of you. The beat and the rhythm of you and me.
We're inextricable now — the making of each other.

A wave of nausea.
I've heard that this should stop after twelve weeks.
I count almost eleven.
The trouble and the joy that you will bring.

Colchester, December 1968

Not a baby.

Mum and George were going out for cheese and wine at their friends on Saturday and they – or rather Mum – had asked Wendy to babysit. Those actual words. Wendy was as mad about this as I was. I am not a baby and my sister does not want to sit her way through a Saturday evening. It occurred to me that I probably wouldn't have to sneak out now – that I could just tell her. But part of me was quite looking forward to furtively stealing into the night. Wendy's only ten years older than me – she can't have forgotten what it's like to be my age.

Almost as soon as Mum and George left, Wendy's boy Jimmy arrived and suddenly it struck me that there might very well be a God so I laid the dress out on my bed, put the lipstick and false eyelashes next to it and then went downstairs.

'Wendy,' I said, 'you're cool if I go to Joan's, aren't you?' Everyone knows she's my best friend.

Just then Jimmy came in with two Martinis and he said, 'Let her go, Wendy.' And I'm assuming he didn't mean for me to see the wink he gave her.

Wendy looked at me and I knew exactly what she was going to say. 'It's your life; it's your funeral.' She said exactly the same thing when she caught me on the high street, when I played hooky from school. 'Your life, your funeral,' she said.

Well, skipping school didn't kill me – but being there threatens to do precisely that. I know what I want to be and I don't need school for it. I am going to be an artist – and to be an artist you need to be a free thinker, and that's something that boring old school does not encourage. My teachers say I'm bright – exceptional, even – but I say school dulls me right down.

So Wendy caught Jimmy's wink and probably couldn't wait for me to get out of the house anyway.

I went up to my room, changed into my handmade dress, and I glued on the falsies and added my cat's eyes perfectly in one swoop of black liner. And then I very casually walked down the stairs, checked myself in the mirror in the hallway and applied more lipstick. I didn't need rouge – my cheeks were pink and glowing with excitement. The sitting-room door was shut and I called out goodbye.

I said, 'Goodbye, kids!' I said, 'Don't wait up!'

It was only Jimmy's voice that replied. 'Be good!'

Of course our mother doesn't approve of Jimmy. She always looks pained when he calls on Wendy. Mind you, there's little in life that doesn't pain our mother. Wendy would have to marry a vicar for Mother to be halfway happy. Anyway, Jimmy was on side and I pretty much skipped all the way to the party, singing to myself thank you God thank you God thank you.

There were so many people! Everyone was like me – like we were a tribe; it was such a groovy vibe. 'Hello, I Love You' by the Doors was playing just as I arrived. It was perfect. Everyone was talking, singing, dancing. Friends from school and new people hanging out. But – best of all I met this boy, this dearest boy, an absolute knockout. None of us knew him – he turned up with Gerald and Martin and that lot. But as soon as I saw him oh! the flutter and the swell and if that's love at first sight then let my eyes see nothing else!

Even when I was really having a good talk with Joan about Sid, my eyes were pulled to him. But it was too much when he caught my gaze! I felt this incredible heat come over my cheeks and my chest, my skin prickled and my breath caught. I didn't know what to do about it – I asked Joan and she said, look! he's over there by the punchbowl. She said, just go over as if your main interest is a glass of punch and see, she said, just see.

So I did.

I went over to the punchbowl and drat! his back was turned but as I took a glass I could sense him, like he was as drawn to me as I was to him. As if our souls were sending out electric charges that were reacting mid-air, propelling us together. My hand was shaking as I spooned punch into a glass. It's excellent stuff to calm the nerves, is punch! And then I hear this lovely voice and I know it's him and he's saying, wow – I dig your dress! Far out!

And that's when I felt I could turn and look at him and I told him I made it and he said that it was the coolest thing. Somebody had put Jimi Hendrix on and everything just seemed magical, so clear and real, so right and so – in the Now.

We chinked glasses and our eyes were absolutely locked as we sipped at the punch. Which was very strong.

'I'm Peter,' he said.

We tapped our feet and nodded our heads in time with the song – and soon enough we were dancing. And when we weren't dancing we were talking. It was as if we'd known each other our whole lives. He's from South Africa but his family don't live there any more, now they're renting on the other side of the park – the well-to-do side. We talked for ages, we drank the rum punch, which was like the best pop in the world but with this hot and sharp delicious aftertaste that made you squint your eyes shut.

'Rum,' Peter said. 'Rrrrrum!' And he said it like a lion starting to roar.

We only had eyes for each other, we didn't care to talk to anyone else from that moment on. We're so similar. We danced and danced and it was as if everyone else at the party just melted into a silent background. Like they were black-and-white cutouts, like scenery. Really, there was just Peter and I. Someone had put on 'All Along the Watchtower' and he kissed me. And then oh how we smooched and I couldn't have told you what was playing then and I couldn't have cared who was looking. Jimi himself could have been right there, wanting to make my acquaintance, and I wouldn't have stopped. And I'll say this: I know that no other kiss will ever feel quite like it.

We smoked some pot and I felt so floaty with it and so springy from the punch. I've never felt so — here! — so alive! So my own person, so in love with being me at this time in the world's history! I felt so high! And 'Everlasting Love' by Love Affair just made me feel this overwhelming sense of YES!!! Me in my dress being the most Me I've ever been — and being kissed all the more for it. Could anything ever match this night, could feelings ever have this strength again? Once you've felt something once, is it diluted by repetition?

And then Peter took my hand and led me away. I know Joan's house as well as my own. I told him, I know where we can go — and we ran up the stairs and then tiptoed up the next flight too. I took him up to the attic, to Joan's brother's room — because he's away at university. We could hear people in Joan's room and even in her parents' room — but I knew Dicky's room would be empty. It was also dark. Warm. Lovely and warm. And so were Peter's lips which were all over me; my face, my mouth, my neck. Oh my, I was soaring and sinking all at once but I was safe in his arms and I was kissing him back. His hands. His hands were moving and finding and squeezing and I thought oh my goodness I'm going to pass out with *the pleasure. I mean, I've kissed boys before and they've had a feel over my clothes. But Peter — well, he discovered the flaw in my homemade dress, which is that the armholes are a bit gapey so he found a way in. And I'm so glad he did. Felt like my breasts were made especially for his hands. He was pressing against me and moving back and forth and I could feel It. It. His desperate hardness. His hardness. His desire. For me.*

He took my hand and led me over to Dicky's bed and we just lay on it, gazing at each other touched by moonlight, or maybe it was streetlight not moonlight. But anyway, he looked so deliciously handsome!

We were kissing so passionately and it was like he was dying of hunger, of longing. I gave his hands freedom because it felt good and nothing felt wrong. He ran them up my thighs and then between my legs and his voice was so soothing, saying, relax baby relax. When your parents call you a baby it's like an insult — but when the man you love calls you baby it's like honey. So I relaxed. It felt — I never knew! His hands, his fingertips — I never knew it could feel so — I never knew that about my body.

And he unbuckled his belt and unbuttoned his jeans and he took my hand down there and I never imagined it would feel so — warm.

And Peter said shall we?

He said I think we should.

He said that feelings like this are so rare and that not many people experience a connection like ours. He said that we have to live in the moment. I believe that too.

And I said I know, but —

And he said don't worry — I'll pull it out in time.

And I said I know, but —

And downstairs the Beatles were singing 'Hey Jude'.

And Peter said relax, baby, relax.

I'm so in love.